# About *The Idea People*

It is 1987: the "greed is good" era. When anxious ad agency whiz Ben Franklin Green accidentally falls through a wall during a hilarious boardroom presentation, he hops a plane and flies west instead of returning to work. During a nostalgic sojourn in the eucalyptus and marijuana-scented playland of LA's sexy Laurel Canyon, he plans to develop a book with his former mentor about the sham that is the advertising business. But his plans are short-lived as they get news that his mentor's outdoorsy daughter has been kidnapped while working in the Rocky Mountain wilds. Ben, with the sharp creativity of a Madison Avenue idea man, becomes an unlikely detective as he is reluctantly drawn into the case.

The brisk, irreverent narrative of *The Idea People* recalls literary voices of nature-loving writers such as Jim Harrison, Ed Abbey, Rick Bass, James A. McLaughlin, and Charles Frazier. Western-style battles, carnal capers, wild animals, and outlaws present uncharacteristic challenges for the urban, neurotic protagonist. There are love interests, bear encounters, wild horseback rides, a gun belt, an arrow wound, back-country brawls, '80s-style boozing, and an engaging amount of Sherlock Holmes-style ratiocination. Ben's interest in nature, loyalty to his friends, and an uncanny ability to see what others miss, just might allow him to become a rare bird who finds a new life and love in the Wild West.

# THE
# IDEA
# PEOPLE

# THE
# IDEA
# PEOPLE

## MIKE LUBOW

gatekeeper press™
Tampa, Florida

The Idea People

Published by Gatekeeper Press
7853 Gunn Hwy, Suite 209
Tampa, FL 33626
www.GatekeeperPress.com

Library of Congress Control Number: 2023940340

ISBN (paperback): 9781662941818
eISBN: 9781662941825

*For my family*

*"Beyond the wall of the unreal city . . . beyond the asphalt belting of the superhighways . . . beyond the rage of lies that poisons the air, there is another world waiting for you. It is the old true world of the deserts, the mountains, the forests...*

*Go there. Be there."*

—Edward Abbey

# 1.

In the summer of 1987, business was good. Madison Avenue, and its kid brother in Chicago, Michigan Avenue, were turning out national advertising campaigns with an optimism that had no end in sight. The creative revolution of the sixties and seventies was over, so ads didn't have to be archly hip any more, as long as they were expensive. And the people who were making them didn't have to be left of center artists. They could be research-led, MBA-led business hacks.

Actually, it was a good time to be in advertising. You didn't really need very much talent. But, like always, it was a good time to walk away from it. Those who make ads for a living are usually frustrated something elses. The something else might be novelist, painter, poet, screenwriter, cowboy, whatever. It was a good day for Benjamin Franklin Green to fall through the wall. Right out of the boardroom at Swift, Pope and Fielding's Chicago office. Whether or not he'd ever fall back in, remains to be seen.

It was also a good time to be hiking through a wildly remote and remotely wild valley in the Rocky Mountains. The girl who was on this hike was twenty-one, athletic and blonde. A real Colorado poster girl. She was looking forward to a midday skinny dip. She liked being naked in the outdoors, although only when she was reasonably sure she was alone. On this sunny day, there was a man watching her from a distance through a pair of high-powered binoculars. She had no idea he was there.

In any case, her immediate problem wasn't him. It was getting lost, which is what she was in the process of doing at about the same time that Ben Green was falling through the wall. Her problem started with a bright red bird that was entirely out of place. And Ben's difficulty started with a drop of blood that was, in its own way, absurdly out of place.

\*   \*   \*

The client was Beeker & Gimble, or the BeeGees, as the agency guys called them. SPF handled their detergent business and one of their brands, Brio, suffered sagging sales. Ben wrote a new theme for them, "Clean is the best thing to wear." He'd built it into ad ideas, or as they called them, "executions." In meetings, Ben would feel a flush of foolishness, using this ad biz tech-talk, saying, "If you thought that execution was powerful, wait'll you see the next." As though their ideas came from death row.

Ben was in the agency's main conference room, the one they called the coliseum because of its seating capacity and occasional gory scenes between inept unfortunates and lions from upper management. Ben was one of twenty or so. Not a large group for the coliseum, so part of the space had been closed off by movable partitions that slid out of the walls on each side, meeting in the middle.

In attendance were the brass of the BeeGee's, hard-eyed MBAs who could fire SPF ASAP if they were disappointed with what they'd see here. Also on hand were agency principals Anthony Swift and Devon Pope. Fielding, the third name on the door, wasn't in attendance, having recently passed away.

Swift and Pope took their seats. The room grew quiet. Around them was a confusion of "suits." These were the account executives and brand managers. There was even a stenographer who sat off to the side. Along the wall were catering carts, all crisp linen and silver trays. One held gourmet cheeses. One had a glistening mound of steak tartar, with onions and little pieces of rye bread. There were buckets of white-collar soda pops, imported waters, quince, gooseberry and ginseng seltzers. One cart just held flowers.

This meant that Ben was in for another major meeting. He hated them. Not every time, but sometimes, when he'd present work he'd become curiously stricken with a mean kind of stage fright. It would make him feel trapped. He'd have trouble breathing. The witch doctors of psychology call it "fight or flight," but neither is an option in such a major meeting. Ben was scheduled to show eight storyboards He just didn't expect to be getting blood on any of them.

In a previous meeting, he got that fight or flight thing and found he could control it with judiciously administered doses of pain, which he supplied by jabbing a paper clip into his hand. He bent it around a finger, out of sight, and when he started to get breathless and felt like he had to run from the room, he poked the point into his palm. The more it hurt, the more it took his mind off the claustrophobic spotlight he was under.

It had worked. So he tried it in this meeting with pretty good results until an MBA in the front said something like, "Uh, you're bleeding?"

And he'd said it nice and loud.

The storyboard had red smears on it. Ben ad-libbed something about putting sweat and blood into his work. He was given a tissue. He apologized and went on. Then the panic attack hit, knocking the wind out of him, literally. No paper clip in his hand could come to the rescue. No Valium or alcohol were in his system. He was suddenly all too clean himself, about to present, "Clean is the best thing to wear." His head swimming from inadequate breathing, lack of oxygen, he pushed forward.

"First I want to review the problem facing Brio according to research."

But he'd forgotten Brio's problem. Blank.

"It's lost its market share." Safe guess.

"That is, it's losing share in the markets. I mean, in the market."

Hard to breathe. Voice sounding like someone else talking, someone far away. Then, ". . . but in the markets, too, of course. *Super*markets, you know?"

Uncomfortable squirming in the room. Devon Pope looked at him with a fierceness, his eyes, saying more clearly than words could, that he was embarrassed that Ben was mumbling such nonsense.

"These executions will reverse that trend."

But he was out of air. Latent autism turned into the not so latent kind and struck with malice. Did they hear it in his voice? Part of him mentally pulled up a chair to watch the show, thinking, *this is going to be good.*

"I've got nine executions, a range of ideas," he squeezed out, realizing he didn't have nine, but eight. High-tension wires began to hum in his ears. His heartbeat became a metronome going fuck upp . . . fuck-upp . . . f-f-f-fuck-upp . . . and that part of him that was the observer of this little soap opera (he was, after all, there to sell soap) stood by, perversely amused at this, and wondered what would happen if he'd inadvertently say out loud, "fuck-upp . . . fuck-upp . . . fuck-upp . . ." instead of what he was supposed to say.

He lifted the next storyboard, blood free, onto the presentation easel and found that all he could say was, "Now, to explain everything frame by frame, is my colleague, Barry Elliot."

Elliot was Ben's art director, a man plagued by professional missteps. Recently, Elliot tried to look good to the big guys by attending Fielding's funeral. But on the way there, he stopped off at a studio party and they'd given him one of those lapel tags that say, "Hi, My Name Is . . ." He'd scrawled in a big BARRY, pinned the thing on and reached for a vodka rocks.

Later, at the funeral, Elliot felt people were treating him oddly as he tried to commiserate. He gave condolences to Swift and Pope, but they moved away. It wasn't until he was leaving the chapel, and snagging his trench coat on the lapel, that he noticed he still wore the "Hi, My Name Is . . . BARRY!" pin.

A pale Barry Elliot joined Ben at the front of the room.

"Barry is the talented guy who drew these storyboards. I thought he'd be the best one to explain them."

Elliot looked at him with an expression Ben used to see on the family dog when they'd take her to the vet. Ben smiled sickly. Sick with guilt. And sick with the aftershock of panic. Yet he was off the hook. Elliot could explain the storyboards. He might be the company's resident sad sack but at least he wasn't a pathologically nervous wreck. Elliot opened, "Gentlemen . . ."

Never mind that there were several important females in the room. Not Ben's problem now. ". . . Our next execution . . ." And Elliot calmly explained their work, dully but correctly, scene by scene.

Calling him up there had been spontaneous, unexpected. Ben guessed his subconscious realized he wouldn't have enough air in his lungs to read the first storyboard, let alone all of them. The group accepted the not unheard of dual presentation format and Ben stepped to the rear of the room, leaning against the back wall behind everyone. He affected a confident, relaxed style, the capable creative director. How good it felt to lean there, blessedly out of the heat of everyone's attention.

Ah, to lean. Lean like a man. The balls-out pelvic tilt, hard guy style. One hip cocked higher than the other and a bit forward. Hands in pockets. Belly in. How many teenage nights did he spend perfecting that macho lean? Leaning legitimizes a guy's presence when just standing at attention would make him feel uncomfortable. A leaning man is a lone wolf coolly regarding everything without participating in the foolishness, above it all. But to lean properly you need a solid surface behind you. In Ben's agitated condition he'd overlooked that simple concept.

With hands in pockets, he settled back against the point where the two folding panels met in the center, forming the movable back wall of their meeting room. His weight parted the seam and in a wink Ben dropped backwards, through it. The seam sprung shut with a snap, leaving him standing in the dark emptiness of the next room.

He had to get back to the presentation! But what would they say? Would they laugh? Did they even miss him? Would this get him fired? He'd literally popped out of the picture. It was possible that some people didn't even see him disappear, as they were watching Barry Elliot.

He left through a back door and turned down the hall, heading for the coliseum's main door. But when he got there, he walked past it, went home, packed a bag, and phoned the airline. Something bigger than a major meeting had taken control. He didn't know what it was, exactly. He recalled a few lines from an old poem he'd always liked. Something by Yeats about the how the center cannot hold, and then things fall apart.

The center of the conference room wall sure hadn't held. He laughed about this quietly to himself several times that day, laughing at his own expense, wincing and shaking his head at the memory. If things were falling apart, well, it didn't feel that bad. Actually, he was breathing easy, feeling oddly free.

# 2.

Around the time that Ben was popping through the wall of Swift Pope & Fielding, the young, athletic blonde woman who'd been hiking all morning in a remote part of the Rockies was standing above a pretty little creek. The clear water moving over red-brown stones was deep and cool. It looked to her like iced tea.

Being in the exact middle of nowhere, she assumed she was alone, but young blonde women are a suspicious lot when it comes to getting undressed, so she double-checked, squinting behind her, scanning the hills, then across the creek into the pines. Seeing no sign of anyone else, she took off her sweaty hiking clothes. The cool air against her skin made a welcome change.

Down by the water's edge the smell of damp stone was strong, overpowering the pine smell that had been with her all day, especially in the early morning before sunshine heated and thinned the air.

A nagging sense of insecurity.

She hesitated, then jogged back to her belongings. She knelt over an open backpack, rooting around, her loose hair falling forward. With one hand she flicked it back, laying it over a bare shoulder, and with her other she withdrew a sheathed hunting knife which hung heavily from a weathered, leather belt.

She buckled this on and returned to the creek, now primitively armed, anticipating the pleasures of a swim. She waded in until the moving water touched the junction of her legs, dampening blondish curls there, turning them dark. She took a deep breath and dove in against the current, swimming below the surface, kicking, arms forward. She broke the surface, stood and tossed her head back, her long hair throwing off an arc of silver spray.

Refreshed, now needing warmth, she waded to the other side, to a flatrock overhang sitting above the water in dry sunlight. In the distant hills, the man with binoculars watched. It was his lucky day. The girl lay naked on the warm rock. Eyes closed. Skin and hair drying quickly in the mountain sun. There was only the steady sound of moving water and the occasional breeze quivering the aspens, making their leaves crackle softly.

She stretched, a lioness at midday. Then a speck of red streaked overhead, crossing the creek into the pines behind her. She turned. A cardinal? Rare for this altitude. Not found in the mountains. The girl happened to be a student of such avian esoterica and became interested, no, not just interested, intrigued . . .

She stood, looking again for hot red against forest green. Nothing. Then a flash as the bird flew to another tree. Red with black. "A scarlet tanager?" she said aloud, to no one (as far as she knew), and walked off her warm rock, away from the creek toward the trees to get a closer look.

The bird flew to another perch and the girl followed, jogging naked on the stony ground, climbing above the bank now, entering the woods, eyes on the bird. It swooped away and down, disappearing behind a rocky outcrop. The girl moved quickly, making use of this temporary screen to shorten the distance without the bird seeing her. The sheathed knife flapped against her naked buttock as she ran, an encouraging *pat, pat*.

She peeked around the rock. Nothing. She scanned the trees but the bird was gone. She thought it could have been an Eastern bird, a species not of these mountains. It would have been an important sighting, but the bird didn't sit still long enough for her to confirm it. She turned, walking back quickly to her place by the creek.

The distance back seemed greater than the distance away. She had no thought of time when following the bird. Suddenly, she felt unsure. Was it this far? The creek had to be just through the trees ahead, and she ran toward them, feeling chilled. She got to the trees and saw nothing beyond but more trees. She stopped, heart pounding, knowing she was lost.

# 3.

Ben was still euphoric from the boilermakers, and his high was heightened by the pink and blue sunset on display outside the window of the 747. He'd asked for a window seat as always, having never grown jaded by the views, always pressing his forehead to the plastic pane, seduced for hours by the sights of cloud tops and patchwork groundscapes.

He'd had two shots of Jack Daniel's neat in the airport standup bar, washed down with foamy drafts that were too cold and gave him a head freeze. The roof of his mouth still ached. On the plane, more JD with extra peanuts he'd wheedled from the flight attendant, a middle-aged crone with uncombed hair. Throughout the flight, so far, she continually wore a look that says, *I only have two hands, asshole!* What lies the airline commercials tell.

In his earphones, Janis Joplin was raging and Ben, losing himself in the rebel yell of old hippie rock, was tapping his foot with the beat. His free-spirited tapping caused a cranky business traveler one seat behind to lean forward and tap, in turn, on Ben. Ben jumped, shocked for a moment, not knowing where he was. The man's neck pressed against the white collar of his shirt. Folds of fat rolled out and over. Ben had the frightening image of the man in a noose, eyes bulging, face reddening.

Ben pulled Janis away from his ears. "Sorry, what?"

"Would you please stop banging your foot? You're shaking the whole floor."

Ben hadn't even been aware that he was tapping, not being the foot-tapping kind.

*   *   *

Until yesterday, Benjamin Franklin Green was VP, Creative Director, at Swift, Pope & Fielding, a multi-national advertising agency headquartered in Chicago. Their stationery listed branch offices in New York, Los Angeles, San Francisco, London, Paris, Milan, Sydney and Kuala Lumpur, in lightface type at the bottom. This projected a smugness in keeping with the image of SPF.

Image is all-important in advertising. Image is also why Ben likes the three-name thing. Benjamin Green, or worse, Ben Green, sounds like your uncle the accountant, or the guy who runs the corner deli. Add Franklin in the middle and the name might suddenly have something of a Colonial American ring to it. Ben likes that. Good for his image in the ad business, and for the image he carries around inside himself, the image of who he really is and what he really feels like. Actually, Ben's late uncle was an accountant named Ben Green. Sometimes image and reality are very different things. Ben thinks about that a lot.

Ben Franklin Green, namesake of the early American savant, rake, inventor and snatcher of lightning, was an introspective guy in his mid thirties with a steady gaze that clients sometimes mistook for resolve. His dark hair was unfashionably long for the yuppified eighties, hanging below his collar. He kept it that way because it was a timeless style in the creative department, and besides, he'd always had a vague affinity for wildness. The prairie over the suburban lawn. Or so he rationalized. In truth, he just looked good in long hair. Short haircuts made him feel fat.

He had a nice face that went crooked when he smiled, but women said the smile was sexy. When Ben scrutinizes this face in the mirror, as he sometimes does, an unmanly lapse into vanity, he thinks he looks something like the movie star, Warren Beatty. The way Beatty looked in *Shampoo*, a pretty good film of the seventies, an era with such an interesting essence, its afterglow was felt even in these sensible times, at least by Ben. (He remembers young Julie Christie grabbing Beatty under the table, loudly drunk, telling the room, "I'd like to suck his cawk!" Ben smiles. Sweet, salty Julie.) But the Beatty image doesn't bear close analysis and an annoying Dustin Hoffman tries to intrude. Ben won't let the little guy in. He turns away from the mirror, embarrassed for caring anyway.

He was in the habit of working out before going to the office. He was strong; always was. At fourteen he surprised a punchy-looking judo teacher by flipping him. "No student throws me!" the man raged. Encouraged, Ben nagged his father for another year's worth of lessons. Maybe the teacher wasn't as punchy as he looked. Things aren't always what they seem. Ben didn't stay with judo, but he knew the moves and was built for it. His arms were thick and his legs had spring. Even at five-ten, he could grab the orange steel rim of a basketball hoop.

All things considered, Ben looked like a formidable young man at the height of his power. A little offbeat perhaps, but full of confidence, a man on a mission. However (and it cannot be repeated often enough in a tale involving the advertising business), outward appearance is not always what it seems.

So Ben, now no longer in advertising and similarly no longer permitted to tap dance (however innocently, unknowingly) on the cabin floor, tuned down Janis Joplin and sat back, slightly drunk and disoriented, wondering what was coming next. He didn't expect to fall asleep. But it happened, the best kind of sleep, the kind you don't try to make happen.

*   *   *

A sudden quietness in the cabin awoke him. It was fully dark outside now, but when he looked down he saw L.A.'s glow, millions of hazy lights woven into gridlines, illuminating the smoggy air hanging over the city like smoke.

The pilot played his repertoire of frightening noises, a performance Ben always associated with the auto racing term downshifting. Ben began to imagine vivid crash scenarios as he always did during landings. The wheels would snag on high-tension wires and the plane would nose over, exploding in flames. Or the tail would scrape on the runway and they'd crack open, tossing out passengers like dice, still strapped helplessly in their uprooted seats.

While he went through this litany of disaster, the plane touched down smoothly as usual, but decelerated with a roar that confirmed there is, indeed, some worrisome violence beneath the superficial calm of air travel. The plane docked and once again Ben found himself in the eucalyptus and ozone of L.A. The place you go when your attachment to another part of the continent has been removed. As though the rotation of the planet slides anything west that's not firmly fastened, all the way west until the country stops and things pile up.

*   *   *

Ben took the familiar route to his usual Hollywood hotel, the Regency Marquis, climbing up La Cienega into the Hollywood hills. The rental car was red, his only request, not caring what make or model, but simply that it be red. This was done with a nod of wistful respect for the young copywriter he'd been years ago on his first TV production trip to L.A.

Back then, by chance, he'd been given a red Camarro. Low-slung, spirited and so hotly red. He'd rolled down the windows, high on L.A.'s heady air, turned up America's *Horse With No Name* until he could feel the music in his chest, and drove, astounded by purple flowers at the side of the road, and the palms, strange science fiction trees from another world.

The Regency Marquis back then was the well-known first choice among Madison Avenue and Michigan Avenue types coming to Hollywood for a week or two of TV commercial making. It was a marijuana-scented swimming pool community of fast-talking men in designer jeans, sleek white-collar ladies, bikinied girlfriends and over-tanned studio reps. It was better than other hotels, because every room was a suite. A little home, Ben thought. You'd have a living room, one or two bedrooms, a kitchen and dining room. Even a balcony, overlooking pool and bikinis.

The Regency Marquis was getting a little beat-up looking. Some of the gloss had faded. Or, maybe it was just Ben. Still, it had been his home ever since he'd started coming to Hollywood and he was glad to see it again. He checked into a second floor suite and went right to bed. The residual buzz from the flight and its hangover exhaustion helped Ben get to sleep but at three in the morning it wore off and he awoke, unreasonably alert, his mind on overdrive, a familiar occupational hazard.

The bed slanted sideways as though its previous occupants had been a couple whose weights were cruelly mismatched. With the heightened imagination of an insomniac creative director in the dark, Ben pictured the husband a scrawny anemic, a man who could never find a dress shirt with a small enough neck. The wife was an enormous Namibian with Hottentot thighs, their marriage being mixed racially as well as morphologically. Her two hundred sixty pounds, which she wore well, having a cute face with a kissable cupid's bow mouth had, over time, pressed the bed down on one side, giving it this irksome slant.

Ben moved sideways on his back, until in a nest of wrinkled sheet he settled into the center point, between the imaginary skinny guy and his whalish wife. Why, he thought, do hotel sheets come out and slide around under you? And why are hotel rooms never as nice as the pictures of them seen on postcards and brochures. More lies.

That's another one for his coffee table book, he thought. That, and the stewardess on the flight out with her surly unsexiness. And he began to imagine the pages of photographs he was going to assemble. He was free to start the project now. Free of Deborah, whom he'd probably call tomorrow, just to say hello. He doubted he'd get to sleep with her, with her schedule. Free of SPF, too, after dropping out of the presentation and never dropping back in. Free of nine-to-five, which, in advertising, often became nine to midnight. Or, to be fair, ten or eleven to midnight; starting hours had some latitude on the creative floor. That's all in the past now, he thought.

He'd talk to Cole about the coffee table book idea tomorrow. Cole could be encouraging. This book, long imagined but never brought to life, was going to be a humorous indictment of advertising, an exposure of the flat-out lies that everyone seems to expect, accept and allow for. Ben first got the idea for it while sitting alone in a Burger Barrel on Michigan Avenue.

Above the counter there'd been a poster of their famed Wow Burger, looking like one of mom's hand-slapped patties. Juices sparkled. Tomatoes were the reddest red. Onions were cut thick. Dollops of ketchup and mustard were artfully applied, and held together neatly. Ben had sat there studying the poster, partly as an ad guy appreciative of compelling work, partly as someone who was hungry. He'd felt good about his decision to order the Wow Burger and unwrapped it with anticipation.

There it lay, dripping and bent. Lifting the bun top, he saw sauces that had run together, looking like water someone cleaned paintbrushes in. The tomatoes were salmon-colored, onions were translucent shavings. And the star of this tired strip show was not the slab of hefty ground beef shown in the poster, but a thin gray disk. Ben gave a mental shrug and ate the sandwich, enjoying it. Once again, he'd understood, as everyone does, that there's a difference between advertising (the burger in the photo) and reality (the burger in your hand).

His book would illustrate this. *"Unreal! Advertising versus Reality."* Photos, side-by-side, would show the advertised version of a thing, then the thing as it really is. He'd shoot the real things himself. The point was not to use professional tricks. Just aim and shoot, like he'd have done with his own sorry Wow Burger. Reality. He'd thought of other examples. Fried chicken, perfect in ads, but shapeless in reality's greasy bucket.

He could fill the book with food products, but he'd go beyond that and show all kinds of things. Flight attendants in commercials are flirtatious starlets. In reality they can be overworked waitresses with PMS. Or even guys. Muffler shop men in ads are fatherly six-footers in company cap, tie and smile. What about the tattooed teenager in reality's muffler shop? He'd show both, side by side. He just had to gather the ad pictures, which he'd do with help from agency friends, then take his own reality shots. If only the night would end, he thought, he'd get going.

As morning light gradually illuminated the room, Ben drifted back to sleep, knowing with certainty that he was lying sideways on the slope of a hill, but forgetting why and not caring.

# 4.

It was a short walk to Greenblatt's, the deli on Sunset that Ben liked to visit when he was in town. He enjoyed taking it slowly, noticing little things as he went, like the matted L.A. grass, different from the smooth kind seen in Chicago lawns. He stopped to watch some Oregon juncos fussing in the foliage. He saw a rufous hummingbird working a row of red flowers, looking more like an insect than a bird. A red-shafted flicker flew over, dipping and rising in the roller coaster flight of all woodpeckers, disappearing into the hills above Laurel Canyon.

Ben had become interested in birds after being forced to do a report about them in grade school. At the time, he'd thought there were only two or three kinds. Gray pigeons, brown sparrows, maybe a robin. He'd lived in the city. But his report uncovered the fact that they came in many different colors, shapes and styles that captured his imagination.

Over the years, he'd quietly kept track of bird sightings and had a respectable life list of nearly three hundred species. The popular image of bird watcher was a little too dweeby for Ben to feel comfortable with, image being important, as it was, to him and his world. He recalled a poem by outdoorsman and author Jim Harrison in which a man's life list ". . . is precise and astonishing, my only secret." And so it was with Ben's, a private thing, even a private pride.

As the red-shafted flicker faded into the smog, Ben turned the corner, into Greenblatt's for one of their famous blueberry muffins and a cup of coffee. He called Deborah from the pay phone in back. Her secretary had him hold for the obligatory several minutes. Then Deborah was there.

"Ben?"

"I'm in L.A. I quit SPF."

"Ben!"

Quitting a job was serious news to Deborah. "Did you get a better offer? Is it out *here?*"

"No. No other job. Don't really want one, I think."

Early in their brief marriage Deborah had told Ben that her career was everything, that it would always come first in their life. (Curiously, this was not an entirely unheard of philosophy back in the 1980s. Hey, greed was good.) He could certainly understand her ambition, she'd said, couldn't he?

They worked at a factory-like Chicago ad agency, two shops prior to SPF. They were on the same account team, devising a campaign for cholesterol-free eggs. He was the group creative chief and she was an account executive. She'd paid him little attention until he'd said something in pre-meeting small talk that made her look at him with new interest. He'd said that the project was going well, and his group had many strong executions. So . . ."I think I'll just send my people home this weekend."

Actually, weekend work was part of the job for some, but Ben felt it was usually unnecessary, a showy kind of overkill, and almost never forced it on his staff. Deborah didn't know this about him, and hadn't realized he'd been joking. The bantering remark meant to satirize the work ethic of the place went right over her head. Taking it literally, she saw something exciting here, and licked her lips. This was a man who took his job by the balls. A guy who would go places.

She was good looking and breasty. Ben, young and unseasoned in the ways of romance, had eventually fallen for her falling for him. In between meetings and business trips they'd courted and married. The marriage was exciting at first. Sex without dating. What could be wrong with that? But it dissolved over the next few years, so gradually that there was never a recognizable last moment. One or the other had always been in late meetings or on out-of-town trips. When they were both home at the same time, it was still kind of nice. But there was an emptiness, their lovemaking having the quality of a one-night stand.

Ben had received an inter-office memo one afternoon from Deborah. It said she'd lucked into an assignment at their London office that would take her away for quite a while and they might as well untangle themselves legally during that time. The sadness of that memo, the failure it embodied, was deep, an almost physical presence in Ben's chest that made breathing difficult for a while.

But he was kept busy by the busiest of businesses, and the long hours, the meetings, the travel to both coasts, served to distract him somewhat, deflecting or at least covering over the sadness until it no longer seemed to matter, or even be there. And when Deborah eventually returned to Chicago, they were still friends, occasionally even bed partners. A practical and familiar outlet for both busy people.

But she'd recently taken a vice presidency at her agency's L.A. office, finally becoming what everyone in the business called an "ad biggie." She must still have her hormones, though, or at least Ben hoped. So he called her first, hoping he could talk her into coming to the Regency Marquis after work.

"Oh, shit!" She'd said in the soft tone some women have that makes a swear word sound perfectly polite. "I'm leaving for New York on the

red-eye. I'm in meetings all afternoon, then I'll have to pack and dash
to the airport. But, Ben?"

"Yes."

"Send us your resume, okay? Something big could open up
downstairs. If I tell you, don't say a word. Promise?"

"Promise."

"Okay. I think we're getting Subaru! We'll need people if it happens
but don't breathe this to anyone. Please?"

"Have a good trip, Deborah."

And he replaced the receiver gently. He left the deli and walked west
on Sunset enjoying the garish billboards endemic to that street, mostly
advertising rock stars, showing them to be surprisingly attractive.

# 5.

The young woman knew she'd have trouble surviving nights alone and
naked in the mountains. Days were mild, but after dark, temperatures
dropped into the thirties.

After becoming lost, she ran in one direction, then another, pulse
racing, surprised at herself, as she was not by nature prone to fearfulness
and took pride in keeping a clear head in all situations. At one point, she
thought she heard a voice in the distance, faintly calling her name, and
she forced herself to stand immobile, listening, but beyond the thump
of her heart there was nothing and she dismissed this as impossible, a
kind of auditory mirage.

Eventually, she calmed and planned a sensible response, based on
something she'd seen in an outdoor survival guide. The memory was
vague, having the feel of those droning schoolroom litanies about
where to go during earthquakes or tornadoes. And like those, it was
probably incorrect. But she believed the recommended procedure
involved walking in a circle.

She did this dutifully, barefoot over broken rocks and bristly
vegetation, widening the circle's circumference as recommended, the
theory being that she should inevitably re-encounter the brook and find

her belongings. Hours later, with the sun lowering above raw peaks that she hadn't noticed before, she'd given up and simply sat on the ground, looking at the mountains, wondering where on earth she was.

A movement in the sky. From the nearest mountaintop a small hawk was approaching, its silhouette unmistakable. In spite of everything, the woman looked at it with interest.

*　*　*

The young male peregrine falcon hadn't killed in days and was weakening. To stay healthy, he'd need about a pound of meat every other day, a grouse, duck or quail, every other day at least. To hunt, a peregrine hovers at altitude, watching for game to take wing. Then as the prey flaps over the ground the falcon dives, splitting the air at more than a hundred miles an hour. As it nears the target, feathers designed for speed can no longer remain still and the bird vibrates with an ominous hum, perhaps causing panic in its target, but by this time the outcome has already been determined.

Either the falcon will miss through bad luck or bad judgement, or it will hit the bird, killing it. Then, if it can avoid trees or landforms when pulling out of the dive, held tightly in the curve of its own momentum, the falcon will calmly fly back to its downed victim. It will pull away breast feathers and rip open the bird's soft underside, first taking the heart and liver, drawing warm blood into its curved beak. It will eat from the inside, so when finished, there will be a hollow game bird to be blown across the grass in the next breeze, weightless, its feathers still shining.

But this falcon was not truly wild. He had been hatched and raised by scientists and their students. In the eighties, there were several programs throughout the country designed to re-introduce these endangered birds into habitats where they were once at home and plentiful.

He was not truly wild for another reason. A small, battery-powered transmitter around his neck gave off a silent signal.

The falcon had been an unsuccessful hunter, catching no wild birds since his release. He had been able to take a few pigeons near a highway overpass. But traffic noise and fumes frightened him, and pigeon flesh had an unnatural taste. So he moved deeper into the back country. Now weakness clouded his vision, and made his wings heavy. If the falcon didn't eat soon, he would simply rest in a tree and patiently starve to death.

Then he saw something in the grass below and with spontaneity born of desperation, dove in for a look. He circled low, impatient, incautious with hunger. The human looked different, all pink skin and unbound hair that blew around like yellow grass, but these subtleties didn't matter. In his experience, such creatures meant food.

*   *   *

The woman was surprised, momentarily frightened, when the young peregrine dropped from the sky, not veering away, coming right to her. It landed on the ground nearly at her feet, and she arose from the grass, all her attention on the bird.

She approached the falcon and knelt. It opened its beak, looking up at her, begging like a hatchling. She noticed that it had a band around its leg. And there was something delicate and technical looking affixed to its neck, a small electronic device.

# 6.

Lara came from the house walking quickly toward them and Ben could see something was wrong. She sat next to Cole stiffly, not leaning back. She swallowed.

"Honey. I just got a phone call. A man, I don't know who. He said he's got Abby, kidnapped her, but she's okay and we should not tell the police. *Kidnapped?* I said. He just said he wants money but won't be greedy. And he said he'd call back."

Lara looked sick. Cole stood quickly, tightening the belt on his robe, his face suddenly gray under the tan.

"Let's call her."

"I did. She wasn't there. Her answering machine only. I left a message to call us. I said, call us right away. Oh my god, Andrew . . ."

The moment was unsettling. Ben didn't belong in it with them. It was unreal. Ben, sitting calmly with them just minutes ago, enjoying their time together, catching up and looking forward to good things with his coffee table book idea, which now seemed stupid, embarrassing, just embarrassing.

Ben wanted to disappear. To call others for help. He wanted to have never arrived at Cole's mountainside haven. It had started so nicely.

*   *   *

Ben thought Cole had it made when he'd first met him more than a decade ago. But Ben, older and wiser now, knew Cole had it made when he saw how the guy was living these days in the hills of Santana, overlooking L.A.'s hazy Valley, standing eyeball to eyeball with snowcapped mountains that appeared out of nowhere on days when the smog lay low.

Cole had the kind of home you see in movies. Actually, you may well have seen it in movies if they were filmed before '85. That's when he and Lara figured they could live just as well without the $25,000 a day that studios paid for location shooting. They preferred not to have their place overrun with cables, lights, props, wardrobe racks, coffee vats, cameras, booms, lounging crew people and sweating actors who were always having their faces sponged off, their armpit stains blown dry. The star would stand, arms raised in the classic stickup pose, as makeup artists waved pistol-shaped hairdryers at them. The Coles didn't need it.

These days they liked things quiet. The alligator made hardly any noise, except when eating. Often there was just the sound of Lara practicing her cello, the whir of hummingbirds, and the occasional clacking of Cole's old typewriter as he hammered the words together, one at a time, that might become another bit of advertising history.

He'd taken copywriting from craft to art. For years his ads were simply thought of as good ads. They'd won awards. Made clients rich. But over time, people in and out of advertising began to wonder: Who did these? And Andrew Beale Cole gradually became known. A New York publisher invited Cole to write a book, which they called *The*

*ABC of Advertising*, a gimmicky but appropriate play on his initials. It collected his work with charming anecdotes, success stories and apologies. It became, fittingly, a big seller.

Cole, who had always made good money in advertising, suddenly found himself in the rarified world of classical income. Giant blue-chip companies, the world's biggest advertisers with budgets to match, came to him. And they paid well for a few executions. Now, with millions stashed, Cole didn't seek more work. His only regular account was his first one, a neighborhood bank in Chicago's suburbs. He'd fax ad ideas to them from his mountaintop and bill the same rate he'd used as an ad kid just starting out. For old time's sake, not money.

Ben called Cole "the old man," but Cole was probably not over sixty. When they'd first met, Ben was interviewing for a copywriter's job at the hot agency where Cole ran the creatives. Cole had been imposing, with a salt and pepper beard, a full head of hair, and bushy eyebrows giving him a hawkish intensity that didn't express his true personality. He was actually a mix of bemused intelligence and a surprising serenity not usually seen in creative directors. Cole had been touched by Ben's earnestness and impressed with his portfolio.

"Invent an ad for me, Mr. Ben Franklin Green," Cole said in the smiling voice no one would associate with that sharply browed face.

"Look over there," Cole said, leading Ben to the window, pointing at a towering hotel that had recently opened near Lake Michigan.

"Walk over to The Saint Martin. Look around. Come back. I'll give you an empty office and in an hour, you give me an ad that would make a business traveler choose this hotel over any other in Chicago."

Other applicants had presented perfectly professional executions. One showed the city's skyline and said, "The St. Martin puts you in the center of things." One indicated a view of the hotel's rooftop pool and said: "A resort in the city." And so on. Hotel ads that looked like hotel ads.

Not Ben's. He came back from his visit to the St. Martin and told Cole he wouldn't need an office. Or an hour.

"Here's what I'd do." He took a pad of paper from his briefcase and sketched an empty parking stall in an underground garage. Grease-stained floor. Concrete pillars. Very unglamorous. There were cars parked on each side of the empty space, drawn loosely in bold line, bloopy taillights, oversize license plates.

Ben's drawing took up most of the page. No picture of a towering hotel. No fancy logotype. Just some small words above the empty parking stall. They said: "Stay at the St. Martin, and you'll get your own private parking space. As well as a room."

Ben broke Cole's silence. "See, they're the only hotel in town that offers that. And in a city like Chicago, people drive. They either come here in cars, or rent them at the airport. They want a place to park."

Cole looked at him, nodding. "Perhaps you could add that to your copy, something brief at the bottom. Do that and we'll get an art director to work this up. I'll take it to the hotel this afternoon. Want to come along? I'll introduce you to their marketing guy."

"I've got the job?"

This reminiscing about that long ago meeting had a familiar feeling, seeming to use mental muscles which had been freshly exercised. Ben realized he'd been flashing back in time a lot lately, replaying professional and personal memories that were quite strong. Perhaps this was because his mind was now free from the demands of office work. Free from having to generate ad concepts the way chickens in factory farms disgorge egg after egg. Free at last, to investigate itself?

And where's the harm? He went through the wall, and now he'll just roam around on the other side for a while if he pleases. He'll freely backtrack the memory banks as often as he likes. Perhaps a kind of solace lies in the past. Maybe more than solace, maybe something that helps us figure out the present. So we can enjoy it, or at least tolerate it.

Ben had wanted Cole's encouragement again in order to get the "Unreal! Advertising vs. Reality " book out of the idea stage. He called him from the Chalet Gourmet on Sunset.

"Come on up," Cole said. He'd just finished his morning writing project, some radio scripts for the bank in Chicago, and was about to spend the rest of the day hanging around the pool.

"Since you're in the Chalet, pick up some live lobsters. Put them on my account."

The trip took an hour but it was good driving, lots of turns on narrow roads overgrown with gaudy California foliage, and there were views of the valleys on either side of the Hollywood Hills. Ben drove with the windows open, enjoying the smell of sun-baked dust and sweet eucalyptus. It was a warm day, and he pictured swimming at Cole's. He changed his mind after seeing the alligator. He'd almost forgotten about Alf.

Last time Cole had come through Chicago, he'd told Ben and some of their old friends a wild story about how his daughter, Abby, had smuggled a young alligator into California against state laws to save it from some kind of science experiment. Ben assumed the alligator was little. How else could Abby have smuggled it?

"He *was* little, sure. But he grew," Cole said.

They were standing at the edge of the pool. In its center floated a six-foot alligator, immobile as the dead log his breed had evolved to mimic. Eyes half shut. Legs dangling. He lazed in pure saurian self-confidence, ending any thoughts of swimming that Ben might have had. Cole, smiling in a big terry robe, said, "I like to feed him *before* I swim."

He took the Chalet bag from Ben. "These are for him."

And Cole dropped the lobsters into the pool. They sank slowly and Alf opened his eyes all the way. Lara came up from behind Ben and hugged him.

"How nice to see you, Mr. Ben Franklin." Still a trace of Swedish in her speech. Its lilt and earthiness.

She took him by the arm, away from the pool and the alligator.

"Come, let's sit in the shade. Would you like a beer?"

Lara led Ben to a patio table under a canvas umbrella that rippled in the breeze. From a cooler she brought out two dripping bottles of Leinenkugel, a butterscotchy regional beer brewed only in Wisconsin in those days.

"Hey, an import," and Ben swallowed deeply, drinking more than he expected before coming up for air, not realizing how thirsty he'd become.

"Andrew loves it. He has a friend up there somewhere who sends us a case every once in a while."

"Cole always did have a friend up there."

And Ben squinted toward the robed figure kneeling in the glare of the pool, watching Alf deal with the lobsters. Ben settled back, staring at Lara now, feeling good to be in this semitropical haven with the rich beer, already working, with ash blonde Lara and old King Cole, his inimitable mentor, whom Ben realized was living the life of a Gauguin up here amid palmettos and sun.

Now in her forties, Lara still looked much like the Lara in Ben's memory. Her eyes were icy blue and her features had that economy of line for which Scandinavian designers are justifiably proud, making makeup unnecessary. That her ash blonde hair was natural was confirmed by wispy pale ringlets under her arms and the fine coating of goldish fuzz on her legs. Ben noticed a little lower belly. This was a charming new development, which came forward in unselfconscious convexity, distracting Ben with the sudden urge to run his hands over it.

Years back, Ben and Cole had to spend a week at the Regency Marquis while filming commercials. Lara had come with them, bringing along their daughter Abby, a tall girl just developing breasts, as Ben couldn't help but notice since she swam only in cutoffs. The family had a Norse casualness about bodies, which had made Ben a bit uncomfortable.

Cole and Ben would be away filming in the mornings, but they spent afternoons around the pool with Lara, Abby and others from the film company. There were jugs of wine and cold cuts. Judy Collins would be singing sweetly on someone's tape player.

Once Cole had sneaked up on Ben and Lara and slipped ice cubes into their bathing suits. Ben hopped around, holding the leg of his suit open until the cubes dropped out, but Lara, standing calmly next to Ben, simply pulled the front of her bikini bottom down, holding it with one hand, reaching in with the other to scoop up the cubes, laughing.

It took several scoops to finish the job, while her front was open to Ben's view, a perfect delta of blonde, shining with coppery highlights in the sun. This was exciting to see, and doubly exciting that Lara was so casual, as though saying to Ben, of course I have this little pussy, and of course you can see it, you're my friend.

Since that incident, Ben had always thought of Lara with a special fondness. He remembered how, on that long ago night in Hollywood, with Deborah back in Chicago, he'd lain in bed alone and sleep being hard to come by, he'd come by thinking of Lara.

Cole swam nude and Lara seemed to enjoy ogling her husband as she and Ben talked, making Ben feel oddly disconcerted. He certainly didn't want to see Lara these days in anything other than a proper, almost aunt-like role, that long-ago vision of down-pulled bikini notwithstanding.

But there was a rising horniness in Ben that he felt now, as much with him as was the recently acknowledged tendency toward reflection of things past. Pretty understandable, too, he thought, and long overdue. He'd been divorced for years and although there had been tentative dating, his energies had been directed, wastefully, wistfully, toward the job.

Now, thrown free finally, he was picking up all these scents on the air, and they'd probably always been there but he'd been too busy to notice. Or maybe it was just California. So what. Cool it, he told himself. The blonde and wonderfully fuzzy Lara is certainly and forever Cole's, and Ben had better get his mind out of her bikini bottom. After his swim, Cole padded over to join them.

"I see Alf still hasn't bitten it off," Lara said, making a playful grab toward Cole as he stood dripping next to her chair, toweling his face.

"Come on. We've got a guest!"

"But I just might," she said giggling, showing teeth. It was just play to her, but Ben, amazed and squirming, turned away to search for another Leinenkugel, rooting around in the cooler, thinking, maybe Deborah will be back from New York soon, and if she's in a friendly mood, well, who knows.

Cole, robed and dry now, sat with Ben after Lara went inside to fix dinner. Cole liked *Unreal! Advertising vs. Reality.* He'd told Ben he could talk it up to a New York agent who worked on publishing *The ABC of Advertising.*

Ben, feeling free and more optimistic than he'd felt in a long time, buzzed on the rich beer, put his feet on an empty chair and slid down in his seat. It was late afternoon and shadow from the mountains spread over them, but in the distance below, the Valley still sat in warm sunshine.

Then Lara got that phone call.

# 7.

Cole took Lara's hand and said, "Let's get in. They might call again."

It felt cold now, by the pool in the shade. Ben followed, wanting to give them privacy but knowing he should stay. *Unbelievable!* he thought. But then he considered Cole's recent high profile and millions of dollars and what a target their daughter must be, working alone as she did out there in the wide open spaces.

No one felt much like talking. They sat in the Coles' living room, waiting. It grew dark and Lara, now in slacks and sweater, got up and went around clicking on lamps. Cole left briefly, returning in Levi's and a blue work shirt, tails out. It was a large room with a Southwestern hacienda feel. Comfortable furniture in white and turquoise. Stucco walls hung with Indian rugs. Beams in the ceiling. Picture windows overlooked the valley, which became a world of lights. A cobblestone fireplace stood unused and cold, smelling faintly of soot.

Earlier, Ben had been brought up to date about Abby's recent whereabouts from Cole and Lara when the threat was still new and before the strain of waiting helplessly for the phone to ring brought them all to grim silence.

Their daughter was a headstrong and independent woman, living in Colorado, working on a university wildlife project. "The PRP," Cole called it. Then, translating, "Peregrine Release Program. They raise endangered hawks. I don't know. Trying to repopulate the earth with these creatures while they can. Abby knows all about it. She's hooked on the thing."

"She likes being outdoors, always did," Lara said, smiling, trying for a light, conversational manner. There is comfort in maintaining the feel of normalcy. But her lips were colorless.

"She certainly didn't care much for L.A.," Cole said.

Then, to pass the hours, to bring their daughter closer, to place her in the room with them, they talked about Abby.

"Did you know why we named her Abby?" Lara said. And Cole told about the raft trip he'd taken more than twenty years ago.

He'd needed time away from the "suits" who were enjoying some ascendancy back then, their interests running more to research papers and power attire than creativity. So he'd signed up for a whitewater adventure in Utah and had fallen into the company of a fellow rafter, a redneck philosopher who lived on royalties earned from a wrench he'd invented.

When the man wasn't lazing down some river, he'd spend his time writing iconoclastic essays and haunting novels while living with much younger women in a trailer he kept out of civilization's reach in the Sonoran Desert. One day the inventor saved Cole from drowning. Their raft tipped in rapids and Cole went over, which can be part of the fun, but his life vest came off in the current and he'd banged his head on the bottom. The man jumped in, grabbing Cole, and the river washed them ahead of the other rafts, floating for hours until the water slowed and the man could pull Cole, dazed but alive, to a deserted riverine beach.

Above them rose ancient redrock cliffs on which the two men discovered petroglyphs, rock paintings made by artists long extinct. Cole didn't know the man's first name, but his last was Abbey. When Cole got home, he found out Lara was pregnant and months later, when she delivered their daughter, they both thought it was a fine idea to give her the name of the man who saved Cole's life.

"She spells it without the "e" though," Lara said, "because that's the way girls spell it," and she smiled.

"It fits that she'd become a hater of crowds and lover of open places," Cole said. "Like her namesake, who's probably still out in the canyons somewhere, raising hell."

Then the phone rang. It was the call they'd been waiting for.

# 8.

Ben was drinking Tanqueray martinis with two olives and a twist each, at Madame Ling's on Rodeo Drive. He'd arrived at 6:30, long before the crowds, and felt mysterious, wearing a pair of stone washed Levi's, old Dingo boots which added inches, getting him up to about six feet, he figured, a black T-shirt over which he wore a comfortable bush jacket. His hair was longer than usual and he hadn't shaved since falling through the wall in Chicago.

Cole and Lara had laughed like kids over the wall thing, carefree, half-drunk, enjoying the smells of chlorine and Lara's coconut sunscreen, long before the first of last night's unreal phone calls. Hard to believe it had only been last night. Seemed like days since Ben took the winding road to Cole's to talk about his coffee table book idea.

With the beginnings of a true beard now and the devil-may-care attitude brought on by the first sips of high-powered gin, he felt people might take him for a movie star. Scott Glen, wanting to be left alone after a day of filming dangerous chase scenes.

He'd come to Madame Ling's as he'd done often when shooting in L.A. because it had great, snob-appeal Chinese food. Also, he often saw celebrities there, and although ashamed to admit it, he was excited by these and all celebrity sightings.

(He remembered spending two days making a commercial with Barbara Eden, whom he'd had the hots for since I Dream of Jeannie. At lunch she asked if she could sit next to him, and he immediately choked on a Frito, causing his eyes to fill with tears and his nose to run uncontrollably. He eventually excused himself to Barbara Eden, saying that he had to check the next camera set-up. Curiously, he'd had no trouble talking to her when they were filming. Then, he would be charming and kind, telling her which words to stress, where to pause. But small talk had always been a big problem.)

This early solo dinner at Madame Ling's would give him a chance to review the bizarre events of the last few days. His quitting the agency and gravitating to L.A. had seemed big enough. But last night's stunning phone calls had dimmed this to insignificance. Ben drained the last few drops of his martini and ordered another from one of the waiters waiting idly in Mao pajamas around the empty restaurant, waiting for the time when normal customers with functioning body clocks would arrive.

The table tops at Madame Ling's were lit from beneath, white glow under white linen, giving everything on the table an artistic underlighting. The Mao pajamas guy set Ben's new martini before him, and the light came into the cold gin in a way that Ben found frankly beautiful. Better than advertising. Better than reality.

Ben realized he was becoming somewhat intoxicated. Enjoying the feeling, he began to drink his second of the night. He'd had some of his best ideas when drinking, but had often forgotten them upon sobering. He took a pad and pen from his jacket and set them on the table. This time he'd take notes.

*     *     *

They'd waited hours for the kidnappers' second phone call. *Kidnappers?* Ben shook his head. *Can this be for real?* Anyway, this call gave specific demands, again emphasizing the importance of not going to authorities of any kind. Cole had spoken to the kidnapper while Lara and Ben watched. Cole didn't say much, taking notes, listening. He'd asked if he could talk with Abby and after he did, showed some silent emotion, his mouth working in and out of an unintentional Bogart sneer. He'd said Abby sounded quite normal but they didn't let her talk long.

It shook up the Coles, and its effect on this stalwart pair shook up Ben in turn. He'd stayed at their place all night, discussing the situation in short bursts, all three coming up incredulous and quiet at the end. They couldn't talk to anyone else. What could they do?

At dawn, Ben drove Cole to LAX for an early flight to Denver and went back to the Regency Marquis where he spent the day napping on his balcony, looking with some guilt at girls sunning by the pool, wives or companions of ad guys on shoots.

*     *     *

The waiter offered a menu. Ben knocked back what was left in his glass, and placing the menu politely off to the side, smiled and signaled for a third martini. He was enjoying the buzz, which he pictured as a gentle force field slowing his movements perhaps, but keeping his mind clear, like the backlit gin itself.

Ben opened the notepad, ready for whatever insights might arise. Other diners arrived and waiters began to hurry around, carrying the scene-stealing Mongolian firepots that flamed at Madame Ling's, her eternal lamps.

The kidnappers told Cole they didn't want money. What they wanted was diamonds. Ben doodled on the pad, drawing a geometrically complex diamond, adding facets inside facets, wondering how Cole would convert all that cash into stones, when he became distracted by a hubbub at an empty table across the aisle from him.

Waiters were hustling, laying out a multi-course meal including dangerously flaming firepots, bringing forth in Ben's ginned-up memory scenes from a novel about Marco Polo in which Mongolian warriors camped around similarly flaming bonfires with their short-legged horses, which must have seemed long-legged enough, Ben thought, to the short-legged Mongols.

Ben had never seen waiters fuss over guests who weren't there. Must be a major financial inducement. He mentally added up the costs of their soups, appetizers, and large number of chrome-domed main dishes. Math was never Ben's strength. Something about it made his mind sit down and clamp hands over ears. But, when drinking, Ben could compute with uncanny speed, skipping the plodding intermediate steps, somehow getting correct answers in seconds, a cocktail-breathed idiot savant.

He figured $500 worth of delicacies would soon be cold. (1987 dollars, mind you). Must be movie stars. He settled back with pleasure, knowing he had an aisle seat, finishing the last of his third, savoring the taste as though it were fine silver wine.

The kidnapper had said to Cole, *don't tell the cops*. Life imitating art imitating life imitating art, and so on. Ben sat amazed at how corny the whole thing was. He recalled Studs Terkel going on about the "banality of evil." The gadfly Chicago philosopher had often used that phrase, attributed, Ben vaguely remembered, to the writer Hannah Arndt.

Terkel said it often when talking about criminals, KKK guys, holocaust monsters, villains who changed the world yet were surprisingly loutish, the banality of evil. *Don't tell the cops.*

Suddenly, Ben, swelling with righteous gin-fueled anger, knew he could rescue the girl and hunt down the banal bastards who'd taken her. He knew it with the same boozy certainty that rose up at these moments and gave him strange powers over mathematics.

The maitre d' rushed to greet the royalty arriving to take places at the fully pre-set table across from Ben. Ben didn't look over there right away, enjoying the suspense, knowing they'd soon be seated in front of him. He flipped the page of diamond doodles, exposing fresh paper. The thought hit that with his pad and pen handy, he could get autographs if the big shots were big enough. He chuckled audibly at this, surprising himself, and cleared his throat as a cover up. Maybe appetizers were needed before Martini number four.

Finally, Ben looked.

*Whoa!* He saw a graying grandmother sitting sullen and unimpressed. Looked a little like his own Grandma Gladys. There was a fortyish man with blow-dried hair flapped over a balding head, egg roll in hand. His wife wore a jogging suit and looked somewhat like Ben's ex, but Deborah only wore business suits. There were three kids, one wearing frayed jeans and untied sneakers. The family was the quintessence of the ordinary and should have been at a drive-in. Shakes, burgers and fries. Or maybe a pizza at some kid-themed restaurant. Ben had the urge to demand his money back.

He signaled to the waiter and ordered appetizers and another martini, smiling too warmly. He felt uncomfortably alone at the moment and wanted even a cold-hearted, anonymous waiter to like him. To be his ally in this place where things don't turn out as expected.

It was probably just an alcohol-induced and therefore unreliable revelation, *but* he'd brought the pad, so scribbling now like some bearded Hollywood screenwriter, enjoying the feeling. He wrote in block letters, FRONTI NULLA FIDES.

He enjoyed the screenwriter impersonation even more when it struck him that this was the essence of what he just wrote. *He wasn't what he seemed.* Not a Hollywood screenwriter but a dropped-out adman. Even as an adman he wasn't what he seemed. Not a boardroom tiger. A nervous neurotic. The table wasn't prepared for stars. Just a guy with bad hair and his ordinary family. Deborah seemed like a great girl to marry. She wasn't. Planes seem safe. Not always. Stewardesses seem friendly. Don't bet on it. Hamburgers look perfect in ads. They're not, though usually edible.

FRONTI NULLA FIDES.

Where did that come from? Again, the idiot savant freed by booze was muttering, not in math talk now, but in Latin, dredging up this once seen, apparently never forgotten expression, first expressed by an ancient named Juvenal. "There's no trusting appearances." Ben's old philosophy teacher, Bech, harped on it, making it the semester's theme. Playing logic games that proved the universe was illusory, and that your desk didn't exist. A sophomoric legacy from a man aptly named Juvenal.

"No trusting appearances?" Ah, the banality of drunks. Why had this hit with the force of a breakthrough? No matter. Appetizers and a fourth martini had been set before him without his noticing. He moved the food out of the way and reached for the top-heavy drink.

Madame Ling's was a different restaurant when Ben left after nine. Hours earlier, lowering sun had filled the place with orange light, throwing his shadow against the back wall. Now the restaurant was illuminated only by glowing tabletops. The place was filled with people, smoke, laughter, the clinking of dishes.

Ben walked up the aisle in the overly precise manner of the overly indulged. He was curiously depressed, disconnected from the normal, connected vaguely to the abnormal of Abby's abduction. What was curious about this depression was that it didn't much bother him. Must be the gin, he thought, gratefully. Four martinis, maybe six.

He searched his bush jacket for the little plastic swords the olives had come on. Two per drink. He always saved these when drinking alone so he could keep count. He couldn't find them.

"Screw it," he mumbled aloud causing the maitre d' to stare. It didn't matter how much he'd had. He'd needed it. "Novocaine for the soul," he said not quite aloud, doing his impression of the world-weary McCabe staggering to Mrs. Miller's candle-lit bedroom. Warren and Julie again. "The old soul needs a root canal." And he pushed through the door into the refreshing clarity of Beverly Hills at night.

# 9.

Ben knew he couldn't drive back yet, thinking again about the olive swords hiding somewhere in the folds of some pocket or other, the lot of them signifying blood alcohol in the red zone.

"We'll walk now," he said aloud, unselfconscious. He strolled around the block, enjoying the cushiony buzz, window shopping the priciest shops in America, whistling at a $7,000 bomber jacket that looked exactly like one he got at Banana Republic back home for two fifty which, at the time, he thought was self-indulgent.

His head cleared slightly, and he remembered a nearby hangout he liked. Le Saloon. He crossed a few streets and headed east on Santa Monica, trusting his sense of direction, which was better after drinking than sober. This, probably because the censoring mechanism gets drowned out, and a man's natural instincts can just do their job.

Le Saloon used to be a fern bar but had matured with the times and now looked like a nineteenth-century pub. Ben found a place at the crowded rail and ordered a beer, suddenly thirsty from the sodium-heavy Chinese, drinking half of it immediately. He downed the rest and then ordered another, which he let sit.

The quick beer ganged with the martinis, brought Ben to a new height, causing the room to roll backwards when he squinted. With eyes wide open, though, Le Saloon looked idyllic, a spiral galaxy with him at its center. The people were comely. The lights golden. The jukebox played a jazzy, "Me and My Shadow," a song Ben felt indifferent to all his life, but here and now, he found himself liking it greatly.

Across the bar a man nuzzled a woman who looked like Deborah, but wasn't, couldn't be. They were sitting, surrounded by the backs of standing people pressing against them. The mass of bodies served as a wall to shield them, giving the two an ironic privacy only found in crowds.

Ben focused in on the couple with the zoom lens scrutiny of the inebriated, peripheral vision gone, a lone man watching TV in a dark room. But the scene was becoming too hot for TV. The man's hand moved up the slim body, cupping a breast of the woman who couldn't have been Deborah, because Deborah was in New York by now, as she'd said, their faces grinding, kissing hard, her hand resting on the seat between his legs.

"Me and My Shadow" no longer played. The mood changed as the jukebox vibrated with the bass tones of "Knights in White Satin," sad sex music from the seventies. Ben had become aroused, and with boozy unself-consciousness, stood up, openly readjusting, pulling at his jeans, pushing the little Louisville Slugger to one side, feeling it against his skin, hot and solid. He looked around temporarily insane with the idea of cuddling up to one of the many beautiful single women in the immediate vicinity, then shaking off the thought, knowing he was dangerously close to getting illegal.

(He remembered how his friend Ricky once got similarly stoned at a Rush Street bar and had drunkenly fondled a total stranger with the hallucinatory certainty that they were long-time mates, she at their kitchen sink doing dishes, he just an impish husband coming up behind, being affectionate. Ricky's dream had been shattered by the stranger's scream. She was a forty-year-old legal secretary in great shape, and could punch like a man. He was knocked silly, taken away in cuffs and sued for psychological damages. The woman had an office full of lawyers to goad her on. A year later, though, she'd called Ricky to apologize and invited him to dinner, but he refused to accept either offer.)

"Ricky, Ricky, Ricky . . ." Ben muttered. He held himself tightly against his belly and, with his other hand, waved for the bartender who was, incredibly, wearing a nametag that said "Ricky." Before telling the bartender what he wanted, struck by the enormity of this coincidence, staring stupidly at Ricky's nametag, Ben thought "this is gonna be a *Twilight Zone* night."

"Ricky," Ben began, trying to talk with precision, unslurry, "please use this," and he pushed a twenty toward the man from his pile of bills on the bar, "to buy those two over there," pointing now, "the ones kissing?" Ricky looked, then looked back at Ben. "Buy them a drink from me. Don't say who it was from. Just say a friend, okay?"

Ricky shrugged. "You got it my man," took the twenty and turned toward the coupling couple. Ben got up, and moving as though holding a folded umbrella he didn't want to poke anyone with, turned and pushed his way through the crowd.

Near the door was a pay phone, and Ben decided to use it to call Lara. This was only right, he mumbled to no one. He'd just force himself to concentrate, get serious, ignore the buzz.

"Hello?" Lara's voice, wary.

"Ben." Then, unnecessarily, "Ben Green."

"Ben, yes, hello."

"Anything new? Did you hear any more?"

"I did hear from Andrew, at the . . . place."

She paused. The silence was uncomfortable for Ben.

"Uh-huh . . ."

"I got the . . . things . . . they wanted. I'm going there tomorrow with them."

Ben remembered the kidnapper's demand that the Coles bring diamonds, a million dollars' worth, small sizes, one to four carats only, to a town called Grandy, somewhere in Colorado. They were supposed to wait in a motel there. They'd be contacted, he'd said.

"Can I help, Lara?"

"I don't know. I don't think so."

"I could do something."

"Just don't say anything about this, please. Pray it turns out okay. Okay?"

"Call me at the Regency Marquis if you need anything. Tell Cole, too, okay? And call me when you get back with Abby."

"Thanks, honey."

She'd sounded small on the phone and scared. Their sobering conversation had given Ben the temporary illusion of sobriety, but as he moved from the phone, he found it took concentration to walk normally. Again he rooted in his pockets for the illusive olive skewers, wondering if he should add his two beers to four previous drinks or six.

"Ben Franklin Green?"

The girl had to tug on his arm twice before he'd noticed.

"Hey!"

She had strawberry blonde hair, a freckly face and mischievous smile. Ben was disoriented by the jump-cut scene change. One moment he'd been brooding about Cole's problem, wondering if he'd been too drunk to make sense to Lara, fumbling for the damn swords, next moment standing nose to nose with this disconcertingly pretty little redhead. Not really nose to nose, as she was rather shorter. It was the top of her head that was directly across from his nose. And it smelled good, like flowers.

"Yes?" he said.

"You work at SP&F, right?"

"Uh-huh."

"I was in a commercial of yours! For soap. Remember? Cheryl Harding? You don't remember!"

And she pouted, giving him a little slap on the shoulder, standing very close in the crowded room. Ben put hand to brow, a self-effacing gesture borrowed from Detective Columbo. He shook his head, smiling down at the cute Cheryl, hoping his breath was okay.

"You caught me by surprise. I've had a few beers. My mind's a little scrambled."

"Maybe we should get you some coffee!"

"You here by yourself?" And he looked around, gratefully seeing no one hanging nearby.

"I was with some people in back, but I'm leaving now. Got an early call tomorrow. Another commercial!" And she gave an exaggerated smile, cocking her head and pointing her fingers into her farm girl cheeks, mocking the business, making Ben laugh.

"But I'd get some coffee with you," she said.

Under the protective wash of who knows how many drinks taken over the last few hours, lurked a shy guy who would normally get tongue-tied at such a moment, but that drag-ass was safely drowned in booze. And from the unlocked back room of Ben's subconscious, an all-male chorus boomed out "Yes!" and began to chant, "Puss-y . . . Puss-y . . . Puss-y . . ."

Ben shrugged, giving her his boyish smile, showing teeth, crinkling eyes, knowing he looked good in the new beard and old boots, feeling tall, having to actually bend forward in order to converse with the petite Cheryl.

"Let's go, sure. You've gotta drive, though," he said.

She pulled keys from her purse, waved them in the air and put her arm in his, pressing up against him as they went through the door. That smell of flowers.

# 10.

Cheryl Harding had a 5-speed Saab and drove with her hand on the gearshift the whole time, even when not shifting, letting her thumb play back and forth across the top of it.

"You know, I could just make us some coffee at my place," she said. "I've got a fresh pie I baked this afternoon. Pear pie."

"Never heard of pear pie," Ben said.

"It's like apple, but with pears. You will love it!"

"Let's go," he said, grateful now that he'd had all the drinks, able to enjoy, without first night fright, the anticipation of Cheryl's pear pie. *Pear pie?*

Her place was above Laurel Canyon on a heavily scented winding road called Wonderland Avenue. He stretched out on an overstuffed couch that had a musty, summer-home smell while Cheryl put Joni Mitchell on and went, Ben assumed, to get coffee.

When he closed his eyes, the world still rolled, the frightening sensation of being on a Ferris wheel, the seat not dangling, but locked in place, carrying him upside down over the top. It was reassuring to know the booze was working, but vertigo wouldn't do, and Ben had to open his eyes to stop the spinning. The room was dimly lit by old-fashioned, yellowish hurricane lamps and one hanging fixture in a corner glowing red through a Tiffany shade. The windows had tiers of potted plants in front of them. Ferns, tropical climbers, cacti, a willowy female marijuana bush. Ben was reminded of the indoor botanic gardens near downtown Chicago. Cheryl's was a greenhouse, and he breathed it in, enjoying the living smells. Damp soil, turpentiny leaves, powdery flowers.

She reappeared in a t-shirt that said LOVE ME HARD in faded letters across the front. It was long enough to cover half her bare thigh leaving hanging the question of what she was wearing for bottoms, if anything. She set a tray on the floor in front of the couch. On it were mugs of black coffee and two slices of homely, homemade pie projecting a gritty, sugar and cinnamon personality that momentarily distracted Ben from Cheryl.

Cheryl upstaged the pie, tiptoeing over the tray. And in a feline flash that Ben couldn't quite follow, she stretched out on the couch, cuddling up spoon style, resting her back against him, her head on his shoulder. Her loose hair tickled his nose and eyes, giving him another rush of flowers.

"She's singing about me, y'know," she whispered.

"Who is?"

"When Joni Mitchell wrote that song, *Ladies of the Canyon?*," she said, squirming into the contour of Ben's arm, "she lived here. Just down the hill from me. And she wrote it about her girlfriends here in Laurel Canyon."

Ben noticed Joni's pure plaintive voice now, singing "... ladies of the canyon."

"Well, I'm a lady of the canyon! See?"

"That's cool," Ben said, whispering back, liking the low huskiness of his voice, sounding like Nick Nolte, king of raspy sweet talkers.

Ben found the nipple of her left breast through the soft t-shirt and pulled it forward, pinching it gently between thumb and first finger, rubbing it back and forth in the universal gesture that, if there were no pliant little nipple in between, would mean "moo-lah."

He nuzzled his face into her flowery hair and crooned, "Mmmmmmm."

Not long ago he'd had lunch in Chicago with his friend, Larry, a recently divorced divorce lawyer who'd been getting a record amount of sex, considering those phobic times. Larry said he'd recently discovered that girls like it if you got more physical with their nipples than you thought you ever could. Ben said he was no Casanova, but had had his share of bare tit and thought he knew all there was to know about it.

"I felt the same way . . ." Larry said, doing a Belushi-style double-take, eyes wide, in case Ben missed the pun. "But this chick was real open and told me, do this, do it harder, do it more . . ." Larry leaned forward, excited.

"I swear, the girl came while I twisted her nipple!"

People from nearby tables turned to look. Ben cringed.

"Keep it down, Larry, okay?"

He didn't know if it was working for her, but it was getting to him. For the second time that night he had a rock hard erection. He took his hand away to adjust himself. Cheryl grabbed his hand with some urgency and pulled it back to her breast, pressing his fingers to her extended nipple, and as he squeezed, she began to moan sweetly. She moaned louder, then spun around to face him, kissing him roughly, running her tongue around his lips, then into his mouth. Cheryl was hot.

*　　*　　*

The morning was chilly. Ben liked that about the Hollywood Hills. It was essentially a mountainous desert and no matter how warm days got, you never needed air-conditioning to sleep and mornings started fresh and cold.

Ben didn't remember much about what happened after they'd moved from couch to bedroom, or even coming into the bedroom. There was just one faint memory, too spectacular not to keep intact, of Cheryl getting up from the couch, standing over the tray with her back to him as he lay there, then she was bending over, bending from the waist, extravagantly and slowly mooning him as she broke off a chunk of pie from one of the pieces on the floor. She'd turned to coax him off the couch with the pie, laughing, holding it out. He got up, but not for pie, apparently winding up here, in an old-fashioned double bed with a brass headboard and lots of feather pillows. This room, like the living room, had plenty of plants. But no Cheryl.

The clock radio read 10:30. He remembered she'd said something about doing a commercial this morning. In the bathroom he found her note.

BACK BY SIX! PLEASE BE HERE! YOU'RE THE BEST! LUV!!! ME!

Hangovers, Ben thought, are overrated inventions by bellyachers who'd probably feel bad in the morning whether they'd drunk the previous night or not. He looked in the mirror. No bags. No redness in the eyes. No problems. He splashed water on his face, enjoying the way it clung to his beard, reached in and turned on the shower, then pivoted toward the toilet, and threw up seventy dollars worth of Chinese food.

# 11.

Ben was sitting on the porch, watching the neighborhood darken as the sun lowered behind him, behind the house, waiting for Cheryl to come home. In the bushes, a couple of broad-tailed hummingbirds appeared, and he amused himself watching them hover and flit, little alien spaceships. He saw Cheryl's Saab starting up the hill, toy-size, then lost it as it went into the switchbacks, hidden behind trees, only now and then climbing into the open, each time larger, closer. Then it whined up to the house in low and pulled into the driveway, crunching stones and sending the smells of both raw and burnt gas barreling up to the porch. Ben waved happily.

Earlier that day, he'd revived himself with a couple of cold Coke Classics and a slab of Cheryl's pie that he ate with his fingers, standing at the sink. It delivered on last night's promise, being sweet, sour, doughy, full of the grit of unrefined sugar and ground cinnamon twigs.

He'd taken a walk, climbing the cliff tops at the end of Wonderland Avenue. He hiked away from the road and sat on a crumbly outcrop that poked through the weeds. The air was clear, and he could see the ocean, out past Century City, UCLA, Santa Monica.

On the mountain below, Ben noticed a dog standing stiff-legged in the weeds. It froze, focusing on something in the undergrowth. Then it sprang in a distinctive arc, pouncing on some small animal, and Ben realized it wasn't a dog, but a coyote. He whistled in appreciation. A wolf whistle. Close enough.

It had all come together for him up there, filling him with a rush of contentment. Ben had a sweet-smelling woman, his pear pie lady, who'd rush home to him tonight. He had a fun idea for a coffee table book that he knew exactly how to assemble. A gut full of earthy food. And the tingling, restorative Classic Coke, a cure-all once available only from pharmacists.

The only off-note was the strange business with Cole's daughter. But there was nothing to do about that, except keep his promise to keep quiet. It seemed farther away from him now, and he examined himself for guilt about feeling less concerned. This reminded him to also examine himself for ticks as he did these days after hiking in wild areas, ever since reading a horrifying article about a new ailment coming along called Lyme Disease. No ticks. No guilt either. He sensed something about the Abby thing that was beneath the surface of his imagination, something he'd deal with later.

*   *   *

Then there was this whole different Cheryl Harding standing in front of him. Not smiling, not pretty, not happy. No smell of flowers in the air.

"I just think you should go, that's all," she said.

"But your note. I thought you wanted me to stay. I thought, I don't know, I thought . . . you know."

Ben was confused. Cheryl was cold. Worse, pissed off. He didn't know why.

"The note was before."

"Before what?"

"The shoot today? The director was Kenny Ziff. That's what."

"Ziff?" Ben recognized the name. A New York commercial director. "Ziff's a friend of mine. I was bidding him for some Brio spots. What's he got to do with anything?"

"Look, Ben. I'm driving down to meet some people. I'll take you to your car, okay?"

Ben's early warning system shifted into yellow alert, signaling a possible anxiety attack. After all, there he was, now achingly sober, with a girl he really didn't know, in a strange house on a strange mountain in a strange city, and he was very alone, and her confounding attitude was making him disoriented. A return to the relative familiarity of the Regency Marquis seemed like a good idea. But wait. There was still her sweet if illiterate note in the morning. An explanation is needed. And what was this about Ziff?

"Listen, I don't want to make you upset," he said as they drove. She kept her eyes on the road. "But there's a big difference between the friendly person who left me a friendly note today . . . and the person who is now sitting next to me."

She handled the gear lever quickly, shifting without lingering on it as she did last night.

"I don't like being tricked."

"What does *that* mean?"

"Kenny told me."

"Told you what?"

"You know perfectly well what!" She faced him for a moment with that freckly face, and he realized that he sort of liked her. She turned her attention back to the road, and he searched the air for her flowery scent, this time sadly finding it.

"He told me you don't work at SPF. You don't even work in advertising!"

She laughed. "He said you dropped out or something! People think you're weird."

"I quit. I'm working on a book. What's weird about that?"

"I don't like being tricked, that's all. I don't dig your act, Ben Franklin Green!"

And Ben understood.

"You slept with me because you thought I'd get you in commercials."

"Mr. Innocent."

"That great old couch of yours? Welcome to Hollywood."

"My career's important to me. If yours doesn't matter to you, I don't care. I'm serious about mine."

And she stopped the car. For a moment, Ben hoped she'd stopped to discuss things, to make up, to tell him she'd reconsider this mercenary philosophy, that she could change, maybe live with him for a while on a mountain with hummingbirds and coyotes, baking floury pies and making love next to house plants and candles.

"We're here. I hope your car's still where you left it."

They were in front of Le Saloon. Ben got out. Before closing the door, he leaned in and said, "I never meant to trick you. I like you." He pulled back from the car, and she stepped on the gas. The door slammed shut on its own as she peeled away.

# 12.

Depressed or not, disillusioned or not, disoriented or not, Ben was hungry. On his way to the Regency Marquis, he stopped at a nearby Chicken D-light take-out place and bought a bucket of breasts and thighs only, having the pretty teenage girl, who could have been a clone of Cheryl Harding, custom make the bucket for him. He'd detected in her eyes a momentary double take on hearing the unavoidable double entendre, "breasts and thighs," but she covered it quickly, asking in professional Chicken D-light seriousness if he wanted fries, corn, cole slaw? Besides, he hadn't meant anything funny. He just didn't like the bony little wings or the gristly legs.

At 7-11 he picked up a Sara Lee devil's food cake with white frosting, his childhood favorite, and two six packs of Coors, which he thought of as his Western beer, even though it had years ago rolled into Chicago, taking away its one-time exotic regionality.

In his Regency Marquis home away from home, now, comfortable

in Jockey shorts and T-shirt only, half-watching the Angels cream the
White Sox, three Coors down, chicken scraps littering the coffee table,
he looked with pleasure toward Sara Lee, her lid pried off earlier, so the
room temperature would thaw her, soften her, get her ready. He put the
cake on his lap and scooped a forkful. The simplicity of living single. No
slices to portion out, no plates needed.

He watched Chicago losing, boozily recalling his once meeting
Minnie Minoso, the superstar left fielder for the Sox during the fifties.
Ben had written a series of public service TV spots that featured former
ballplayers. When he'd guided Minoso into camera position, he was
stunned at how solid the man's arm still was. Minnie had to be well into
his sixties, but the old ballplayer's arm was like stone.

Ben, beered up and high on chocolate in the empty room, felt his
own biceps. Respectable, but still the biceps of an adman. He resolved
to use his new freedom to get into shape, to get Minoso-hard arms.
He'd do more pushups. He'd run miles. Spend mornings working on
his body and afternoons working on his coffee table book. He'd stop
eating rich food, stop drinking so much. This would be his last Sara
Lee. As a farewell gesture, he scooped up another piece, which came
out too large, but he crammed it into his mouth anyway, just as the
phone rang.

It had to be Cheryl Harding. Who else would call him here? His
certainty was immediately galvanized by one of those rare coincidences
that turn normal people into mouth-breathers, no longer sure of an
orderly universe, instantly open-minded about the supernatural.
*Twilight Zone* strikes again. At the moment the phone began to ring, a
commercial came on and Cheryl was in it.

It was one of those young-people-at-the-beach spots for a mass-
market beer whose brand identity apparently had something to do
with volleyball. Cheryl, one of the bikini girls, was laughing, having an
implausible amount of fun. Ben had the split-second thought that of all
the people in the Angels and White Sox television audience, he alone
knew what that freckly beach bunny looked like without her bikini.

"Brrrrrrt! -Brrrrrrt!"

The phone had a foreign double-ring, damnably loud, downright mean sounding. Not like phones back home, which had sensible, Midwestern voices.

"Brrrrrrt! -Brrrrrrt!"

His mouth was jammed with cake. He couldn't talk yet. He chewed madly, watching Cheryl jump for the volleyball and fall into the arms of a muscle-bound pretty boy. Obviously they'd both need beer.

"Brrrrrrt! -Brrrrrrt!"

Ben chewed crazily, trying to mash the cake into something manageable enough to let him talk. Finally, fearing Cheryl would hang up if he waited any longer, he blew the mess into his hand and with his other hand grabbed the receiver and shouted into it.

"You're on TV!"

Silence.

"I'm watching you! Right now!"

A man's voice said, "Excuse me? Is this Mr. Green"?

Ben admitted that he was and began to stammer something about expecting a call from someone else but was interrupted immediately.

"Sir, I completely believe California is our nation's nuthouse. I have to tell you that I am not the least bit surprised by how you answered your phone."

The man's tone seemed friendly enough but his words and lack of interest in an explanation were somewhat insulting. Ben didn't know what to say. He realized he still had the blob of cake in his palm and asked the man to hold while he went into the kitchen and rinsed off. The comfortable beer buzz gave Ben a bit of boldness he might not otherwise have had when talking to a stranger. Especially a stranger who sounded older than Ben, and had an authoritative edge to his voice.

He turned the TV down before picking up the phone.

"Okay. I'm back. Who's calling?"

"Nick Van Dyke is my name. I need a bit of your time. If you don't mind?"

*Dick Van Dyke*? Ben's mind scrambled, trying to understand why some old actor (actually, a favorite of his from the '60s *Dick Van Dyke Show,* with Dick's wife being the oh so pretty Laura Petrie, exactly the kind of girl to marry ...) would be calling. The neighborhood was full of TV and movie people. Maybe Dick Van Dyke was staying at the Regency Marquis, too. Maybe he was in the next room calling to complain about the ball game being too loud.

Maybe he'd recognized Ben from an ad shoot, saw him coming up to this apartment after the blow-off job by Cheryl, and was calling to pitch for a part in a commercial. No, he was too big a star for anything like that. Although he hadn't been doing anything lately that Ben knew of.

"The actor, right? Dick Van Dyke?" Ben said.

"Nation's nuthouse ..." the man said again, and barked a gravelly cigar smoker's bark.

"Name's Nick, my friend. Nick for Nicolas. Like my Greek mom wanted. Van Dyke, like Van Dyke, from my dad's Dutch family. You can call me Van. That's what everyone does. Now listen. I'm a very close and very old friend of Cole's. Andrew Cole? Not Nat King Cole, or Cole Slaw. Understand? Cole hired me today, because I can help him and I think you know what I mean. He asked me, among other things, to get ahold of you. You're the Ben Green who worked with Cole in the ad business, right?"

Ben sat, shaking his head, wishing life were a VCR so he could hit reverse, backing things up to before the phone rang.

"Sorry, Mr. Van Dyke, you caught me at a bad time."

"Listen, call me Van."

Ben recalled telling Lara to call him at the Regency Marquis. There was a hazy vision of their phone conversation at Le Saloon after the beers, before Cheryl came along.

"Cole told you to call me? Is everything okay?"

"Hey guy, you know it's not."

"I mean, new developments?"

"Don't want to go over this on the phone, my friend. Which is why I called.

I want you to see me in Colorado, if you will. Actually Cole wants you to come. Asked me to work it out with you. You're free I believe?"

All Ben wanted to do was eat more cake, drink the rest of the beer and watch the ball game. Still, if Cole asked for his help ...

"I don't think I've ever been this free . . . Van. Yeah. I'll come. But first I'd like to talk to Cole."

"I thought you might. Sure. But keep it very, very short. We don't want to tie up the phone. Don't want it to look like they're talking about what's happening."

"How'd he get you in on this?" Then, fearing his question sounded blunt, potentially offensive, he added, "I mean, without looking like they've been calling in help, or whatever."

"Later. Call Cole now, quick. Then call me back." And the man gave him the two phone numbers, both in Colorado's 303 area code.

Andrew Cole answered the phone before the bell stopped ringing. Ben could hear it fading in the background as Cole said hello in a tight voice. Ben asked about Van Dyke. Cole was emphatic.

"I'd appreciate it if you do exactly what he asks, Ben. He's a friend. And a good . . ."

Cole paused, apparently reluctant to say detective, after being warned about talking to authorities, ". . . guy. Point is, it's blue-sky time, Ben. That's when you shine."

And he broke the connection.

"Come ON!" Ben said to the empty room. This was too much like a movie. What was he doing here? Far from home, from normal life, normal people. He had a sudden urge to take the next plane to Chicago, maybe ask for his job back. He'd spend time at his parents' house in Evanston, eating his mother's overproduced meals, each containing her five basic food groups. Beef, chicken, potatoes, bread and cake. He'd sleep after dinner on their gold-on-gold couch. He'd live like a kid again for a week, maybe forever.

Instead he called Nick Van Dyke at his Colorado office, not knowing where in Colorado it was.

"What do I do?"

"Come to Denver. Brown Palace. Ever been there?"

"No."

"Great hotel, right downtown. Tomorrow we'll go for a ride. You'll see mountains."

"I couldn't get to Denver until tomorrow."

"Nonsense. Leave now. I'll arrange a charter as soon as I hang up. Go to Charters International at LAX."

"Don't I need a ticket or anything?"

"Listen, you'll love it. It's like taking a limo instead of the bus. Ask at the desk, and they'll show you to the plane. You'll be here by midnight. In the hotel by one. They'll have your room waiting. I'll pick you up at seven. See you in the morning!" And he hung up.

The Sox had turned the tide and tied the game. Ben wanted to dial up the volume, pick up Sara Lee and lie down on the floor. Instead, he threw some things into his canvas duffel. It was after nine when he left. On schedule.

"What the hell," he said to the back end of the silver Stingray driving in front of him on Sepulveda, "I've never been to the Rockies."

Besides, he thought, when Andrew Cole invites you to a blue sky, you really should go.

# 13.

Somewhere in the Rockies, the young woman with wild hair, naked but for a knife belt, stretched out in surprising comfort, preparing to spend another night in the wilderness. She luxuriated in the warmth of her unexpected bed and the security of her unlikely campfire. She even had the companionship of the young hawk, with its deep eyes that watched her from somewhere in the dark pines overhead.

Before drifting into sleep she wondered again about the mysterious presents that were making her nights not only survivable, but comfortable to the point of sensuousness. She was a person who was accustomed to getting answers to her questions. She was going to get some answers, somehow. And she moved under the musky fur robe with impatience.

\* \* \*

After the peregrine came to her on that first afternoon, things changed. Perhaps some latent maternal juices got fired up by the falcon's helpless condition, or simply, the hawk, being another soul, made her feel less alone. But in any case, she took command for both of them and with several hours of light left, she abandoned the idea of going in circles and struck out in a straight line, figuring if she stayed on it long enough she'd eventually cross some sign of civilization.

For hours she moved through a valley between two snowcapped ranges, but had seen no sign of civilization. This hadn't surprised her. She could recall the topographic map of these mountains fairly well and remembered liking how vast the undeveloped areas were. She'd sat on a rock, the feel of it cold against her bare skin, and watched the world gradually darken, blue pine forest heavy all around her. A chill in the air.

And then she saw it. A thin column of translucent smoke was rising straight into the sky above the trees. It stood tall in the twilight, holding at its top a pinkish light from the lowering sun, and she felt it beckon. She ran through the trees, ignoring the needle grab of boughs, the bite of broken rock, eager for the warmth of fire and company. The hawk flapped silently above, following. They found only the fire.

It was neatly constructed, having been kindled with lichen, which had now burned to ash except around the edges. In the middle, dry twigs flickered gently, and a few larger, slow-burning logs were arranged above these in a pyramid. The well-made little fire smelled sweet, autumnal, and the woman bent over it, taking its warmth into her skin, its scent into her hair.

Near the fire a leather pouch lay open, spilling wild berries. She'd noticed such berries growing on bushes earlier that day, but hadn't known if they were edible. Presented as they were by the fire, there could be no doubt and she ate, realizing she'd become ravenous. Also in the pouch were strips of dried meat, looking like the jerky sold in saloons and at convenience store checkout counters, but this leathery stuff had no spice. And to get the flavor of meat and salt, she'd had to chew for a long time with strong teeth and strong need.

She tossed the little falcon a strip of dried meat, made soft and pliable by her chewing, and the bird gulped it down. There had been one other item by the fire. A bulky tan fur, folded neatly into a square the way a blanket might be folded. She'd opened it and discovered it was a vast and sharp-smelling cougar skin, leathery on the inside, and heavy with dense winter-strength hair on the outside.

Every part of the lion's hide was there, even its tail which was fully as long as its body. The head was surprisingly small, with eyeholes, pointed ears and long-whiskered jowls. Its legs spread out in two great spans, front and rear, and the fur around the paws was dense, fluffed almost as though for decoration. She'd wrapped the skin around her that first night, and hunched by the fire. Her blonde hair, tangled with pine needles and dirt, spilled out of the fur, framing her face. Her chin was sticky with berry juice and fire glowed in her eyes as the night grew black.

She'd chewed and stared at the fire, not thinking, just being, knowing she was going to survive.

# 14.

Cole stood at the front of the room, and Ben hoped his old boss wouldn't turn and start writing things on the blackboard. He felt like he was back in the agency with Cole leading another of these notorious sessions. "Blue sky" means every subject is open for discussion, no limits, no censorship, everything said is written down for group analysis.

Cole had insisted on such sessions. Some creatives found them useful. Ben thought they wasted his time and had felt confined, being closed up with a bunch of schizoids, ad people whose self-images fluctuated with the regularity of pulsars, going from cocksure to unsure, back and forth forever. Ben suffered from the same confidence swings, but had always gotten ideas alone, away from this kind of structured business setting.

At any rate, he figured, if this was a blue sky meeting, they picked a good place for it. Outside, the sky was bluer than any sky Ben had ever seen. They were in the Alpine Visitor's Center at Rocky Mountain National Park, elevation 11,796 feet. Snow lay in the shadows, and the temperature was a crisp thirty-three at ten in the morning.

Cole thanked Ben and Van for coming, saying he'd fill them in quickly, because he'd borrowed the room for only one hour. While Cole talked, Ben was struck once again with the unreal feel of the thing. It was as though he'd dropped out of his semi-normal ad life into a B-movie with faded Hollywood motels, troubled rich people, one wearing the requisite tiny bikini, a freckly starlet trading rolls on the couch for roles on TV, a wisecracking private eye and now a clandestine briefing in the wilderness.

The morning had started with Van's phone call at seven, as promised.

*   *   *

"I'm downstairs," Van said. " You ready?"

Earlier, Ben had the hotel operator blast him out of bed with a 6 AM call so he'd be up in time. He was showered, dressed and ready to go by 6:30, but having had only four hours of fitful sleep, he'd dozed off in the room's old easy chair while waiting. So when Van called, he was at first confused, seeing he was not in bed.

He'd had the momentary sense of having made an awful error, of having never actually gone to bed but of simply having fallen asleep fully dressed, sitting up. As he came back to reality, he had the thought that tiredness makes quite a potent mind-altering drug.

Before responding to Van's question, he flashed on former first lady Nancy Reagan's artless "Just Say No" slogan that had been somewhat ridiculed in the eighties by ad people who thought she could've come up with something more clever. And while thinking he couldn't have just said no to the events causing this current overdose of tiredness, and in the microsecond it takes to have a parallel thought, the philosopher Timothy Leary's suggested improvement to Mrs. Reagan's attempt at copywriting popped into his head: "Just say no, thank you."

So still groggy, partially dreaming actually, he'd followed that thought and spoke clearly, as though perfectly awake, into the phone.

"No thank you."

"Wasn't exactly an invitation, Mr. Green."

What must this man think of him?

"I'm in the restaurant. Big guy, tan jacket. Bet I spot you first."

And he had. Soon after entering the rancho-riche style restaurant with its paneled walls and mounted buffalo heads, he heard Van.

"Over here, Ben."

Van was a large man in his fifties with thin brown hair and a jowly face. He had a road map of tiny red capillaries on his nose and small blue eyes full of sparkle. The eyes of a class clown in the face of a Chicago cop. He wore a starched bush jacket, jeans in a waist size that jeans weren't intended for, and beat-up sneakers.

"Mr. Dyke? You *did* spot me first. I didn't even knock over a table to tip you off."

"Van Dyke. But we're just using Van. And you didn't even tell that buffalo up there you'd seen him on TV!" The big man offered his hand. Ben shook it and sat.

Van said, smiling. "I just looked for an aging hippie."

"That what Cole said?"

"He thinks you're great. His Mrs. thinks you're cute, too. Want something to eat?"

On the table were the remains of Van's breakfast, chewed up T-bone on a yolk-smeared plate, empty beer bottles, half a tomato juice, toast crusts and a pile of jelly packages with their tops peeled back, their insides scraped out. Ben wasn't hungry and said he'd just as soon get on with whatever they had to do. Van signaled for the waitress, but she didn't seem to notice.

"So," Ben said, "Where're we going?"

"Look at that one over there, whew-eee," Van whispered, gesturing toward a woman several tables away.

Her back was to them, but Ben could see she was very overweight, overweight in the way young rural women sometimes can be, looking like grandmothers at twenty-nine. She was sitting with a pretty little girl, about five years old, who had wispy blonde hair and a party dress that was too short. The child alternately stood and sat, obviously impatient.

"Just sits there chewing," Van said, aloud, as though he almost wanted others to hear.

Ben looked again. The woman was wearing synthetic slacks, and her buttocks stretched them hard and tight. She turned, mouth full, and scolded the little girl, who quickly sat. As the woman turned, Ben could see her profile, a porcine archetype, small upturned nose, down-turned mouth, multiple chins. Ben didn't know what to say.

"Yeah," he agreed. To be polite, although the direction of this conversation didn't feel polite at all.

"I've watched her graze for an hour while the kid's bored silly."

Van picked up an empty jelly package and, to Ben's amazement, tossed it in a high arc toward the table where the overweight woman sat. It dropped short, and she didn't notice. The waitress saw it, though. Assuming it might have been meant for her, a summons, she came quickly, totaling Van's check as she walked, slapping it down, then doing an about-face, as though she'd had some previous unpleasantness at their table.

On the way out, Van put a big hand on Ben's arm, stopping him where he stood.

"Hold it a minute."

The heavy woman was just biting into an oversize powdered sugar doughnut. Van walked to her table, and in a friendly, confidential manner, placed one hand on the back of her chair as he talked. Then, smiling, he gently removed the doughnut from her hand. She sat mouth agape, lips framed with powder sugar, as he turned and left the restaurant with Ben.

As they walked along the plush corridor of the Brown Palace, Van offered Ben the doughnut.

"Want this? Practically new."

"Come on," Ben said, befuddled, uncomfortable.

Van tossed the doughnut over his shoulder. It bounced behind him on the lobby's carpeting, a white splash.

"What did you say to her?"

"Said I was a safety engineer with the Polyester Fabric Institute of America. The PFI of A." His eyes twinkled.

"And I was duty-bound to warn her that for the safety of herself and other patrons, she'd better stop eating, since I'd calculated that the tensile strength of her pants wasn't great enough to offset the size of her ass and there could be an ugly explosion."

He laughed and slapped Ben's back.

"Then I took her donut. She didn't even bite me!"

* * *

"Mr. Van Dyke . . . Van. I'm sorry, but I gotta ask, why'd you do that back there?"

They were in Van's Jeep Cherokee, which had a car phone, CB radio, dash-mounted rotating light, and to round out the lawman image, there was a shotgun sitting erect between the bucket seats. It was held by clamps that reminded Ben of the devices that lock skis to ski boots. Ben had no experience with either skis or shotguns, and this added to his continuing sense of disorientation, driving through country with signs advertising ski areas, while sitting next to the big gun.

Van looked at him. "That thing with the doughnut?"

Ben, a lifelong nice guy, could never imagine insulting someone as Van had done.

"Because I thought it." Van said to the road ahead. He turned and winked at Ben. "And if I think it, I say it."

"Some philosophy," Ben said, sensing there was more to come, hoping Van would go on.

"For fifty years I pretty much kept my thoughts to myself."

They were out of urbanized Denver now, and both men eased back in their seats, settling into the rhythm of an open-road drive.

"Strict home, strict schools, the military. After that, the bureau. I was an FBI agent for years and years."

"There's a theme there somewhere," Ben said. "Bureaucracy?"

Actually Ben knew little about the kind of bureaucracy he was referring to, having come from a blessedly unstructured background and a profession that rewarded freewheeling ideation.

"Ho man, did I live by the book!" Van said. "Know that thing they used to say to kids? 'Don't speak until spoken to?' My whole life was like that." Van tilted his left hip up off the seat and noisily passed gas. Ben's first impulse was to open the window. He hesitated, thinking this would embarrass Van. Then he thought, what the hell, and lowered it.

"Yep. I said and did only the correct thing. At the correct time. Until age five-oh." And he glanced over at Ben to emphasize the point.

They were driving into the beginnings of mountains now. The rock formations were on their left, and the sun was still low in the sky off to the right, so it sent direct yellow light into the boulders and pines. Ben saw three deer grazing in a distant meadow, following them with his eyes as the car moved, so he was practically facing Van when the man turned toward him.

"At fifty, something gave."

Ben encouraged Van to go on, enjoying the archaic pleasure of being told a story, person to person. "Yeah?" he said.

"Let me put it this way. I figure a man's mind is like a bladder. It fills up with stuff naturally. You know, ideas, opinions. And it has to empty itself naturally, too. Like a bladder."

He paused, a half smile on his plump face, steering with obvious enjoyment as the road curved back and forth in a series of serpentine turns. This was the kind of driving you could only find in the mountains. Never in Chicago, Ben thought, at least not since the early eighties when they'd taken the fun out of Lake Shore Drive by straightening the deadly S-curve over the Chicago River.

"So at fifty I started emptying. Ideas. Gripes. Every bottled up thought. Out they came. I quit my job with the bureau. Had to, after my ideas about them started popping out."

They were climbing through a gorge, and the shoulders on both sides were piled with fallen rock. Garish long-tailed magpies could be seen along the roadside, and Ben mentally added them to his life list. But their discovery was being overshadowed by Van's story, which Ben felt had the quality of a rare sighting, too, similarly worth collecting.

"I started my own agency then. I say whatever pops into my mind. The bladder's comfortable, see? I'm happy. Probably for the first time in my life. That large lady back there? If I hadn't said what I did, I'd be storing it up. Sitting on it. Letting it stew. Just won't do it."

They came over a rise in the road and began to descend into a valley. In the distance Ben saw the high Rockies now, their snow-covered peaks starkly white in the morning sun.

"Hell," Van said, "She might go on a diet. Maybe I helped her. Everybody else ignores the poor thing."

"Maybe . . . I guess," Ben said, finding himself talking with a slight western inflection, unintentionally aping Van's, though still not in agreement with the man's rudeness. But, who knows, maybe after fifty a guy goes a little crazy. Fifty was still a lifetime away, something to be thankful for.

They passed a sign that read "Rocky Mountain National Park 9 mi." At the side of the road they saw a horse and rider. The rider wore a cowboy hat and had a gun on his hip. Within an hour they'd arrived at the Alpine Visitor Center and found the private classroom that Cole had arranged for their meeting.

# 15.

"Maybe I shouldn't have listened to Lara," Cole went on. "We should've called the police, FBI, whatever."

He spoke softly in a weary voice. The kind of voice people use in hospital waiting rooms. "But I did listen. I cooperated with them completely. Now, nothing. I'm out of ideas."

Van put his feet on the table and scowled. Ben leaned forward and said, "Maybe you should call the cops now. Maybe it's the best thing to do."

Cole looked over his shoulder at the blackboard, and Ben knew his old creative director felt the impulse to write down Ben's suggestion. The rule of Cole's blue sky meetings: Every idea goes on the board. But this wasn't advertising, and Cole made his note on a yellow legal pad, bending over the table, writing quickly.

"Duly noted, Ben."

"And seconded, my friend," Van growled.

Cole pulled a chair over and sat heavily, staring at the yellow pad. Minutes of silence, and Ben realized Cole wasn't focusing on the words that had been written there, but on some unexpressed thought. He'd seen the look on Cole's face before. The man was struggling with a concept.

"Okay," he said after a while, "but I didn't ask you up here to tell me that." Boring his eyes into Ben's. "Ben. Nick Van Dyke is a superb investigator. I want him on our side. He has hi-tech capabilities. Contacts all over Colorado."

Van grunted.

"Van . . ." Cole turned to the reclining detective. "This guy, Ben Franklin? Ben Franklin Green? He can see the same problem everyone sees, but he'll find a new slant. A way to solve it. He's an idea man. Best I've ever known."

Van looked at Ben. "Ben *Franklin* . . . ?"

Cole looked at the yellow pad again, talking quietly now, becoming conversational.

"What I need, and my wife and daughter need, in addition to the authorities which I will call now, is a good private detective. And an idea man."

Cole looked up. "I want to hire you guys to help get Abby back. As a team. Money's no object."

Ben remembered that one of Cole's strengths as a creative director had been to team up people who'd catalyze each other. Separately they might produce average or uneven work, but together they'd create breakthroughs. His teams often stayed together throughout their careers. Even when jumping from agency to agency, they'd jump together. Cole was doing it again.

"If you're interested, I'd like to give you as much background as I can."

Van and Ben exchanged glances. Van said, "Interested?"

Ben turned to Cole. "Absolutely."

Cole told them he'd delivered about a million dollars in diamonds yesterday morning. Abby was supposed to be dropped off in Denver that afternoon but never appeared.

"You'll be interested in this, Ben," Cole said. "A bird took the diamonds."

Cole stopped, looking like he'd just thought of something new. He said to Van, "That's another way we can use Ben. He knows ornithology."

Ben saw Van turning slowly, fixing him with a sidelong glance. *Ornithology?*

"Look, I got a phone call the night before . . ."

And Cole went on to explain the transfer in detail. He'd been told to take the stones sealed in a plastic bag, and walk on Grandy's main street until he found a car which he'd know by its license plate. It was unlocked, with keys under the visor. Inside was a map of Rocky Mountain National Park. A red circle had been scrawled over a point on a service road near the Alpine Center where they now were.

He was told to drive to that spot and look for a coffee can at the side of the road. Ben was following this closely, wondering how a bird would figure in, but Van interrupted, impatience in his voice.

"Tell me. Before you did this. You get to talk to Abby on the phone?"

Cole nodded quickly, "Yes. Insisted on it. First thing I asked when they called."

"Tell me what you both said," Van asked, his voice deadpan, doing a pretty good Joe Friday now, without trying.

"The guy held up the phone for her. Like she was across the room. She said something like, I'm okay, Daddy, Daddy, I want to come home . . ."

"You sure it was her?"

"I know my daughter, Van."

"She say anything else?"

"The fucking guy. He came back on." Cole's face reddened. "He said, 'enough socializing,' and told me to just follow his instructions."

"You were telling us about a coffee can?" Van said gently.

Cole found the can on a seldom-used dirt road that ran for about nine miles through heavy woods on the side of the mountain. In it there was a typed note that said OPEN TRUNK.

"Still have the note?"

"Sorry. I'll tell you why in a minute."

In the trunk Cole found a staple gun and a dead duck, fully feathered and soft to the touch. Cole told Ben he thought it was a female mallard. Brown with a blue wing patch. It had a slit in its breast but hadn't been gutted.

A leather rope, looking like a dog leash to Cole, had been knotted at one end around the duck's tail feathers and the rest of it lay coiled next to the bird. A note taped to it said, PUT STONES IN DUCK. STAPLE SHUT. SWING DUCK OVER EDGE.

Cole took the duck to the rim of the cliff. He could see water boiling white against boulders in a brook far below, but couldn't hear it. He swung the duck with the diamonds stapled inside, feeling ridiculous, he said. The hawk dropped out of the sun and took the duck in a burst of feathers.

Cole stopped talking, still struck by the experience, looking surprised. Ben flashed on a pillow fight he'd had at overnight camp when he was ten. His old pillowcase had unexpectedly burst, feathers suddenly everywhere, hanging in the air around him.

Cole couldn't identify the species, just a dark hawk with pointed wings. Cole made his hands into claws as he talked. The hawk pulled the duck free of the tether, and disappeared into the canyon with it.

Cole told Van. "The instructions said to put the can, the notes you asked about, the rope, everything, in the trunk and return the car. Cole obeyed, he said, meeting Van's gaze. He'd expected to hear from Abby that day, believing that since he'd done his part, others would do theirs.

Cole said again that he'd contact the FBI and police now, although he was still worried about the kidnappers clear warning. Meanwhile, he thought Van and Ben might come up with something. They arranged to meet the next day at Van's office so Cole and Lara could give them background about Abby's job and people she knew in Colorado.

Then Cole's blue sky session ended and it was fitting, Ben thought, that clouds had built up low and gray over the building as they left.

# 16.

The Van Dyke Agency: Confidential Investigations, Private, Corporate, Local, National, International, was headquartered in downtown Denver. In addition to some quiet clerical workers, there were three key people, including Nick Van Dyke himself.

There was an associate named Tina who was tiny, about four-eleven, Ben guessed, making it easy for him to remember her name. She was a

Native American with dazzling eyes and high cheekbones. Her straight black hair was pulled rather severely into a single long braid. She wore large glasses that gave her a bookish look, the look of a no-nonsense librarian. Still, she had some elemental appeal, and Ben had the absurd thought that he could probably fit his hands around her little waist and have his fingertips meet. She wore a tailored gray business suit, but there was a rawhide belt around her middle, its silver buckle set with turquoise stones. And on her feet she wore well-used moccasins that looked handmade, somewhat offsetting the serious suit and glasses.

Van's second in command was a former college basketball star who was as tall as Tina was short, easily six-six. And while Tina had long black hair, the man had a smooth bald head. This was a look that worked for such dark-skinned African-Americans. A look that would never quite work for totally bald white guys, who just wind up looking sick. His name was Harrison James but he liked to be called HJ.

Van said HJ had done unspeakable things for the CIA before getting fed up (Van stressing the word *fed*) with the bullshit there. Ben later learned that "unspeakable," although literally correct, was Van's playful way of misleading him into imagining HJ terrorizing terrorists in hidden torture chambers. But HJ's job had been to work with the electronics involved in eavesdropping, unspeakable only in the sense that some of the equipment was secret and HJ was never to speak about it.

They had a large, surprisingly luxurious suite in one of those mirrored skyscrapers that Ben believed were pitifully out of place in downtown Denver, as though a group of CEOs in pinstripes and power haircuts were standing around a campfire. There were several furnished offices that were unoccupied, and Van explained that when they got a big case they'd bring in free-lancers who'd use space without actually becoming employees.

"Same thing happens in the agency business," Ben said.

"This is the agency business."

And Ben realized that the word no longer automatically meant ad agency. He was part of a detective agency now. Unreal.

The Coles were expected at the Van Dyke Agency in an hour.

Meanwhile Ben was feeling stranded in the private office he'd been given, an office properly furnished and ready to go to work, even if its occupant was somewhat dazed and suffering from new-kid syndrome, an all-too familiar malady for anyone who had been in the job-jumping world of advertising.

The meeting would give Cole and Lara a chance to amplify details touched upon at the blue sky session and it would be a chance for Van, and maybe even Ben, to input some ideas. *Input ideas.* Would he ever stop thinking that way? Stop thinking in the language of meetings?

Feet up now, reclining in a comfortable office chair, Ben looked out at Denver's movie set skyscrapers, so reflective, all glass and chrome. And feeling reflective himself, Ben remembered the first time he'd had to input ideas.

He'd been suffering from new-kid syndrome that day, too, which is maybe why the memory is now so accessible. But the skyscrapers back then, back there, were the real thing. He'd been sent to the agency's New York office and had arrived early, wide-eyed as a hayseed in Manhattan, which wasn't far from the truth, being a twenty-two year old from the north side of Chicago, now in Manhattan for the first time.

He'd stood alone in deep, white carpet looking at a black marble conference table that seemed as long as a bowling alley. In its gloss were the reflections of crystal chandeliers. A man entered with the bearing of one who owns the place. He was about sixty, silver hair, flawless black suit, looking like the elegant British actor, Wilfred Hyde White, but without the mischief in his eyes. The man made his way over to Ben and inquired as to his identity.

"Ah, yes," the man said. "From our Chicago offices."

When they shook hands, Ben noticed that the man's nails were artificially round and highly glossed. He hadn't seen such nails on males before. This was big time. But who was the guy? President of the agency? Ambassador from Great Britain?

After the meeting began, Ben discovered the man was simply their stenographer. In those days, the doings in fancy meetings were recorded by hand. The stenographer gentleman was such a classic touch. What an image. Ben went on to input ideas. And the stenographer sat against a wall, writing into a leather notebook while his superiors, including Ben, argued about whether the dancing strawberries in Ben's commercial should cha-cha from left to right around the big cereal box, or right to left.

Ben, fully tilted in the big chair, eyes closed, enjoyed the replay of that long ago meeting with a self-indulgent smile. He was nearly asleep, not the sleep of the relaxed, rather of the overtaxed, when he sensed, then caught the sweet scent of the tiny Tina.

She was standing in front of his desk, actually leaning into it, so unexpected a sight he couldn't prevent a sudden twitch from rocking both his body and the chair, momentarily off balancing the whole set-up. He might have tipped over backwards if he hadn't shot out his legs and grabbed the desktop with his hand. Not a pretty move. And in front of such a pretty woman.

"I didn't hear you come in." Trying for the calm tone of a man long accustomed to the instability of executive chairs.

"I move quietly," she said, not moving, still close upon the desk front. And Ben thought, *Indians*, the word adventuresome and romantic in his mind.

"So, what are you doing?" as she cocked her head, her eyes hard upon him behind those librarian glasses.

"Waiting for the meeting. Daydreaming. I'm a little sleepy today."

"Well, I came to tell you not to listen to those tapes. I didn't have a chance to lock them up. Van would be mad if he knew I left them out and you played them."

In advertising offices electronic equipment is part of the decor, so the hi-tech player on Ben's desk didn't seem exceptional, and he'd paid it no attention. Now he noticed it, and a box of cassettes nearby. In the simple era of the eighties, such equipment represented the height of technology.

"I wasn't going to play anything." But now, wondering if he should. Why the concern? "What's on them?"

She looked straight at him, a steadier gaze than one normally sees in ad circles, still leaning into his desk that way, pointedly occupying a piece of his territory.

She calmly said, "Oh, people fucking."

Prim Tina. Those glasses. That tightly drawn hair, the corporate tailoring. People *fucking?* Not people *having sex.* She'd said fucking. And he hoped she couldn't sense that she'd startled him again, although he knew he'd probably done a bit of a double take.

"Like porno?" Then, realizing he'd never heard of audio porno. Ben wondered if such a thing even existed, and if the question sounded pathetically naive.

"Oh, they're better than porno."

Ben, no longer sleepy, completely up now, found this exciting. Her use of the word "better" must mean she thought porno was somewhat good. And she was so implacable standing there, so close, a scent of wild aboriginal perfume tantalizingly slight in the closed office.

In the more playful days of the previous decade, the famous porno *Deep Throat* had been shown in SPF's large conference room, an unofficial but fitting spectacle for the coliseum. Ben had found himself blushing in the dark next to a 19-year-old secretary. When it ended, the girl invited Ben to lunch, saying she felt like a hot dog. But in the clanging reality of a nearby diner the movie's spell dissolved, and the girl simply made witless small talk, approaching her lunch with no special relish.

"Better?" Ben said, wondering where this was going and how long until the meeting would start and why Tina looked so planted there.

"We bug bedrooms," she said, whispery as though sharing a secret, but smiling now, having fun with him, amused at this new kid.

"Of course," Ben said, finally getting it. Didn't these agencies spend much of their time snooping on cheating spouses? Documenting infidelities? And wouldn't it follow that they'd use bugs as well as photos? Ben once read that this was the meat and potatoes of the private dick's trade. Ben's phone sounded a sharp tone, a disapproving comment on the carnal direction his thoughts were taking. Tina picked up the receiver, even though it was supposed to be his phone, on his desk.

"Sure," she said. "He's ready." Then to Ben, "Van says to come to the conference room."

As Ben came around the desk, she put her arm in his and walked him to the door. Tina, looking up, gave him a promising zap with those dark-shining eyes, and she was warm to the touch. She whispered, "We'll listen to the tapes another time," then winked and pulled away. "Besides," she said smiling," if we played them now, someone might have heard and thought it was us."

Ben stood flattered and uncertain, late for another meeting. Some librarian, he thought, smiling now. Libertine, perhaps, if the word works for women. Libertina? Libber Tina? How foolish to have been fooled by such simple symbols. Prim eyeglasses, severe hair, gray flannel tailoring. Advertising versus reality, with a carnal thrust this time. Why did the idea of listening to real people on mere audio tape ("Fucking," Tina had said, so casually) seem exciting compared to the banal embarrassment of pro porno? Porno versus reality? A further extension of the concept? No time for extensions now. Ben had a meeting to attend.

# 17.

It was after five. It was after work. The subsonic insect whine hanging in the air around every office building had faded as the humming and drumming of another day ended. The Coles had gone. Tina and HJ had gone. Ben stayed on, wondering about the tapes, wondering if Van would leave, too, leaving him and the tapes alone. But Van stayed on.

Ben joined him in the corner office where the big detective sat, his stocking feet on the desk. He wore thick wool socks, gray around the foot and red above the ankle. It wasn't that he'd taken his shoes off out of respect for the smooth polished walnut of the expensive desk. He simply hadn't worn, didn't ever wear, shoes around the office. His habit was to kick them off next to the front door when entering. Earlier, he'd said to Ben, "Don't let the informality around here fool you. Dress codes don't work. But our people do."

They were drinking cherry wine coolers laced with 100-proof Russian vodka, which Van would pour into the narrow-necked cooler bottles very carefully, until the level inside the bottle rose about an inch.

He poured often, and the bottles never emptied, but got less cherry as time passed.

"You know," Ben said, pausing, squelching a burp, dissipating it silently, then going on. "Back in the old days, one of the agencies I worked in? They wouldn't start working 'til now. Guys would come in late morning, take two, three hour lunches . . ."

Van, listening, took a gulp from his bottle, grimaced as it hit bottom and sucked on a tooth, nodding at Ben, encouraging him to continue.

". . . and they'd basically just do nothing all day. Then the office people would go home. And the CD, that's the creative director, he'd call us in, shut his door, pass out dope. Grass, you know? And wine or beer. And we'd do ads 'til midnight or so. Then we'd all go out for pizza. Or Mexican."

"First time I had grass, it was Tina who gave it to me," Van said, his voice gravelly. "She was working in a massage parlor in St. Louis. Shitty city, St. Louis. Mosquitoes there'll give you sleeping sickness. Know Joseph Conrad's *Heart of Darkness? Bend in the River,* by Naipaul? Doesn't matter. They're about this horrible place in Africa, deep in the Congo. The humidity. Reminds me of St. Louis. America's heart of darkness, as far as I'm concerned."

Tina, in a massage parlor? Ben became suddenly interested, wanting to know more, something erotic and itchy inside him. But he wanted to say that, yes, he did know those books, too. Van kept talking, though, and when he stopped, Ben, feeling the vodka now, lost both trains of thought.

Finally, he said, "What about Cole, Van? What do you think we should do?"

"I think the diamonds are out of the country. And the girl? She's dead."

"She's not, no way," Ben said with off-handed casualness, as though it were obvious, not even worth discussing.

"We humor Cole," Van said. "He'll face it himself soon. Then you go back to what you do. I go back to what I do."

"I don't do anything now."

"Y'know, Cole and I go back. Long way. Guy's a good guy." Van sighed, and took a swig. "One of the good guys."

"How's an advertising writer like Cole go back a long way with a G-man hard guy like you?

"There's a bond some people have. Some don't. Strong as blood sometimes. Know what it is?"

Ben stared at Van. Both instinctively knew that such a stare between two drinkers signifies one has the other's complete attention.

"Neighborhood!" Van growled. "He and I grew up on the same block! Played football in the street. Used cars for goal posts. Sometimes the goal posts drove away in the middle of a game. He remembers that, see. He knows I remember it. Know what I mean?"

"Tina and the massage parlor. What happened?"

"This little college girl, moonlighting. Good hands. Jeez!"

Ben laughed politely, fighting a pang of irrational jealousy.

"Well, I met her gettin' a massage there, I admit it. I'd been drunk already, and she got me stoned like I said, my first and only time, and I offered her a job, shitfaced as I was. Gave her my business card. Never expected her to take me seriously. So she comes to Denver and calls."

He looked suddenly surprised. He laughed out loud, then took a swallow from his bottle. "She's got a Master's from Washington University. Political Science. Who'd have thought?"

"I don't know. She looks smart to me."

"She is! Does surveillance for us. Plants microphones. Such a cute thing. Has an interest in you. The hots I'd call it. Started as you walked in. She told me."

"See, she *is* pretty smart."

"Horseshit." Van poured vodka into his bottle, then gestured for Ben to hold his out. Ben watched the clear liquid wash down the insides of the bottle. He took a drink, and it burned his mouth, throat and stomach. Volatile fumes hung below his nose, then went right up in there, so when he breathed they burned his lungs, causing him to cough urgently, foolishly.

Van shrugged, "Cole could be right about O'Brien, I think."

"He's behind it, huh?" Ben asked, his voice hoarse.

Earlier that day, Cole explained that a certain Dr. O'Brien was the director of the PRP, the organization that was engaged in the captive breeding of peregrines. O'Brien was Abby's supervisor. What made him stand out was that he hadn't shown up at the office for the last few days. No one knew where he was. He had no family in the area, and his phone wasn't being answered. The man worked with falcons, and that made him an obvious person of interest, under the circumstances.

The problem with receiving a ransom payoff is that it can immediately implicate the recipient. Transfers can be watched, and whoever does the collecting can be followed and arrested. But the falcon simply flew away with the ransom, disappearing to a place where it could eat in private. Where? A modern falconer wouldn't have to guess.

Falconers equip their birds with radio transmitters, and as the bird eats, they can home right in on it. A trained bird will release the catch for a reward of raw meat, which it's been conditioned to enjoy even more than the taste of captured game. The kidnapper, they believed, probably used this technique to retrieve the diamond-stuffed duck at a location impossible to know in advance and impossible for anyone to stake out.

An expert like O'Brien could have managed it. Cole suggested that the Van Dyke Agency start with him. Maybe they'd find something the FBI would overlook. The Bureau was involved now, and hadn't berated the Coles as they'd feared, but quickly mobilized, putting a number of agents on the case. They didn't mind that the Van Dyke Agency had been engaged privately, as long as no information would be concealed from them.

"You know, I don't care if O'Brien did it," Ben said. "Know what I care about?" And he put his feet up on Van's desk, too, shoes off, following the big man's lead.

"O'Brien's a cocksucker," Van said, "and I'm gonna put a bullet in him. Don't tell me you don't care!"

"I only care about Abby."

"O'Brien took her, my friend. Probably threw her off a mountain. Maybe sold her to slavers in Columbia. Or Arabs in Turkistan. She could be in a fucking harem right now!"

"I'm not so sure." Ben said.

Thirsty from the sweetness of cherry-flavored sugary wine and the ravaging diuretic action of Russian firewater, he looked at the bottle in his hand, and too buzzed to see any irony in it, swigged deeply. Then belched a belch from hell.

"Listen," Ben said, swaying, fighting dizziness. "I think I might just know who's got her!"

He stood and leaned forward, hands on Van's desk, pushing his face into Van's. "You do, too. You spotted the culprit!"

Van squinted up at him, showing he not only wasn't getting Ben's meaning, but wasn't seeing Ben too well either, up so close as he was. So Ben spelled it all out. Like Gregory Peck before the jury in *To Kill A Mockingbird*. Measured delivery, patient with righteous passion.

"The fat lady. The white powdered sugar on her face? That was the tip off!"

"You've had too much to drink," Van said, matter of factly.

"Little Abby," Ben said. " Skinny little blonde girl, see. Can't get away from the fat lady."

"And, frankly, you're pretty weird even when you're not drinking. Let's call it a day."

Ben, smiling a smartass smile, backed away from Van's desk and sat. No chair was there. He fell onto the carpet, smacking his tailbone hard, and it might have cracked if he weren't so loosely drunk, joints and muscles all relaxed and elastic, then rolled backward out of control, legs up, knees bent, into a partial back somersault, stopping just short of it. Never could do one of those.

"You okay?" Van said, standing now, behind his desk.

"Never better," Ben said calmly, as though nothing had happened.

"Let's get something to eat," Van said, taking a large black revolver out of his desk, jamming it into the empty holster he wore on his belt around in back, above his hip pocket.

Ben was momentarily sobered by the sight of the gun, but Van's nonchalance had about it the feel of a normal, leaving-the-office ritual, and Ben remembered seeing TV cops doing the same thing. Filling empty holsters before going out.

"Pizza?" Van asked.

"That's the way we did it," Ben said, getting up from the floor. "Or Mexican.

# 18.

The young woman awoke as usual in pre-dawn darkness, struck by the purity of the black punctuated by so many blue-white points of hard, clear light, more stars than anyone from LA could imagine. LA nights are never truly black, having instead a pale darkness, the color of dead TV screens. *I'll never live in L.A., no matter what my parents say.*

She lay in her own warmth, well wrapped in the lion skin, thinking that no Indian maiden, hell, no Indian chief had ever been more comfortable under the open sky. Still, she guessed she was in some danger. Beyond the matter of being lost, there were the regularly appearing campfires and provisions. She'd needed them, sure, but there was the question of who had sent them her way. There were unseen hands out there. Watchers in the woods. But danger had never really scared her. It seemed to scare men more than women anyway, she thought. And she nestled more deeply into the heat-softened robe, enjoying this quiet time to think. The hours before dawn are the best time of day. You have no obligation to do anything.

Perhaps men feel it's their business to deal with danger, while women can take it or leave it without guilt or blame, making it less of a problem for them. But no. Such gender distinctions have been sensibly blurred in recent years. And besides, she didn't think she'd be overly concerned by the dangers of this situation whatever her sex. The cozy lion robe was too reassuring. How could anything this protective be connected to danger? Really.

At any rate, she'd been gone for days now, and rescuers must certainly be searching everywhere for her. They'd probably be flying over this exact spot after sunup.

A breakfast of berries, a leathery chunk of jerky for herself and the falcon, a trip to a nearby clump of bushes, an unnecessary modesty, absolutely no feeling of being spied upon on this beautiful morning with its birdsong and sparkling dew, and she was on her way.

She rolled the cougar skin tightly and tied it with its own tail, carrying it now, by habit, as though it were a suitcase. She'd flung the pouch of berries and jerky over her bare shoulder and was heading, according to plan, in a straight line as much as the landscape would allow.

Every morning, when leaving camp, she wished she could take the fire with her, but then, every evening another seemed to be there at dusk, with more berries, more dried meat. Even if a new fire failed to appear, she could stay warm without it now. The lion skin worked so well, trapping and holding body heat, that she'd found it too warm sometimes, and had to flap it open during the night, allowing cool air to come in with her.

And she'd stockpiled some of the food. She'd walk all day if need be, eating her berries, drinking only spring water found seeping through cracks in rock walls, avoiding the flowing water of creeks, knowing that it could be tainted, that an animal lying dead in the headwaters of the creek, out of sight, could make her sick. That, she couldn't afford.

The falcon followed and surprised her by its willingness to sit on her wrist when it wasn't circling overhead. She'd cut a small strip of cougar hide, and fashioned it into a protective sleeve so the bird could perch there without its talons cutting into her skin. That night at dusk, she saw it again. A tall, thin spire of smoke rising before her, calling her into camp. Next to the fire was a freshly cleaned quail, and the sight of it caused the falcon to flap his wings in excitement.

There was also a crude but sturdy pair of deerskin moccasins.

# 19.

Ben awoke before dawn with the urgent and opposite needs to take in water and let it out. But the curtains at the Brown Palace were dense as lead, keeping out all light, giving him no clue as to where he was. A chilling panic. Where was he?

He sat up, reaching his hand quickly to the right, some dim memory of a lamp in that general direction. He touched the soft fabric headboard *what is this?* and pillows. He'd become turned around. What if he fell off this unknown bed? What if he couldn't find it again?

As with all panics, this one ran out of gas as Ben ran out of patience with the foolishness of it. He sensibly groped in all directions until banging into what must be a lampshade. He felt under it for the plastic knob, which was located, as always, on the lamp's backside, requiring unnatural hand contortions to twist it . . .

"Click!"

And there was light. He'd thought he was on the bed's left side with the headboard in front of him, while actually on the right side, facing the foot. He was at the Brown Palace, of course. Denver. Van. Abby. Falcons. He'd been enjoying himself. Why? Something about drinking cherry wine coolers and vodka last night.

But where is the bathroom? With the shuffling, bleary-eyed casualness of one who hadn't just awakened, heart banging, not knowing where he was, Ben made his way to the sink, the toilet, to drink, to urinate, dynamic equilibrium. While in the bathroom, he realized that those moments in limbo weren't wasted.

In the dark, something had popped out of his subconscious that explained the nonsense he'd babbled to Van last night. Explained might be an overstatement. Deciphered would be more accurate. Whatever, it had the comfortable feel of old information. *Large ladies with powdered sugar on their faces are like mountains. And skinny blonde children in their company are trapped, perhaps, but are nevertheless alive.*

The scene in the restaurant must have served as a mnemonic, a symbol to be filed alongside Ben's inexplicable but certain hunch that Abby was alive in the mountains. Mountains with powdery snow on their plump faces. Well, he thought, the mental basement is a messy place, and for the moment, he didn't care if it sounded silly. Alone, he was talking sub-conscious, not self-conscious.

Workers in the imagination industries are rewarded for their ability to make associations, and good copywriters like Ben sometimes over-exercise this talent, one stimulus becoming quickly connected to another, so that, for example, when he stands at the curb and sees a yellow cab drive by, he remembers his last ride in one, and that the driver seemed to be a Pakistani, and that in college his girlfriend had been duped into having dinner with a Pakistani who said he'd tutor her but tried to seduce her after forcing her to eat a nauseating curry, and the curry reminds him of an unwanted lunch date with his boss scheduled for tomorrow at an Armenian restaurant which pushes not curry but garlic, which is also a strong flavor long detectable on one's breath, and the Armenian restaurant is on 14th street, which is the same street where he'd seen a dog get run over by a car years ago, one of those French cars with the funny suspension systems, a Citroen maybe, and there was that girl in his French class during his first year at college . . .

All this, while the man standing next to him, a nice guy from accounts payable, simply sees a yellow cab.

Luckily, most of this takes place below the surface, but occasionally, such mental overkill sneaks out, especially when the conscious mind is otherwise occupied. Or, he added, standing in the bathroom, going with the spirit of digression now, when lulled into carelessness by uncountable martinis. That, Ben figured, must be how he could solve math problems when buzzed. If he simply takes his conscious mind politely by the elbow, *here, have another drink*, the hyperactive hard drive in his subconscious could be freed. And for it, ordinary math is child's play.

The panic attack must have been similarly addling. While mindless during those moments in the dark, the subconscious showed a piece of itself, revealing the curious mental connection Ben had unknowingly made days ago, and now at least he understood why he'd told Van that embarrassing nonsense about the fat lady. Van, on the other hand, would never understand.

Ben shuffled out of the bathroom, searching for a clock which he eventually found, uselessly hidden in an armoire which also contained a TV he hadn't realized was there. 4:17 am. He yanked open the heavy curtains letting grayish street light into the room. He clicked the table lamp off and flopped back into the big bed. Too big a bed for one person, he thought. And suddenly he felt sorry for himself, so alone there in the dark.

The feeling was probably just a byproduct of Van's vodka-spiked wine coolers. But it would have been nice to have someone to share this bed with, to share the insights of all this recent mental self-examination, talking about the fun you can have with your subconscious in the dark. They might have had a laugh about that. They might have talked about all kinds of fun you can have in the dark.

Deborah would have liked that bit about the yellow cab, he thought. Once, after making love to her, he rolled over and said, "On top of everything, its sugar free." A normal wife might've taken offense, but Deborah knew the difference between pillow talk and a smart ad slogan.

The product he'd been ruminating about for days was a diet whipped cream that the agency was struggling to promote. Ben had been on top, and at the climactic moment, when the conscious mind shut its eyes, much like actual eyes shut during sneezes, the slogan came up from some trusty subway station in his imagination. Must have been waiting for days, embryonically, it having the vague familiarity of an old memory. And it was perfect.

Ben did ads and TV spots showing the topping on varieties of desserts and fruits. Bananas had just the right amount of sex appeal, and the accompanying words were correct from both sides of the pun. On top of everything, it's sugar free.

Idea man. The idea of making love to Deborah made him surprisingly horny, and he found himself thinking of Tina, looking forward to seeing her at the office tomorrow, yawning now, remembering that tomorrow was already today.

# 20.

As informal as the Van Dyke Agency was, it was still part of an environment that Ben called, with a gentle contempt that had taken years to acquire, office life. Of all life forms, Ben thought this the least appealing. And in the eighties it was running wild everywhere. Gimme nightlife, he'd say. Wild life. Still life (O'Keefe's not bad). But office life? Too deadly!

Its essence is most strongly felt in the morning. Fumes of freshly applied aftershave, deodorant, cologne and mouthwash rise off well-dressed crowds pushing through marbled lobbies to vaulting, vault-like elevators.

There's the scent of coffee, the hum of hurrying. Caffeine and speed. Same thing, aren't they? Doughnut and yogurt vendors in white shirts and caps, snap up money and dispense to-go orders in time with the same double-time beat with which the workers march and march. There's the tang of fresh newsprint in the air. Everybody's grabbing a paper, flicking it up under an arm. Or they've come in with one already planted there, firm as a drill instructor's baton.

Secretaries and deliverymen. Executives in suits and ties or high heels and shoulder pads. All are slaves to Styrofoam coffee cups. All pretend to have esprit de corps. All would rather be in bed. Or anywhere free. It's only seven thirty!

Ben, in army jacket and jeans, long hair and healthy new beard, stood in the rear of a crowded elevator nervously watching the little numbers one by one, another floor safely passed, another. No cable snap this time. No power failure (". . . *They were in their underwear when rescued nine hours later. It was believed temperatures in the packed car reached a hundred and ten degrees.*")

He'd had enough of this. Put up with it for years. He hadn't quit SPF a moment too soon. He thought of Van's oddly charming bladder theory of self-expression and wondered if there weren't a similar explanation for his disdain of office life.

Maybe a guy could smell only so much coffee, newsprint, English Leather, only take so many production line elevator rides, only so many seven-thirty surrenders. That's what they were. You gave up. Gave up your whole day, letting yourself become fuel to be ingested, digested and egested by some fluorescent-lit, gray corporate engine. This dismal dismay. Every day.

So Ben was pleased to learn that Van's plan for him would keep him away from their downtown building, away from office life. In fact, far from it.

"I think maybe you should join up with the bird people, Ben.".

Detective work was much like advertising, apparently. You zeroed in on the obvious. It was obvious that the Peregrine Release Program was central to Abby's situation. She'd worked there. Her boss was a suspect, since he'd skipped town. And the only known member of the kidnapper gang was a falcon.

"I can't go in," Van said. "I look more like a redneck duck hunter than some nature lover. But you can. You even know a thing or two about birds. Lucky, isn't it?"

Ben thought of mentioning that falconers used peregrines to hunt ducks. Less noisy than shotguns. But he let Van continue, eager to soon be out of the office.

"Your objectives," Van said. "First, we want to recreate Abby's day, the day she disappeared. You're going to attempt to do that. Next, we want to recreate O'Brien's day, the day Abby disappeared. You're going to take a shot at that, too."

Ben thought, what am I getting into?

"Next, we want to know about any other people out there." Van rubbed his chin as he talked. The skin moved in thick, loose folds. Ben thought, you just turn to rubber, the older you get.

"We don't know what to expect. You must be very open-minded, open-eyed, open-eared, open in all ways in this business. Get impressions from everything. Soak up!"

Van pointed at Ben. "You'll surprise yourself. Odd things will maybe come together, but later. You might see a connection when you're not even trying. Maybe when you're in the shower, that's what happens to me."

Ben flashed on his early morning shock in the dark, nodding, remembering that he'd confirmed that the old subconscious was still putting things together for him, still surprising him. Van went on, the old coach now, Pat O'Brien's Knute Rockne. *O'Brien talking about O'Brien,* Ben thought.

"For all you know, here we are saying how we want to crucify O'Brien, but who knows. Maybe he was trying to stop the kidnapping. Maybe the guy you're looking for was his partner and he killed him. Who knows? Someone else up there could be the bad guy. You tell me."

Ben thought, once again, what am I getting into? But it was kind of exciting.

"Now," Van went on, pacing in his stocking feet. "Time's critical. If they killed the poor girl, this is for nothing. We'd like finding who did it, but our mission is to get the girl. Maybe, who knows, they're still holding her and they're going to ask for a second ransom. That happens."

And he popped his eyes at Ben, staring him down as if Ben were the bad guy himself.

"Look at you," Van said. "Absolutely perfect. The typical environmentalist type. Long hair, unshaven. Even your clothes. Now, there's one thing you'll never need, but just to be safe . . ."

Van opened a drawer and brought out a gun. It wasn't the same one he'd taken last night when they left. This was bigger. He set it on the desk, and Ben could tell by the CLUNK that it was heavy.

"HJ has all the appropriate documents you need for this, saying you work here. Everyone who works here carries. Even Tina."

Ben thought, *wild*.

"We rushed things but it's legal. Out West it's no big deal. Everybody's got guns."

He reached back into the drawer and brought out a black leather holster, attached to a rolled-up gun belt. The belt uncoiled, coming to life. Van held up the gun.

"This is a nickel-plated, Smith & Wesson .357 magnum with a four-inch barrel. Could stop a grizzly bear, okay?"

He went into the drawer again, coming back with a box of bullets.

"Ammo, okay?"

He pushed the pistol into the holster, and slid it and the bullets toward Ben.

"I never shot a gun," Ben said, nerves changing the sound of his voice. "I don't know anything about them. How to load it. Anything."

"Watch," Van said, unholstering the gun. He flicked it open, pulled six bullets from the box, dropped them in. Freud could have a field day with the sight. Then clicked the chamber, and jammed it into the holster.

"Now come on, guy," as though Ben were delaying things. "We got to get you into the field. HJ will cover your ID, and some tech stuff. He can check you out on the gun if you want. Then Tina will do logistics and transportation."

"Van? What'll you be doing?"

"I'll be watching. Listen, just don't you worry."

Ben didn't like it. People never said don't worry unless there was something to worry about.

# 21.

"The places I find myself," Ben said to the trees growing along the side of the road. They were exotic, unfamiliar Western trees. He knew from lifelong dabbling in nature and outdoor exploration books . . . Annie Dillard, Barry Lopez, Tim Cahill . . . that these trees had names like juniper, larch, mesquite, pinyon, but he had no idea which were which.

Yet he instantly knew the make and model of any American bird seen even in silhouette on the wing a half-mile away. Selective knowledge. Selective ignorance. Too much to know, to know everything. He chose birds. The irreverent *aves*. A-V's? Audio-visuals? And so they were. Free spirits who might have been in Guatemala yesterday, who unlike trees must have no word in their language for roots but probably have, like Eskimos and their snows, many words for sky.

Besides, he's no naturalist. He's an adman. Nothing natural about that. But not even an adman, now. A would-be debunker of ads, defender of realities with an honest camera that won't lie, exposing cameras that do. No, that'll have to wait. For now, Ben's a detective. A truth finder, true to his namesake Ben Franklin, himself.

He was driving a rattling, old brown Jeep that was similarly undercover, designed to pass for something a struggling grad student could afford. It was actually a mechanical overachiever belonging to the Van Dyke Agency, with a high-powered Chevy .427, four-barrel under the hood. It had a transmission that shifted so smoothly Ben pictured the gearbox packed with clear gelatin. And the heater worked, filling the interior with air singed by hot metal, a nostalgic winter morning carpool scent.

He drove into the Rockies, north and west of Denver, away from the 4-lane, away from condo tenement ski towns with their lift lines littering the summer mountains, looking like high tension towers among the trees. As he drove, he played back the morning's events. No wonder Van was brief in his briefing. It was HJ who explained most of it. And little Tina did her small part.

*   *   *

"It's a short-term assignment," HJ said in a soft Harry Belafonte voice. "Six days have passed since the girl was snatched. We figure, fourteen days, she's got to be history. We'll pull the plug. Van'll tell Andrew Cole we're out of it."

They were in HJ's room. Ben took in the jumble of electronic gadgetry, tape machines, VDTs and computers with about as much understanding as a polite Springer Spaniel might have. He sat listening, eager to please, impatient to get on with the hunt.

"So the plan is to have you go up there today and become a *hacker*?"

Ben knew the term and nodded quickly, figuring it was the only tech talk he knew that HJ might not know, enjoying the irony in this place of computers because hacker also meant one who played with computers. HJ was a hacker.

"Hacking," Ben said, "is when they raise baby falcons in captivity, then free them."

"Right," said HJ, grinning kindly, acknowledging a curiosity of no practical value.

"Now look," HJ went on, "You've got IDs here in your own name. You're a grad student specializing in raptor management."

And HJ slid papers toward Ben, who sat there, mildly surprised how naturally HJ said raptor, as though it were an everyday word, not the ornithologist's name for certain birds of prey. And it dawned on Ben that HJ surely knew all along what hacking had meant.

"There's a letter here, too," HJ said. "Van called the PRP office and told whoever was taking O'Brien's place that he was your dean, and

you'd arrive today. Said it was arranged weeks ago with O'Brien. Won't
be a hassle."

"Great," Ben said, not so sure.

"Besides," HJ said, "They want to check on you? They'll get me. Hi,
I'm chairman of Brown University's *Brown-in-the-Rockies* Wildlife
Field Management program. Anyone calls the school, they get
connected here."

Ben remembered Cole saying that Van had hi-tech capabilities and
good contacts.

"Anyway. You'll just be there a short time. Snoop around. Encourage
gossip, you know? They'll tell a guy like you shit they'd never tell the
law."

"Yeah. Their boss is missing. This girl is missing. There should be
shit to tell," Ben said, trying to convince himself.

"Exactly," HJ, smiling now. "One more thing. This is for me. I hear
they use satellites to follow animals? Radio collars send up a signal. It's
tracked from space and relayed home."

"I saw that on National Geographic," Ben said. "They do it with
bears, I remember."

HJ nodded, "So, I was thinking. The falcon that took Cole's diamonds?
Had to be wired. I figure this PRP group, being big time, funded by the
state, public donations, the University, probably time-shares a satellite,
right? Maybe there's a printout of their birds. If you could get your
hands on the one from the day Cole dropped the diamonds, maybe
I could place one of those birds there. We'd know its frequency, and
maybe we could track its signal ourselves. Find out where it is now, and
who's got it."

"I look for what, a printout?"

"Could be on a map. Little numbers clustered in patterns."

Ben felt lost. There was something cold and artless about computers.
He'd resisted professional pressure to use them, never learning to
operate SPF's word processors, writing ads on an old typewriter. He
figured when the nineties finally came along, he'd have to switch. But
he was in no hurry.

"I don't know much about computers. Printouts . . ."

"Don't sweat it. You don't see a printout, no problem. But keep your eyes open. If you do see what I'm talking about, take it. I want it. Okay?"

Van and HJ had made it sound easy. But the nearer he got to the PRP the harder he felt it would be. He'd have to pass for a grad student ("At my age?" "You look the part," HJ said, patting his shoulder. "I've never seen Brown University." "Shhh," HJ said, his finger in front of his smiling mouth).

\* \* \*

And he'd have to look for some kind of James Bond satellite printouts? He knew less about computers than he did about these mountain trees. He was less than an hour away, according to Tina's directions. It was high noon, the time of day when mountain scenery is at its plainest, lacking shadow play from the slanted sunlight of morning and afternoon. Still it was the most seductive landscape Ben had ever seen.

The road was a seldom used two-lane, and the only other vehicle on it in the last hour had been an ancient pick-up with an Indian couple in the cab and beautiful terra-cotta-skinned kids in the open back, their wise-seeming black eyes, staring at him. Ben didn't want this drive to end. He liked being in between here and there. Open places are havens for the unprepared. Can't do anything until you arrive. Can't do anything if you never arrive. Freedom isn't nothin' left to lose, Janis; freedom is being in transit.

On the next switchback, a hairpin turn with a reddish wall of fractured stone on one side and a pebbly shoulder overlooking a valley of old forest on the other, Ben decided to take a break.

"Noon break" he said aloud. "Warning—this vehicle brakes for breaks."

And he pulled over, tires crackling, parking near the edge, getting out, stretching, inhaling, the air surprisingly cool, arms back like a diver before leaving the platform, the diver image suddenly striking him as inappropriate so near a cliff. Or was it.

# 22.

Ben sat on a rock in the shade of nameless pines, soft rust-colored needles under his feet. It was quiet except for an occasional metallic ping from the cooling Jeep. After a few minutes, these stopped. When his ears got accustomed to the silence, he noticed subtle sounds. A raven calling in the valley. The wind moving in the branches. A brook somewhere close but unseen, lightly coursing. Ben felt he'd done this once before. *Deja vu*? Must be. He'd never been in the Rockies. Never been on his way to the offices of a falcon release program. But it was all so familiar. A feeling of going in unprepared, stopping at the side of the road, enjoying the green, the fragrance of the place.

*   *   *

He'd been asked to drive to a small brewery in Michigan to talk about promoting Schmidt's, a regional premium beer that was about to go national. Some New York bosses would meet him, but Ben was the only one from the Chicago office, and as creative director, he was expected to present executions. He'd procrastinated and had no ideas, thinking maybe he could reposition the meeting once there, making it simply another fact-gathering session. If the client accepted this, the New Yorkers wouldn't beat him up too bad for coming to a presentation with no presentation. And the clients just might accept it, Ben felt. Clients love to answer questions about their product, feeling the more their agency knew, the better the results would be.

He'd left for the 200-mile drive uncharacteristically confident, feeling something would save the day. An hour from the brewery, he pulled off the highway into a camp grove, to rest, to stall. He sat on a picnic table. It felt much like the rock he was sitting on now. He'd let his mind wander, and just as though he'd planned it all along, he drafted a simple idea that could make his client's beer a household word.

He sketched a hand peeling back the pop-top tab from a beer can. Out of the opening he drew an explosion of lines, and in the middle of it he lettered in *"Schmidt'ssss!"* It was, he thought, the exact sound a can makes when you pop it open. Or, if you have a bottle, and he sketched a bottle being opened, it makes the same sound when the cap pops off, "*Schmidt'ssss!*"

Later that day, Ben would tell the clients that this sound is also the sound every other beer makes when you open it. Or, for that matter, every other soft drink. Once Ben's ad campaign establishes that the sound is "*Schmidt'ssss,*" every time someone opens any carbonated beverage, they'll hear the brand name. Free advertising. Billions of name impressions a day. He pictured them carrying him out of the conference room on their shoulders. They didn't do that, but he liked picturing it. Actually, they really did like the idea, although, being beer guys they expressed their enthusiasm with macho nods and opened a couple of cans raising them in a toast to him.

*       *       *

Now, the falcon office was an hour up the road. Ben was similarly unprepared and yet, as he did before the long ago beer meeting, he felt uncharacteristically confident. He'd think of something. But first, he'd sit for a while enjoying the pine smell and cool silence.

He had driven more slowly than necessary on the way into Halfway, Colorado, the former mining town where the Falcon Release Program was headquartered. He liked being on the road, especially this winding wilderness road with mule deer brazenly grazing in adjacent alpine meadows and fluttering, iridescent magpies which had been exotic novelties the day before but were now common as pigeons.

Tina had given him a quick course on the place. She'd apparently been researching while HJ was arranging Ben's cover story. Ben laughed to himself, *I have a cover story.* Be careful, he thought, or you'll become a cover story. *Adman drives off mountain in souped-up Jeep.*

She said, "Want you to have the lay of the land when you go up there." And Ben loved her voice, sweet and strong and mischievous. Maybe he loved her a little, too. They were in his office, he behind the desk, she in front, with an oversize U.S. Forest Service map spread between them. She was wearing a loose top and as she leaned over, Ben got a clear look at the swells above her bra. Was that a little half circle of darkness peeking out? Hard to concentrate.

"Come on!" She said pulling back, friendly but bossy. "You must pay attention." A soft laugh, a hard tap on the map. "Here's where we are now."

She tapped another part of the map where there wasn't much writing. "Here's where you're going."

And she traced the route, taking a pen from a cup on his desk, writing on the map, showing where to turn by drawing little arrows at junction points. She was fast, sure of her knowledge.

"The town's called Halfway 'cause it's half way between two old gold mines. It was a boomtown once, but these days it's not much. People go there to fly fish in summer. Someday, maybe it'll get built up for skiing. Now it's just a small, out-of-the-way place. Old hippies, our bird people. Lots of wildlife in the hills."

Ben was still thinking about the hint of Tina's nipple. He tried a Mickey Rourke smile on her, that mysterious leer Kim Basinger mysteriously fell for in the absurd *9 1/2 Weeks*. Tina ignored this, and Ben got the feeling such a smile might work for Rourke, but it made him look like Steve Martin.

"The Falcon Release place is in an old building, used to be the high school."

"Halfway High." Ben said, showing he was paying attention, ignoring a background static of possible bad jokes running around in his mind.

"It's perfect for them," she said. "They turned the gym into a lab where they hatch the eggs. They have an antenna tower on the roof, and HJ thinks they use it to communicate with a cabin in the mountains. Hackers use it when they're out there." So she knew what falcon hacking was, too. These people are good.

"Let's go get your Jeep," she said, folding the map. She brought a canvas bag off the floor and set it heavily on the desk. As she opened it to drop in the map, Ben saw the butt of the revolver Van had given him. This was it, Ben realized. He didn't feel ready, and was struck by a familiar pang of nervousness. Almost like the feeling of leaving the office with storyboards in a big art case, off to make a client presentation. Well, maybe not that bad. He was merely leaving with false pretenses and a real gun, no comparison.

Tina had taken him to the multi-leveled underground garage below their building and shown him the Jeep. She gave him the Van Dyke Agency IDs including vehicle and firearm registration for emergency only, she said. After all, he was supposed to be a grad student, not a secret undercover operative, and the thought of this gave him a curious zap of excitement, not nerves, more of a fun kind of thing. He tucked the IDs deep into his wallet. The Jeep had been loaded with camping gear, insect repellent, first aid kit, flashlight, compasses, matches, blankets, hunting knife, freeze dried food, granola bars, potato chips, chocolates, a canteen, plastic baggies, bottled water, and a twelve-pack of Coca-Cola.

As he revved the overpowered engine, Tina blew him a kiss, then turned and walked away, bouncy, sure-footed. Bet she blows kisses to all the secret undercover operatives, Ben thought. And he left the underground for the high country.

# 23.

The PRP's old school building still looked and smelled like an old school although there was a slight zoo-like aroma coming from the gym on the first floor, where Ben, figuring it's a detective's job to sniff around, assumed they hatched hawks. The school's old team trophy case in front of the gym was empty now except for a life-size wooden falcon standing guard in there, staring fiercely out at Ben. Come to think of it, Ben's high school gym had smelled something like a zoo, too.

Ben met the man who'd be the boss of any real or unreal falcon hacker in an office on the second floor. According to the somewhat confusing signage of the place, it was at one time the principal's office and most recently had been Dr. O'Brien's. But that was when people knew where O'Brien was.

Today, the man behind the big desk was Darren Altman, the PRP's official number two person according to Tina's briefing, although at the moment he was shaking Ben's hand in the perfunctory style of an officious number one person. His nails were neatly rounded, highly glossed, the nails of a corporate VIP, and Ben flashed on the manicured and presidential looking male stenographer in that long ago New York ad meeting, thinking Altman has city-guy hands and wondering why the man bothers out here.

Ben said, "Nice to meet you Mr. Altman, Darren?

"Doctor Altman, actually. Only recently got the doctorate. Wildlife management. Finally! Love using the title."

Ben recalled an old friend who, upon receiving his Master's, a cowardly ploy to extend college in order to defer and delay getting a real job, had said "Just call me master." Ben smiled at this, and Altman, not realizing he was dealing with someone prone to watch instant replays of his past at random, assumed the smile was for him and returned it, revealing a set of unusually small teeth.

But small teeth and needlessly nice nails weren't the most unusual things about Altman's appearance. He wore mirrored sunglasses throughout the handshake and introductory pleasantries, and these clearly stole the show.

The rest was fairly conventional, although Ben had the impression Altman enjoyed looking older than his age. Acting and dressing forty something, the man was probably not much more than mid-thirties. His dark hair was cut short, overly neat, with wet-looking comb marks visible and an extremely crisp, white part. He wore a white dress shirt and a string tie held together with a little silver falcon, wings spread, talons clenched.

Once Altman and Ben were comfortably seated for Ben's indoctrination, it seemed unusual that Altman would continue wearing the sunglasses. But there they stayed, one-way mirrors, inscrutable little barriers, preventing Ben from seeing not just the man's eyes, but the man himself.

Ben remembered a book he'd seen passed around the agency. It was about office power games, ways to one-up corporate opponents by doing things like positioning your chair higher than your visitor's, or keeping the window behind you, silhouetting you so your visitor can't see you clearly. He'd told friends that the book must have been written by an asshole, about assholes, for assholes.

Strong language for Ben. His verbal style didn't favor profanity, although like everyone who was young in the sixties and seventies, he'd been happily desensitized to the harshness of the word "fuck," and found it merely spicy, even somewhat humorous, considering its literal meaning, and especially when used by females. Tiny, tawdry Tina. How long until they could listen to the tapes?

But the book's ideology had been outspoken on one subject. When some asshole wears dark glasses indoors, you're at a disadvantage. You can't read his reactions. You don't know where to look. It's like you're being watched, vulnerable to social or professional ambush. Mirrored glasses worn indoors must surely be the cheapest power trick in the book. Ben couldn't ignore this. After all, he wasn't really a student and didn't give a hoot about currying favor with the man. Kind of a nice thing, this undercover operative feeling.

"Dr. Altman, may I ask? Why are you wearing sunglasses indoors?"

"Does it bother you?"

"Me? No. I just thought maybe you were hiding a black eye or something." Ben said this with a laugh, hoping to warm the moment, establish some informality, friendliness, even. That would be the way to play it. The man was supposedly going to be his superior on this make-believe mission. A make-believe superior. And Ben thought, should there be any other kind?

Altman smiled, an attempt, perhaps, to return some warmth, but it was impossible from behind the lifeless lenses. At any rate, it gave Ben another look at the little teeth, a small reward, of sorts.

"Oh, I haven't had a black eye in years. But I've given a few."

Ben thought, *you don't look so tough.*

"Now," Altman said, "let's talk about your duties, Mr. Green."

And Altman, not knowing he was not, in reality, Ben's superior, went on to outline Ben's responsibilities as their new hack site attendant. He had a voice and attitude Ben had encountered in past bosses, a kind of whispery confidentiality, a phony holding back, as though the so-called superior would have preferred dialing up the volume but was going to some length to keep it modulated, a begrudging civility.

Ben had been thinking about this and about the audacity Altman was showing by so readily accepting the role of Ben's superior, when Ben shamefully but with pleasure, calculated that he'd happily left a salary that was certainly quadruple that of this cocksure doctor's, and his eyes must have glazed temporarily, becoming little soulless blanks themselves, which Altman, an apparent expert on eye wars, noticed. It happened during a particularly monotonous monologue about the preparation of hawk food and the importance of keeping out of the hatchlings' sight.

"Mr. Green? Are you following this?"

"Sure. Can't let the birds see you. Of course."

"Should you be taking notes?"

Ben had left his pad and pen in the Jeep. Had this all been for real, he'd have run for them. Now, annoyed with his own carelessness, he stood his ground.

"No. I've got it. Really."

Altman was quiet for an uncomfortable moment. He looked down at the forged letter Ben had given him earlier, reading it again, going slowly.

"This letter to Dr. O'Brien highly recommends you. He didn't have a chance to go over your placement with me. But I must say, we could use the extra help. One of our volunteers just up and split on us, no notice. Some of these people are rather free- spirited, I'm afraid."

He leaned forward and whispered, as though uttering a dirty word, "Undependable."

Ben thought the Coles would settle for undependable over kidnapped, and he wished it were that simple.

Altman nodded toward the letter in his hand. "I'm pleased to see you've had experience with raptor management in Massachusetts. That could be useful in our program. But I hope you're not going to split on me if you find it a little wild out in the back country."

Altman smiled, signaling a doctorate-level witticism to come, "See, I've been to Massachusetts, Mr. Green and, believe me, this is no Massachusetts."

Ben, though thoroughly briefed by HJ on the letter's contents and his cover background, quickly blanked out on all of it, and had to change the subject.

"Is Dr. O'Brien here? I wanted to meet him."

"Yes. No. Not at the moment."

"Will he be back before I go off to the site? My department chairman asked me to give him his regards, you know."

If Altman' eyes had been visible, Ben sensed they'd have been looking off into the distance.

"Dr. O'Brien said something to me once. He said, no man lies on his deathbed thinking, I should've spent more time at the office."

Ben had heard this platitude before, and although trained in ad agencies to dislike the unoriginal, he had to admit he endorsed it himself, original or not.

"You mean, he's gone fishing, right?"

"We can't blame him if he did. Do you have any idea what the rainbow trout are like around here?"

Altman placed the letter on a neat stack of papers, setting a paperweight atop it. The paperweight was a little stuffed lizard. Its shiny black eyes, not eyes at all, but tiny beads, seemed to take in everything that was going on. Ben was pleased to be moving the conversation away from the sham letter, the sham identity.

"Well, when Dr. O'Brien returns from his trip, maybe you can get out there yourself."

"How right you are, Mr. Green. I'm learning that the director's job can be, well, tiresome. A bit of fishing is definitely on my calendar."

Would it be possible to actually like Altman?

"Now, Mr. Green, let me repeat what I expect you to do on your first day at the site." That patronizing voice again, the bored superior, and Ben thought, no, go with the gut. Look at the sunglasses. The guy's simply an asshole. And once again, Ben, inveterate job hopper who had no great love of jobs, found himself being the new guy in another new job. It was a feeling he knew.

# 24.

Ben couldn't sleep. He was in what Altman had called their "line cabin," in mountain forest about seven miles from Halfway. He had no idea what the word "line" meant as applied to cabins, although he vaguely recalled hearing the term in westerns. He thought about it as he lay in the cold.

Maybe the cabin had been on a line, like a stagecoach line, and people "rode the line" bringing mail and goods in. Maybe the cabin was on a property line, marking a claim site. Maybe it was where they stored line. Fence line. Fishing line? Maybe it was the end of the line.

He twisted around inside the down sleeping bag, reminding himself of a caterpillar he saw once in a nature documentary, squirming in its cocoon. All that nervous motion just below the surface. Ben Franklin Green's life story. Ben had three or four hours to kill before it would be light. Would be nice if he could sleep, but the more he thought about it, the more awake he became. It's a vexing part of life, at least Ben's life, that the degree to which a thing is desired is directly proportional to the difficulty of attaining it.

"Ben's Law," he called it. How many times had he lain on the couch trying to watch a ball game, really caring about the next play, only to fall helplessly into sleep, awakening in the after-game recap show, refreshed and dumbfounded. Yet, when sleep was wanted, required actually, where was it?

How about all those unwanted erections that marched throughout his life to their own inscrutable drummer. In school classrooms from age twelve on. In business meetings. Important interviews. On airplanes, crowding up under that flimsy dinner tray. Even once at a funeral, hiding behind his prayer book as the group was endlessly put through stand up, sit down exercises while his own member of the congregation only knew stand up. And, after all that, where was it when he really needed it, during a visit to a whore at sixteen? The plump mascara-stained lady coaxed, but it wasn't buying, though she still got paid.

Ben's Law. He remembered being able to shoot ten, even twenty baskets in a row, earning a big schoolyard reputation and having friends enter him into a city-wide free-throw contest. Much behind-the-scenes betting on deadeye Ben. But alone on the court when it counted, his eye went truly dead, and he hit one for ten, eliminating himself in the first round.

It took years to gain this wisdom. Don't fight the law. Just don't want the thing you want. Someone once told him this was a Zen concept. Zen's Law? No, he'd thought of it first. Can't sleep? Fine. Don't. Get up. Get dressed. Fuck sleep.

He unzipped the bag which he'd spread atop the bunk-style bed built into the side of the one-room cabin. He reached for his flashlight, having had the foresight to put it in the bag with him so he wouldn't run the risk of waking to black limbo as he did at the Brown Palace hotel, flailing around for an on-off switch. The flashlight was warm with body heat and gave him the feeling that it was somehow, for the moment, an extension of himself. The two of them against the night.

The beam arced through the room, and lit on his wristwatch. A little after two AM. He'd been in the cabin about eight hours, having arrived around six o'clock, after four-wheeling up an old logging road, turning at exactly 7.5 on the odometer, then following a two-track rut that took him to the cabin after the odometer said 4.3. Odometers were like addresses up here, he thought. What's your address? Seven point five, what's yours?

Eight hours. At first, he'd amused himself by hiking in a wide circle around the cabin, always keeping some part of it in sight through the trees, correctly fearful (thanks to the finely honed instincts of a semi-phobic personality) of getting lost. He'd looked for birds, figuring he'd be likely to find species as remote as this backcountry location, but all he saw were large black ravens, roosting in surprising numbers in the tops of trees, giving the place an eerie feeling.

He remembered that the presence of a large predator can sometimes attract these opportunistic birds who like to clean up the scraps after a kill. And he wondered if a bear or mountain lion were watching him. Lion cabin? Could that be it? So he went inside.

The cabin was dark, dusty, easily the most foreign environment Ben had ever found himself living in, even if it were only for one night. The plan, as it had been explained, was for Ben to overnight there. "Your last taste of civilization for quite a while," Altman had said, smiling, showing those little teeth. Then Ben would hike up the mountain in the morning, following a trail on a topographic map until he found the hack site.

"The site's supervised by someone we affectionately call Rambo. I suggest you make plenty of noise as you approach. Perhaps you could sing or something?"

Ben had just stared at the map, such a meaningless tangle of lines and circles. "Sing?"

"You must learn the backwoods courtesies, Mr. Green. Always avoid giving the appearance of . . ." and Altman whispered, "sneaking in."

He explained that Rambo was somewhat post-traumatic and didn't like society, preferring to live alone in the woods, taking hack site assignments for little pay and lots of solitude.

"Could be, oh, a slight bit touchy if you don't announce yourself properly. Rambo's quite the independent type, you understand. Won't be expecting an assistant. Short-handed as we are, I'm afraid there's been no chance to get word up there. But I'm sure you'll get on fine together. Watch and you'll learn something." Another blank-eyed smile.

And Ben readily agreed to everything Altman said, knowing then as he nodded that maybe he'd check the cabin for clues, but would never go up any mountain trail singing to himself, looking for somebody they called Rambo, affectionately or not.

Ben sat on the bunk in the dark, flashlight off, conserving batteries. Can't turn on the lights. No electricity in the cabin. Could start a fire, he thought. There was a fireplace built into the wall. He flipped on the flashlight, playing the beam around the room, seeing things in its moving circle that he hadn't noticed before. Wood and kindling were set up on the hearth, looking new against the background of old soot.

There were holes along the flooring through which mice probably commuted freely. The old plank table was covered with dust except near the corner, where it had been scraped clean in a half-circle. Under it was a crumpled up pretzel bag, empty except for some crumbs the mice must have missed.

As he swung the beam around, it crossed in front of his face and caught the fog of his breath. Frost in July, he thought. And he remembered the bright snow he'd seen on the mountain tops earlier. He thought of hot Julys in Chicago, the sticky, insomniac nights, and decided he liked July in the mountains better.

If his mind weren't all balled up with thoughts of Altman and Rambo . . . undercover missions, the telling of lies, his determination to skip out on this lunacy at first light, disappointing both the spiers and the spied upon . . . he'd probably enjoy a fine sleep in the chilled room. He played the beam back and forth through his foggy exhalations, playing with light and breath, passing quiet minutes in the middle of the night in the middle of nowhere.

The white circle thrown by the flashlight on the ceiling caught his eye as it moved over the old timbers. Something had flashed in the beam. He carefully ran the light over the area. The flashlight segregates its illuminated circle from everything else, simplifying the job of being attentive.

Like Sherlock Holmes with his magnifying glass, Ben used his circle of light to bring into view something he might never have seen otherwise. A wire. A simple electrical wire covered with ordinary black insulation, gray with dust. Wasn't there supposed to be no electricity here?

Ben remembered the neatly stacked firewood and kindling in the hearth. Maybe he'd start a fire and take a better look at that wire. He pulled on jeans, socks and boots, then aimed the flashlight into the duffel, looking for a lighter to use on the kindling, packed just for this reason. It was nowhere to be found in the clutter. As he searched, he thought it was interesting that he only noticed the thoughtfully prepared firewood after shining the flashlight's beam on it, completely ignoring it through the evening hours when the cabin was well lit by the setting sun.

An idea. Maybe just using the narrow eye of the flashlight would be the best way to investigate the wire. It felt better. More detective-like. And didn't fireplaces have flues and dampers and things he was unfamiliar with? Besides, a fire would send smoke signals, and with crazed vets in the hills, he felt it best not to advertise his presence. So he wouldn't make a fire.

At the moment of making this decision, he located the lighter. The Law's busy tonight, he thought, smiling.

# 25.

The wire disappeared into a crack at the juncture of ceiling and wall, reappearing again at the floor, having been run through the wall in a curious attempt to keep the untidy room tidily wired. The harsh scrutiny of Ben's searchlight made the wire stand out as it never would in ordinary room light, and Ben could see it had been snipped off close to the wall, only a stiff stub, craning itself upward as though interested in all the midnight commotion. Its core shone, shiny new copper, suggesting it was recently cut.

Outside, there was a rustling in the woods. Not everywhere, but seemingly in one spot, somewhere off to the right and downhill. Would the wind be so selective a rustler? Could a bear be rooting about? Why didn't line cabins have locks on their doors? Don't think about it. So there was a wire and it had been cut. So what? Ben sat on the bunk and regretted not bringing a bottle of whiskey, a wine cooler, a beer, something to make the night move its tiresome butt.

Tiny Tina had loaded his Jeep with campout foods, which Ben had no interest in eating at the moment, and didn't know how to prepare anyway. Freeze-dried Beef Stroganoff? *Come on.* But no medicinal alcohol. Those detectives, private eyes, shamuses, dicks, (did they really call themselves dicks?) weren't so smart. Ben mused, Tina's in the dick biz. St. Louis massage parlor, Denver detective agency. All dicks to her. Didn't she say there was a cabin in the mountains that had a radiophone or something? A cabin from which the hill-bound hackers could send messages back to civilization, or at least, the PRP office?

Ben clicked off the light. There was probably no reason to care if this was or wasn't their communications cabin. Probably wouldn't have any bearing on the kidnapping. And yet, what? That itchy feeling. A need to nose around among apparently irrelevant details. This itchiness had done him a good turn when he'd been assigned to advertise a new kind of potato chip, hadn't it?

\*   \*   \*

The chip, if it could be called that, was formed and pressed from powdered potatoes. SPF'S client had been firm. "Make it fun food. Write a jingle. Show kids eating my chips at the beach."

But Ben didn't go to his typewriter, going instead to the food lab where the potato flour was developed. Nosing for random information. There, a potato-headed Ph.D. in a lab coat, hair cut in homage to Larry of the Three Stooges, told him that they didn't use one kind of powdered potato, but several kinds. Russets, Reds, Idahos, Irish and others were blended into the powder that made the new chip. Bingo. Ben's nosing paid off.

He blew them away in Mr. Chips' boardroom, first presenting the spot as requested. Kids going crunch at the beach. It was titled, "Join the crunch bunch" and the client smiled. Ben smiled back, but it was the indulgent kind, as he was about to pull the rug out and present what he said should be done.

"It takes seven kinds of potatoes to make one perfect chip." He said, showing a storyboard of a pink-cheeked farm mom standing, cute in a big apron, in a big country kitchen. She displayed seven potatoes and talked about the virtues of each. One is mild, one perky, one meaty, wouldn't it be wonderful if all these qualities came together at the same time? She moved to her great old stove where our chips are sizzling in a family-size skillet. And she said, "Now you can, in the ONE chip made from nature's SEVEN tastiest potatoes."

Cut to the chips on a platter surrounded by gingham napkins. Everybody in the boardroom got hungry. Ben said, "See, you're not selling the beach. You're selling . . . simply good food." They bought Ben's approach, repositioned the brand and sales were, like the chips . . . simply good.

\*   \*   \*

Ben got hungry, thinking about it. He had a can of these chips in the Jeep. Maybe he'd get some. Besides, he hadn't found any other sign of communications equipment in the cabin. Might be good, he thought, to nose around outside a bit, being as how he was a detective and all.

The sky was lightly salted with stars, but there was no moon and on the ground darkness was nearly total. The small noises Ben made opening and closing the cabin door, boots scraping frozen pebbles, seemed unnaturally intrusive in the silence of the woods. They were enough to spook something big out there, something that careened off at speed, banging through trees, snapping brush as it went. Ben's spine was electrified. Primeval fears of night, woods, bears.

He listened. Nothing. Must have been a bear. They were supposed to be plentiful in these hills, and night was their time to scrounge around, especially near cabins and jeeps where there might be something to eat. Ben quickly went back inside.

But soon, the ceaseless middle-of-the-night boredom combined with a growing need for potato chips and the itch to nose around. It had been reassuringly silent out there for a while, so Ben decided to give it a shot.

In daylight, he might not have noticed the two ancient oil drums at the end of the rutted drive where he'd left the Jeep. They fit naturally into the cluttered landscape back there among rust-colored heavy equipment of a sort Ben couldn't identify. But the white beam of his flashlight brought its selective scrutiny into play again, and the drums stood out brightly, especially their lids, which seemed cleaner than they should be, and unnaturally well fitted.

He assumed these drums had once held fuel, or some substance unknown to him, but commonplace to the rough-hewn, do-it-yourself types who lived everyday lives in wilderness areas, who by necessity understood gas and oil, chain saws and water pumps, compressors and generators, things with which Ben was rather sheepishly unfamiliar. He aimed his beam at the first can and with his free hand worked the lid off. It dropped to the ground, rolled like a wheel into the weeds, and fell onto its side. Ben illuminated the inside of the drum and peeked over the rim. "Ah," he said aloud. And he didn't care if bears heard him or not.

It wasn't easy lifting the radio out, so he laid the drum on its side, then upended it. The radio slid out with an afterbirth of tangled cables, all inflexibly coiled, stiff with cold. He opened the other drum and dumped out an Army surplus field telephone and two 12-volt car batteries. He didn't know what it all meant, exactly, but figured since these things were hidden, they were clues. He'd take them to Van in the morning.

He loaded the radio, wires and phone into the Jeep, moving aside the provisions put there by Tina. What was it about those provisions? And he remembered his earlier reminiscence about potato chips, his original motivation for leaving the cabin. He rooted around and found the can of chips. He pulled a Coke out of its plastic webbing, well chilled as was everything up there at that hour, and went back to the cabin for a snack. He hadn't noticed the fire burning in the fireplace until he'd opened the front door and saw the room filled with inviting orange light.

# 26.

There was little doubt that it was Rambo who'd started the fire. A battered Army jacket was draped over the back of the room's only chair. The jacket had letters stenciled in cracked orange glitter across its back. R A M O. Any doubt that might have remained was instantly eliminated by the ugly pistol pointing its wide black eye into Ben's wide, white eyes. An automatic, something with a big caliber, needing two hands to hold it steady. Probably a .45, the old standard sidearm of the military. Time stood still. No words spoken. The fire crackled. The pistol clicked as a large, dirty thumb moved a metal lever from one position to another. Ben assumed it was the safety being taken off.

"Who are you?" Rambo said.

Ben looked beyond the black hole into Rambo's face. Then dropped his eyes to take in Rambo's bare chest, becoming more interested in her fire-lit breasts than in the gun. Rambo had an interesting face, wild and frizzy dark hair with auburn in it, and she was definitely not a guy. Something in her expression communicated fear, her fear. Ben remembered earlier thinking the bear in the woods was afraid of him, too. He'd wanted the bear to run. He wanted Rambo to stay. But without the gun. Then he realized the gun was clearly for defense, not offense, and relaxed a bit. After all, he'd intruded on her while she was changing her clothes from the look of things.

Her pack lay on the floor, unzipped, and Ben could see she'd been taking out items of clothing. Somewhere underneath his understandable tension from being in a gun-sight, the recently liberated horn section in the orchestra pit of his mind cheered at this good timing and played a few bars of *Night Train* in salute to this woman's truly top-form form, noting how her bosom shook when she talked, holding the pistol forward in both hands, and didn't stop after she'd stopped, but kept on jiggling, suggesting the rollicking stubbornness of a waterbed.

Ben, frozen in the unexpected firelight, the unexpected gun-sight, the unexpected everything, found it difficult to deal with, or even remember, her question. It came again, louder,

"Who are you?"

He looked up, face to face now, the only polite thing to do.

"From the Peregrine group," he said. "In town? A man sent me. Man named . . ."

And he went blank on the name.

"Wait," he said. "Mirrored sunglasses. Small teeth. A lizard on his desk . . ."

"Yeah?" she said, still aiming the .45 at him. (Her 38s—the horn section took a secret ballot and came up with that figure, "C" probably— were similarly aimed at him, but he, unlike the guys in the horn section, was still keeping his eyes off them, all business, talking fast.)

"I'm supposed to work on a hack site? Work with someone called . . . Rambo. Could that be you?" And he gestured with a glance to the army jacket, the stenciled letters. She lowered the .45, holding it in one hand now, but the 38s were still aimed straight on.

"My nickname," and she smiled showing a wide mouthful of healthy teeth. When she did this, her blue eyes got crinkly like Bette Midler's, but her mouth was Carly Simon's.

"My god . . ." she said.

"What?"

Shaking her head, but with the tiniest, self-amused smirk, she moved her free arm across her chest, covering up.

"If you don't *mind*?" And she made a pirouette gesture with the gun, clearly suggesting he turn away.

"I've been living alone out here way too long," she said.

Ben looked toward the fire, turned somewhat, but not entirely, feeling she didn't really care anyway. Rambo tucked the gun into her waistband at the small of her back and pulled an oversize orange jersey from her pack. It said Denver BRONCOS across the chest, and when her head popped through the opening, she was smiling.

"Hi, my name's Rachel. I gotta say, though, that I do prefer *Rambo* these days."

That smile of hers.

"Ben," Ben said. Then quickly said it again, "Ben," inadvertently making it sound like his name could be Ben Ben, which he corrected by adding, "Ben, just Ben."

He wondered briefly if he should mention the Franklin part, then thought, *what am I doing!* The guys in the horn section booed him, slapping their foreheads in frustration at his eternal ineptness as a charmer. But he fooled them all by simply smiling, a smile he meant, eyes crinkling with warmth as hers had, and he could feel an invisible bolt of energy connect them.

He liked Rachel inexplicably, instantly, feeling with some psychic certainty that the feeling could be mutual. He wanted to ask her why she'd appeared at the cabin in the middle of the night. How could she have traveled on foot through the black woods? He wanted to ask her if she knew where O'Brien was. And if she thought that Altman (*that* was the asshole's name!) was a bit odd. He wanted to ask her if she knew Abby Cole. On some level, he wanted to ask her if it was absolutely necessary that she wear the shirt.

"Potato chips?" he asked.

"Sure." Was there shyness there? He uncapped the tall can, pouring a few of the pre-fab chips into her hand.

"Some Coke?" he asked.

"You only have the one."

"I'll get another!" he said, and handed the can to her. He stood, not leaving to get another, not wanting another. Why had Altman clearly led him to believe Rambo was a guy? He couldn't remember if Altman actually said anything about Rambo's gender. Pretty crafty, and this reminded him of those childhood monster films in which an expert scientist is called in, known only by the title "doctor," who turns out to be a woman, ultimately even the love interest, although in childhood Ben was bored by that part of it. Suckered by that old trick. But why? Was Altman just being playful, or did he want Ben to chicken out before even getting started?

Rambo popped open the can and took a good, long pull. Her chest moved under the Denver logo with its big letters, and Ben couldn't help thinking, *bucking BRONCOS.* A Wild West moment.

# 27.

Ben had never been much of an extrovert, but the last few days had brought uncommon stretches of solitude, causing a hunger for conversational contact. Being alone in the mountains and spending so much time knocking around inside his head had given him a spooky malaise for which Rachel, with her warm orange fire and hot orange Bronco's shirt, was a welcome remedy.

They sat side by side on the bed, backs leaning against the cabin wall, knees up, feet tucked and cozy. This room that was an hour ago darkly alien to Ben now had about it the secure fellowship of a slumber party. As they talked, Ben realized the remaining two hours before dawn, which earlier had seemed an interminable sentence of solitary confinement, would be over in a wink.

Rachel was kind of pretty, Ben thought, but maybe not according to the pop culture doll-face definition. Her mouth was too wide, her eyes a bit squinty. Ironically, these slightly off features contained items of resounding purity, teeth bright and powerful, a bit large perhaps, but of exuberant health, suggesting untold biting and smiling power. They caused Ben to flash on the old-fashioned expression, soul satisfying, though he had no idea why.

Similarly, the girl's ... woman's ... eyes that peeked out behind her squint had a lively shine and seemed to change colors, at once greenish brown, then lovely brown-gold. His grandmother had had the same color eyes. Hazel, she'd called them, and he remembered that she had owned a large, single topaz, set into a pendant kept locked in an ancient jewelry box. Her birthstone, she'd said, and it was the color of clear tea, like her eyes.

"Your eyes are pretty, " Ben said, surprising himself, not having meant to say this aloud, remembering vaguely having spoken those words once long ago to his grandmother, and feeling as if he'd just said it to her again, her memory strong in him.

Uncomfortable with the lies that had to go hand in hand with his deep cover secret agent detective false identity, Ben deflected Rachel's questions about his grad school studies, his supposed interest in hawking and hacking (the words conjuring up visions of old tuberculars in his mind), and steered her into talking about herself. All it takes, he thought, is the unease of living a lie to make one into a better conversationalist, turning talk to your partner's favorite subject anyway.

Rachel, though now warming to the moment and, in any case, stranded for the night, seemed willing to be friendly. She told him she'd grown up in suburban Denver, but went to college at UCLA, graduating in the same year Ben had, and he felt pleased at this, believing that people of the same age share a bond, belonging to some amorphous cult in which all members watched the same TV shows as kids.

But she was reluctant to talk in depth about her recent background. Could she, too, be undercover? Stricken, as Ben was, with the inability to craft a plausible identity? This Ben ruled out absolutely. Just a feeling. He sensed there might be something in her she wanted to keep away from. With the nosiness of an adman snooping for another unique selling proposition, he overstepped politeness and frankly pried. This was uncomfortable for him to do, as he found himself caring about what she might think of him, and not wanting to offend. But still, let's not get entirely carried away, he thought. After all, wasn't she essentially an unknown roughneck who could actually have shot a bullet into him if she'd hiccuped back there with her finger on the trigger?

"You married or anything?" he said. "Have any kids?" After all, she was well into her thirties.

Silence. She stared at the fire. The convex profiles of her hazel eyes were so clear when seen from the side, and Ben thought, *falcon eyes*, no wonder she likes the job.

"Yeah. Married. A kid. But no more married. No more kid. I don't want to get into it, " she said softly, talking to her knees, to herself.

Ben wanted to change the subject then, change the mood. He groped for something quick to say, but she said it first as he knew she would, knowing that "I don't want to get into it" often means you're going to.

Rachel and her husband had worked for a big-ticket LA law firm. They'd been caught up in the power careering of the early eighties and had both made partner by thirty. The story was simple and grim. Their little boy of three was in the care of a nanny all day, and both lawyers would work until ten on many nights. One day Rachel wondered if being a workaholic mother couldn't really be a form of child abuse and decided to quit, figuring she'd go home and play Donna Reed for the rest of her life.

She gave the firm a generous month's notice, but during that month her son toddled into their swimming pool while the nanny had The Grateful Dead dialed up to eleven on her Walkman. The nanny found the kid's body on the bottom and drank a whole bottle of Johnny Walker Black Label, not even calling the paramedics. She was on the floor when Rachel got home, but unlike the child and the marriage, the nanny had survived.

"I'm over it now," Rachel said. Then she looked at Ben and smiled, or tried to, and said, "I'll never get over it."

Ben didn't know what to say.

"But at least I'm out of the city now. I just like being where it's totally wild, you know? And raising my little guys up there in the hills. Think of it. These birds might have become extinct. But we're bringing them back. Giving life?"

Ben knew he'd forced her out of bounds, and felt guilty. But she seemed to be perking up.

"Anyway, I'm no Donna Reed."

"You're more of a Mary Richards, I'd say." Wanting to move her into the mindless world of sitcoms. His dad used to call them shitcoms.

"I never missed a show!" she said. "Think I'm like her, huh?"

" Cute. Thirtyish. Big smile. But one thing, though . . ."

"Yeah?"

"You can fill out a Broncos jersey a lot better than Mary Tyler Moore could."

She bammed her shoulder into him, roughhousing, playful, the grim mood gone, or at least put back where she kept it.

"You have to forget what you saw before," she said. "I'm embarrassed about that!"

"You even sound like Mary now."

"Did that on purpose. I'm not the least embarrassed."

"I knew."

"You didn't."

It was nice to talk to someone who, like Ben, had stayed home with a pizza on high school Saturday nights to watch Archie Bunker, then Bob Newhart, then Mary Tyler Moore. When Carol Burnett came on, then they'd go out. Hell, most girls he met only knew those shows from reruns, or not at all. And so . . .

"Remember Mr. Grant falling for Sheree North?"

"That silly turtleneck he wore to impress her?"

"Remember Newhart's group of weirdos . . ."

"His 'Fear of Humidity' group!"

"How about Mary's party . . ."

"When Johnny Carson was coming . . ."

"And all her lights went out?"

Yeah, it was good to be with someone who'd been there.

Ben did not find it welcome when a few pre-dawn birds shook free of their little reptilian sleeps and broke the frozen calm of the forest with tentative chatter, as though they really had anything much to say. Except that *day is coming.*

As a hack site attendant, Rachel was not supposed to leave her young falcons unguarded. Her job was to protect them from predators who'd be attracted to their flightless vulnerability, and to feed them, which she explained was done by sliding chunks of raw chicken and whatever mice she could catch and mash, down a long cardboard tube that led from Rachel's perch out of the chicks' sight, to the ledge where they sat in makeshift human-built nests, waiting stoically to grow up.

To the falcons, food just magically dropped at their doorstep. This is not quite the way it would happen if they were fed by parent birds, although it's close enough, and experts think it's better than having them see a human directly feeding them, thereafter associating humans with handouts.

"That only works if you're going to raise the bird for falconry-style hunting," she said, and went on to tell Ben more than he cared to know about that ancient sport. Seems Rachel was a little in need of conversation, too. Sport was a strange word for falconry, he thought, since the falconer did nothing much but stand around while his or her bird did the athletics. As she talked, he remembered having similar doubts about horse racing being called the "sport of kings" when all the king did was sit on his fat butt in the stands. And what kind of sport is fishing, anyway? You can do it while sleeping. His mind wandered and Rachel rambled. This lady was really into falcons.

But when she said why she abandoned her post, especially after all she'd said about how she was never supposed to leave, Ben perked up. It was a bizarre story. To tell it she used a bizarre prop, which she brought out at just the right moment. She'd jumped off the bed with a girlish grace that only enhanced the kids-on-a-campout feeling, rooting around in her pack, pulling it out. She stood up, wheeling to face Ben, holding the thing away from her as though she was afraid of it, letting it dangle by a thread in front of him in the firelight. He leaned forward to get a better look. Then he gulped like a kid at a Friday the Thirteenth festival.

It was a human scalp.

"Isn't this the damnedest thing?" Rachel said with a kind of mild astonishment. A brow-furling expression, mouth half open, as if she were showing off a baffling but harmless curiosity. She stared at the swinging hair. Ben stared at it. The scalp slowly spun. Was there some contingent of lost Arapahos living in these endless wooded hills, lost in time as well as place? Just like the fabled and enfeebled old Japanese troops said to be living in South Seas jungles, keeping ancient rifles clean and ammo dry, not knowing about Hiroshima, blissfully unaware of the bomb age, not knowing the war ever ended, or that the world suddenly could? Injuns? Could they have been responsible for the noises he'd heard in the woods? No. Indians move quietly. Like Tina.

"A scalp?" He said, almost stuttering the word, almost sounding foolishly like some pop-eyed ham actor in an old black and white movie, *s-s-s-s-scalp?!* But he managed to pronounce this question whole, thankfully, and Rachel didn't catch the catch in his throat. She laughed and flung the scalp at Ben. He had an urge to dive aside, avoiding it, but resisted doing so as he'd vowed he'd always resist that particular cowardly move, since as a kid he'd spun around to avoid a writhing grass snake some older boys had tossed at him, letting the snake bounce off his back, while to his distress (to say nothing of the snake's) little girls laughed. Especially the one little girl in a pony tail whom he'd had his eye on. Never again!

Ben caught the scalp in one hand, decisively, as though it were that snake that day, while Rachel, Rambo, whatever she called herself, watched him, sexy envoy from the world of all girls. Hands on hips, head cocked in certain approval. And somewhere in the sub-basement of all the synapses that made Ben who he was, the pony-tailed little girl revised her opinion. Ben wasn't such a pussy after all.

A pussy? The soft, lightweight clump of curls in his hand resembled that particular mysterious item more than it did a human scalp. Ben knew something about scalps from reading frontier novels, and even U.S. Marine horror stories (no wonder those Japanese were still hiding). So he knew that scalps generally have leathery undersides which give them some heft. This was simply a weave of lightweight hair on a mesh backing that had all the solidity of a nylon stocking. It was no scalp. It was a toupee.

"What the hell?" Ben said, calming, finding himself using the same curiously amused tone as Rambo had.

"A toupee?" He pronounced the word "toop," with some derision, as he'd always felt these things to be hopelessly tacky and maybe actually tacky. Didn't they need to be held in place with glue? He tentatively touched the underside. Only a little tacky. But of course, it hadn't been on the job recently.

"Wait'll you hear how I found it." Rachel, said, and joined him on the bed again, taking it from him, staring at it now as though there were some serious words in the salt and pepper hairs. She quietly added, "And why it kinda worries me."

They sat against the wall, wiggling their butts around atop the billowy sleeping bag, getting comfortable. Outside, the darkness seemed less intense, but there was no obvious dawn grayness yet, in spite of the early birds.

"I might know this hairpiece. That's why I broke the rules, left my falcons on their own, and came down here."

She'd wrestled with her decision most of yesterday and only decided to make the hike after nightfall. She knew the trail and had a good flashlight. It took hours, picking her way slowly over the rocks. Several times she'd heard noises in the trees, more than usual she'd said, having spent enough nights in the mountains to know what was usual, and she was worried at so much nocturnal animal activity. Worried because along with her toupee discovery, it could spell bad news. Ben asked why, and she explained, telling him about the ravens. This was a good place to start because Ben, alert to unusual bird sightings himself, was especially interested, remembering his own sighting of ravens crowding treetops in watchful silence near the line cabin.

"I always see ravens where I am," she said. "They're more common than hawks. And, you know, they do almost the same thing. They eat small birds, rodents. Even carrion, like vultures will. They like the higher altitudes, so you see a lot of 'em in the mountains. Anyway, last few days? I noticed they'd disappeared from my area, but there was a whole raven convention going on downhill. Near here."

Not only did Rachel have Bette Midler eyes, her voice had that silky resonance, like in Bette's torchy *Do You Wanna Dance* . . . and Ben enjoyed the nostalgic pleasure of being nestled in bed while being told a story. By a lady with a pretty voice. But it wasn't going to be a pretty story, he guessed.

"I figured, okay, they found a dead deer or elk. They're feeding on the carcass."

"Near here?" Ben asked. "I've seen them, too. Lots of them."

Rachel nodded, looking at him, looking good in the firelight, her frizzy hair wild and floppy, throwing off the faintest scent of baby shampoo. "And on my way down tonight, I heard animals moving, not trying to be quiet. I think they're working on something dead. Something big."

She fingered the toupee, staring at it, then glanced at Ben and went on.

"A raven flew up to my mountain with this. I saw him coming from far away. He had the damn thing in his beak. Must have wanted it for a nest, although it's late for nesting. Who knows what's in a bird's mind?"

She said the raven put the toupee on the upper branch of a Douglas Fir near her hack site. Curious, and with nothing but time up there, she climbed the tree and snatched it

"Ben, I may know this hair. I think it could be my supervisor's. Dr. O'Brien. I'm worried something happened to him. See, either he misplaced this while camping out or something . . . I don't know, and the bird grabbed it. Which is all I hope happened. Or, the bird got it . . ."

She looked through the window. Dawn was definitely underway now, black trees beginning to stand out from the dark gray of the forest. ". . . off his body."

As macabre as this statement was, the moment was quietly comfortable. All the more so for being completely unanticipated, and Ben didn't want it to end. He could tell by her posture that Rambo-Rachel, felt the same. She had her back against the wall in a soft, girlish way, pressing shapelessly into it, her slumping posture showing relaxation and pleasure at being for the moment, anchored. Ben found this flattering since her anchorage was so close their shoulders touched and he could smell her wild scent, tangy feminine sweat, and that humid nostalgia of baby shampoo.

Ben knew what lay out there. With idiot savant simplicity, the accounting department working nights in his mental basement put two and two together and got one dead O'Brien, who was playing smorgasbord for the wildlife nearby. They'd deal with him later.

Ben found it surprising that he was thinking so casually about a body in the woods. Until recently, he'd lived the innocent life of an average man, untouched by criminal actions or even the routine violence associated with city life. He'd seen a few bloody schoolyard fights years ago, as every kid did. But he hadn't been in any of them, although he did have his triumphs on judo school mats. People hear about crime in Chicago, but most Chicagoans have no first-hand experience with it.

Still, he figured a body was out there. Surprising, too, that he'd earlier stared down a mean .45 so casually he'd almost forgotten about it. In normal times such an experience would have created a cyclone in his psyche, setting off angry electrical fires for weeks to come. How come so calm?

But these weren't normal times. And let's not forget Rambo's twin distractions. Could they be why the pistol threat left so little an impression? The math guys in the basement immediately went to work on an equation expressing this interesting observation. $(2)38c=(1).45$, thereby using algebraic principles to prove that one side of the equation serves to neutralize the other. While occupied with this nonsense, his eyes slowly closed and he got the first sleep of the night which had moments earlier come to an official end along with the arrival of a band of loudmouth Steller's jays screaming in the pines around the cabin.

# 28.

How long had he slept? Five minutes? A half hour? Rambo was gently pushing him awake by wiggling the shoulder that rested against him. He opened his eyes to the pleasant shimmying of her free-flowing chest as she nudged him. Even though he'd only been sleeping a short time (the woods were still merely gray with faint sky light, the sun not yet having risen over the hills), he felt quite rested.

He'd always awakened feeling refreshed after short naps, and tried to find time for them during each day. Especially back in his desk-job life, which, after all, was only last week. He remembered reading somewhere that Jack Kennedy, his favorite president, took similar short naps often, having the ability to lapse into them at will. Ben envied such control of the autonomic, a part of the nervous system that, in his case, had a particularly ornery mind of its own.

Frequently, upon waking from such a mini-snooze, Ben would flash on this Kennedy reference. He did it now, only the picture played too long, Ben reluctantly remembering the gruesome Ziprouder film of the assassination, shown to death on TV, an 8-mm real life horror movie which Ben, after seeing it once, could never stomach again. The reason for going as far as remembering Dallas wasn't hard to figure. The sleep-warm girl cuddled next to him had a .45 tucked into her jeans. He himself had a .357 somewhere in his gear. Shit. What is it about the West and guns? And they were about to hunt for a corpse, another man with part of his head missing. Even if it was a fake part.

"I'm up," he said softly.

"I'll make coffee," and she unfolded herself from the bed.

"I think there's some there," Ben said, pointing to a dusty cabinet he'd looked into earlier when he was exploring, tracking the wire's origin.

Rambo found the coffee along with an ancient blackened pot and took them outside. Ben heard a *crunk crunk* as she worked the pump out front, a thing Ben would never have dreamed of doing, knowing he'd subsist entirely on bottled liquids until they ran out or he did. He sat there, wondering if he should bring in some food from the Jeep and set up breakfast on the table.

The table. Why so dusty on one side, but wiped clean in that wide half circle along the other? And why would mice leave crumbs on the floor next to a pretzel bag? Didn't they find crumbs just the right size? He got up to take a closer look. Rachel came back in and kneeled in front of the fireplace, tinkering with the coffee pot, poking the fire.

"Be ready in a minute," she said. "Now, 'scuse me while I go find a powder room out there somewhere." She stood up and brushed off her knees.

Ben said, "Does O'Brien have a heart problem?"

Rachel stopped. "He does. Not serious, I think. I know he takes pills."

"Just wondering," he said.

She looked at him a moment, as though wanting to ask *now, why were you just wondering?*, but smart enough to realize the pointlessness of the question. She gave him a shy, brief smile. Shy because she was off to the powderless powder room of the woods. And all too brief, he thought, realizing this morning how exciting she looked when she smiled, all teeth and eye sparkle.

She turned and left the cabin, and he picked up the little nitroglycerin tablets, the same kind of heart pills his grandmother used to take, that lay under the table like crumbs. And he put them in his pocket.

*     *     *

"Well, guess I made a mistake coming here," Rachel said. They were sitting on the fender of Ben's Jeep, blowing on their coffee, sipping it, watching steam billow from the mugs into the sharp morning cold.

"I thought there was a link-up here with the office. A telephone or a radio."

Before Ben had walked in on her last night, she'd looked around, eager to contact the PRP office and make sure O'Brien was okay. She'd lit the fire, but it soon became obvious that there wasn't any communications gear in the small room.

"There was," Ben said.

"Oh?"

"Someone disconnected it. "Put it into oil drums out in the woods. Recently, too."

"Seriously?"

"I saw a wire, probably to a roof antenna. I'm no expert, but it looked freshly cut. I couldn't sleep so I looked around. After I found the stuff in the drums, I came back and found you. Pointing a gun in my face," and he smiled, showing he remembered exactly how she looked at the time.

"You make quite a first impression," he said. "I see why they call you Rambo."

She smiled back, those squinty eyes again. Zapping him. Then took a sip from her coffee, and stared into the trees. The Steller's jays they'd heard earlier were out in force now, flying back and forth with inexplicable purpose in the branches above the cabin. The first horizontal rays of unsullied mountain sunshine shone on them, bringing out the radiant blue of their tail feathers.

Rachel was quiet. Ben guessed she was uncertain about what to do next. She should get back to her post, but there was the unspoken worry that O'Brien had lost more than his toupee near here. Someone could check by homing in on the ravens.

Having already decided to blow the scene (an expression Ben and his high school buddies had used, not to be in style, but rather in the way of brighter kids, to be making fun of it), Ben figured he might just as well also blow his cover. A kind of sluggish symmetry in that. Besides, Rachel had a right to know about O'Brien.

"I gotta tell you something . . ." he said into his coffee.

He could feel her eyes on the side of his face, and in spite of everything, he couldn't help wondering how his profile looked to her, hoping his new beard somewhat mediated the Mediterranean cant of his nose that only seemed apparent on the right side, and wished she'd sat on his left side which was slightly handsome. Trivial and banal conceits can never be underestimated! He once saw a man hit by a truck on Michigan Avenue, who, while fairly flattened into a mess of broken leg bones and puddling urine actually reached into a shirt pocket for a comb, which he used to neaten his hair as sirens wailed in the distance.

"First," he said, "you've got a right to be worried about O'Brien. He's been missing for days. That's why it was that guy Altman who sent me here, and not O'Brien."

He went on to tell her that Abby Cole had been kidnapped, and as the result of an unbelievable chain of events that he didn't want to bore her with, he'd found himself working with her father and some detectives. Working to find information about Abby's kidnapping.

Rachel said she'd known Abby slightly, having seen her at parties for eco-activists in Boulder. "I kinda liked her," she said. "She was much talked about, you know, for swiping that laboratory alligator that was going to be experimented on."

"Really?"

"They were going to implant this new kind of transmitter into its spinal cord? Very complicated, all kinds of electrodes. They'd worked on it for years. It would let trackers know everything the animal did, not just where it went, but when it was eating, sleeping, making babies."

Ben looked at a jay, which had alighted on the ground near them. The jay looked at Ben.

"It was going to be taken to Texas in the lab's pick-up truck. They planned to let it loose, then track it by satellite. We heard that the batteries in the implant would leak after a year or so and kill it, but the science people didn't care. They'd get a year's worth of information first. As the story goes, Abby sneaked it away before the implant surgery and paid the pick-up driver very well to take it somewhere else. Then she notified PETA and they protested the project. It kind of dried up after that."

Ben remembered Alf dozing in the pool at Cole's home in Santana. Cole had dumped in the lobsters and Alf had opened his half-closed eyes, all the way . . .

"The guy in charge? Was he pissed! He'd seen the thing as a way of getting famous or something. You know, publish or perish stuff. He wanted the cops to arrest Abby, but O'Brien calmed him, told him falcons would be the next big thing, then brought him into the PRP. He's all gung-ho about it now. He's the guy you told me about."

"I did?"

"Guy wears sunglasses inside? Darren Altman?"

For the first time since he came to Colorado, Ben felt a sense of direction. He knew what he was going to do. He had a plan. An agenda. *Agenda.* A formerly sensible word, he thought, remembering good old days when it simply meant a list, something to guide you through a meeting or a day of office work. That was before the word had been changed by media usage and special interest groups into a hackneyed war chant. The liberal agenda, the conservative agenda, the black agenda, the gay agenda, the women's agenda (would that be a shopping list, little lady?). Then, suddenly, a new thought: *Ben, chill.* You're in the peaceful woods. Cowboy country. Let the birds do the squawking for a change.

Whatever, he now had the Ben agenda, and with the sun off the horizon finally, and Rambo's severe black coffee sending high-octane caffeine into his system, he was ready to get his mission off the ground. This sudden impetus was impelled by a feeling of certainty that he'd learned what he'd been sent out to learn. Sometimes when researching a thing you get to a point where you say, *enough! I know what to do next.*

*       *       *

As a young copywriter he'd been assigned to Granny Annie's, a premium chicken soup that came in clear glass jars instead of common cans. The food scientists, guys who threw around terms like "mouth feel," working behind Granny Annie's fictitious skirts harped on the advantage of their jarred soup: "No canned taste," they said. No trace of tin on the tongue. No sub-sensory smack of aluminum. "It tastes better than canned soup," they insisted.

Ben thought then, as now, *say no more!* He'd wanted only to leave the jarheads for his office. Once there, he wrote the utterly simple headline that said it all and won a New York Ad Club award, which is bestowed begrudgingly on Chicago-based writers, making it even better. He'd merely shown the jar with Granny Annie's smiling face on the label, and the rich soup visible inside. Above it, he'd put one simple word in bold, tightly packed letters. UNCANNY.

*       *       *

He felt a touch uncanny himself just now, certain he'd found more than enough plot thickening agents for Van. Look, he'd say, Altman disliked Abby. And look, somebody hid the radio. Why? And listen, O'Brien was taking heart pills. Maybe O'Brien didn't skip town, but had a heart seizure of some kind up here. The altitude and sloping terrain are hard on any heart. Maybe he's lying out in the woods somewhere. Ben had to get back, had to let Van know. He stood up, tossing the coffee dregs to the ground, a black slap on the stones.

"Nice meeting you, Rambo. Rachel," he said. And looked at her, planning to shrug, to convey some regret at having to leave, but she wasn't looking. She stared into her coffee, swirling it, watching the sky in it.

"Stay a little longer?" she said.

"I have to get to Denver right away."

"I'm hiking to the place where I saw the ravens. With what you said about O'Brien missing? It's got to be done."

"How far?"

"I'd do it alone, but together, if we find something? You can drive out and tell people. I've got to get back to my falcons. If there was a radio here, like it was supposed to be, I wouldn't have the problem."

Eager as Ben was to lay his clues on Van's desk with the same impatient pride he used to feel when laying ad ideas on his boss's desk, he'd started feeling a curious inertia, keeping him on the spot. Actually, it was not so much an inertial inability to get moving, but a gravitational pull from Rambo, whom he was starting to see as more of a Rachel. She looked good, even in bright morning sun. She had a wildness about her that was attractive. Literally so, apparently. And if she was mad or disappointed over his original misrepresentation of his mission up here, she didn't show it. No huffiness. No coldness. No reproach. This was something to appreciate. And if she was asking for his help, well . . .

Ben looked at the wall of trees behind them. Rachel squinted up at him and said, "I could really use some help, what d'you think?"

The way she said this, her look, the twinkling eyes, it all sent a small electric charge through him. There was the unfamiliar pleasure of familiarity there. Intimacy. Like they were old friends.

"Sure. Of course. But I've got to be in Denver tonight. I'll leave by noon. Okay?"

She jumped from the fender and put her arm around his shoulders, giving him a brief roughhouse hug, one jock to another, saying, "Let's move!"

# 29.

The going wasn't as tough as it looked. From the air these pine-covered hills gave the appearance of tightly packed broccoli, and from the clearing where the cabin stood, the trees still looked jungly and impenetrable. But once among them, there was little ground vegetation, so walking was surprisingly easy. The air still held some of the cold bite of night under the shady canopy. But Ben had to walk quickly to keep up with Rambo, enjoying how she moved in those tight jeans, unintentionally wagging a prehistoric invitation, and he was soon sweating under his army jacket, not minding the temperature.

Mountain forest was new to Ben. He'd hiked in Midwestern woods all his life, casually bird-watching with binoculars and field guide, enjoying being away from the press and mess of city life. But this was different. In Chicago's forest preserves there were well-worn paths. You couldn't get into the trees, and wouldn't want to. The ground would be a tangle of poison ivy and weeds that would stick burrs onto your legs. And there were plagues of bugs, mostly mosquitoes from midsummer to the first hard frost, following you like a cloud of electrons as you went anywhere in the woods.

But here there were no ivy, burrs or bugs. Just stony ground, fallen pine needles, big and little boulders covered with lichen. There were wildflowers, too, and he was sure Rambo would know them by name. (Once again he thought of Sherlock Holmes, how the great detective had not cared to know the names of planets, as they would be immaterial clutter in the limited space of a busy mind. Similarly, Ben had no interest in flower names.)

And these woods had a great, heady scent. Midwestern woods smelled of pollen, leaf, mulch and mud. Fair escapist pleasures for the city-bound. But here was the high smell of unrestrained pine. There was an antiseptic bite in it. And while it was as coldly indifferent as starlight, it brought out in Ben some faint racial memory that gave him contrary signals of danger and well being at the same time.

Rambo carried a compass and topographic map. Every so often she'd slow her militant trudge to a feminine flatfooted walk, a dancer padding off the stage, wiping her neck with a towel. Then she'd look at her compass and check the map. She'd peer off into the trees as though fixing on a green light somewhere in the monotonous green light filtering through the branches, and she'd trudge off again at speed, Ben panting behind her, his lungs working hard to open up new avenues in the rarefied mountain air.

After an hour, Rambo slowed, did her usual compass and map check, then instead of resuming, she slipped her pack off and let it rest on the ground. She stopped, turning to Ben. When he reached her, he was breathing hard, and trying not to show it.

"Why're we stopping?"

"This is the place. Where I saw the ravens?"

She looked around, taking some time, squinting into the distance, checking the ground, looking up into the trees.

"I think it's the place."

Ben sat on a rock, his pulse loud in his ears, hearing it from the inside. Hiking at altitude takes getting used to.

She said, "Let's rest a few minutes. Then . . ."

She sat on a flat-topped rock, next to a tree, opened her map wider, looking at it. Then the compass. Then she looked at Ben.

". . . I think we'll go that way for a mile. We don't see anything, we'll go right, north. Make a square. Then we'll walk back and forth in it."

Ben nodded, still rather breathless, preferring not to speak.

"Until noon," she said. "Then we'll go back. Promise."

Ben looked at his watch. Ten after seven. It wasn't going to be an easy day. He leaned against a tree, remembering he'd hardly had any sleep last night. But neither did Rachel. She was wiping her eyes with a bandanna, staring at the map as though it were a puzzle. Ben had to urinate. He lifted himself up, groaning like an old man. Maybe she'd take pity on him and call off this forced march. Ignored, he headed around the tree where she couldn't see him.

"Gotta be a men's room here somewhere. Be right back," he said.

But standing there unzipped, holding his pants open, feeling fairly and unfairly obscene, cooling that way in the open air, he couldn't get anything going. She'd surely hear the splash, run-off, squeezed-out finales and encores. So he left that spot and walked some distance away, stopping when he judged he was far enough, and took his shot, comfortably out of earshot, onto the side of a shaggy, old evergreen.

Done. Zipped and feeling some comical animal pride at having marked a territory, he turned around and walked back over the rocky ground, picking his way through the trees, returning to where Rambo had been, but as he came around the tree she'd been under, she wasn't there. What was worse, it wasn't the tree she'd been under. No flat rock in front of it. Disorientation hit. He turned around. Which direction had he come from? He looked left, right. Where was Rachel? All around him were . . . trees. Just trees. Standing like vertical spikes, stockade pales, prison bars, reaching to the sky, trapping him, closing in on him. His heart clanged and misfired. His vision got fuzzy around the edges. Adrenaline shot into his neck, swelling it with heat. His breath rushed, quick and shallow, more breathless now than when he'd been hiking.

Wait. He may be lost, but he can't have gone so far that Rachel wouldn't hear him if he called out. Still, what about a man's dignity? He liked Rachel. He wanted her to think him tough, the cool detective. He decided to walk around a little. Maybe he'd just step around the next tree and there she'd be, reading her map. He'd act like nothing had happened, saying, "Ready whenever you are."

But wait. Too much time was passing. Hell, she must be thinking that he's really going to the bathroom in a big way out there. Now embarrassment overrode panic. Got to get back! He walked. Then ran. Then rushed wildly, pushing through the trees. Then did an about-face, running the other way, panic-overriding embarrassment. Where was she? Nothing left to do. Forget male pride, lose face, yell for help. Wasn't funny anymore. He steadied himself against a tree, took in a deep lungful of air and . . . wait a second.

It didn't smell nice, that air. He followed his nose to the right, and a short distance away saw what was left of a man's body, lying partially covered with branches and twigs. Such a discovery would disconcert a normal person, but Ben, already disconcerted, had the contrary response. His anxiety attack stopped as abruptly as if it were some discordant music merely switched off with a click. Silence. Peace. And clarity. Of vision, and of purpose.

Ben moved a few steps away from the body. There was some pink internal stuff visible there, tangled with a strap that held a pair of broken binoculars, and he preferred not to see it. He was calm now, realizing that he had just been given a perfectly legitimate reason to call out loudly through the trees for Rachel. She'd be here in a minute. And he and O'Brien would both be found.

# 30.

It was almost nine. They'd been going over Ben's discoveries since six. He'd swiveled his chair around and was looking at the front range of the Rockies from Van's conference room window. The sun was setting behind the mountains, turning them dark against an aqua light that shaded upward into deep blue, becoming pure navy black at the top of the sky, revealing stars so clear and pretty as to seem faked, added by a Michigan Avenue airbrush artist.

"Enjoy the sight," HJ had said. "It's rare here."

"Rare? Here?"

Irony is not native to the West, but like all too many transplants from the inscrutable East, it had taken root in the Denver area, causing this outpost between windblown prairie and cold mountains to be surprisingly dirty during the 1980s. In fact, Denver was currently one of America's most polluted cities. Forget the invisible grit of plutonium from the local H-bomb factory and the chemical leaching from the neighborhood nerve gas arsenal. Can't see those things. What you could see on most days here was the yellowish fog from countless gassy enterprises and infernal combustion engines, held in a curious airlock by the very mountains that symbolize environmental hygiene. Irony.

Ben, figured HJ was probably right. He'd looked out this same window at other times during his three days here, seeing no mountains. The view had been the same as that from Chicago's corporate towers.

Industrial low rises, slum flatlands, the dismal geometry of suburbs dissolving into haze. But today the winds of Denver had blown well. Chamber of Commerce photographers must have scrambled to take publicity shots, city skyline in front of white mountain peaks. White lies. And Ben remembered the book he'd planned to begin so long ago. Weeks. Months. What was it? Six days?

Recent adventures had knocked his sense of time somewhat senseless. The relativity of subjective time speed. He had a curious craving to talk about this with Rachel while sitting side by side as they'd sat that night in the cabin. That night? Hell, he thought, it was only this morning. Just before sunrise. Now it was the sunset of the same day.

Van, who'd been silent while HJ and Tina examined the radiophone Ben had brought up from the Jeep, spoke suddenly.

"How'd the girl take it?"

It startled Ben, and he realized he'd been half-sleeping while looking at the mountains, not so much thinking these random thoughts but dreaming little random dreams. He turned to face Van, who was manipulating his spongy jowls, waiting for an answer.

"The girl . . ." (and Ben smiled at the quick thought of Rambo, bare-chested and militant, aiming her big .45 at some guy calling her a "girl") "was upset, Van. Like I said, she'd worked with O'Brien and seeing him like that, anybody'd be upset."

This meeting, so far, hadn't been quite as difficult to sit through as most advertising meetings, Ben thought. After all, they were discussing motives, dead guys, abductions, covert identities. Not dancing strawberries. No talking eggs.

*　　*　　*

Talking eggs? Once Ben had commented on such lunacy, only to be chastened for thinking others saw things as he did. He'd created a TV spot for cholesterol-free eggs which were sold frozen in the carton. He'd had a talking egg explain how "shattering" it was to have become obsolete. This spokes-egg was sitting on a wall, in a silly bow tie and medieval cap, and was clearly Humpty Dumpty.

But an argument about the obviousness of the egg's identity had started. One faction favored superimposing his full name on the screen, Humpty Dumpty. Others said it wouldn't add anything to the ad's effectiveness, might even distract viewer attention from the product. They insisted on no name. Early in the discussion Ben said it might be funny to use "Mr. H. Dumpty," but Humpty Dumpty in full would be artless.

Some saw this as a good compromise, but Ben, his own voice echoing in his mind *Humpty . . . Dumpty . . .* felt suddenly foolish, withdrawing to watch from the sidelines. What he saw were powerfully dressed, over-educated men and women captains of industry debating the Dumpty dilemma. He eventually jumped back in, saying, "Look, all this high-priced talent actually arguing about an *egg's* name! From a kid's nursery rhyme! Can you believe us?"

Instead of the expected comradely chuckles, there were icy stares. A silver-haired honcho harrumphed, suggesting with great sobriety that the matter be tabled, and broke the meeting for lunch. Ben, crestfallen, was not invited to join them, even though the talking egg execution, roundly endorsed by everyone, had been his in the first place.

*   *   *

No such foolishness in the world of private dicks. Although, meetings are still meetings, and this one, like those in the ad world of public dicks had gone through its tiresome life cycle. A classic bell curve. Faltering beginning when participants arrive, bump chairs, pour coffee, *pass the cream over here?* and figure out who's going to do what. Then mid-meeting, a high point when things happen, notes are taken with energy, decisions are formulated. This evolves into the degeneration phase. Groups splinter off, as HJ and Tina had done. The same questions and answers get asked and answered. Van's question about Rambo had been asked and answered earlier.

The sunset darkened into night, and as the light differential on each side of the window pane reversed, inside now stronger than outside, Ben no longer saw mountains but instead saw reflections of those in the meeting, fluorescent-lit images on the dark glass. Van looked pasty, fat. Ben, with his daily-thickening beard and unkempt hiking clothes looked uncharacteristically untamed, which gave him a rush of vain pleasure. He'd always admired the whiskery, buck-skinned Indian scout standing among uniformed soldier boys, reporting on what he'd seen out there, using insolent language, free of regimental constraints, better for being freer, dirtier, proudly un-uniformed.

HJ said, "I wish we could see their receiver, see if they tape incoming transmissions. Could confirm your theory, Van."

"You ought to hurry," Tina said. "This is, what, day, no, night seven? That the daughter's in their hands?"

Ben watched her reflection in the glass. He shifted in the chair, shifting his attention now to Tina, giving into the distraction, figuring, after the meeting, maybe a drink with her? Some strong martinis . . .

Van cleared his throat, a bark and growl at the same time. It had the effect of a gavel slamming. He looked at Ben.

"Let's go back up there, my friend. This time I'm going with you. We'll do a little B&E, I believe. Might be fun. We'll leave now. Kids, I really do mean now."

To HJ, he nodded and said, "Get everything ready, please?"

HJ and Tina left the table, moving quickly. Van turned to Ben. "You'll sleep, I'll drive. Couple of hours and you'll be fine. You look like shit now." And he joined the others going through the door.

"Going back?" Ben asked. "Why?"

But they were well on their way out of the room and no one turned to answer, ignoring him, treating him not like the grizzled Indian scout in the window, but once again, like the new kid who asked dumb questions. Actually, he thought, pushing away from the table, slowly getting to his feet, it made sense. Van had laid out a scenario for what "might-maybe," as he called it, have happened in the mountains around the time Abby disappeared. To be fair, Ben had contributed some of the ideas. Maybe no Indian scout, he thought, catching a sidelong glimpse of himself in the window as he walked around the table toward the door.

Idea scout?

*   *   *

It should have been easy to sleep. The car rocked gently on the 2-lane's frequent curves, and it was certainly dark enough, the only light coming from the diffusion of their headlamps into the night and from the instrument panel's reddish aura. The bucket seat was comfortable, and Ben had it notched back 45 degrees. The heater sent out a mix of somnolent white noise and dusty warmth.

Van was quiet, concentrating on the case or, probably, just watching the narrow road, not wanting to miss the turnoffs that would take them through the mountains to Halfway. He'd put on a long-playing Duke Ellington tape, and Ben liked the music even though it seemed out of character out of the city, giving the mission a vague, 1930's film noir feel. But as they drove through a notch in the mountains, with steep walls rising on both sides, creating a claustrophobic channel of stone, Ellington went into "Harlem Air Shaft." It was one of those perfect little coincidences, Ben thought, that you have to shrug off because there's no sane way to explain it.

He should have been sleeping. The closest he could get was this feeling of anesthetized comfort. Maybe the conference room catnap at the end of Van's meeting had sufficiently recharged the mental batteries. Soon after they'd left Denver, he'd discovered a six-pack of Coors in the back seat, and helped himself to one, which now mainlined through his empty stomach, smoothing his psyche. Peace. Comfort. Who needs sleep?

Instead, he replayed the meeting in his mind. He was good at recalling things in detail at times like this, times when he was essentially trapped in place, yet physically at ease, unrequired to do anything but sit and think. Once during an endless lecture about FTC regulations he'd been required to attend for a client, he'd replayed an entire movie seen on TV the night before. Kirk Douglas as an anachronistic saddle bum in the modern West, and remembered it with such clarity it was as if he'd seen it twice, even noticing new things the second time around.

In this state of mind, he eased back to review the Van Dyke Agency's observations, decisions and plan of attack

# 31.

Van had a large pad of paper on an easel next to his chair. They'd used marker pens to scrawl down key points as they went along. Meetings are, after all, essentially the same everywhere, Ben thought. Everyone agreed there was no obvious evidence tying the PRP people to Abby's disappearance. "But the place has a funny smell, I say," said Van.

This caused Ben to remember his experience in the woods, lost and ready to scream for Rachel, the stench of O'Brien's body. Something he didn't want to remember. Don't do it now, he thought, then, unable to stop, what was it? Fecal? Ammoniac? Methane? Gouda? Don't think about it. They agreed that with the information brought back by even so inexperienced a dick as Ben, they'd better focus on Halfway, and the people working there.

"Theories?" Van had asked the group.

Ben, feeling more observer than participant sat back, watching, listening, exercising the excusable non-involvement of the new guy.

HJ said, "I'd like to know who took down their radio linkup at the cabin. And why."

Tina said, "I don't see how anything up there, even the dead gentleman in the woods, has much to do with finding Abby. What's the tie-in?"

Van sat quietly, looking at the heart pills on the table in front of him, the ones Ben found on the cabin floor. He made a little spring out of his finger and thumb and flicked a tiny tablet at Tina. She caught it quickly, snapping it out of the air. Good hands, Ben thought.

"You didn't mean that," Van said. "If you did, it was a dumb-ass question, and you wouldn't belong here, but back in the massage industry."

He looked red-faced and serious, but winked at Tina. "You were just asking, so we'd get to the heart of the matter, right? Forcing us to make the tie-in, as you put it, right?"

Tina sat, unruffled, toying with the little pill, and Ben assumed Van's rough talk was business as usual. She said, "Make the tie-in, Van."

"Okay. Maybe the birdman of advertising here brought back good stuff." And the big detective leaned back in his chair, hoisting his stockinged feet onto the table. "Now, lemme think out loud for a bit . . ."

Van rambled, talking to the ceiling in a muffled, liturgical style while the others waited. ". . . told the bureau 'bout the body. They're up there now. Forensics'll be done tomorrow. Might tell us something. Might not. They'll be checking the car Cole used, his phone records. Won't come up with shit . . . It's in the birdman's stuff, I'm betting."

He glanced downward, over his belly to Tina. "Honey, write up what we got here." Tina took a marker pen from a basket on the table and walked to the easel. Van told her to make five columns, and the pen squeaked as she drew four wavy vertical lines, as though making a score sheet for a game they were about to play. The easel was taller than Tina, and she had to stretch to reach the top of the page, causing her skirt to move up. Ben hoped Van would have her do a lot of reaching.

Two hours later the page had been filled, and Tina was back at the table musing over the chart she'd drawn, as they all were doing, while she fondled the marker pen with disconcerting hand movements that distracted Ben momentarily. But only momentarily. The chart was just too interesting to be upstaged. It had five names running across the top, each heading its own column. "O'Brien, Altman, Rambo-Rachel, Abby and Kidnapper."

Under each, in the columns divided by Tina's scrawled lines, were key facts pertaining to the person whose column it was. The "O'Brien" column read:

HEAD GUY
DEAD GUY
BAD HEART
PILLS IN CABIN
H. ATTACK?
WHY WAS HE UP THERE?
WHY BODY IN WOODS

In the next column, under "Altman," these listings appeared:

BEN'S GUT—ASSHOLE
2ND IN COMMAND/TAKES OVER TOP JOB
AMBITIOUS?
TRICKY SUNGLASSES
"RAMBO" WARNING—SCARE TACTIC?
DISLIKED ABBY (ALLIGATOR STORY)

Then, in the "Rambo-Rachel" column:

HAS A GUN
KNOWS FALCONRY
TOUPEE STORY?
IS NOT A GUY
LIKED O'BRIEN

Below "Abby," they'd written:

LAST HEARD FROM AT PRP
ON BACK COUNTRY ASSIGNMENT
WHO GAVE ASSIGNMENT?
ASSUMPTION—O'BRIEN OR ALTMAN
HEALTHY ENOUGH TO TALK ON PHONE TWICE
CURRENT STATUS UNKNOWN

The final column, written in a downhill slant because Tina had to reach across the easel, stretching not just up but to her right, read, "Kidnappers . . ."

HAVE ABBY
HAVE DIAMONDS
HAVE A FALCON
KNEW OF COLE'S WEALTH
HAVEN'T RELEASED ABBY
FBI INVOLVED. NO NEWS FROM THEM.

It had been just like the brainstorming meetings ad agencies have. Everyone throwing out ideas, someone writing them down. But it had been Ben doing most of the talking this time, since he was the one who'd gathered the impressions during his foray into the mountains. He sat, relaxed, feeling that he could pull back now, be less involved again. It was only fair to take a break, like a schoolyard basketball gunner scoring repeatedly, then taking himself out, having proved something, letting someone else have a chance.

"Now?" Van asked Ben.

"Now what?" Ben said, surprised at having been singled out. Was he expected to say more? After having said virtually everything on Tina's chart?

"You did good. Gave us some facts. Still, they're isolated. What do you make of 'em? What should *we* make of 'em?"

"You're the detectives," Ben said.

"You're the idea man. I'm told," Van said, voice hard.

Silence. The hum of ceiling fluorescents.

"Let's make the connections," HJ said, rising, walking to the easel. He casually held out his hand to catch the marker Tina threw in a little end over end lob. He drew a diagonal line across the columns, connecting two items. One was in Rachel's column. It said KNOWS FALCONRY. The other end of the line was in the kidnappers' column, HAVE A FALCON.

Ben leaned forward, feeling uncomfortable because this drawing of lines to show relationships between columns was apparently a normal part of the process, and maybe Van had expected him to suggest it, to show them he thought the way they thought. But there was something else to the uncomfortable feeling, something under the surface.

"There's another one," Van said.

Without being told, HJ connected the first item in O'Brien's column, HEAD GUY, with the items in Altman's column that read 2ND IN COMMAND/TAKES OVER TOP JOB and AMBITIOUS?

At that point Van had thrown down his big feet and popped out of his chair with the surprising agility of the healthy overweight. He moved to the chart, half facing it, half facing the group, a weatherman on the morning news. He underlined Altman's name, running the marker back and forth until the paper was wrinkled with wet ink. Then he drew a looping circle around the Altman entry, BEN'S GUT—ASSHOLE, and turned to face the table.

He said, "I'll try a little scenario here. Might be what happened. Might not. Gotta start somewhere." And he paused, touching the marker to his chin. Then began.

"I believe Altman is at the heart of it. Ben had this gut feeling about the guy. Totally unprofessional, but I'm listening to it." Ben felt a rush of contradictory emotions, pride at the respect Van had for his instinct; insecurity, even guilt, at the possibility that he was wrong.

"But gut's only part of it. Altman must know Abby comes from money. Her dad's kinda famous."

Van drew a circle around the entry in Altman's column that said AMBITIOUS?

"The guy's ambitious. Likes power, and money gives you power."

Ben realized he hadn't even mentioned Altman's nails, that dandyish affectation so out of both time and place in Halfway, but perhaps indicative of the man's uspcale pretensions.

Van quickly drew another circle, this one around the entry that read 2ND IN COMMAND/TAKES OVER TOP JOB. And he tapped the marker there. Then Ben recalled enjoying the secret knowledge that his own salary had probably been four times that of Altman, no matter how well manicured the man was.

"And there's something not entirely straightforward about the guy."

He circled, TRICKY SUNGLASSES and "RAMBO" WARNING—SCARE TACTIC?

"If Altman had something to hide up there, why not make their new kid here feel less than enthusiastic about taking the hack site job? Let him take a powder instead. Plus . . ." and he pointed to DISLIKED ABBY (ALLIGATOR STORY), "there's this, for whatever it's worth."

And Ben remembered the lizard paperweight, knowing now that it wasn't a lizard, but a very young alligator, probably a hapless relic from Altman's days as a notorious experimenter.

"Now, here's what happens." Van moved the marker casually over

the entry that read WHO GAVE ASSIGNMENT—O'BRIEN OR
ALTMAN, and kept it on ALTMAN.

"Altman sends Abby into the sticks. Tells his girlfriend, Rambo
here . . ." and he tapped the page at Rachel's name, "to snatch the kid.
Which she does."

Ben shifted in his chair.

"Then she and Altman get the diamonds, using this Rambo's bird,
the falcon, see? Which she knows how to work, see?"

And he circled Rambo's KNOWS ABOUT FALCONRY.

"They take the girl to the cabin. Make phone calls from there to Cole.
A wireless phone system. That'd be possible, right, HJ?"

"They did have a transmitter. I'd like to see what their receiving
equipment looked like at the office. But, yeah."

"Right," Van went on, "so that's what they do. This Rambo chick has
a gun, remember? She uses it to guard the girl. You with me?"

Van had talked rapidly, to no one in particular. He walked away
from the easel, pacing in front of the table. Ben thought, *the guy's in
his glory.* This is the way ad people get when they're presenting a hot
execution. He'd been this way himself. He knew the feeling. Hearing
the idea come to life while explaining it, liking it even more after
verbalizing it, seeing yourself how good it is.

"After the calls, they hide the communications equipment. Makes
sense, right? They figure people will come looking around eventually.
That Cole will call in the troops, right? But they don't have to hide it too
well, because after they get the ransom they'll split, right?"

Van tossed the pen into the little basket in the center of the table and
put his hands in his pocket, looking finished, but still pensive, adding,
"If there's some loose ends to this, fine, let's discuss."

HJ said, "The neighborhood stiff. How do you ignore a dead guy?"

"I make this assumption," Van said quickly, showing he'd thought
about it already, "O'Brien was walking around up there, probably
falcon watching or something. He had binoculars on him when they
found the body, right? This is strenuous for him. He gets a pain.
Makes his way to the cabin, figuring he'll call for help on the radio,
right? Finds no radio. He's hurting. Takes a nitro pill. In his agitated

condition, he drops a few of them. Then he leaves. No choice, he has to try to hike back. Dies in the woods. No connection to anything else. It happens."

Tina said, "A dead man unconnected to the case. It's a weird coincidence, Van."

"Life is full of weird coincidences."

HJ said, "Why'd the Rambo lady come to the cabin?"

Van said, "Don't know."

"She's in on it like you say, Van," said Tina, "why'd she tell Ben all that stuff? About the alligator thing. About her boss, the toupee. All that?"

"Don't know." Van answered making it clear by the staccato cadence of these last two answers that he wasn't apologetic about not knowing, that it might not matter, his not knowing certain things, all things.

"If you're right," Ben said, "where was Abby when Rachel was with me?"

"That's not a pleasant thought," Van said.

Ben, still struggling to accept the concept of a real-life kidnapping, it being almost too far-fetched, too fictive in appearance to be taken seriously, found himself absolutely balking at the idea of the girl having been killed.

"But Cole heard her on the phone," he said.

Van sat down heavily, leaned back and said to no one in particular, "That was before the ransom was paid."

"Even then," Tina said, "it might not have been her talking live. If you'll remember, Cole wasn't permitted to have a regular conversation with her. He said the kidnapper just held up the phone so she could say things from across the room."

"Not her talking live?" Ben asked. But at the same moment understanding, Tina nodding at him now, and he remembered those tapes of hers in his borrowed office. *"Besides . . ."* she'd said, smiling, *"if we played them now, someone might have heard and thought it was us."*

And, of course, Ben realized, *of course* a person's voice heard over the phone didn't necessarily prove the person was actually there. It didn't prove the person was alive. Ben had spent countless career-hours in recording studios working with tape, reels of words that sounded so real, but they were just lifeless inches of thin brown *tape*.

Hadn't he adjusted and altered advertising voice-overs long after the announcers themselves had left the studio, the city, the world for all it mattered? Once their voice was recorded, they were expendable, and his thinking of this treasonous word gave him a momentary chill.

"So," he said, "you're thinking it could've been a tape of her voice, and she was . . . not there . . . even that first night?"

"I'm not saying that," Van said. "I'm just worried about what happened after the ransom was paid."

"But," HJ said, "for the sake of conversation, understand that those people do work with recording equipment a lot. You know, they record observations of their studies. I think they even record and play back the calls of wild falcons to attract the birds and study their behavior. I wish I could see what they use, the fidelity they get."

Van said, "If they made her say things on tape for the phone calls to Cole, we're way too late to help her. But anything to do with tapes and such, you're interested, huh, Aitch?"

"Very much so," HJ said.

The meeting, which earlier had the familiar feel of any corporate work session, had moved into dark territory and Ben refused to follow. He supposed their pessimism made some sense, but there was an optimism in him, and it was there with such surprising backbone that he was able to fend off any thoughts of Abby having been expendable.

He wasn't, however, able to fend off the old feeling of meeting burnout, and when Van said, "Let's start at the beginning, run through it again," Ben found himself drifting from depression to distraction to reluctant daydreaming.

And then they were out. The meeting had ended, everyone mobilizing to send Van and Ben back to Halfway, into the night, to commit the felony of breaking and entering, which compared to the felony of kidnapping, is nothing to lose sleep over.

# 32.

They entered Halfway at two forty-five in the morning, self-conscious about their headlights and motor noise in the sleeping, dead-quiet darkness. Ben directed Van to the old high school where the PRP had its headquarters. They pulled around back, the crunch of gravel under the tires sounding to them loud enough to wake every cop and hound dog in town. They parked, killed the engine and clicked off the lights. Car sounds seemed to hang in the air around them like the gravel dust they'd kicked up, but soon dissipated into the night, giving them a feeling of having arrived safely.

"Let's go," Van whispered, reaching into the back for a small leather case, which he'd earlier shown to Ben. It contained industrial-strength burglary tools, carbon steel picks, miniature crowbars. Everyone expected the break-in to be easy. Ben hadn't remembered seeing any sign of an alarm system, although he should have made a point of looking for such a thing, apologizing in the meeting, saying, "I don't think there's one," feeling some new kind of detective demerit being chalked up against him. Still, the others agreed that a wildlife research station in a hick town probably wouldn't be wired.

They got out of the big Jeep Cherokee quietly, not clicking their doors shut, but replacing them silently, leaving them slightly ajar. Ben had done this, exactly as Van had, without being told, and he couldn't help feeling a tinge of pride. This cat burglar stuff was exciting, and he was taking to it. Van fiddled with the door hardware while Ben stood behind him, a shadow behind a shadow, an impatient lookout.

As a kid, he'd had friends who regularly broke into neighborhood schools, writing obscenities on walls, chalking juvenile murals of outrageous sex organs on blackboards, tossing books around, tipping over desks, doing nothing really destructive, simply expressing a little righteous outrage against the totalitarianism of public education. Ben had never participated, being by nature a well-behaved kid who secretly agonized over his niceness, feeling it might be a cover-up for hereditary timidity, something shameful but chromosomal, as unstoppable as having brown eyes or a tendency toward jowliness in old age.

He remembered reading a favorite philosopher of his describing something a dying friend had said. "If I regret anything it is my good behavior. What demon possessed me that I behaved so well?" And Ben had nodded, feeling a sad kinship with the man. But he'd always hoped that someday he might stray from this programmed program. Tonight was a step in the wrong direction, and the feeling was great, although somewhat mitigated by the fact that the burglary was ultimately for a good cause.

Still, he wondered, as a thief in the night, shouldn't he be packing heat? The .357 lay buried in his duffel with the other stuff in the Jeep. Shouldn't it be strapped heavy and tight against his hip, under the bush jacket, making him dangerous and secure? He dismissed the thought as unreasonable. There were simply no circumstances he could imagine in which he would shoot the gun. Van moved into the door. There was a sound of splintering wood and a sudden blackness where the big man's back had been faintly visible in the dark. The door was open now, and Van had gone into the building.

As they moved through the dark hallways of the old high school, Ben was reminded of scuba divers entering a sunken ship, flashlight beams becoming, in the blackness, as vital as bottled air. The divers would float with strange lost fish through rusted companionways looking for the room that held treasure . . . .

That made some sense though, Ben thought. Unlike this mission. And he took in some extra air, appreciating the breathable if thinnish atmosphere of landlocked Colorado, shaking off the faint claustrophobia that would inevitably show up whenever he attended or even remembered undersea movies. He'd once hyperventilated during the German submarine film, *Das Boot*, when the U-boat sank to the bottom. Only thing then that prevented an all-out panic was the reassuring English subtitles, reminding him it was only a movie.

Van whispered, "Which way to the guy's office?"

Ben took Van briefly by the elbow, indicating that the detective should follow him. Ben was looking for a stairway to the second floor, trying to remember where Altman's office would be, wondering, again, why they were doing this.

Van's hypothesis had Altman making two radio-telephone calls from the line cabin so Abby could tell her dad she was all right. HJ said he'd like to see the radio receiver here, in order to know if that's what actually happened. Ben didn't fully understand the technology involved, but it had to do with radio signals being converted to ordinary phone calls. Apparently Altman would have had to have rigged up his radio to patch into the phone system. Van would know by looking at it, or he'd simply steal it for HJ.

Ben couldn't ignore it. There was something about Van's scenario that bothered him. At first he figured he'd just been tired and unable to concentrate on the fine points of the big detective's reasoning. But he wasn't tired now, and even if he'd been, it wouldn't have mattered. When it feels right, it feels right. Instead he had that subsonic itch that always signals him when he's on the wrong track.

Maybe there was no treasure, but the sea-hunt fantasy persisted as darkness hung between them and their point of entry. Where was their point of entry? Back to the right? The left? Rush of adrenaline! *Calm down, you pussy!* On the staircase, their light beams rose, floating upward, the only things visible in the blackness.

Luckily, there was a sign at the top of the stairs pointing them to the "Office of the Principal." The door to the outer office was unlocked, and they walked in, clicking it shut behind them. Inside, it looked like every student's first painful brush with bureaucracy. The wooden bench. A long counter. An ancient reception desk, which in days past had probably been the lair of some sour-faced school secretary. A nostalgic scent of industrial floor wax, books, ink, and asbestos insulation hung in the air. Behind the secretary's desk, their beams picked out two doors, each with pebbly shower-glass window panes, one marked Principal, the other Ass't. Principal.

Ben was struck by how intensely he was noticing details that he'd overlooked on his first visit, of which he could hardly remember anything except the brief talk with Altman. This was much the same thing that had happened last night in the mountain cabin, the flashlight isolating things, forcing them into focus, insisting that he see them. But still, hadn't he been here before? Wasn't it his job to guide Van?

He whispered, "Okay, O'Brien used the Principal's office. Altman's office was the other one. But, when I met with Altman, it was *here*." And he shone his light on the Principal's door, reaching his hand out into the beam, turning the knob, finding it rigid, locked. Van shone his beam on the other door, tried the knob and found it also locked.

"Enough of this shit," Van said, and he swept the beam back and forth, near the outer door, holding it in place when he found a bank of switches. He walked over and flipped them all. There was a flickering hesitation as the ceiling fluorescent took the voltage, blinked, flared, then flooded the room with an almost audible blue-gray brightness causing Van and Ben to squint at each other like sleepers rudely awakened.

Van switched off his flashlight. No longer whispering, he said, "After three in the morning for god's sake. Who's gonna see a little light up here?"

He opened his tool kit on the secretary's desk, selected a small L-shaped device and used it to open the Principal's door as easily as if he'd had the key. He reached into the room and switched on the light. Then he did the same at the other office. He turned to Ben and winked.

"Piece of cake."

# 33.

Ben stood in the doorway while Van busied himself in O'Brien's office. Or was it Altman's office? The name on the door said O'Brien, but Ben thought of it only as Altman's. It was where they'd sat together talking about the hack site job *"Call me doctor..."* Besides, there was some mechanism at work again in the back room of Ben's psyche, attempting to block any non-essential dealing with the concept of O'Brien as an actual person, someone who had a desk, a chair, a toupee.

Best to keep a lid on that particular mental dumpster which held the image of O'Brien rotting in the forest. But, like all dumpster lids, this one was warped and ill-fitting, letting out vapors that attracted flies and ravens, and Ben flicked them away, flicking away the memory, switching to something else. Yes, this was Altman's office. Altman, with his haughty sunglasses and polished nails.

There was something comical about Van barreling his way into the office, as though Abby herself were waiting bound and gagged at the desk. Now, standing in the overly neat, disconcertingly empty room, Van looked large, ragged and out of place. Worse, he looked unsure. Even from the doorway Ben could see there was no radio equipment attached to the ordinary desk phone. Van smiled and gave Ben a shrug, looking for a moment like a big kid. Ben couldn't help smiling back and shrugged, too. Then Van moved behind the desk, opening and closing drawers, looking slowly, methodically at the contents of each, back to being the detective again, in control, snooping for clues.

Ben, feeling uncomfortably useless, recalled long-ago childhood visits to his dad's office where he'd spend endless afternoons, a squirming spectator, intent not on his dad's routine of punching adding machines and talking on the phone, interested only in afternoon snacks of doughnuts and cokes, waiting impatiently for quitting time, when he could quit feeling out of place.

"Mac, I'll check the other office," he said, still feeling the need to whisper. Mac grunted something in reply, his head now lost below the desktop, looking under there for whatever it is detectives look for.

On the wall between the two offices, Ben noticed a stack of maps pinned to a bulletin board. They were "topos," the topographic maps that wilderness savants used, the kind he'd heard about, and should have paid attention to before going off to find Rambo, but didn't. Now, waiting for Van, being in a mood to browse, maybe even to find something useful, he stepped up to the top topo, wondering if he could read anything understandable in its impassive math-book personality. Perhaps he could locate the place in the mountains where the line cabin was. Yes, there was the name, Halfway . . .

But he might as well have been studying printouts for a cardiogram. (He tried to read his own EKG once, sneaking open the medical folder while the doctor was out of the room, becoming panicked at the irregularity of the wavy lines, figuring any such bumpiness must indicate serious problems. He went on to provoke his kindly doctor to impatience at the third-degree style questioning he gave the man's normal diagnosis). The page was covered with wavy lines. Precious few place names, and a confusion of colored dots clustered with cryptic numbers.

He was about to give up and enter the other office to snoop in a more accessible environment when some colorful notations at the top of the page caught his eye. "Beanbrain," it said in red ink. "Milty," in green. "Redeye" in blue. "Cracker" in brown. Somebody had a nice set of colored pens. Then, he noticed that the spots on the map had been drawn in corresponding colors, indicating that . . .

Wait.

*Keep your eyes open, HJ had said.*

This could be what HJ had talked about. A map, a plotting of radio signals given off by the PRP's released falcons and picked up by a satellite. A tiny date was printed next to each dot, providing a daily record of the monitored birds, up to and including today's date. So the colored spots showed where nicknamed birds (save us from the cutesiness of scientists) were.

Beanbrain's red spots were clustered here. Milty's green ones were there. And so on. They were evenly distributed around the area south of Halfway, which was apparently free of towns and roads for about fifty miles, until the map indicated a small state highway and a town named Stretch. The birdwatcher in Ben studied the distribution of colored dots with some interest, noting how they were segregated into roughly defined territories. Predators like their own space. Dots were clustered in fairly random patterns, as you'd expect from free-ranging birds, except for the eccentric Milty who seemed to like to go across his territory in a straight line.

Ben checked the map carefully to see if it included Rocky Mountain National Park, where the diamond-snatching falcon could be traceable, as HJ had hoped. But the map only covered the hundred or so square miles south of Halfway, north of Stretch, and that was a good hundred miles west of the park. He lifted the crinkly sheet and saw that, below, there was a similar map for the previous week. Other sheets went back for several months. None showed a wider range. Nothing to interest HJ.

Ben heard desk drawers open and close as Van continued searching. Enough birdwatching. Time to check out the other office.

Jackpot. Bingo. It was obvious that the assistant principal's office, or wasn't this actually Altman's?, was their target. On a table behind the desk sat a radio, which was clearly not simply for listening to the local C&W station. You didn't need to be an expert to see that. It had a police car type speaker and a satisfying confusion of buttons, knobs and wires. Even better, there was a telephone next to it.

His immediate impulse was to call Van. But caution (or was it some burgeoning private dick vanity?) intruded and he thought, *first find the big clue.* The unmistakable tie-in. A scrap of paper with the phone number of Cole's motel on it. A ticket to Rio. Who knows? A diamond that rolled unseen onto the floor? Then he'd casually walk next door, drop it on the desk, and watch Van drop his teeth.

There was a box of cassette tapes on the radio table. He pulled them out and, fanning them like cards, read the titles which had been scrawled on their labels. Maybe there'd be something particularly interesting, like one marked "Abby Cole." And he remembered that in their meeting, Tina had said, . . . *it might not have been her talking live.*

As if on cue, he saw that one of the tapes was in fact labeled "A. Cole." A chilling feeling. There was a tape player hooked up to the radio. He could just slip this into the machine and see what it had to say. Mac would hear it, though. He might as well get him in here now. He turned to call for the big detective but before he could say anything, the secretive atmosphere of deep night was explosively broken.

From the next office came a massive *BONK!* A solid smack as of a baseball bat connecting perfectly, sending a new hardball high and long. This was immediately followed by a monstrous cry, spontaneous and primitive. It was Van's voice, and it chilled Ben, literally causing a shiver to run through him in the still office. He couldn't breathe. Neck hairs bristled.

Then there was the sound of breaking glass, of heavy furniture scraping, unyielding wood shimmying, vibrating the floor under Ben. The same sickening sound again, *BONK!* Ben was somehow sure that it had been Van's head making the BONK, both BONKS. This latest wasn't followed by that outrageous cry of outrage, but by an anticlimactic scrape and slap as something heavy moved over one surface, dropping to another.

Ben imagined Van sliding across the desk, dropping to the floor unconscious, bleeding from a gash above the eyes and from both ears. And Ben knew with that strange, primitive knowledge that often comes in moments when circumstances . . . sudden shock, an unholy number of martinis, whatever . . . let loose the instincts, that this imagined picture was exactly right.

# 34.

Maybe if Ben had been in his own office, or anywhere he could call home territory, a righteous anger might have seeped out of his glands, fueling some kind of respectable response to a hostile intruder. Even the most passive get tough when their space has been violated. Trouble is, hostile or not, it was Ben who was the true intruder, and holding someone else's cassette tape, he was struck immobile with guilt and elemental deep-night fear. He felt the need to swallow, but couldn't.

Still, just as under winter ice a fish can sometimes be seen flickering, somewhere within the frozen Ben an idea swam, barely visible through the opacity, but moving with urgency. It said, *Mac needs help!* It said, *a guy helps his partner.* It said . . . *move it!*

This growing awareness of his proper obligation to help Van, followed by an inner debate about the pros and cons of various possible courses of action seemed to go on for an unconscionable length of time, but in actuality, took less than a half-second from the second BONK. Then Ben was jamming the tape into his jacket pocket, moving through the door from the assistant principal's office in long strides, his mind devoid of a plan, his body high on fight or flight chemistry now, (at last, both a possibility), his mission simply to get into the next office.

As he turned toward it, he collided with Altman hard enough for both men to let out an uncontrolled "Ooof!", the same graceless sound Ben had heard himself make automatically, surprisingly, when his car had been rear-ended at a stoplight years ago in Chicago. It had the effect now, as then, of sharpening his senses, filling him with rich adrenaline.

In the instant before they bumped each other, Ben saw himself in Altman's mirrored sunglasses. A flash of beard, long hair, dark eyes. There and gone so quickly as to be somewhat subliminal, and Ben thought all at once, *It's Altman. Why does he wear those stupid sunglasses even at night? Hey, I like the way I look. Definitely gotta keep the beard.*

They ricocheted off each other, standing apart now, facing each other like Sumo wrestlers.

"Son of a bitch," Altman, said, hoarse and low. An attempt to sound menacing? If so, it worked. Ben felt frozen again. Not so much afraid, but unsure of what to do. "I thought there was something funny about you. Mr.. Green, isn't it?"

Altman's question sounded foolish in the quiet office, having the pseudo-sophisticate phoniness of a James Bond villain, ("Mr.. isn't it?") Hell, Ben thought, this guy's nothing much to worry about. Except for that thing in his hand.

He was holding the carved wooden falcon Ben had seen in the trophy case downstairs on his first visit. Must have been cut from a solid chunk of wood because, from the way Altman was struggling with it, needing both hands, it was heavy. There was blood smearing the bird's chest, and shining wetly on its beak, which meant Altman had hit Van with the front of it, going for a puncture as well as a clout.

What about Van? Ben had to get to him. See if he's okay. Slap his loose old cheeks. *Wake up big guy!* Maybe throw water on his face. Maybe drag him to the car and drive to some midnight hospital, skidding around corners on two wheels. He was strictly using visions from old movies now, as his life experience in this area was really very weak.

"Van?" Ben said, loud, hoping. Then, to Altman, "Get out of my way, please!"

And the force of these words fed Ben's sudden and surprising fear-induced anger, anger equating with strength in such situations, anger becoming desirable now, and, wanting to add to it, added . . ."NOW!"

*Where'd this version of Ben come from? Lot of pent-up something in there, buddy.*

Altman smiled, thin-lipped and small-toothed, then came at Ben, swinging the wooden falcon by its feet, bringing it down with blurry velocity, using its top-heavy heft to whip it hard, aiming at Ben's face. Ben, with the instincts of a basketball player dodging slashing elbows under the boards, arched backward as the falcon sliced through the whiskers on his chin and was gone. He could feel a cold rush of air in its wake, and the hum of its motion seemed to echo in the room.

"Works better when you sneak up on a guy, doesn't it?" Ben said. He felt hot and somehow freed-up now, no longer the guilty trespasser. Van's blood had sprayed off that chunk of sharp wood. This mirror-eyed man had tried to bash Ben's innocent face. And Ben hadn't done anything to deserve it! Righteous and wild, he felt ready to spring, ready to smash into Altman, to lift him off the floor and throw him against the wall so hard he'd stick there, or to fling him out the window in a spray of glass.

He'd always led a civilized life, bookish and artistic, being the shy ad writer, nervous dreamer-upper of slogans, and had had only one other fight since grammar school. It hadn't been something he wanted to relive, although now, with his blood up he recalled it in a blink, and knew he'd be as invincible in this ornithology office as he'd been in that suburban bookstore . . .

*       *       *

It was one of those rare Saturdays when Deborah wasn't working at the office. They'd had a pleasant deli brunch at the local shopping center, and had gone to browse the books. Since their interests were antithetical, they drifted apart, she to Business and Careers, he to Fiction and then Nature. On this day, as he wandered past Health and Family Living, the *Illustrated Joy of Sex* caught his eye. Illustrated?

He leafed through the pages, astonished at the drawings which were somewhat pornographic, yet made acceptable for polite company by genteel graphics and lofty text written by doctors. This was better than the girlie magazine display. No sense of disapproving browsers behind him, condemning his lust. And the pictures were even better. Blow jobs. Soixant-neuf. Group sex. Wild positions.

There was one drawing that he couldn't wait to show Deborah. In it, the man was lying back while his girlfriend fondled him. The man had a silly smile on his face. Deborah, just that morning had remarked about Ben's "dumb grin." She'd probably like the other pictures, too, he thought. She and Ben were somewhat newly wed, after all, and were still interested in trying out all the positions.

Book in hand, thumb keeping the place, he walked over to Business and Careers, and came up behind his wife, her head twisted sideways scanning titles. So as no one nearby would notice, he nudged her elbow and whispered, "Look at this," and he held the book open to the very graphic picture.

"Remind you of anything?" he said, looking at her with his dumbest dumb grin, the one he'd had this morning, the one the guy in the book had.

One problem. That wasn't his wife . . . that was a lady! Ben had mistakenly nudged up to an attractive thirtyish brunette he'd never before seen. From behind, she'd looked exactly like Deborah, and he'd just assumed . . . But now he was holding the obscene picture in front of this perfect stranger.

He lost the dumb grin and the ability to move his feet. He wanted to explain. He urgently wanted to say, *Oh, excuse me, I thought you were someone else.* But when he tried, he found he'd lost that ability, too, and could only manage, "Ooh . . . ooh . . ." coming out in a whisper that could have been misconstrued under the circumstances.

The brunette slapped the book away, knocking it to the floor, and disappeared up the aisle. A couple of shoppers heard this and turned to look. The lady told her husband, who must have had previous troubles with perverts, because his approach was wildly unreasoning and unreasonable.

Even though he was Ben's size, his anger made it no fair match. The guy charged up the aisle, and before Ben knew what hit him, the Guide to America's 100 Best Companies did. Across the mouth. This unfroze Ben who did what any red-blooded and bloodied man would do. He backed away from the book-swinging maniac. Then the man threw the book at Ben.

Browsers had come from every part of the store now, watching with wide-open eyes and mouths as Ben ducked first one, then a barrage of books. Finally, his back up against Best Sellers, Ben made a stand. The guy, giving up on books as weapons now, pushed Ben violently in the chest, causing him to hit the shelves, dropping the top row of books onto his head. This, finally, made him mad. Deborah was screaming. People were watching. His mouth was bleeding. And he really hadn't done anything to deserve this.

Righteous fury popped up, the head of a maniac jack-in-the box, and Ben pushed back, hard. This used the muscles a man uses when doing push-ups, and Ben had been doing that particular exercise to the tune of fifty a day since Judo school. So when he pushed, the man flew. Deborah screamed. The man hit the fiction aisle's shelf system, and the thing went over. More screams. Novels everywhere.

The man, eyes mad slits now, crawled to his feet. There was a freestanding wire rack nearby, the kind that holds crossword puzzle books. The man lifted it by its base, and swung it in a circle, crosswords shooting out in all directions. Ben bent over backward to avoid the thing, and it kept going, its momentum twisting the man around. A golfer exaggerating the perfect follow-through of a textbook swing . . .

\* \* \*

And so, when Altman swung the falcon at Ben a second time, and Ben again bent backward to avoid getting clocked, and the weight of the circling bird brought Altman around, making his body twist, looking like a golfer exaggerating a perfect follow-through, Ben knew why he'd flashed upon the bookstore battle.

When the enraged husband had swung the wire rack, it, too, had twisted him around and Ben, operating on instinct, heat, and ingrained judo principles from his teenage lessons threw himself forward while his opponent was off-balanced, grabbing the top of the rack as it came around behind the man's head, pulling it away, causing the guy to spin to the floor, face down, vulnerable to a quick hammerlock, a hold from which the guy could not budge without Ben's permission as Ben waited victoriously for the police to take over. It's irrelevant that Ben was the one actually cuffed, and until the facts were sorted out, was in some trouble.

Altman's bird had reached the top of its swing and was suspended motionless behind his head, above his shoulders in that instant of equilibrium before Altman could untwist and bring it forward, slashing in the other direction, the blunt object a double-edged sword.

Ben made his move. This being the second time he'd had the opportunity, it was executed with greater speed and strength. He lunged toward Altman—probably could have punched the guy's face, or grabbed his ears with both hands—but sticking to plan, he put his hands on the bird's cold, carved head and pulled it quickly down and away.

Altman reacted like any textbook guinea pig on a judo mat. Completely off-balanced, he spun over backward and hit the floor, landing on his back, immediately rolling over, trying to get his hands under him, to push into a standing position. Ben flung the bird away and threw himself toward Altman's back, hearing glass shattering somewhere as the bird hit one of the doors. He grabbed Altman's right arm, going for the proven hammerlock, but Altman rolled, causing Ben to fall off, finding himself now awkwardly under Altman's kicking legs, as the man scrambled to stand.

Ben propped himself on an elbow, unsure of his next move, only knowing he had to get to his feet, had to somehow restrain and contain Altman, his heart racing, his mind a hellish stew composed of guilt for having been caught, fear for Van's health, fear at being alone here without Van's help, fear of this wild man Altman, fear of his own ability to perform with grace and athleticism during the rest of this fight, a real-life fight, he thought. Like in the movies, and the idea awed him.

Then, as he leaned forward on his hands to prop himself up, to stand, to see where Altman had gone, to deal with whatever the next moment would bring, Altman kicked him in the mouth. The blow was delivered with more force than any Ben had ever experienced. His left upper bicuspid popped down his throat like a pill taken with hot salt water, which he knew on some non-verbal level, was his own blood. He didn't pass out, although a tweedy pattern of gray and silver overlay his vision. In it were little flashbulb pops, appearing and disappearing, actually kind of pretty.

Folk wisdom has it that a good kick in the teeth will knock the fight out of a guy. But sometimes it can have the reverse effect, and knock the fight into a guy, as it did with Ben. He had no sense of crossing the intervening space between where he'd landed and where Altman was standing. He was just there, upon Altman in a clumsy impact of bodies, fists filled with folds of shirt, spinning, falling, crushing cabinetry, cracking back tilted chairs, breaking everything breakable, hearing nothing of the splitting wood, shattering glass, sliding furniture, bouncing phones, feeling no new pain.

Mindlessly, they spun. Ben shifted one hand and got a fistful of Altman's hair. It felt crisp and oily at the same time, but was well anchored in the scalp and gave him good leverage for pulling Altman. Altman got a hand in Ben's mouth. Ben felt fingernails gouge into the tender flesh under his tongue with sudden blinding pain. He bit down, but with the newly missing bicuspid and its painful gum, this was ineffective. He pulled Altman's hair harder, pulling the man's head back. Still, Altman's nails dug in.

(Such is the shameful reality: A real life fight is mean and desperate and utterly artless.) Ben ripped Altman's mirrored sunglasses away. Altman shook his head to prevent Ben from grabbing his face, but Ben got a grip on Altman's left ear and pulled. Altman's hand came out of Ben's mouth, fingernails no longer gouging blue and pink under-tongue, a moment of sudden ecstasy as pain departed. But only a moment. Altman made a quick fist and drove it hard into Ben, aiming perhaps for Ben's stomach, an honest target, but hitting instead, with all this spinning and staggering, the hollow of Ben's neck, bouncing off the vee of his collarbone, up into the delicate underpinnings of Adam's apple.

Ben, stunned, released earhold and hairhold, falling backwards, unable to breathe in or out, feeling as though a bucket of the Colonel's chicken bones were wedged sideways in his neck. He didn't feel the floor coming up to hit him from behind, but now he was looking up at Altman, into the man's naked eyes.

Altman was on him, swinging with both hands now, his face shocking, all drool and blood and something else, those eyes! Pale, pink little eyeballs staring down. Hard eyes. But unlike any Ben had ever seen. *Pink. Imagine, pink.* And Ben couldn't breathe. The tweed pattern came again. Tweed with little flashbulbs.

# 35.

Even though Ben's body hurt, he was free of the psychic discomfort that had been dogging him. His throat was raw and swollen, but he felt none of the nervous depression caused by being far from home and familiar acquaintances. His tooth, or rather the ragged pit his tooth once occupied, throbbed and dribbled, but his guilt over burglarizing the PRP had disappeared.

A fair tradeoff? At the moment, Ben was too tired and beat up to judge. But through this uncomplicated physical pain, his tiredness, equally uncomplicated, was almost enjoyable. And he lolled back in the big bucket seat of Van's Cherokee, enjoying the simplicity of the moment, confident that Van would bring him out of the night, out of the pain. His confidence was well placed.

Apparently he'd only been unconscious for a few seconds, probably from bad breathing, hyperventilating during the mad pirouette with Altman. Too much air too fast, then the smack in the larynx causing it to go into a spasm, blocking all air suddenly, making him pass out. Altman might have really hurt him then. The guy was clearly crazed. And, also having something to hide (there could be no doubt about that now, Ben felt), Altman fought with the motivation of the cornered, completely neutralizing Ben's bush league judo training, such as it was.

But Van, as he'd later explained, had awakened, and hearing the war in the outer office came to the rescue, calmly walking up behind Altman and knocking him senseless with one ham fisted punch to the back of the skull. The elementary brain concussion. The fabled coldcock.

Invisible little birdies circling around Altman's smiling, sleeping face. Probably little falcons, wearing radio collars. Well, this was Van's line of work, wasn't it? Ben thought. Let's see him try to write a slogan.

Van had picked Ben off the floor, a father collecting his kid after a schoolyard fight. He'd brushed bits of broken glass off Ben's clothes, wiped his face with a shirttail and led him to the door, saying, "We gotta get outta here."

"Okay by me," Ben croaked.

"Must've been a silent alarm, after all."

So that was why Altman had suddenly shown up in the middle of the night. Van probably figured others might do the same.

Then Van propped Ben against the doorjamb and went back to where Altman lay amid overturned desks and office litter. He knelt over him, opened one sleeping eye with the deft authority of an ER doctor, then the other. He shrugged, grunted, and put a big palm on Altman's chest, satisfying himself that the man's heart and lungs were conscious even if he wasn't

"The guy'll be okay," he said, standing, then wobbling, almost falling as he came toward Ben. And Ben noticed for the first time, a swath of blood down the right side of Van's face. There was a loose piece of scalp, skin with hair on one side, pink flesh on the other, hanging away from Van's head, a loose flap about six inches long. It bobbed as he walked. Van, regaining his composure, didn't seem to notice.

Ben couldn't remember the details of their walk back through the dark school. Maybe he'd drifted off again, but he remembered Van guiding him into the Jeep's front seat. Van had jogged around to the driver's side and driven quickly away. After they were out of town, he'd pulled over, turned on the interior lights and looked at Ben in that combat doctor style he'd used with Altman, impassive scrutiny, a man looking at his watch.

"You're fine," he said. He took some pills out of the glove compartment and told Ben to swallow them with a swig of whisky from a flask also stored there.

"Tylenol Codeine Three's, with Jack Daniels neat. You'll be just fine . . ."

Then he twisted the Jeep's oversized rearview mirror toward himself. He lifted the flap of scalp and pressed it to his head. When he took his hand away, it dropped back, a sheet of wallpaper that wouldn't stay glued.

"Holy shit. And I hate stitches," but he laughed.

*This is a tough guy*, Ben thought.

Van shook his head, making the flap swing ridiculously, then twisted around to look in the back seat. He found an old baseball cap and jammed it down tightly on his head, holding the flap of skin in place. He looked at Ben and grinned.

"Away we go!"

He darkened the interior, and they drove into what was left of the night.

"We didn't get anything to show. But we got away. We did do that," he said.

"We did get something to show," Ben said, dimly remembering his chill upon seeing the "A. Cole" tape, and putting it in his pocket just before things went crazy back there. He reached into his pocket for it, but fell asleep in the middle of doing this and stayed that way, sleeping drugged, beat up and content, hand in pocket, as they drove back to Denver.

# 36.

Ben was sitting puffy and despondent in a Denver dentist's chair. The dentist's spotlight was over bright. And morning sunlight was coming through carelessly adjusted mini-blinds in painful stripes, one of which lay across Ben's eyes, adding to the discomfort.

While Ben sat there, mouth open, eyes shut, a wild-haired blonde woman was walking somewhere in the Rockies. She was naked, carried herself with perfect posture, and wore a living falcon on her wrist. She was a breasty and muscular vision reminiscent of those seen on covers of Edgar Rice Burroughs' adventure paperbacks.

Actually, she was even better, more real, with streaks of cakey soil smearing her tan skin, a profusion of pine needles in her careless hair. She moved with long, determined strides into the camp of a man who called himself Ute Sommers. She didn't know his name yet. She didn't know anything about him except one thing. And that one thing filled her with confidence and the tight-lipped kind of feminine energy that moves mountains, men, mountain men. What she knew about him was that he'd been saving her life for the last week. And that she'd finally found him.

Dr. Bernard Cass liked patients to call him Buzz, a lifelong nickname admittedly better than Bernie, Ben figured. But when applied to a dentist, it had either disturbing or thoughtless implications. The man was either sadistic or stupid. Two traits to be avoided in dentists. It was all out of Ben's control, though. Buzz was Van's dentist, probably because his office was in the same building as the Van Dyke agency.

Van had arranged a special, early appointment for Ben by calling Buzz at home at dawn, and the whole thing was served up as a kind of special favor. So there he'd sat in the pre-Muzak, pre-workday hour, listening only to the suck of dental hardware, and Buzz's wet breathing as he strained for air under his sterile facemask.

"Okay," Buzz said after awhile, theatrically pulling his mask over his head. "Got 'em. Those last few chunks of root. Came out clean." And he smiled. Ben, ever the polite soul, smiled back. He felt a little rush of cold air come into his mouth. A door had been left open somewhere in his smile, and he wondered what he looked like now but was too tired to ask for a mirror.

They spent the next hour taking impressions so Buzz could fabricate a single temporary false tooth. Buzz called this device a "flipper," as though it were a common word known by everyone, with no other possible meanings. Ben merely gave this curiosity a mental shrug and settled more deeply into the contour chair, thinking of tame porpoises, his mouth filled cheek-to-cheek with wet cement, not even having the energy to gag.

Buzz said he'd rush the flipper as a favor to Van, a further statement of the man's insensitivity, Ben thought. Better it were a favor for the guy in the chair, right? Buzz? Ben agreed to stop in tomorrow, at day's end, still working the periphery of Buzz's appointment book, for the flipper fitting. And he left, the rest of the day free for rest.

Ben, on his way back to the Brown Palace for a good day's sleep, was enjoying the curiously superior attitude of the night shift worker, tired and going slowly upstream against the current of the new day's neat, combed and cologned corps of day workers, all squinting in morning sun and cigarette smoke.

He wanted that big hotel bed, and he wanted it soon. He'd flop face first onto it, covers and pillows still neatly tucked and smoothed in that military hotel maid fashion. He wouldn't pull them apart, nor would he take off his clothes. He'd drop onto that hotel-made bed in boots, jeans and bush jacket, close his eyes, sleep all day . . .

The thought of the bush jacket triggered something. What? No matter. Time to get some sleep. He stood across the street from the Brown Palace, waiting for the light to change. So close was the old building and the new bed, it made him all the more tired. And the red light was long. He leaned against a lamppost, waiting, enjoying the pleasure of leaning instead of standing, remembering suddenly something associated with the old joy of leaning, something funny. What? Like the other thing, the bush jacket thing, it was impossible to bring into focus. No matter. He simply leaned, high school hard guy style, hips cocked, jamming hands deep into the big patch pockets of his bush jacket, completing the pose, letting his arms relax, supported there by the pockets.

His right hand wrapped itself around the cassette tape, and the elusive thought relating to his bush jacket came clear. He jumped to attention, causing himself to slip sideways off the post, back-stepping in a clumsy stumble, not enough to cause attention, but enough to also bring into focus the leaning memory. This one, something to do with falling through a wall at SPF wasn't worth dealing with. The stolen tape, though, that was important.

The light switched to green, but instead of crossing the street to the Brown Palace, Ben turned and headed back toward Van's building. He walked through the morning crowd, now going with the flow instead of against it. The ease of movement, of being borne along, ironically made his tiredness more burdensome. Everywhere he looked he saw beds. A bus groaned by, every seat a contoured pillow, inviting rocking, gas-scented sleep, sweet sleep, sleep until the end of the line.

Ah, the dreams of the deprived, he thought. When dieting or otherwise empty-bellied, you see food everywhere. To a dieter the same bus is notable only for the ad it carries on its side, a long, horizontal cheeseburger, juicy and hot, backed with piles of fries, a poster created by McSadists. And when sexually deprived, a man is taunted by shimmying breasts, rolling buttocks. Every woman who passes possesses within the confinement of the most insubstantial kinds of garments, the most private and sweet body parts, so close. Deprivation creates compulsion.

Ben's compulsion now focused on the couches in Van's waiting room. He made plans as he rose in the elevator to Van's floor, impervious for the moment, to phobias about elevators and their vault-like confinement. Let it stall between floors. He'd lie down and close his eyes, cozy and contained. He made plans for those couches. When he got there, he'd lie down for a while. Five minutes. Then he'd be refreshed enough to find Van, to present the tape. They could have it. He wouldn't stay. He'd say, "Thanks for the dentist appointment. Goin' to the hotel for a nap. Oh, thought you'd like to see what I picked up last night while you were out of it."

Tina sang out, "You're here!" And she came across the reception area, right into him with her tiny body, hugging him in apparently genuine happiness, confusing him because, incredibly, he'd all but forgotten her.

"I told Van you'd come in today. But he said I was wrong!"

She yelled over her shoulder, "Van, look who's here like I said he would be!"

Now, with some faint sense of disappointment, Ben picked up on the possibility that her enthusiasm was not so much that he'd survived a night in the so-called field, but that maybe she was merely winning some kind of inter-office bet on whether or not he'd come in after the pounding he'd taken.

This meant that the others in the office might have pegged him as being so soft as to need a day of recuperation. And he remembered a jowly old gym teacher who looked a lot like Van. (Or maybe over the years, the teacher's face had grown so amorphous in Ben's memory that Van's similar one had simply superimposed itself there on the man's fat neck, hung with lanyard and whistle.) The teacher had routinely lectured his scrawny seventh graders about the need to *play with pain*. He'd no doubt heard this from football commentators, and with the muscle-headed meanness of coaches, had adopted it as a motto.

So, Van and HJ must have assumed Ben wouldn't play with pain. An insult. Ben had encountered that dubious challenge as far back as junior high. Of course he'd show up for work. Of course he wouldn't let missing a night's sleep or missing a front tooth change anything. Tina knew. And he couldn't be any less of a man than Tina thought he was. She knew what he was made of, all right, and his tiredness didn't seem to matter at the moment.

Van came padding across the carpet in his stocking feet, bright-eyed, red-cheeked, perfectly rested, hair neatly combed. Ben dimly remembered a flap of gory scalp dangling from Van's head after the fight. There was no bandage there. Had he imagined the injury?

"Never thought we'd see you today. Ad guys are pussies, generally, I figure. Thought you'd be headin' home or checking into a clinic or something." All this, while smiling. Then he slapped his hand into the side of Ben's shoulder, making him feel more welcome than insulted, but insulted nonetheless.

"Come on in, there's lot's to do." And with a big hand on Ben's shoulder, Van guided him toward the corner office.

Ben hadn't had a chance to say anything since being spotted and fussed over by Tina, and now, the thing he'd planned to say, that he wasn't there to stay, suddenly became out of the question as a matter of pride.

"There might be more to do than you think, Van."

And he walked with Van, his tiredness making him feel now not so much sleepy as intoxicated, and he remembered reading once about sleep deprivation experiments causing the experimentees to react as though they'd been drinking. Not an altogether bad feeling. Kind of takes the edge off, eliminates the natural nerves of the moment, the shyness, lets a guy's personality come through. Ben smiled at Van and slapped his hand against Van's shoulder. It was hard, like the flesh of a saddle horse.

"I've got something to show you, big guy."

Ben noticed the neat rows of stitches visible under the comb strokes of Van's hair. They made a geometrically precise rectangle, and the skin around them was stained with a purplish disinfectant. He was reminded of Frankenstein's monster, and slightly giddy now, this struck him as funny, causing him to chuckle, which surprised both him and Van. He passed it off as an expression of excitement at his having something important to show, although there was nothing funny about what might be on the tape. They'd know soon.

# 37.

Ben dropped the tape onto Van's desk.

"Forgot to mention it last night. Found this in Altman' office, just before you got hit. By the way, how's the head today?" Actually, this last question was added to minimize the possible importance of bringing the tape back from Altman' office. Van looked at the tape, then raised his eyes to meet Ben's.

"I'm fine. Just don't much like getting stitches is all."

Van looked again at the tape, taking some time to read the name, slowly nodding his head. Softly, he said, "Forced the doctor to do them without shaving much hair. So that's not too bad, you know? Listen, Green, this could be what we talked about awhile back. You know?"

\* \* \*

Four hours later, Ben pushed his chair back from the long table in Van's conference room and put up his feet. The table was littered with lunch leavings. Paper plates and bread crusts. Pickles going dry and empty potato chip bags. Soft drink cans, coffee styro-cups. Another luncheon meeting. Another day spent in conference. And Ben thought, as he had on countless past occasions, *this is going to be my last meeting.*

Normally, this vow had a whiney insincerity to it. A chain smoker saying through yellowed teeth, *my last cigarette, swear..* But this time, it had a different feel, and it gave him a rush of ambivalence, a familiar enough feeling, though not an altogether pleasant one.

The meeting had been a status report, as Van described it. But Ben privately pegged it as another rehash and felt a growing impatience, which seemed fueled not so much by the tedium of this (and all) meetings, but by something below the surface he couldn't yet identify. Something made him feel they were spinning their wheels, as ad guys say.

Once again Tina had rolled out the big easel with its oversize paper on which Van had dictated features of the case. Tina, Ben thought, our Vanna White, our Wheel of Fortune teller, spelling out words, revealing our hunches to be true, teasing us.

Van's analysis pointed to Altman being guilty of kidnapping Abby. Altman had his motives. He had opportunity. He'd acted guilty by responding to the office's silent alarm, not with cops as any honest alarmed party would, but alone with a deadly weapon which he used enthusiastically. He had the technical equipment that could have transferred a radio phone call from the mountain cabin to a land line, which could have been used to contact the Coles, letting them hear their daughter's voice and his demands.

Also, as they'd touched upon in the last meeting, if the kidnapper wanted to pretend Abby was there after she wasn't, he could have faked her responses by using recordings made earlier, if such tapes existed. Ben proved one did. And Altman had had it.

The tape, which they listened to earlier, crowding around HJ's tape player in his tech room, was at the same time discouraging, encouraging, and depressing. Discouraging because it proved Abby's voice had been available not live, but on tape. And encouraging because it didn't contain anything even remotely similar to what Cole had heard on the phone. No "Daddy, help me." No "I'm all right, I want to come home . . ." Just observations about falcons at hack sites and in the wild.

It could have been a recitation from any monotonous monograph in wildlife biology.

Even though Ben knew it was technically possible to make new words from others, to splice them together to form sentences never actually spoken, his ear for this kind of thing was good, and he believed the tape contained nothing that could have been tampered with in order to create the illusion that Abby was responding to Cole.

And it was depressing because Abby's voice was pretty and young and ironic. There was a self-deprecating quality in it, a valley-girlish way of acknowledging the inherent dullness of the material. Abby was funny and full of life on the tape. And something bad had happened to her.

Van said he'd contacted the FBI agents working on the case as soon as he'd arrived, before Ben had gone to the dentist. They agreed with him that Altman looked, as they said, "dirty." Van didn't tell them about the breaking and entering or more accurately, the entering and breaking, knowing never to admit lawlessness to lawmen. He simply told them he'd had suspicious evidence come to light concerning some phone and radio equipment recently removed from a mountain cabin used by Altman and his staff. At the same time, he recommended to the agents that they bring Rachel in for questioning and warned them she was armed. That got them interested in her.

More scribbling on the big board. O'Brien's death . . . a murder? It was too early for the FBI's medical report on the cause of death, and Van was leaning toward the idea that maybe Altman had murdered O'Brien. He thought maybe O'Brien discovered the kidnapping and had to be eliminated. Or there was the chance that O'Brien was in on it, but they'd had a falling out, and Altman decided to take all the ransom for himself.

At that point, Ben found himself defiantly, yet indefensibly, positive that poor O'Brien hadn't been killed by anything more criminal than his own unhealthy heart. Again Van and his theories sounded like material from cheap detective novels, TV shows, B movies.

Isn't mystery fiction simply a form of pop culture? Like advertising, the simple truth is that it's simply not the truth. Ben's original reason for running away from Chicago ran again through his over-tired mind. He could see his would-be book as it would be, hefty, glossy-covered, big as Life (the magazine), though thicker. *Unreal! Advertising versus Reality* on coffee tables around the country, each copy contributing royally to the payment of royalties, making him rich. Well, that's for later. Beware the dangers of *Daydreaming Versus Reality*.

But wait, there was a reason for this, a connection: Detective fiction versus reality! The *gap*. Is it as great as between ads and reality? Ben guessed it was. Maybe greater. Could this be the reason behind his growing skepticism regarding Van's conclusions? Recent experiences made Ben not just worry, not just weary, but all the way to wary. And he smiled at the memory of a hyperactive female voice-over chortling cleaner than clean, whiter than white, all the way to bright . . . in the first TV spot he'd written for Brio.

Yes, too much like a detective story. O'Brien murdered? *Unreal.* Rambo? Could be that she's just a girl who smells sexy, the scent of baby shampoo in her hair, living in the mountains, watching birds. What about the big .45 in her hand? Okay, sometimes reality has a little spice in it. But she's no kidnapper's moll. What about the kidnapping itself? Phone calls asking for diamonds. Frantic parents. Pleading victim. The FBI. The Van Dyke Agency. Was this reality? Reality enough, Ben figured, reluctantly, but once the comparison to his dreamed-of coffee table book was made, it was hard to let go of certain implications.

"Ben!"

It was Van.

"You with us, man? Want to lie down in my office awhile?"

Ben had been so absorbed in the undeniable nature of reality that he'd left reality himself, snoozing while sitting there, hand on chin at the table.

"Just thinking. I'm fine."

"We need you to be thinking. That's what you're here for."

And Van pointed to him, a gesture meaning, you've got the floor. "So?"

Ben, still fuzzy. "You want to know what I was thinking about?"

"Anything good?" Van said.

"I was thinking . . . what if Altman didn't kidnap Abby Cole?"

Van nodded but didn't say anything. He was leaning back in one of the big tilt chairs they had at the conference table, his stockinged feet up. He seemed to grow interested in his toes, wiggling them inside his socks. Tina and HJ stared at Ben.

Then, from somewhere in his subconscious, a part of him all too loosely hobbled due to extreme tiredness, Ben found himself adding, "See, the guy was an albino."

\*     \*     \*

The afternoon ground on.

The conclusions Van led them toward during the morning-cum-luncheon meeting were neatened up for presentation later that day to Andrew Cole, scheduled in at two.

Ben's absurd albino comment had been largely ignored as a lame non-sequitor, a joke by an overtired amateur. Although Tina had tittered politely, a courtesy Ben didn't want, overcome as he was by a rush of embarrassment for revealing this little piece of subconscious mental fussing. The subconscious is one of the body's private parts and, as such, is properly kept zipped up, tucked away during business hours.

How had that thing popped out? He had to assume the intoxicating effect of sleep deprivation had relaxed certain censoring mechanisms, just as not long ago, in Van's office, alcohol caused him to blabber about little girls and sugar-powdered fat ladies, indicating Abby was somehow in the grasp of snow-powdered mountains, unhappy as a squirming child, but alive. Van had discounted that easily enough. Although, after this new remark, Van might wonder about Ben's sanity. *Join the crowd*, Ben thought.

Still, why the albino reference? There was no doubt that Altman with his mind-blowing pink eyes was a member of that accidental race. Ben had noticed a few of Altman's dyed hairs stuck beneath his nails after the fight, having apparently yanked them out by their white roots. What was there about albinos? The symbolism of white? It led to an absurd vision of plump sheep which could have been a legitimate association, or just a sneaky way of reminding himself it was past bedtime, sheep unaccountably countable, the most effortless of cliches, readily available to an exhausted mind.

But the white sheep led to his recalling something Winston Churchill said about sheep, a funny remark wasn't it? And he looked over at Van thinking, *give the guy a bowler and cigar* . . . Then the faintly remembered quote came into the foreground, accompanied by an adrenaline hum because he realized he wasn't hallucinatory after all, but was, tired or not, still working. Churchill had described political rival Clement Atlee as "a sheep in sheep's clothing." An innocent posing as an innocent. Why? Does this mean anything?

Does anybody care?

The afternoon continued to grind.

Cole had come into the conference room looking ten years older than he had four days ago. There had been a sudden and unhealthy weight loss causing his skin to bag, especially under the eyes where it went dark. His color was no longer Santana tan, but a sad gray. And Ben, perhaps inside still mulling over the curious hair yanked from Altman, noticed that Cole's hair had gone dead, now lying there faded, of indeterminate color. Cole's posture was poor, and his movements were slow, appearing arthritic, painful. He looked at Ben with none of the hearty enthusiasm that had always been Cole's trademark.

"Ben," he said, "You look terrible.

# 38.

By four, Cole had shuffled out of the Van Dyke Agency heartened and disheartened. He'd thought it promising that evidence suggested Altman was their man, and there'd been a conference call with the FBI agent running the case. The agent said they were about to pick up Altman anyway, but there was a feeling that Van's information had tipped the scales.

They'd also passed on their information about the radio-telephone gear that had been recently removed from the mountain cabin. And they'd mentioned "Rambo," living up there, armed and working with falcons. They'd made discoveries the FBI hadn't made, and there was a feeling of unspoken pride in the room. The disheartening part was that Abby hadn't been heard from, and nobody knew where she was, or how she was. After Cole left, Ben asked Van what more there was to do.

"Nada, my friend. The Bureau will get Altman soon. They'll find out what he did with Abby Cole's . . . uh, with Abby Cole."

And he padded off to his office. Over his shoulder he said to Ben, "Go to your hotel. Get some sleep. You look like hell."

But Ben stayed in the office. He went to see HJ.

"Could use some technical advice," he said.

"Or . . . you could use some time off," HJ said.

Ben slid one of the workbench chairs across the floor. It was on rollers, and he brought it around in a wide half-circle in front of him, then straddled it cowboy-style, his elbows resting on the backrest.

"Here's what's happening," he said. "I have this feeling we're missing something."

"Something to do with guys being albinos and shit?"

"Maybe," holding HJ's gaze. Then he said, "Everything we told Cole sounds right. But underneath, it's incomplete. You know?"

"I don't," HJ shrugged. "Sorry, man."

"Okay. Altman looks bad. I thought that right off. But when I try to picture him doing it, grabbing this girl. Tying her up, whatever. It feels kind of . . ." Ben paused, searching for the word, looking at the floor as though there might be words lying around down there, then finding it, looking back up at HJ. ". . . fictional."

"I like you, Ben," HJ said, "But you and me, we're from different places, man. You're all mental and creative and feelings. I know. I've known people who worked in advertising. But in my job? I deal with the realities. The tangibles. That's why I love math. Why I got into this side of things. It's quantitative shit, not qualitative. I admit even Van'll use hunches. Sometimes good investigators have to. But that ain't my style."

He stood. "Besides, I don't see much future in basing decisions about a guy because of his pigmentation. Know what I mean?"

When HJ stood, he was very tall. Ben bent back to look at him.

"I must be nuts." Ben said. "Buy you a drink?"

*　*　*

Off the lobby of the building there was a large bar and restaurant just crowding up with office lifers, drifting in for the habitual winding down ritual of happy hour. It was a dark, friendly enough place reminding Ben of Disneyland for a reason he was too tired to try to deal with. They slid into the last available booth along a wall covered with framed corporate logos and artificial plants.

The cold beer burned the raw socket where his tooth had been, but there was some perverse pleasure in the astringent carbonation, a feeling of sanitizing, the illusory promoting of quick healing. After two beers, HJ got a bit more talkative, and Ben got philosophical.

"You happy here, HJ?"

"Happy? I was happy playing basketball. Now I'm just making a paycheck. Van's generous, though. And easy."

"Yeah. I was happy playing basketball, too," Ben said with a wistfulness falsely suggestive of a glorious lost career on the court. HJ squinted at him.

"You played?" Fair question. Ben was white, creative and under six feet.

"Not like you." Unconsciously, Ben put his head back, sitting more erect now, taller in the booth. "But I had a shot. Deadly at horse. Once beat a kid who played for the University of Illinois."

"At horse," HJ said.

"Isn't that what the game's about? Putting the ball in the basket?"

"Shit," HJ said.

Ben, finding himself feeling slightly combative now, chafed by HJ's attitude toward him as a basketball non-entity, said, "You don't, yourself, then, have much of a shot?"

HJ laughed. They both seemed as though they'd had more than just the two beers.

"That's okay," Ben said. "Game needs Boerwinkles and Cartwrights. Good passers. The heady types. Not everybody can be another Michael or Magic."

He took a swallow of beer and added, "Or Bird in his prime."

"Bullwinkle?"

"Boer-winkle," Ben corrected, smiling at the intentional ignorance HJ was pulling . . . probably. "Tom Boerwinkle. Big center for the Bulls back in the seventies. Don't know him? Probably a lot like you, HJ. Good moves, no shot."

"You're beginning to piss me off, just a little."

"Let's change the subject. I wanted to talk about the Altman thing anyway."

Ben hadn't actually articulated it as such in his mind, but he was right. He'd wanted to have these beers with HJ to informally brainstorm about the case. He knew from past experience with similar problems, that talking randomly, freely, preferably while drinking, could sometimes bring about a breakthrough.

*     *     *

Once, he'd sat in a bar much like this one, griping to his art director about an unusual assignment they'd been given. The agency had donated Ben's services to the fire department to create a public service commercial. Big ex-firemen in suits wanted him to show a couch that caught fire after a cigarette fell between its cushions. They said, "Film the couch on fire. Show flames. Make it scary." Ben asked how long it takes for a cigarette to cause such a blaze. "Hours," the chief had said. "That's the danger. It smolders invisibly, then when the family goes to bed, it flares up. The smoke kills 'em in their sleep."

Over drinks with the artist, Ben had wrestled with a vague annoyance, a little fire alarm of his own. "See," he'd said, "showing a burning couch doesn't tell people anything new. It just says, hey, couches burn. People will say, that's not *my* couch."

He'd thrown back the rest of his drink, and with no conscious forethought, had simply said, "We should show a couch *not* burning. A nice, normal couch that anyone would see as their own. And have the announcer voice-over calmly say, 'This couch is on fire. It's been on fire for three and a half hours." Now that was scary. Ben's friend had pantomimed a little silent applause. Ben went on to sell the idea to the fire people. The commercial went on to win awards, and probably prevented some deaths.

*   *   *

That was the kind of thing Ben was hoping for in this conversation with HJ. A way to get beyond whatever it was that felt funny about the Altman and Abby and Rachel and Cole business. Instead, they'd gotten sidetracked, bantering about basketball. What good could come from that?

"Tell you what," HJ said. "There's a health club next door, baskets and all. Let's play some horse. Teach you a little lesson, or are you too tired?"

"Sure," Ben said, feeling the current of events just pulling him along, as though he were on a raft, enjoying the scenery, not even trying to steer anymore. But as he moved across the bench on his way out of the booth, he bumped into Tina, who'd just started sliding in.

Exhaustion, once gotten used to, works like a tranquilizer, and beer works like beer. Mixed together inside Ben's over-revved system, they produced the heightening effect that substance enjoyers are warned against. He had wits enough to know he was heading for a crash but he was, for the moment, carefree enough to enjoy the flight. He felt surprisingly light and strong, for the moment full of the most elusive of all drugs in his experience, self-confidence.

Maybe this was part of the natural balancing act he'd always expected from life. Over the last couple of days he'd been frightened, anxious, lost, found a decomposing body, got his throat punched, and had a good tooth kicked down his throat. He'd missed a night's sleep and had been worked on by a strange dentist. Enough yin. Time for some yang.

He took Tina's tiny hand and said, "Come on. We're going to play basketball."

She'd emitted some bird-like little enthusiasm, which he couldn't hear over the growing din of the lounge. With her free hand she grabbed

Ben's glass and drank off the last of the beer. This seemed less a sign of thirst than a signal of intimacy. That inch or so of flat beer couldn't have looked too appetizing. HJ threw some bills on the table and led the way out. Ben, happily holding hands with Tina, was vaguely aware that it was he who'd offered to buy HJ the beer. No matter. He wasn't able to fire up enough psychic energy to fuel guilt or any of the usual neuroses at this point. Everything was devoted to keeping the tired body moving, the tired mind smiling.

As Ben wound his way through the suits, he thought, no wonder the place had reminded him of Disney. It was to a real bar what Frontierland was to a real frontier. All ambience, no reality. Still, what's wrong with that? Frontierland is more fun than a frontier, anyway.

Or is it?

So self-confidence had come to visit and Ben, glad to be in its rare company, wasn't asking questions. He'd score some baskets. Maybe score with Tina. Then sleep for a week. Tina? Score? He supposed he should keep things Platonic, as it's best that workplace relationships be as non-carnal as possible.

But there were excuses to be made here! Ben was not, after all, of their workplace, but merely a free lance. Tina was playfully inclined and certainly liked him, drinking off the rest of his beer the way she did. (Or was he making more of that than there was? He never liked drinking from the glasses of others, and perhaps was attributing it greater significance . . . ) What about her past profession? And her coquettishness regarding the sex tapes in his borrowed office upstairs? *We'll listen to them another time.* And she'd winked, or did he imagine the wink?

Above all, there was the recent self-acknowledgement that until coming West, he'd been clearly overworked and underloved. That night at Cheryl Harding's could be just the beginning of a new life as a cocksman, and he was lightheaded enough now to find the idea mildly interesting. But first he'd show HJ what it means to put the ball in the basket, in the style of John Paxson, another Bull from their winning days.

The guy who ran the health club sold Ben a jock and tennis shorts.

Ben's hiking shoes were really just gyms done in brown, so they were given the okay for floor wear. To everyone's amusement, Tina came with them as they went into the men's locker room. Who says that the double standard is dead? If Ben or HJ had walked into the Ladies', offense would certainly have been taken, and maybe the cops would be called. But little Tina's company in the Men's brought smiles from the few men in there. One bear-shaped old guy in gray hair with an enormous belly and no discernible privates casually called out, "Hi, Tina honey."

Tina stayed with Ben as he changed, while HJ used a locker on the other side. A thoughtful guy, Ben thought. Tina ripped the plastic wrap off his tennis shorts and set them on the bench. Then she opened the box and took out the new jock. There was a moment of indecision when Ben should have been unbuckling and stepping out of his pants. But with the quick impatience of all-knowing moms, little girls and kindly massage parlor veterans, Tina clucked and took control, pulling him toward her briskly, undoing belt and sliding down pants.

"Here," she said, "pull those shoes off."

She sat him on the bench and he kicked his feet free of the soft hiking shoes. If tiredness was indeed a drug, he was totally stoned and went with the bizarre program as it played itself out. She lifted pants and jockeys free, smiling happily at his nudity, her face the face of fun, his blown mind totally dazed as she folded his pants neatly, actually caring that they were neat. She tossed the new jock at him and stored his pants on the shelf of one of the lockers.

"Get your shorts on," she said. "HJ's already out."

In old thermal undershirt, unfresh but comfortable, crisp new shorts and dusty trail shoes, Ben followed Tina to the courts, wondering, how does she know the way? The gym was empty except for HJ at the far end taking some lay-ups. The guy looked smooth, picking the ball off the rim, getting way up there. Tina went over to a canvas bag of basketballs, which lay, on the floor near the wall. She got one out and tossed it to Ben.

"Go get 'em!" she said, then sat down on the shiny floor against the wall, tucking her skirt in under her thighs, a little junior high schooler.

Ben bounced the ball. It felt good. Good tread, good dampness on his hands. The floor was live. The varnish shone. The rubber of his soles gripped as he walked. Coolish air blew around his bare legs. He dribbled across the court toward HJ, liking how Tina had said *go get 'em*, liking the smile on HJ's face now. When he got to the top of the key, he shot the ball, a nice, easy one-handed jumper. His fingertips had a mind of their own, a mind that remembered everything about shooting baskets, and the ball went out in a smooth, back-spinning arc. Yang was still upstaging yin. The ball went in.

*    *    *

At eleven that night Ben was finally able to take a swan dive into the king-size bed waiting all day for him at the Brown Palace. The detour starting at seven that morning, when he'd remembered the tape in his pocket as he was virtually on the hotel's doorstep, had taken instead of the expected fifteen minutes, more than fifteen hours. But the last four of those hours were a blur of pleasure, filling him with the feeling of having had a good dream, one so nice you just want to go to sleep again, if only to be in the same neighborhood as such a dream.

Sleep. He was ready at last to sleep long, druggy, innocently. He lay fully dressed, face down on the made bed, his face deeply impressing itself into the spread where it covered three oversized pillows. It smelled sweetly of detergent and starch. Totally out of fuel now, unwilling— worse, unable, to move—his mind sputtered a last few thoughts before being hauled away. This evening had been a going-away party for him. Yeah, that's what it was. He'd never had a going-away party when he'd gone away from Chicago. Or when he'd gone away from anywhere.

He pictured the echoing gym the way it had been, replaying his best shots out there, the ball swishing through the net, impressing HJ, actually managing to outshoot the big guy at horse as promised, and with Tina watching. He remembered Tina laughing with him later over a Chicago-style pizza taken out and up to Van's office after HJ had gone home, before Tina and he had stretched out on Van's couch, listening at last to the forbidden tapes, finding them ultimately boring. But Tina wasn't bored or boring. She was a cat. Small, strong and wiry, full of quick movement. She even purred, while generously doing most of the work, as he was really just so tired.

He felt himself descend into sleep now, like a diver dropping into the sea, a warm sea, comfortably dark. And he only wondered—if that was my going-away party, where am I going away to?

# 39.

*They were in a large conference room with walls that weren't walls, but sliding partitions. Every once in a while a puff of wind would open the partitions a crack and Ben could make out mountains and pine trees. He wondered if he could spot some interesting birds out there. Steller's jays. Clark's nutcrackers. Bald eagles. He waited for the walls to part again so he could look.*

*Van was presenting storyboards. His scalp had flapped open, and must have been bleeding because there was blood on the storyboards. And Ben thought—not again.*

*Tina was there, and so was his boss, Devon Pope. Pope wasn't paying attention to Van but was staring at Ben with those popping eyes, saying wordlessly, I could kill you, I'll fire you.*

*Ben was stretched out atop the conference table, lying on his stomach, his face resting cheek down on a soft layout pad. Nobody cared that Ben was on the table instead of sitting at it. It seemed normal even to him. Barry Elliot was there. So was Abby Cole—the young teenage version, blonde, very pretty—and next to her sat Cole and Lara. Lara wore no clothes. Her hair was pulled back into a pony tail, held by an orange ribbon and she looked very young. Seeing her nude, her tan breasts outrageously nippled there over the conference table, gave Ben an erection which he didn't want anyone to know about, and he was grateful he was on his stomach.*

*The table was hard there, hard on hard, and he wanted to lift up his hips, give himself some breathing room. But then everyone would know his secret, so he just lay there unmoving, uncomfortable. Lara looked worried and Cole was unshaven and old, the silverish stubble on his face shining, refracting the room's ceiling light.*

*Van was droning on about the execution of O'Brien, and Ben without moving his head—too heavy to move—strained his eyes to see the storyboard frames. They were smeared red and showed pictures of O'Brien's body on the forest floor covered with little cartoon ravens. Some art director had even cut out pictures of Disney animals—B'rer Bear, B'rer Fox—and put them around the body. Must have been Elliot, still mad at Ben about that stunt in the Brio meeting. Elliot knew these innocent pictures in that gruesome place would annoy Ben.*

*It was a well-drawn storyboard, but O'Brien's body was showing pink stuff, and Ben shut his eyes. Very wrong to show that in a meeting.*

*HJ popped the tab on a can of beer, and it made a sound that Ben liked. There's a big idea there. He wanted to tell Van about it, to make him pay attention to that sound, but he couldn't lift his hand to get anybody's attention, couldn't even speak. Nothing was working. He'd wanted to tell Van that the sound reminded him that sometimes you have to trust the instincts. And the instincts were warning him that something was wrong with Van's presentation.*

*Van slammed a new storyboard onto the table. More executions. This one was about Altman, but Ben wouldn't look at it. Instead he looked at HJ's face but HJ just drank his beer, not wanting to argue about anything Van did.*

*He looked at Tina, but she wasn't paying attention. She was writing a letter to the fat man in the shower, the man with no visible privates, and she had a silly, little girl's handwriting in which she drew smiling cat's faces instead of dots over her "i's." He was disgusted with her. She couldn't pay attention to anything that was going on.*

*He turned his eyes toward Cole, but was distracted as Van banged yet another storyboard onto the table. This one was about Abby, Van's voice said, and Ben looked at Abby and she was squirming in the big white chair, bored as a young kid should be. She had a green felt-tipped pen and was using it to make a series of round green dots on the chair's arm.*

*Ben wanted to tell her not to do that, not to deface that expensive upholstery, but then felt glad she was doing it. He became unreasonably*

*excited about it even, and felt like laughing but couldn't move, even to*
*smile.*

*Devon Pope looked at her and popped his eyes. Ben looked at Pope*
*and tried to say, get fucked—I quit, but, again, he couldn't speak. Too*
*tired. And besides, Pope was already having it socked to him. The little*
*girl was marking up one of his pretentious white chairs, and Van was up*
*there selling the client on a campaign that was all wrong.*

*Jeez, his erection was getting uncomfortable. He had to lift up, just a*
*little. He'd do it. Hell with what people thought. He gathered his strength*
*and pushed off. Coming up. Up, like a diver surfacing. He woke for a*
*moment, turned over and went back to sleep without noticing the light*
*streaming into his room.*

# 40.

"Altman disappeared on the way to a hospital, somewhere in Atlanta,"
Van said. "Never did find the diamonds." He looked down and said
to his desktop, "Still, the guy's gotta be guilty. Why else did he run?
Twice! And the poor kid's most certainly dead. 'Til they find Altman
again, we've just got to wait." He looked at Ben and went on, "The Coles
know."

He leaned back, sighed, and his chair sighed along with him as it
strained under his weight. He put his feet up. He was wearing light
gray socks and the bottoms were dirty from walking shoeless, making
them dark gray. Ben was noticing everything. On this, his last day as
a detective, he found himself hyper-observant. The irony in this was
observed, too, but wasn't worth thinking about. He had other things
on his mind.

It was late afternoon. Ben had slept through the previous night and
most of the day, waking after noon with a new sense of mission. He
dressed quickly and went to the Van Dyke Agency. Tina had given him
a big smile, saying, "Your dentist called. You forgot to go yesterday
after work." Nothing about their pizza and couch party last night. He
looked at the papers on her desk to see if her handwriting was ditzy as

it was in his dream. No cat's faces, but as she smiled up at him, he saw the cat's face was her face. He smiled back, very sober now, aware of the air blowing through his front teeth, through the gap.

The dentist. His temporary false tooth, the flipper, had been created for him with same-day-rush service. *For cosmetic purposes, of course,* Buzz had said. Ben brushed aside any thought of seeing the dentist, no time to worry about a missed appointment or a missed tooth, no time for cosmetic purposes. He'd hugged Tina briefly, getting a bit of sweet scent off her shiny black hair, and brushed aside further thoughts of her, too.

Van explained that Altman was picked up after arriving at Hartsfield from Denver via New York. He didn't have the diamonds on him, but they were going to check out the possibility that he might have swallowed them in the time-honored tradition of jewel smuggling. Altman told the FBI he'd had a bad hit on the head, describing Van as the hitter, gaining from the FBI a little credibility, perhaps causing them to relax their guard.

He'd said he thought it was fractured and was for that reason feeling too disoriented to answer questions. He couldn't remember if he'd even known a girl named Abby. They'd sent him to the hospital for x-rays which showed he did have a cracked skull. Hairline fractures in the hairline, Ben thought, impatient for Van to be done with this part of the story.

But Van paused, and made a fist. He looked at it, slowly rotating it as if it weren't part of his body, but a thing to be valued for craftsmanship. He winked at Ben and continued. On the way from the hospital, to a federal holding facility, Altman disappeared. The Bureau expected to recapture him, but so far, no news.

Until Altman could be questioned, they'd have to wait for answers to the questions they'd struggled with. Where was Abby's body? What was O'Brien's role? Was Rambo, or Rachel, or whatever you called her, a player? Only a matter of time, Van said. Then added, "I don't give a rat's ass anymore. Hearing Cole on the phone . . . his voice? Thinking about the girl? I don't want to deal with any of it any more. How about a drink?"

And he dropped his feet soundlessly to the carpet, bending forward in his chair, taking a bottle of vodka out of his bottom drawer along with a couple of cups.

"Van," Ben said, "I have an idea."

Ideas gestate in warm internal juices, and they must like it there because they don't come out without some labor pains. Artistic types, and there should be no apology for including ad people here, know this. They know from nerve-bruising experience that the process takes an unpredictable course but, predictably, there will come a moment when they stop wrestling with their personal sloth. Not because sloth won or they won, but because the time has simply come to stop. Stop stalling, stop complaining, sleeping, drinking, looking out the window. The idea has formed, and now it is time to go to work.

Ben leaned forward and said, "Suppose Altman didn't kidnap Abby?"

He put his hand up, a stop sign, refusing the vodka, refusing the invitation to put feet up and relax, contradicting Van's implication that the case was closed, stopping Van from saying, you're fulla shit.

"You're fulla shit. Altman escaped!" Van's tone carried hostility as well as some disgust. As though he were annoyed that he'd treated a dumb kid with respect, let alone a small degree of friendship.

"Wait," Ben said, exerting power they each hadn't seen from him before. No longer the new guy out of his element, asking silly questions, getting drunk, drooling over Tina, clumsy with the simplest assignment. And Ben said it again.

"Just. Wait."

Then he told Van that he had come up with a new slant. It might mean Abby was alive, needing their help with no delay.

"The new slant," Van said, nodding, showing he'd remembered Cole using those words in the Alpine Center when he gave Ben the big build-up. Then he squinted at Ben, sighed, and said, "Tell me about the new slant." And he poured some vodka into one of the cups.

Ben wanted to tell Van about his *Unreal! Advertising Versus Reality* coffee table book idea. About waiters fussing over empty seats in a Beverly Hills Chinese restaurant for what had to be celebrities, not just a guy with bad hair and his family. But this would sound eccentric. He had no taste for the eccentric at the moment. Besides, Ben didn't care, now, if Van understood the genesis of his thinking. Just that he hear it. And buy it.

"Assume Altman only *said* he kidnapped Abby. To get the diamonds." Ben said.

"This is bull . . ."

"Assume Abby's not kidnapped!"

"You're wasting your time. Listen, my dentist called me and said you blew an appointment."

"Van. I worked it out last night."

A lot of it had worked itself out while Ben was dreaming on his belly, not so much asleep as out cold with exhaustion. But he didn't want to say that. He'd put the rest together after waking up. It hadn't taken long. The unconscious think tank had done most of the work.

"I wanted to see what would happen if I imagined that things weren't so melodramatic. See, I think kidnapping is a little melodramatic. Like something in a story, not real life."

"You haven't seen real life, I think."

"Please." And he held up his hand again. "Say Abby is out looking at the birds that they released. Maybe checking the sites. I don't know. Maybe listening for radio signals. Doing whatever they do out there."

Van took a sip and smacked his lips, smacked them loudly.

"Say she gets lost. It's easy to get lost in the mountains. I know."

"Bet you do," Van said, and smiled.

"Now. Van. You said yourself, *life is full of weird coincidences,* remember? I was thinking about how you said that, and you're right, okay?"

Van laughed. Ben continued.

"My coincidence is this: O'Brien's also in the mountains. Somehow, he knows that she's lost. Maybe they had walkie-talkies, and she told him. The kind of walkie-talkies that only carry for a mile or so. So she could reach him, but not people in the town." Ben paused, letting this sink in, hoping it was sinking in.

"Or maybe he saw her from a mountain. He could've been up on a ridge and seen her through his binoculars. The guy carried binoculars,

Van, they were on his body. These bird people are always scanning the hills. Never go anywhere without binoculars."

Van settled back into the chair, tilted, and put his feet up, getting interested.

"So maybe O'Brien goes to get help. He's not the one who's lost. He knows exactly where the cabin is. The cabin's got a radio-telephone. He uses it to call Altman and says something like . . . *Abby Cole needs help. She's in so and so valley* . . . I don't know. Then, because he ran to the cabin . . . it's high altitude, hard to breathe . . . and he's got this heart condition, you know, so he has chest pains. Takes out his pills, the little nitro tablets? The pain's bad, so he spills pills all over, see?"

"He tells Altman about the pain, too, right?" Van said, looking at the ceiling.

Ben sat down, feeling Van might be with him now. "Right! So maybe Altman drives to the cabin to get O'Brien and take him to the doctor. Here's an assumption I take the liberty of making, based on Altman disliking Abby as we know he did, okay? Altman comes to get O'Brien but doesn't tell anyone about Abby. He figures he'll first get O'Brien out. Then after Abby sweats it a little, he'll send in some help."

"But in the meantime, O'Brien, well . . . he dies, right? " Van said.

Van's participation in the scenario was encouraging, Ben thought.

"Right again! When Altman gets there, O'Brien's had the heart seizure or whatever and is dead. Now Altman is this real asshole, remember? Here's where he decides to commit a crime. Not kidnapping, Van. Extortion. A crime of opportunism."

Ben stood again, pacing as he talked.

"Altman thinks Abby's lost and will probably stay that way for a day or two. No one else, now that O'Brien's dead, knows she's lost. Altman realizes he could call the rich father, say she's kidnapped, and maybe get a ransom. *Without* kidnapping anyone. See?"

"Go on." Van was shaking his head. What did that mean?

"Van, the guy never has to hurt anyone. O'Brien died naturally. Abby'll be okay, he figures. It's summer and she's tough enough to live through a few nights in the mountains. If he times it right, he can get some ransom money before she walks out. I like it that nobody gets hurt. Even Cole's rich enough to not even miss the money he pays."

Van stopped Ben with his hand, then picked up the phone and pressed two buttons. "Aitch, Van. Come in here, will you?"

A minute passed, while Ben looked at Van and Van looked at the drink in his hand, swirling it, playing with it.

"It's the gunner," HJ said to Ben. Ben waved a quick hello, going with the momentum, not wanting to think about last night's basketball game. There'd be a temptation to relive those feelings out there on the court, and that would be distracting. He was working now. Doing what he'd come to do.

He said, "See, that's what so believable about this concept, this . . . idea. Altman doesn't really hurt anyone. He just gets some money."

"'Cause he's an albino and all?" Van said, looking at HJ.

"I'm not being funny, okay?" Ben said, some forcefulness there. Then, with a disarming shrug, "Well, it did get me to think along these lines."

"Why?" Van asked. "Just curious."

Ben didn't want to explain about the sheep in sheep's clothing quote he'd remembered from Churchill, the innocence of sheep. There was no logic to it. It had just set his mind in a direction that led to this scenario. Van wouldn't understand.

"What's going on?" HJ said.

Van said, "Just listen."

Ben ignored Van's question about the albino, ignored HJ, and went on.

"Maybe Altman puts O'Brien's body off in the trees, downhill, away from the cabin. The guy might not be a kidnapper, but he's still an asshole, right? Then he comes back, scoops up the pills O'Brien left on the table, leaving the sweep marks I saw in the dust, but he misses a few that are on the floor. Then he takes out the radio-telephone gear. He does this, see, in case Abby finds her way to the cabin. Now she can't call for help, so she'd have to spend another whole day walking out. Giving him time to get the ransom."

"Will you guys tell me what you're talking about?" HJ said.

Van briefed him on Ben's main points. Detectives have a way of doing that, Ben thought, feeling some respect for Van's ability to tick off everything Ben had said in four or five quick sentences. Just the facts, ma'am.

After Van finished, HJ said, "I'm not too sure about this." He looked at Ben apologetically, and kept looking, losing the apology as Ben met his gaze. Finally, he knit his eyebrows.

"Now," Ben went on. "*Doctor* Altman is smart enough to dream up the ransom arrangement. Maybe he has a trained falcon. Rachel told me O'Brien got Altman into falcons. So, he gets the diamonds. He comes to his office when we trip the alarm in the middle of the night. Doesn't call the cops, because he's feeling guilty and doesn't know what's happening at the break-in. Sees us. Assumes we're on to him. Decides to take the diamonds and run. But, he wants to take us out of it for a while. Maybe to give him time, I don't know. Maybe he's just pissed at us for messing into his stuff. Then he does run, right?"

Ben took a breath. This monologue hadn't made him tired as similar performances in rooms full of idea buyers had in the past. Instead, he'd become strengthened by it, feeling more powerful than when he'd started. Abby could be waiting in the hills. He knew it. They had to know it, too.

"The point is, Van, HJ, maybe Abby Cole is still out there. We've got to find her. This is what? Eight, nine days? She could be alive, but for how much longer?"

Van leaned forward.

"Now let me tell you why your new slant is bullshit. Entertaining bullshit. Brilliant bullshit. But bullshit." He looked toward HJ. "Want a pop, Aitch?" And he held a cup toward him.

"No, Van. Thanks." HJ was looking thoughtful.

Van said, "What's he forgetting, HJ?"

HJ sat back comfortably, elbows on armrests, bringing his large hands together, lacing the fingers, pointer fingers aiming straight up, pressed against his lips. It looked as if he were saying "Shhh" . . . with both hands at once.

Van took another sip of vodka, again smacking his lips, the only sound in a room now profoundly quiet with HJ simply sitting, thinking, not saying anything.

"Come on," Van said, loudly, a little incredulous laugh in his voice, playing the gruff guy with the kind side.

"See," HJ said softly, looking sidewise at Ben while talking to Van. "I'm not sure he *has* forgotten it, Van. I'm wondering if he knows something we don't."

Then he turned and faced Ben. "Ben, what do you know about the phone calls?"

Van leaned in and slapped a fat palm on the desk.

"The phone calls, kid. You say Abby's not kidnapped? Cole heard her on the phone. Twice!"

"Right," Ben said, nodding, impatient to get past this.

"There was always the chance, as we agreed in the meeting, that Cole might only have heard a tape of Abby's voice. We'd hoped it hadn't been the case, because that would have meant she'd been killed, you said. Then I found the tape in Altman's office, and we all figured, oh shit. But we played it, and it was just field notes. It didn't have ordinary words that could've been cut together to make the kinds of sentences Cole heard her say on the phone."

"Which means," Van said, "whether she was talking live on the phone or whether Cole heard a different tape—one Altman might've forced her to make for him under duress—she still had to have been kidnapped. She said 'I wanna come home.' 'I'm okay, Daddy . . .'" There was a cruel edge in his voice, and he was making his free hand into a fist, opening and closing it. Ben could imagine that fist busting Altman's head again, this time like a clay pot. In Van's other hand he held the vodka. He looked at it as though surprised. Then took a deep pull.

"But if Altman didn't have Abby . . . like I'm saying . . . then, of course, it rules out his using any tape she made for him under duress. He'd have to have taken her voice from a tape she made previously. And edit her words to make a few sentences he could convince Cole with. Remember—he'd told Cole he was holding the phone so Abby could talk from across the room. There was never a give and take conversation. Interesting, huh?"

"But," Van said, "the tape you found was all numbers and statistics and you, *we all*, agreed it would have been impossible for him to edit her words. Not in the time he'd have had since finding out she was lost." He looked at HJ. "If she had gotten lost."

Ben said, "I agree. He'd have needed pretty good editing equipment. It wouldn't have been possible. Not with *that* tape." He looked at Van. It would take plenty to break through the skepticism and vodka. "Van. Stick with my premise that Abby's never been kidnapped."

"There'd have to have been another tape," HJ said, "one that had regular words, easy to edit."

"Right!" Ben said, reaching into his pocket. But Levis aren't designed for easy access and he had to struggle to get his hand in and out, making them wait, and this seemed staged, a theatrical pause. No matter. The words on the folded paper still filled him with excitement.

A simple message, several lines hand printed by Ben on a hotel note pad. In places he'd drawn circles around words or parts of words.

"Took me three phone calls to get this down, word for word."

He held the paper, teasing them like he used to tease clients, doing his little preamble before unveiling storyboards, making them want to see what he had.

"I remembered that afternoon when Cole and Lara first heard Abby was—supposedly—kidnapped. Lara got the call and came out where Cole and I were having a few beers. She looked upset."

Ben paused, thinking of Lara in a bikini. Remembering the day she pulled the suit away, reaching in for the ice cubes. What a power to distract, that woman had. Even here . . .

"Damn you, Ben, what have you got there. Just show it for Chrissakes already!" Van. Loudly.

"Wait a second," Ben said. "Right after the call, first thing, Lara said she called Abby's apartment in Boulder. All she got was Abby's machine. See? There was a tape of Abby *there* saying regular words. I called it this morning. Her machine still works. Nobody shut it off. Funny, isn't it? Look what it says."

He laid the paper on Van's desk, flattening the folds, tilting it sideways so HJ could lean in and see it. Van would have to cock his head. Both came forward, reading quietly.

"It's the kind of message you'd expect from someone like Abby,"

Ben said. "Apologizing for having one of those machines. Informal. Kind of funny. In a loud, clear voice. This isn't like the tape I found. This is a piece of cake to cut. All you'd need is a razor blade and some splicing tape."

The message said: HI. I'M NOT ABBY . . . JUST ANOTHER DAMN MACHINE. NO BIG DEAL. LEAVE ME YOUR NAME AND NUMBER. ABBY'LL . . . COME HOME, AND I DO WANT TO TELL HER YOU CALLED. OKAY, NOW, AS THEY SAY, WAIT FOR THE BEEEEP . . .

Ben had drawn a circle around HI, I'M and OKAY. He'd circled WANT TO, and COME HOME. Also, the first two letters of DAMN, and the first two letters of DEAL. And the word DO, and the words, AS THEY SAY.

"Now, I'm not saying it happened exactly this way. But it could have. Altman could have recorded that tape over the phone. Made as many dupes as he wanted. Then cut them into little blurbs. 'Hi—I'm okay.' Or, 'I just want to come home!' Or, 'Please do as they say.' He could've even combined the first half of 'damn' with the first half of 'deal' to make 'Daddy.' It's surprisingly easy. I've done it myself for scratch tracks of commercials. 'Daddy, I just want to come home . . . '"

"Holy shit," HJ said.

"Horse shit," Van said.

Ben ignored him. Slowly, very low-key now, he said, "Altman calls Cole. Cole says 'let me talk to my daughter.' Altman says, 'I'll let her say something.' He holds up the phone. Altman says, 'Say hello to Daddy.' Cole hears a voice from across the room. Not into the phone, not real clear, but unmistakably Abby. 'Daddy, I want to come home.'"

Ben leaned over Van's desk. He looked into Van's eyes. "Altman would get the diamonds. Cole wouldn't get his daughter, though, because Altman doesn't have her."

*   *   *

Ad people call it kicking an idea around. Massaging it. Bouncing it off each other. Whatever detectives call it, they apparently do it, too. Ben called it bullshit. Finally, he'd had enough. Van said he certainly wouldn't want the Coles to hear a word of this because it would be cruel to give them false hopes based on an idea that was, (with a shrug and a smile to Ben) "Frankly . . . contrived, unsophisticated, inexperienced, based on hocus-pocus, unsubstantiated, fuckin' weird shit, etcetera and etcetera, meaning no particular disrespect, of course."

Ben admitted that it could very well be all those things, but he just had a feeling about it. Enough of a feeling to make him decide to leave the room, the agency, the building, the whole well-groomed city. Someone had to go out and get Abby.

"You guys just go on with your little debating society here," Ben had said. "I'll see you later. Abby must be getting a little impatient by now." And he left the room.

Tina watched him go past her office on the way to the front door, and cocked her head, throwing him a "what now" smirk. Ben reached over and gave her firm little shoulder a squeeze. "See you, Tina."

She waved at him, not with the whole hand, just her fingers lined up like little people, all bending at the waist, up down, up down. He wondered if he'd ever see her again and pushed through the door, on his way to the elevator. As he waited, he had the feeling that this sudden call to action, although seemingly of his own making, had put him in a position that could quickly become out of his control. He felt like a passenger bouncing inside a runaway stage again, no driver up there, horses pounding through wild new country, with him inside holding on, trying to enjoy the scenery, wondering, what next?

"You can't go off into the mountains just like that." A grainy Harry Belafonte voice. HJ had followed him to the elevator, and stood waiting with him now. "You don't know where the hell you are. Gonna get lost right off."

"If I do, you guys'll have a reason to send a search party, get the planes out."

In their meeting Ben had pleaded for Van to get some people out there looking for Abby. Van said there was no way it could be done. Not enough information to warrant it. Even if she was lost, he'd said, after nine days she would have walked out or was already dead.

The elevator doors opened. The car was empty. It looked like a bank vault with those thick mechanical doors. HJ stepped in first.

"Maybe I'll come along for the ride," he said.

Ben took this to mean the elevator ride, a ride that to him was almost never casually taken and could be made better by having company. But that couldn't be what HJ meant. He turned to the big guy, having to look up to see his face, not far from the flashing numbers that described their descent through the shaft.

"Coming with? To the mountains?"

"You'll need help," HJ said. "You have no idea where to start."

Not exactly, thought Ben. There was one thing he had neglected to tell Van and HJ. It was even more unsubstantiated and hunchy than the rest. And he didn't want the abuse. Besides, if they weren't buying the over-all theory, it made no difference. So he'd kept it to himself.

He didn't tell them he thought he knew exactly where Abby was.

# 41.

Somewhere in the Rockies, Abby Cole was accompanying Ute Sommers on what seemed to be an afternoon ritual of his. This was her third day in his company. On each of the previous afternoons, he'd stopped whatever he was doing when the sun got "under the eyebrows," as he'd put it, and hiked up the side of the mountain.

Today, Abby followed him, the hawk wheeling above in easygoing circles. It kept an eye on Abby during days, coming in to sleep near her at night, having breakfast with her every morning. Abby and Ute took the footpath that had been worn just enough to be visible, but not so overused as to expose bare ground like so many trails Abby had hiked near Colorado's resort towns.

She was wearing hand-made deerskin trousers he'd given her the first day, and a too-tight old white T-shirt that said HARVARD in maroon letters across her chest. Those letters, Ute said, had never looked better, and she didn't catch his meaning at first, still dazed from her days of solitude, until he winked. It was a friendly wink, and hell, he'd been watching her strut across the back country bare-assed, as he'd put it, the words giving her a little excitement somewhere deep down. He'd been not far away during all those days, leaving food for her, helping her stay alive. That gave him a right to kid about her tits a little, didn't it? Besides, he was really old, and hadn't seemed interested in anything physical. She'd just smiled and shook her head, as though saying *you men!*

Abby had become accustomed to walking naked through the day, smearing her skin at noon with wet clay to avoid sunburn, enjoying the free feeling, her breasts swaying comfortably, the wind moving cool around her thighs. The soles of her feet had grown some callous, and she was able to take the long, strong strides she preferred. After the fires started appearing for her with fresh food, and after she'd gotten the cougar skin for sleeping, she knew she'd survive. She'd begun to take pleasure in the wildness of the place, wearing only its clay, its dust and pine needles, its bugs, its smell.

Still, where Ute went these afternoons was cold, and she was glad for the clothing he'd given her. As she walked, she thought how it was kind of funny, being glad for clothing only because of the cold, and not even thinking about covering up in front of a man. The shirt was tight, especially under the arms, and she guessed it would be okay to take it off when they got back to the camp and the fire. Maybe get rid of the pants, too. They got sweaty after walking, and they chafed. For modesty she could simply use the big old poncho he'd given her on the first day in camp.

After climbing for an hour, the path curved and crested over a hill of stubby foliage and chunks of rock. The wind blew up here and had the taste of winter in it. The sun was lower now, coming right into their eyes as they walked toward it. The path sloped downward and curved around a bank of raw, gray stone revealing on its other side, a small sheltered meadow set amid rock wall on three sides, the fourth side open to the valley below.

The meadow was green with the short wiry grass of high country and had crusty snow dunes around the edges near the rock shadows. In the middle of the grassy area, seven bighorn sheep were resting on their bellies, legs folded, chests puffed out, calmly chewing. The sheep must have sensed Ute and Abby before they'd come around the rock because all heads were turned in their direction. Impassive gold eyes stared at Abby, unimpressed.

Three of the rams had heavy horns growing thickly out of their skulls, curling back and down behind their ears, then up and forward into a point. Full-curl males, Ute said. The others had smaller horns that only went halfway. Young guys, Abby thought. The teenagers.

Ute went to a place that he called "his spot," a ledge near the wall that was free of snow. It was in shadow now, but felt warm from having been in sun earlier. Abby sat next to him. Above, the hawk hung in the sky. Below lay the meadow, its small summer-time grouping of bachelor bighorns, and past them, the cliff's edge beyond which they could see green forest in the valley.

Above the forest, on the neighboring mountain there was rock and stunted vegetation, then above it, snow all the way to the jagged crests. There, resting on the skyline now, was the sun, getting ready to drop behind the mountain. Clouds lay full and round up there, and the sun moved behind them, poking straight shafts of light through random openings. The sun wouldn't redden and soften until it got near the flatland horizon, which was something else altogether. Up here, it was white-yellow still, and when it finally dropped behind the mountain, shadows quickly darkened the meadow, yet the sky remained surprisingly blue.

"They saved my life once, those sheep," Ute said quietly, almost a whisper. "Was in a blizzard up here. Stupid of me. It was too early for blizzards, I thought. I was wrong. But the sheep, they were still here. Hadn't left for the valleys and the females yet."

Abby watched the last bit of sun drop down, its light shining on the wide horns of the resting rams. Shadow crept across the grass now, and Ute told her how he'd had to nestle in there with the rams to stay warm in the blowing snow that day. "So much snow all you'd see was white in front of you," he'd said. The rams let him lie right in there with them, between them, getting their warmth. "Their wool smelled like wind," he'd said, "and sweet tobacco, for some reason."

# 42.

In the garage, HJ asked to see Ben's gear. It was still in the back of the Jeep that Van had let him use.

"I'm no camper," HJ said, "But I did do a survival course once. Mountain survival. Almost killed me. They made us read case histories, too. Of lost guys? Ever do that?" And he looked up from the boxes he'd been sorting through. "You know, to see what they did wrong? Why they died?"

This was the first time Ben had slowed down since he'd made his pitch upstairs. He leaned against the side of the Jeep while HJ bent over the tailgate, poking around in there, and the reality of the situation caught up with him. It was as though he'd been pulling it behind him and, when he stopped, it kept coming, heavy enough to plow into him with some force.

A tactical-sized anxiety attack started in his stomach and mushroomed upward, gray and puffy like every ugly mushroom rising out of the musty places that fungi favor. It bloomed through him, dimming the garage's dim lights, causing HJ's voice to sound far away. Ben had lived through such A-tests before and hung on, determined to out-muscle the bastard, knowing it would pass. And it did, but as always the fallout was unhealthy, and he'd found himself now not so confident, thinking, *what the hell am I doing*?

"Hey, HJ?"

"What?"

"Any beer back there? Or whiskey? I think we gotta get some, HJ."

*       *       *

It was near midnight when they pulled into the gravel parking lot of Steve & Marie's Fisherman Lodge on the outskirts of Stretch, Colorado, Pop. 1250, Elev. 6975. Ben saw the numbers as a kind of score, and thought, these hicks are getting their asses whipped.

They got two cabins and asked the owner if it wasn't too late for some food. Steve was a friendly bald guy with poppy eyes and a brushy mustache that was too big for his face. He looked pained. "The grill's closed for the night." Then the mustache smiled. "Bar's still open. Guess I can find ya's some cold sandwiches. How's that?"

The stuffed deer heads on the wall behind the Fisherman's Bar had a wide-eyed look that Ben found tantalizingly familiar. Then Steve came in, wiping his hands on a towel, and Ben realized they looked like him, permanently startled. Steve opened two longneck Coors and set them on the bar in front of HJ and Ben. Foamy strands of beer ran down the sides of the cold bottles, puddling on the bar. A friendly sight.

"Guys gonna do some fishin'?"

HJ took a pull on the bottle. He looked at Ben for a moment, then back to Steve.

"Little hunting."

Steve's eyes widened. Not a pretty sight. He glanced at two men sitting at the far end of the bar, the only other patrons. Rough-looking locals. Big men in overalls and peaked caps, the universal uniform of country boys. Their hands were big and fleshy, with dirt ingrained around their nails. The two looked past Ben, rather pointedly at HJ, and their faces didn't offer much in the way of rural hospitality. Ben turned away, not wanting to encourage a staring contest, a particularly inane expression of misguided machismo, which he'd known since high school could preclude senseless violence between strangers. HJ didn't seem to notice.

Steve looked at HJ now. "Come on," he said. "Ain't season. You boys know that."

"Hunting goose," HJ said. "Wild goose."

Steve wasn't about to understand, and HJ wasn't saying more. Ben felt compelled to break the silence, defuse the cryptic mood with a little friendly talk and a smile.

"Hey, he's just kiddin'. We're going fishing. Heard it's great up here. We'll be horse packing out of Archie's. Know the place?"

Archie's Wilderness Outfitters arranged horse pack trips, and HJ had called earlier to make a reservation for tomorrow. HJ calmly turned and smiled at the two men now, then motioned to Steve.

"Man, did you say something about sandwiches?"

Ben had to admit, HJ was cool.

Two homemade ham and cheeses, two more longnecks, and Ben was feeling pretty good. Just about ready to call it a day. Lots to do tomorrow.

On the ride up to Stretch, Ben told HJ why he thought he might know Abby's exact location. His personal bombshell. Either a dud or the real thing. He had a feeling it was no dud, and the more he thought about it, the more confident he became.

"I saw something in the PRP office when Van and I went there. Actually you're the reason I noticed it, because of something you'd said. This was right before I found the tape, before the attack by Altman. After the fight and all the excitement, I'd forgotten about it. Didn't seem like it could be important anyway."

Ben was driving. HJ had his feet up on the windscreen, his long arms circled around his knees. They were the only car on the winding two-lane. It was dark and clear. The heater was working. The moment was peaceful, and HJ was doing what good listeners do. Nothing.

"So," Ben said, "last night I had this dream? Very psychedelic. I'd missed a night's sleep the night before. Then we'd shot baskets. And I'd gone out with Tina . . ."

"She'll make a guy tired," HJ said in a whispery calypso rhythm.

Ben had a flash of Tina there on the couch. Hard little breasts. Tan all over, she was. Surprisingly easy-going about everything. Ben felt himself getting excited and wriggled in the bucket seat. HJ laughed.

"What'd you dream about, Ben?"

"Abby was making these marks on a white chair with a green felt-tip pen. They were in this straight line?"

HJ just stared at the road, resting his head back on the seat now. And Ben was struck by the real reason HJ had come with him. Van sent him. They must have talked about it right after Ben had walked out, while he was saying goodbye to Tina. It didn't take long. They both knew they couldn't let this ad guy from Chicago go into the mountains alone. Besides, what about the outside chance he was right? So HJ was going through the motions. Van's babysitter was keeping an eye on things. I have, Ben thought, no problem with that.

"Wait. I know it sounds strange. But it won't in a minute," Ben said.

"What I saw in the PRP office that night was a satellite tracking map, the kind you told me to look for? It was the U.S. Army "Topo" sheet for Eagle's Nest Wilderness Area and Gore Range. And there were these marks on it. Green dots."

Ben said the colored dots, as HJ had expected, did represent daily locations of each of several peregrine falcons being tracked by radio. HJ nodded, showing some interest.

"The dots came in other colors, too. Different colors clustered together, which you'd expect from territorial predators. I was interested because birds have always been kind of a hobby. There was something strange about those green dots, though. The most recent six or seven were in a straight line."

"Like in your dream."

"I stood in front of the map wondering about it. Maybe the bird was following a river. The map said STRETCH CANYON where the dots were. I thought maybe it was just a real straight valley, but that didn't seem natural. Then I thought, come on, Van's working in one of the offices, I ought to look in the other. I found the tape. Then Altman came and I forgot about the map."

"Why's the girl in Stretch Canyon, now?" HJ looked at the yellow line in front of them. But he sounded interested.

"Okay. The bird whose signal was indicated by green dots, Milty was its name I think, was accustomed to being fed by humans. Those people up there go to great pains to avoid having young birds imprint on them, but it happens. Say Abby Cole is walking around lost, and this bird sees her. *Mama! Food!* So it flies to her. It follows her. Now, Abby's doing what a lost person would do. Walking in a straight line, figuring eventually she'll come to a highway or something. The bird tags along. Its transmitter is still sending and being picked up at regular intervals, showing an unnatural pattern, a human pattern. The straight line. That's how we find Abby."

"Assuming Altman never kidnapped her."

"Yeah," Ben said with some strength there.

HJ looked away from the road now, looked at Ben with that same thoughtful expression he'd had in Van's office. He didn't say anything. Ben took this as a compliment.

They'd agreed to save time by going straight to the Stretch Canyon country instead of Halfway to see the PRP map again. Ben had a good memory of where the dots were, having paid closer than usual attention to the map's markings, thinking he'd never have felt so miserably lost back there by O'Brien's body if he'd known how to read one of these charts.

The dots had extended from the top of the S in STRETCH CANYON to a little cross symbol with the words, GAUGING STATION, whatever that meant. At first, he'd read it as GAGGING STATION and had pictured himself lost and puking over O'Brien's reeking remains.

They figured if they could just get a look at this map they'd know where to go. There was only one U.S. Geological Survey Topographic map of the area, and they'd pick up a copy at Archie's Outfitters. Even if they'd gone to Halfway to check the dots again, chances are no new ones would have been added, with Altman as well as O'Brien gone, and the PRP probably in chaos. They'd follow the pattern as Ben remembered it.

So they headed for the town of Stretch. HJ had called Archie's to reserve a guide, two saddle horses and a pack horse. The place was run by a man HJ said he knew from his FBI days. It was only ten miles from town, virtually at Stretch Canyon's doorstep. They didn't have the time or the inclination to go after Abby on foot, and the Jeep couldn't go into the Canyon.

Tomorrow, they'd mount up and maybe rescue the girl.

After the beer and sandwiches, on the way back to their cabins, they passed a dirt track that went into the trees. Ben paid it no attention, but HJ stopped, sniffing the air, and looked down it into the darkness.

"Those two guys. Bet they're in there. I thought I saw a light. And I smell 'em."

"They looked a little rank, but . . ."

"I smell their pick-up. I think they turned in here."

"You sure you were just an office guy at the FBI, HJ?" Ben said, moving away from the dark intersection, hoping HJ would follow.

"Now, I got a theory of my own for you. Not about kidnapped girls. Somethin' else," HJ said.

It was cold. Totally dark except for some weak porch lights on the cabins up ahead. No moon, but the mountain sky was heavy with cold, pinpoints of stars. Ben wanted to get to his cabin, get warm, get some sleep.

"We made those guys nervous, mentioned hunting, you notice?"

"I don't know . . ."

"I don't look like a local. Or a trout fisherman, really. Know what I look like? Law. Maybe a federal game warden."

"So?"

"I'm guessing they're poachers. Steve knew. He 'bout popped an eyeball onto the bar when we talked about going hunting."

HJ said these backcountry lodges usually had outbuildings where hunters, in season, hang and clean game. He said he thought such a building must be up that dirt track and those two guys, with Steve's help, had some illegal kills they were working on right now.

"Probably give Steve a couple hundred pounds of meat for the freezer. They'll sell the horns, claws, whatever. Big black market for bears' gall bladders. You believe that? They can get $600 for one. To these rednecks, that's real money."

"We got a lot to do tomorrow . . ."

"They'll be gone by then. Besides, there was something in their attitude. Y'know what I'm sayin'?"

"Leave it alone, HJ. Or tell somebody. Phone somebody. I don't know."

HJ shrugged and followed Ben to their cabins where they said goodnight. Ben was in his small, saggy bed listening to a mouse—he assumed it was a mouse—scuttle around the floorboards, not at all tired, wired somewhat from three beers at 6975 feet, when he heard HJ's cabin door shut with a quiet click. Too quiet, that click.

Ben got up and pulled the curtains open. He saw HJ's lanky body disappear in the shadows, up the dirt track they'd seen. Two separate and powerful feelings struck him. First he felt alone, and it wasn't comfortable. After all, where the hell was he? Second, he felt he'd have to do what HJ had done for him: Follow. Watch your buddy's back. See that he comes out okay.

He pulled on jeans and boots. Put on a baseball cap, down vest, and grabbed a flashlight from the duffel which, thinking as a city boy thinks, he'd brought into the cabin, not trusting it to stay overnight in the unlockable ragtop Jeep. He left the cabin and started after HJ.

The night was colder now. Clouds had blown under the stars, making the darkness even darker. He stopped, overcome by something akin to the familiar anxieties he'd grown to accept, but this had a new flavor. Fear. An honest emotion. Healthy, un-neurotic but nonetheless uncomfortable. He remembered the loaded revolver, holstered and wrapped in its belt, the black leather smelling of the cowboy toys of childhood.

He hurried back, found the gun, and strapped it around his waist under the vest. On the way out he let the door slam behind him, not caring about the noise. He jogged up the road HJ had taken, the gun patting him on the butt, encouraging him.

# 43.

Ben's flashlight, which had shone itself admirably in the contained darkness of the line cabin a few nights ago, was overwhelmed now by the black night all around him, and its beam looked thin, diluted. To divert his understandable fear out here, Ben played around with the scientific ramifications of light actually having weight as he'd read somewhere, imagining some light to splash out like rich German beer, and other light to flow in puny streams, like the watered down lite and diet beers of America, these all protesting-too-much in their jock macho TV spots. Heavy light. Light light. Lite light for today's litestyle . . .

This ruminating did the job, taking his mind off the fear so he could hurry up the path to the shed that HJ had said might be there, and was. Ben pressed the soundless rubber switch, turning off the flashlight, and stood in the shadows. The shed was a wood frame structure with a peaked metal roof. It was lit up from inside, and light spilled out through an open window so Ben no longer needed to bring his own.

The taller of the two men they'd seen in the bar was going backwards around the side of the shed, as though he were returning to the open door after circling the place. He moved on his toes, not so much walking as stalking. He looked from side to side and carried a rifle in the attack position, barrel pointed straight out, hand firmly on the trigger. When reaching the door, he relaxed his posture and went in, letting the door swing shut behind him without clicking.

Ben stood like a forest animal, ears cocked and straining, eyes wide, catching everything. Even his nostrils moved, searching the air. The night smelled of pine and frost. A tang of gasoline. He wasn't thinking, for a change. Or planning. It was as though he'd handed over the controls to some new side of him, some battle-wise, gap-toothed veteran squinting there in the trees, ready for action. In the quiet, it was easy to hear the tall man's words as he entered the shed.

"No sign of nobody. Fucker's alone like he said."

Ben processed this non-verbally, easily. HJ was in trouble. Ex-FBI or not, and big as he was, HJ was still an office-lifer. He'd underestimated the situation, allowing himself to get caught and was now being held by armed men who were guilty of something, probably of poaching. HJ must have told them he was alone, but they'd checked to make sure.

Once again, timing . . . Ben had always heard it meant everything in sports, the stock market, sex, cooking, comedy . . . had indeed meant everything. If he'd come up to the shed a moment earlier, flashlight waving, he'd have been seen and captured as HJ must have been. He might even have been shot. A moment later and he'd have missed seeing the armed man's reconnaissance, and probably would have blundered into the cabin unaware of the danger.

He stood in the dark. Afraid, but not as afraid as he might have been. Just the other night, hadn't he gone *mano a mano* with some guy the FBI itself had hunted and was again hunting? Violent detective work was like anything else. You got experience, it got easier. Okay, he figured, now: Options. One, get to a phone and call for help. But the only phone was in Steve's office. Steve could be buddies with the poachers. Other option. Go in and get HJ out.

And do it personally.

Ben, .357 in one hand, door handle in the other, felt his eyebrows flick. A little facial shrug. If he were using words, they'd have been, *Here goes nothing*... But he was running on nonverbal automatic now, letting instinct tell him what to do, actually enjoying the feeling, probably brought on by much recent disorientation, capped by their arrival in this dark wilderness with its unexpected dangers.

His adman, city-kid, divorced yuppie, neurotic dreamer identity was becoming ill-defined, leaving him feeling disconnected and strangely full of possibilities, as he'd briefly felt in the early seventies listening to The Doors, nodding with the music, *The time to hesitate is through*...

He crashed through the door, gun out, waving wildly. He surprised everyone—dead bears, dead eagles, live poachers and HJ (but no one was more surprised than Ben, himself) by yelling a hoarse and wild, "Police! Freeze, Motherfuckers!"

Some underground voyeuristic part of him howled at this, knowing it was big-city, even cliched ghetto-style talk, and not for the Rocky Mountains, where something like "Reach, ya' shit-heads!" would've been appropriate. No time for recriminations. Moving on fast-forward now. And Ben fired the pistol into the ceiling.

A .357 fired in a small, enclosed room doesn't go bang or boom. It goes something like BLAAAAM! And white fire blooms out, a sulfurous flashbulb, freezing the scene. The noise vibrates under the chest bone, drop-kicking heart through lungs. It stings the ears, making them seep red blood hours later. It scares the shit out of people.

HJ was standing in a corner staring at him, all eyes, a lampoon of their host, the goggly Steve. The taller of the two men had just been setting his rifle against the wall. He jumped at Ben's shocking entry, and the rifle clattered on the shed's cement floor. The other man also jumped, unfortunately for HJ, as this guy was holding a fearsome weapon on him.

Ben's first blurry impression was of a spear gun, like one he'd once seen in Jamaica, an ugly arrangement of pulled elastic and barbed points. Poachers don't spear fish. Couldn't be that. *But a crossbow!* And in the frozen moment when Ben correctly identified the thing, the crossbow, as though wanting to show that he was right, giving him a little demonstration, went off. This, probably because the poacher's trigger finger jerked unintentionally at Ben's shot.

HJ must have known it would happen. He spun, turning his back to the arrow, moving to the side, an honest reflex, a childhood snowball fight stratagem. The arrow disappeared from the crossbow, invisible in flight. It missed HJ's target parts, heart, stomach, Adam's apple, gut. But pierced the side of his buttock, entering at the outside seam of his back pocket, exiting at the other seam, feathers and all. Not slowed by denim or muscle, it zipped invisibly on, burying itself with a thwack into the wallboards.

"Ow!" HJ screamed.

"Jay-sus!" screamed the man with the empty crossbow. Anger, shock and frustration, all there in a word. And there was a whiny edge to it, suggesting that some of this was directed to himself, that he probably hadn't meant to fire, that once again in his life he'd screwed up.

"Don't shoot," screamed the taller poacher.

HJ, holding his butt, fell to his knees, face pinched in pain. The other two stood unmoving, staring at Ben. He didn't know what to do next. Instinct said he'd gotten the drop on these guys through dumb luck, and—again—timing being everything, he could quickly lose control unless he took some decisive action. No time to think. Act. He fired the gun into the ceiling again.

BLAAAAM!

Everybody jumped. He fired it again. (This was kind of fun.)

BLAAAAM!

While Ben was aiming this last shot into the ceiling, the taller man spun and ran out the front door holding his ears. Ben turned and saw the crossbow bouncing on the cement where the other man had been. It made no noise over the ringing and stinging of the .357. The man who'd been holding it was half out the shed's open window, stuck with his knees on a sink that was mounted against the wall there. Then he popped through the window and disappeared. Both had run away. A sensible thing for them to do, Ben felt.

The upshot was that HJ had been shot in the ass. The old-fashioned way, by an arrow. He wouldn't be going anywhere on horseback for a while. It was a surprisingly clean wound, patched up at two in the morning by a pretty ski bum who made her winter money by nursing during the summer at an all-night clinic the state cops took them to.

She'd used a scalpel to connect entry and exit punctures, the channel being close to the skin, so she could clean the wound and allow it to heal evenly. She gave the anesthetized cheek twenty stitches, looking housewifely with needle and thread. HJ had commented on this, and she told him with a friendly pat that she wanted to see it again in a couple of days.

The cops had confiscated the shed's five bald eagle carcasses, two of which were brown immatures, lacking the white head feathers of their elders whom, Ben thought, had reason to grow white with age under such worrisome circumstances. One of the troopers, a tobacco-chewer with a Wyatt Earp style pistol swinging halfway down his thigh, a guy whom Ben thought must surely be a seasonal murderer of elk, deer, moose, bear, grouse and dove, was outraged by the eagles.

"These sons of bitches sell the feathers and claws. There's people make Indian souvenirs out of them. Anything for a dollar, huh?"

They'd also found three black bears who'd been gutted for their black market gallbladders. The troopers put the dead animals in tarps and loaded them into their four-wheel pickup, an unlikely police vehicle in other parts, but right at home in the mountains with its mount of flashing lights and police decal on the door. They didn't expect to find the poachers, and innkeeper Steve wasn't much help, claiming to know nothing about them. He did have some dressed game in the freezer, but said he'd taken it last fall, legally, and had his hunting license to prove it.

The cops hadn't been much concerned about Ben's gunplay, other than to say it was generous of him to have aimed only at the ceiling. No talk of gun permits or registration. By four, their business was wrapped up as neatly as HJ's wound.

# 44.

At one time, Archie's might have been called a dude ranch. To Ben, "dude" had always carried an unattractive image. Who'd want to be known as a dude? It wasn't surprising to him that these places now called themselves guest ranches, horse packers or outfitters. Better to go horse packing on your vacation than duding.

Archie's had a ranch-style arch over the unpaved road leading up to it, made of lodge pole pines hammered together crudely enough to pass for the genuine article. This was cowboy country. The crossbar of the arch held a wood plank by two chains, and the plank had a big "A" painted on it in the typeface known as P.T. Barnum. Good execution, Ben thought.

It was not even nine in the morning, and the road was already crowded. Their Jeep was eating the dust of at least two other vehicles, one a four-door Caddy with an Avis bumper sticker, and the other a road-worn RV with New Jersey plates and a big rear window through which three kids and a dog could be seen. The rutted powder made slow going, but bumps were unavoidable and with each one HJ tensed. He was sitting tilted over on a pillow, taking his weight on one hip, worrying not about the pain, he said, but about popping a stitch. The speedometer bounced between 0 and 5. Slow going.

Ben had awakened that morning feeling something was missing, or maybe he'd forgotten something. No jitters, that was it. After all that had happened, the Ben he knew should be rooting around in the baggage for Valium. He'd fired a gun last night. He'd seen those grotesque dead animals. HJ had an arrow wound! And he was in strange country, to boot, about to head into stranger country. Worse, he'd now have to make the ride alone since HJ could barely sit on a car seat, let alone a saddle.

Ben had lain in bed, casting around in his psyche for some complaint like a man checking himself for broken bones after an accident. Nothing. No whining "*Who am I?*" or "*How did I get here?*" He was about to start worrying about this when he shook loose the thought and jumped out of bed. If he was going to start worrying about not worrying, he must be okay.

HJ had insisted on coming along. Although Ben went through the motions, telling HJ to rest up and not subject his butt to the bouncing Jeep, he was pleased to have the company. On the way, HJ said again that he'd known Archie years ago when they were both FBI agents, and Archie was known by his full name, Coladarcci. He'd retired early, shortened the name to its less intimidating and anglicized last half, and opened the horse-packing ranch. It was Archie who'd hosted the survival course HJ said he'd been on when they were loading the Jeep yesterday.

*   *   *

Ben leaned against the corral while HJ looked around for his old acquaintance. The air was still sharply cold, and breath came out of people and horses like steam. The place smelled of pine, coffee and animals. You could bottle that smell, Ben thought. A million dollar idea for a room freshener. Call it *Ponderosa*. Stop, he thought, and kicked the ground. Got to get that ad thinking out of me.

"Harrison, you walk like you gotta stick up yer ass!" bellowed a red-faced man in a white beard, pointy boots and a black derby. He looked like a Western character who wasn't trying to look like one. The best kind. Ben had always wondered why there was always some fool in every cowboy movie standing apart from the action wearing a derby. But real pictures of those times, as seen in museums and books, often do show these ugly round hats on ugly round men needing shaves, standing ankle-deep in mud.

HJ said something Ben didn't catch and Archie laughed, a thin staccato noise, the noise a horse makes, an appropriate noise for a corral. HJ waved Ben toward them and made the introductions. Archie shook Ben's hand, holding it firmly in his callused grip, and wouldn't release it. He looked at Ben, shaking his head side to side as he talked.

"Now listen. You're expectin' a guide to go out with you, I know. But today, I just ain't got any. I'm sorry."

He turned his head to face HJ, but still held Ben's hand, making Ben feel uneasy standing there like that.

"Harrison, I'm sorry. Two guys quit on me. And we're full up with tourists today."

HJ just shrugged. "You still got the horses, though, right?"

"I got one good one I saved, and one not so good."

"Ben'll take the good one. We won't need the other."

Ben pulled his hand free. His throat suddenly felt dry. He needed to swallow.

"Be needin' him overnight, like you said?"

"Could be a couple of nights, Arch."

"No problem, Harrison," Archie winked at Ben, then led HJ toward a log house that had a sign over the front door that read "Office."

"We'll just go do the paperwork, and he'll be ready to move out any time."

They left Ben standing there in the cold.

Moments later, Ben found himself leading a horse, holding the reins delicately, not wishing to offend. He guided this towering animal toward the Jeep where he'd agreed to meet HJ before riding into the Wilderness Area's well-mapped canyons and his own private future, which he knew now, more than ever, was a coy thing and stubbornly un-mapped.

He walked, and the horse clip-clopped past the log office building, around the ranch's central plaza with its picnic tables empty and wet with morning dew, tilting on pebbled ground under a canopied structure that looked to Ben like a carport without a driveway.

They passed a stone barbecue pit with a heavy, blackened gridiron over a smoking fire of snapping and fragrant pine logs. There was a leathery old woman there, holding a skillet full of sizzling eggs afloat in fat. Next to the skillet stood a cauldron of bubbling beans showing bits of red pepper and curls of onion. Black-chinned hummingbirds shot back and forth overhead, making little whirring noises.

Archie had said the horse was a "strawberry roan," and he'd named him, with common sense respect for the obvious, Ben thought, "Strawberry." There'd been a brief lesson back there in saddle strapping, bit fitting and bridling, since Ben would be doing these things alone next time, after overnighting in back country.

This was a frightening proposition, and he didn't want to picture it happening just yet. Maybe he'd miraculously find Abby waiting on the trail an hour's ride from the ranch. Such an outcome was probably no more unrealistic than the idea that she might be out there at all, un-kidnapped. Still, he'd watched how the buckles buckled and what went where.

Archie had slipped Ben an apple as Strawberry drifted off to the side, snuffling a tin plate that had earlier held oats. He whispered, "Pat the horse nice 'n feed 'm this when you two're off by yourselves. Make yourself a good friend, son."

He then startled Ben silly by screaming, "Heeyah! Git over here, Strawberry!"

This was so explosive and unexpected that Ben jumped visibly, making him feel foolish in front of both Archie and the horse. Strawberry trotted to them, head back, ears cocked, eyes bright and if horses could smile, as dogs do, this one would be smiling. Archie grabbed the dangling reins and handed them to Ben. He then turned and clomped off, bow-legged and wobbly in his high heels, leaving Ben alone with Strawberry.

Ben held the apple out but dropped it when the horse came for it, lips back, huge yellow teeth bared. "Sorry," Ben said.

\* \* \*

At the Jeep, HJ was throwing back the last of his coffee from a big mug he must've gotten when he'd gone inside to work on the paperwork. Ben was leaning against the fender now, quiet, moving the dusty ground around with the toe of his boot.

He had Strawberry's reins tied around the rear bumper, and the horse was zoned out, perfectly horse-like, just waiting, doing nothing. HJ set the empty cup on the Jeep's flat canvas roof and reached inside for the silver suitcase he'd thrown in before they left Denver yesterday. He hoisted it onto the hood, unlatching it, swinging the top open.

"Well, here comes my 'M' routine."

Ben didn't understand. "What routine?"

"Know the guy in the James Bond movies? 'M?' Guy who gives Bond a whole bunch of goodies to play with? Exploding pens, two-way cufflink telephones?"

"It's 'Q,'" Ben said, not enjoying the allusion as much as he might have if they'd been in Istanbul or Moscow.

He noticed a hawk riding the first morning thermal winds, high above the ranch. Strawberry shuddered a patch of neck skin and whisked his tail. The sun was warming. The parking area smelled of manure, American cars, dust. No place for James Bond. Jesse James, maybe.

"What do you mean, 'Q?'" HJ said over his shoulder, not really caring, working on the gear in the suitcase, getting it ready.

"Not important. What've you got there?"

HJ ripped open a plastic-wrapped pack of batteries and loaded them like bullets into something Ben hadn't seen before.

"Wasn't 'M' the guy?" HJ said as he worked.

"That was the head guy. 'Q' was the guy who made the wild weapons. Guy with a mustache? Big British accent?"

"Not important, Ben." As though Ben had thought it was in the first place. Was this to make Ben feel glad to be rid of HJ, instead of abandoned?

"Now listen," HJ said. "Pay attention because *this* is important."

HJ removed what looked like a Walkman radio from the suitcase. He held out a lightweight set of earphones at arm's length for Ben to see, then plugged them in, exaggerating the move, making a demonstration of it. Ben nodded. He understood the principle.

"A tracking device. Picks up your bird signals. If you're right, and the bird's transmitting, this could help you find it."

He pointed to a concave dish-like depression in the center of the little device. "Aim this in the direction the strongest signal is coming from. It'll sound like a beep, I think. Trouble is, I can't set the frequency for you. We don't know it. So just move this dial . . ." and he held up the device while twisting a little knob back and forth, ". . . and you'll go through the band that animal trackers normally use. Might get lucky, who knows."

The lesson went on. HJ's 'M' routine. Strawberry stamped and shook more often. Ben began to sweat. HJ gave Ben the topographic map of the area. There was a trailhead near Archie's that went into Stretch Canyon, and they traced it on the map with yellow liner pen.

They did the checklist: Compass, flashlight, matches, lighter, canteen with fresh water, water purification tablets for creek water refills, saucepan, freeze-dried meals for a week, chocolate in the melt-retardant form of M&M's—several half-pound bags, crinkly, looking good anywhere, anytime—a newly obtained sweet fifth of Jack Daniel's Tennessee Sippin' Whiskey (black label), small hatchet, jackknife, the .357, reloaded after last night's excitement, two boxes of cartridges, rain poncho, a bedroll that fit behind the saddle, down vest, heavy turtleneck, and two capacious saddlebags to hold everything except the bedroll.

"Saved this for last," HJ said. "I designed this myself to make it light. And very small . . ."

He brought out a red plastic box the size of a paperback book. Ben, distracted and antsy now, flashed on the fact that he probably should, in fact, also take along a paperback to read, something to do when not searching.

"Ben? You with me?"

"Sorry. What is this, Aitch?"

"An 'ERB.' Same thing planes and ships use worldwide. 'Emergency Rescue Beacon.'" He pointed to an on-off switch on the top of the device. "Flick this, and you'll send out a signal that will be picked up by any commercial airplane flying over. They'll radio that someone's in distress, even give your exact coordinates. A helicopter'll be over you in hours, maybe less."

An escape hatch, Ben thought. Next best thing to a horsephone. He wouldn't be that alone out there after all.

"Batteries will only work for about ten hours. Use it if you have an emergency. Or, if you find the girl and need to get help. If you can walk out on a trail, don't use the ERB. Okay?" HJ pronounced it *"urb."*

"This is great. Thanks, man."

Ben held the ERB, admiring its compactness, its kindness.

"Thing is," HJ said, "In a few years I think people will carry phones, little phones that'll work on a system of cells, relaying calls . . . ."

"Communicators."

"Huh?"

"Star Trek, Aitch."

"Yeah, well, anyway. While you pack everything away, I'll go call Van one more time, make sure this is still necessary. Maybe they got Altman. Who knows. Maybe there's no reason to look . . ."

He let the thought trail off and walked stiffly across the parking area toward the office.

Ben found that "packing everything away" wasn't as easy as it sounded, but eventually got his gear in decent enough shape to get on the trail. By that time, HJ was back with the news that there was no news.

Van had said Altman was still on the loose. No trace of Abby. The medical examiner said O'Brien died of natural causes. Bad heart, no foul play. The FBI had finally gotten into the hills and found Rambo. They'd brought her down for a polygraph, which she passed, and they didn't think she was involved in any of it. Ben felt a momentary flush of annoyance at the thought of her strapped to a machine. Van was sticking to his original vision of the case. Real kidnapping. Real dead victim. But he was still somewhat amused by Ben's "new slant shit," as he'd put it, and told HJ to wish Ben luck.

Archie arranged for HJ to stay in the wranglers' quarters until Ben came back. It would give him some time to heal the first arrow wound they'd had in those parts for far too long, he'd said. They all figured that Ben Green, green as he might be in the mountains, could follow a 'topo" map and even if he couldn't, the horse would come back if given its head.

HJ was standing uncomfortably, shifting his weight from leg to leg, the arrow wound obviously paining him, as he watched Ben swing the fully packed saddlebags over Strawberry's back. They were both trying to figure out how to buckle them under the rear of the saddle when Archie came over.

"Got something for you, Ben. Comes with the horse," Archie said.

He had a beat-up, once-white, now dirt-gray cowboy hat in his hand. It had an enormous brim, curled up at the sides, down tilted in front and back.

"Gotta keep the sun outta your face. Rain outta your shirt back there." And he spun the hat to Ben like a Frisbee, then quickly adjusted the saddlebags and hitched them tight.

The old hat was soft around the crown but strong enough to want to hold its shape. Ben popped it on. Might have been a bit too large for him, but his hair had recently grown even longer and fuller than usual, making up the difference in hat size. He tapped it into place and it rested perfectly above his ears. He enjoyed the shade it threw on his face, now no longer needing to squint in the hard morning sun.

"Thank you, sir," he said solemnly to Archie. "Appreciate it." Sounding like something a guy in a ten-gallon hat might say. Archie and HJ laughed.

"Better get going," HJ said. "Follow the map. You won't have any problems. Happy trails, Ben."

"Happy trails, HJ," Ben replied mindlessly, his thoughts already somewhere up in the hills. Time for this adman to mount up and ride.

# 45.

Ben had stretched the truth a little, an occupational habit, perhaps, by letting Archie assume he was an experienced rider. Truth was, he'd ridden as a kid, but only on dispirited day camp horses, dragging their tired butts along the level bridle paths of suburban Chicago, occasionally trotting during the return trip when the stable was in smelling distance, and almost never galloping. *Cantering,* the more experienced called it, but Ben could never distinguish the difference between this word and true galloping.

Strawberry was different, moving with the responsiveness of a sports car. The horse seemed to dislike trotting as much as any sensible rider does, and had just two speeds. Walk or gallop. With the merest touch of Ben's heels against his ribs, he'd surge forward. Ben would have to grab the saddle horn with one hand, his hat with the other.

After the initial whip-lashing jolt, a bit of boisterous fun, the galloping would smooth into an undulating rush through slapping grasses and overhanging leaves. Ben felt like yelling out loud, as though on a roller coaster, but there seemed a need to maintain dignity in the quiet mountains, especially in front of the horse.

He sat tight, knees squeezed to the saddle, releasing his grip on the horn gradually, holding only the reins, allowing his elbows to bounce outward with each stride as he'd seen cowboys do in countless westerns. Strawberry's hooves drummed the ground with authority, an exciting sound, stirring elemental memories.

At first, the trail had been easy to follow, a good place to let the horse show what he could do, a test-drive. Then the path narrowed and became rocky as they began to climb through stands of birch, pine and other trees Ben recognized, but not by name. They were moving uphill now, on their way to the first mountain pass of many shown on the map to Stretch Canyon.

Strawberry moved deliberately, picking his way over slippery stone while Ben, a helpless passenger no longer feeling he was in the driver's seat, let the reins rest in his hand against the front of the saddle and gave himself up to the pitch and sway, enjoying the heady atmosphere sharp with the ever-present scent of evergreen, the squeak of leather from a hundred complicated connections in and around the saddle, the scrape of metal-shod hooves on grit.

His was a sunny trail this morning, and he nodded his head, going with the motion, as in agreement that this was just a pleasant '80s-style *perk*, part of doing a job well. If he twisted around in the saddle, he could still make out the red dust road that wound toward the ranch. In the distance, Archie's arch could now and again be seen, as well as white smoke rising from what must be the barbecue fire. He wouldn't really be on his own until he topped the rise and got it between him and this outpost of civilization, with its telephones and HJ, his partner.

The idea of being cut off plunked an atonal chord somewhere under Ben's heart, and adrenaline flushed out from it, filling his chest and neck with nervous heat, making his pulse race and flutter, the thin air becoming slightly suffocating. He was reminded of the feeling he'd had, lost and crazy when separated from Rachel that day in the woods. No way, not this time. He had the stalwart Strawberry for company. And all the comforts of home riding with him. You can't be lost when carrying food, clothes, shelter, fire, water, map, compass, even a radio beacon, his ultimate safety net, the *urb*.

This calmed him somewhat. Only trouble now was that a depressing sadness had inched its way forward, surprising him, something new to this, caused by the very insight he'd just found reassuring. The well-packed animal was indeed now house and home. It was his only true address in the world, having left Chicago with bridges burned for a series of strange hotel rooms with no comfortable or comforting destination in sight. What was to become of him?

A scarlet tanager flew in front of the horse and sat on a trailside branch, unconcerned with Ben's problems or proximity, not having been conditioned to fear horses or anything growing out of a horse's back. It had a deep red body, sharply delineated black wings and tail. This bird didn't belong here. It was a Midwestern bird. An Eastern bird. A rarity here in the West. And this distracted Ben from nerves, funk and self-pity. They looked eye to eye as he passed, two strangers in these parts. A wordless greeting. And the bird was gone.

When Ben turned his attention back to the trail, he saw it finally had topped out, leveling off between two rises. They were in a green clearing now, and sudden strong sunshine. The horse blew a snotty Bronx cheer to announce his arrival in the meadow, a raspberry from Strawberry, and dropped his head to feed on the knee-high grass, sending up clouds of tiny flies which attacked both horse and rider with enthusiasm, excited as insects will be by sweat and blood.

Ben dismounted. He'd only been in the saddle an hour, but his legs were feeling funny, as after ice skating, and he stamped them, walking in circles around the horse. He'd tied the reins to a sapling, ignoring trace remnants of the recent nervous buzz still resonating somewhere inside.

He opened one of the overstuffed saddlebags and had the faint impression of himself as a kid, unwrapping presents. The Jack Daniel's still carried the morning's coolness in glass and contents. He twisted the cap, breaking the seal with a satisfying snap and took a long swallow, enjoying how it bit back. Then there was the immediate rush of warmth and serenity, diffusing from his empty stomach into every extremity.

He replaced the bottle, and it clanked against the wrapped-up revolver, which had been jammed in there near the bottom of the bag.

Behind him stood the tightness of trees they'd ridden through. Ahead, the meadow sloped down and into a V-shaped landform that reminded him of a woman's inviting legs. It was well grown there with early summer's healthy vegetation, making the comparison— undoubtedly coaxed along by the hot-breathed JD in his veins—all the more inviting.

The horizon lay green and rolling, with some hazy, silver-tipped mountains hovering above it, seemingly unconnected to the land, floating like clouds. The adman in him poked his head out of a crack somewhere, saying . . . *fade in theme from Magnificent Seven, Marlboro Country, lotsa French horns . . . music builds and swells* . . . but Ben shook the guy off. This was too good for theme songs. Too big to need help.

He went back to the saddlebag, this time pulling free the gun belt and its heavy, loaded holster. He buckled it on, enjoying the weight of it. He adjusted his hat to keep the sun out of his eyes, untied the horse and swung back onto the saddle. Ben didn't look back again. He touched his heels to Strawberry's sides and lit out across the meadow at a gallop, the old Stetson tipped forward, his long hair flying out from under it, the six-shooter hefty on his hip, good whiskey hot in his blood.

# 46.

For the moment, Ben was riding faster than his misgivings. But they were back there. In addition to the blessedly half-hearted agoraphobia he'd managed to deflect with bird-watching and whiskey, there was the truly substantive concern: What on earth made him think he was right about Abby being out here?

Strawberry slowed after a while, panting, or *blowing*, as horse people call it, Ben remembered, dropping from a hard gallop to an easy walk. This seemed natural, and Ben assumed no horse maintains a sustained run for much longer. Those seen in Westerns, endlessly galloping, must be yet another media exaggeration, akin to the often simultaneously seen six-shooter endlessly shooting. Just more lies. Hey, "Unreal! *Hollywood* versus Reality?" A coffee table sequel?

But once slowed, the exhilaration gone, the aloneness having an almost tangible quality, he couldn't avoid the question. Was he right about coming out here? He alone had seen a connection between some outrageously unrelated information. A map with green dots. A telephone machine message. None of it would have made sense if he hadn't done a little trick he'd learned during years as an upstart copywriter. It was simple, something done without conscious thought, never actually verbalized before. Now, somewhat pressed to justify his putting himself so literally on the line, he named the process: "Premise reversal." And he smiled.

Fancy name. Truly academic sounding. The Business School professors of advertising should know about it as they grind out their little advertising masters and advertising doctors. Doctors of advertising? Maybe they'll find a cure for it.

*       *       *

Example of "Premise Reversal." He'd been asked to work on a national brand of coffee. His orders were to create a commercial in which a guy complains about his morning cup, and leaves without finishing it. Neighbor pops in to cheer up the man's devastated coffee-failure of a wife. Tells her to use client's coffee. Next day, husband loves it, loves her. Case closed.

But Ben didn't love it. Too pat. Made the wife look stupid. Stymied, he tried simply reversing the old premise that husbands hate their wives' coffee. Assume husbands love it. He did a commercial showing husband after husband in quick cuts, all singing, "I love my wife's coffee!" At the end, the client's coffee was shown with the words, "He Loves It!" Women across America loved it, and the brand's market share shot up.

The horse walked, moving lazily now in the late morning sun. Ben, picking up some of the laziness, let his mind wander further, remembering more of this "Premise Reversal" business, wanting to strengthen still further his case for being here.

A dairy asked Ben's agency to boost milk sales by getting kids to drink ten glasses a week instead of six. Bullshit, Ben thought. Kids already drink too much milk. Reverse the premise.

Kids shouldn't drink more milk. *Adults* should drink more milk. Research said adults drank practically none. But there are a lot more adults than kids. Get just a few of them to drink merely one glass a week more, and sales would soar. Ben did a humorous campaign in which a famous comedian played a psychiatrist telling TV viewers to stop rebelling against Mom! Now that you don't *have* to drink your milk, do it because you want to! With cookies. With chocolate cake. With a shot of Scotch.

He remembered this with mixed feelings. Milk sales rose. Even a slight increase among adults caused this easily. And he won a film festival award. But he'd felt some guilt about promoting the scummy stuff with its Strontium-90, isotopic iodine and cholesterol.

*        *        *

"Premise Reversal." You say there's been a kidnapping? Okay, let's say, there *hasn't* been a kidnapping. Now, what happens? She hiked alone in remote mountains? Feasible to figure she got lost. Right?

"Right," he said aloud.

Strawberry cocked an ear momentarily, but otherwise this went ignored.

Say a guy claims he kidnapped her. It looks bad. But wait, according to the reversed premise, he must be lying. He lets you hear her voice? Then he must have a tape of it. How could that be? Feasible that it came from her answering machine. Feasible, too, that she's been followed by a falcon conditioned to recognize people as food givers. Why else would it send signals from positions in a straight line? Birds don't move that way. Lost hikers do. Everything is feasible.

Yes, Ben thought. This is more than just a hunch. She's probably out there.

Probably.

# 47.

After lunch, Ute would sit on a flat rock not far from camp overlooking the tangled gorge where Ute Creek, his namesake, ran. And he would play his cello. The strings made a soft, lowing sound, not exactly music but not exactly anything else. He didn't seem to play the same melodies twice. After about an hour, he'd stop, lay his chin on the stock of the big fiddle and sit for a while. Then he'd carry it back, pack it gently into the velour lining of a cracked old case and rest it against the cavern wall. At least that had been his routine for the three days Abby had been there.

He was playing the cello now. Abby was sitting on the ground, finishing the last of some Oreo cookies and trout. Ute's menu, like his cello playing, seemed habitual, and she accepted this easily, assuming the least you could expect from a hermit was that he'd be set in his ways.

He'd been there with his cello on that first afternoon, when she'd finally caught up to him and strode into camp feeling two contradictory feelings—triumphant like Stanley uncovering the elusive Livingstone. But also, like Livingstone gratefully meeting her own Stanley.

"Thanks for the fires and all!" She'd shouted up to him, so crusted with clay sunblock and trail dust that she felt, for the moment, no awareness of her lack of clothing.

"Have a cookie," he'd said over his shoulder, then turned his attention to creek and cello.

She tossed the wrapped-up cougar skin to the ground near his campfire, which was smoldering inside an ancient circle of stones. This was clearly the man's home. A rock wall rose nearby, and in its face was an opening over which a canvas awning had been erected. It had the familiar green and brown camouflage design popular with soldiers and duck hunters.

She could see furnishings within. A bed, old kitchen chairs, a chest of drawers. The walls had been painted in colorful abstracts. Around the fire and scattered nearby on the grounds were various possessions. Cookware. A crate of books. A basket of empty bottles. Chunks of firewood and an ax. Against the rock wall much firewood had been stacked already. Near the fire lay a large metal chest, its lid open. In it she saw crisp cellophane bags of Oreo cookies. Cases of beer in longneck brown bottles were stacked off to the side.

"That hawk yours?" he'd said after putting away the cello.

Abby had momentarily forgotten about the hawk. She noticed it sitting on the overhanging branch of a tree in the direction the man had been looking. Before she could answer, he seemed to have lost interest.

"Here," he said, walking from the cavern to join her, "put this on."

And he tossed her a large, square poncho. It was rough cloth with red, white and black markings, some kind of Indian design. She accepted this kindness gladly, having become somewhat self-conscious (though not uncomfortably so) as he'd approached and could see her up close, naked except for the knife belt. She found the hole in the center of the poncho and popped her head through. The cloth lay upon her with its uncomfortable texture, making her warm, but she gave it no thought, all her attention on the man now.

"Hi. My name's Sommers," he said, "spelled with an oh."

His pronunciation was slow and careful. Then he touched a hand to his forehead, a quaint salute which Abby found charming. He was silver-haired, probably well over sixty, she thought. He looked quite a bit older than her father. He was full-bearded, pony-tailed, and wore a suit of tan hide, roughly stitched by an unprofessional hand but fitting him comfortably. It smelled musky and leathery. Out here in the fresh air this was not unpleasant. He had a red plaid bandana tied around his head, holding his full hair flat and this crossed his forehead, giving him the look of a movie Apache, the famous Cochise himself.

"Why not call me Ute?" He said.

"Yoot?" She said. "Like the Indian tribe?"

He didn't answer immediately, but smiled pleasantly. Then, seconds later, said "like that creek."

"Mine's Abby. Abby Cole."

"Abby Cole," he said nodding, as though making it a point to remember this name.

"I'm lost," she said, shrugging, a shy smile.

He was of medium height and seemed agile, moving with the grace of a man a generation younger. He had penetrating black eyes, and when he smiled, he showed good teeth, straight and white. He had a gentle voice and spoke with a cultured style that seemed out of character for a man of such rugged appearance.

"I was thinking," Ute said, "you certainly can't be as lost as those who must be searching for you."

She'd had this exact thought herself, many times, during her ordeal. But she had put it out of her mind, along with the confusion and anger it brought. Not a plane. Not a helicopter. No searchers. No barking dogs. What the hell! Didn't anybody notice she was missing? In a way, it was pretty embarrassing.

"So," he said. "you get that hawk for a pet?"

"It's a long story, sir."

In a manner she would soon become accustomed to, Ute ignored this line of conversation, tabling hawk talk for later, probably when least expected. He nodded his understanding in regard to her previous statement about being lost, saying, "I know how you must've felt. Got lost myself. Big department store in Boston. Just wandered off, and . . . bang. Lost. I was five."

He'd offered her some food and beer, then told her she was only a day's hike from a two-lane highway that, if followed to the left, would eventually take her into the town of Stretch with its telephones and other "civilized inconveniences." He'd show her the way and could even spare her a compass, but couldn't guide her.

"Too busy just now," he'd said.

Since it had been late afternoon and she was hungry, she agreed to eat, then stay that night and start out in the morning. She thought, *too busy?*

Mystery is often the most engaging of human stimuli, and the front part of a mystery, in which the mystifying happens, delivers twice the pleasure as the back part in which explanations come to light, ending the suspense. This worked to Abby's advantage during her wanderings, in that it was partly her desire to solve the case of the mysterious campfires that kept her going strong.

But when she'd achieved this, there was a letdown, not that the answer wasn't interesting. But the fun had come to an end. An inertial weightiness set in, causing her to go idle for the moment. She sat, just sat, doing nothing, enjoying doing nothing. She finished her meal, really loving the Oreo's nostalgic flavor, finding herself wondering why she hadn't had any since girlhood. Sommers sat next to her, saying nothing while she ate. She grew appreciative of the poncho's scratchy protection as the sun lowered and the air cooled quickly.

"Actually, I didn't do it for you," he said, "at least not the first one."

He sat back, resting on his hands, taking in a lungful of chilly air, as a smoker pulls a drag off an after-dinner cigarette. "I did it for me. It was my fire, my dinner, my lion robe."

He looked her straight in the eye, smiling with his eyes as he talked quietly.

"Then I smelled you on the wind. No offense intended, young lady."

She couldn't tell if he were for real or what.

"And heard you coming about a mile off. Stomping through brush. Talking to yourself. I moved out of sight, and you came in and took over. Took over my campsite like it was made for you."

"But why'd you hide?"

He said nothing. It looked like he was never in much of a hurry to respond to a question. Perhaps having lived alone for what was apparently quite some time, he'd lost his sense of conversational cadence. Abby, like the rest of polite society, had the clear impression that questions were like skywriting, and would dissipate after a reasonable time if ignored, leaving nothing in the air. This man, though, acted as though an asked question were built to hang around until dealt with.

He sipped from his coffee mug and popped the two wafers of an Oreo apart with his fingernails in a smooth, well-practiced maneuver, using only one hand. He dunked the part retaining the frosting into his coffee and placed it whole into his mouth. He kept it there for a long time, and Abby thought he might have dropped off to sleep sitting up, or else was far too unreasonably enraptured by a silly cookie.

He said, "Don't know. I guess I just wanted to assess the situation."

"You watched me from the trees?"

"They don't call me Ute for nothing."

"That's another thing. I mean, I like it, the name, Ute, but you're not really one, are you? An Indian? A Ute?" He was tan enough, but there was that full beard.

"Course not. I thought I told you about that."

"Oh, the creek. That's it? You took the name of that creek?"

Ignoring this pointless question, he answered an earlier one.

"Better to control the event, you see, than to have the event control you." This, she assumed, was in response to the question as to why he'd hid.

And so the mystery had gradually been revealed. She'd stumbled by luck into a trail camp he'd prepared for himself on his way back from visiting a forest ranger who obtained beer and other civilized pleasures for him. He relinquished that camp to her, and on the next day he'd watched as she walked by luck along the straight northbound route she'd chosen, which was the same general direction as his hermitage. Toward day's end he made a fire in front of her, correcting her course, bringing her in line with the place. And again, each night thereafter.

He said he didn't know what he'd have done if she'd walked off in another direction. After some silent reflection, presumably about this, he'd said probably he'd have done nothing. With the lion skin for sleeping and lots of clean running creeks in the area, she'd be fine. A person would walk into a road before they'd starve in that situation.

"But I knew you'd walk straight. You'd been walking straight. And any sensible lost person would do the same."

"Why didn't you say anything?"

"Maybe I'm not so comfortable about ladies in the buff." He smiled and said, "Been awhile. Got to watch my heart. And maybe the sight of me coming at you in the middle of nowhere wouldn't have been too pleasant for you. Might have given you a shock, yourself."

He went on to say he just assumed she'd get here to his campsite soon enough. He planned on giving her some supplies, then aiming her in the right direction so she could go home.

"It's not far, really," and he pointed off-handedly over her shoulder beyond the forest, toward the east.

Three days later she was still there. She'd leave tomorrow, probably.

At least she promised herself she'd try. She laughed silently, thinking about the bighorn sheep he'd shown her, thinking, *was she too busy to leave?* Three days with Sommers, it was possible.

# 48.

On her second day in camp, after morning coffee, Ute sat with her near the fire, and she asked him about himself. He said he'd come into the mountains seven years ago because of the plague.

"Huh?" She'd said, her mood darkening as she ran through the possibilities. Bubonic? AIDS? Lyme? Was he carrying some bug?

"People!" he said, with unusual—for him—intensity. "Too many fucking people. I mean that in both senses of the word fucking. Not that there's anything wrong with fucking, but when it's done wrong it just makes *more* fucking people!"

He picked up a stone and threw it some distance away. She heard it bounce on rock. "Excuse the vulgarity, please."

She figured, what do you expect from a hermit? Complete mental stability? A conventional world view? Now, although no longer worried about germs, she still felt uncomfortable. Could the old guy be dangerous?

"Sorry," he said after a span of silence. "I don't get into many conversations up here. Guess I'm rusty. And impolite. I was about to say I don't much care for talking. But I just realized that's not right. Truth is, it's been too long since I've had the pleasure of a person to talk with."

She had so many questions, and she'd asked so many that morning, she felt like a wild-haired, ponchoed Barbara Walters of the wilderness, shamed by her rudely intrusive prying, yet captivated by Ute's charms as well as his answers.

Eugene Sommers had been a magazine publisher based in New England and had lived the life of a white collar commuter, "going with the flow," as he'd put it, raising kids who were now grown, having his wife of twenty-seven years run away from home to work in off-

Broadway theater, producing "unremittingly silly plays in which ego-maniacal showoffs thump around on the stage, shouting at each other, making fools of the audience."

He'd stayed in their suburban home alone, commuting into the city, not really knowing another way to live. His company had purchased a small outdoor life magazine that was becoming popular with growing numbers of aging baby boomers who had become disillusioned with power-careering and had taken, if only vicariously through the magazine, an interest in stylish camping, biking, climbing, the environment.

The magazine had been put under his control and with nothing else to occupy his days or nights, he threw himself into the assignment, reading whole bodies of work previously written by the magazine's contributors, accepting advertisers' invitations to field-test tents, boots, windbreakers.

In two years he became as much of a wilderness expert as an office-lifer could be.

Perhaps it was his new awareness of what Gretel Ehrlich (a then recently discovered favorite of his) called *"the solace of open spaces,"* but the increasing population density around him increasingly irked him. Growth for the sake of growth, *the ideology of the cancer cell . . . another of his favorite writers had called it*, had come to his formerly pastoral suburb.

Both residential and commercial development, the latter in the form of monstrous "office campuses" clogged the area's narrow lanes with cars. He became obsessive on the subject of overpopulation, reading everything published about it, and these writings, not known for their sunny outlooks, just made him crankier. *Too many fucking people.*

It was between six-thirty and seven one morning, and he was on his way to work when the idea of escaping to Ms. Ehrlich's open spaces hit. He'd been leaving for work an hour earlier than in days past, just to avoid delays caused by cars newly arrived in the area. But there he sat, waiting at a light prior to his turn onto the freeway into the city. Even this early he found himself confined by cars, amid appalling exhaust from countless idling engines.

His progress could only be measured in the number of green lights it would take to get him to the intersection. He estimated no fewer than three. The freeway, seen through chain link fence bordering the road, showed itself to be a steaming creep of vehicles. This, prior to seven AM! Everybody had arisen while it was still dark to avoid the rush, causing this rush to happen daily. Madness.

And it hit him. This isn't traffic. We're waiting in line. In line to go to the city. Then at night, we wait in line to leave the city. "I don't like waiting in line," he said. "I figured there and then, Abby, no more."

He U-turned and wound up here. "Goin' with the flow" again, but it's the flow of Ute Creek, as the map calls it. And liking it so much he renamed himself in its honor. " I never much cared for Eugene anyway."

The more Abby's questions got answered, the more she had. Where did he get the groceries? Did he hunt animals for food? Did he stay out here in the winter? How's the fishing? Does anybody know he's here? Does he ever leave? What was he doing on that hike when he discovered her?

She leaned in, head cocked, projecting cutely attentive curiosity, framing her lips to ask these, when Ute held up his hand.

"Sorry," he said, "I'm a bit talked out, for now." He smiled shyly, stood up and stretched.

"Sure. Of course." Abby said, feeling she'd been pushy. After all, the guy lived alone out here for seven years. Surprising he'd said as much as he did.

"Besides, I've got to go now," he said. "Meeting some friends for a drink. Be back by dark."

He pulled a quart bottle of bourbon from the food crate that lay open nearby. He carried it loosely, swinging it in one hand as he walked into the trees, disappearing immediately. After seeing him leave, Abby's hawk flapped down from a giant pointed pine tree, and landed near her on the ground, looking, as was his habit, for breakfast.

To the hawk she said, "Meeting some friends? For a drink?"

# 49.

Ben's first night sleeping under the stars had gone surprisingly well, causing him to approach the second night with a sense of competence. The old trail hand now. But in reality, he was literally still a babe in the woods, and not above making mistakes.

He'd ridden into the wildlands along Stretch Canyon following no marked trail, navigating solely with a compass and map. By sighting certain unmistakable landforms—twin cones called The Witch Sisters, a distinctive star-shaped lake, and the like—he'd been able to verify his position and measure his progress.

On that first day he'd ridden fifteen miles only, stopping by a clear pool in late afternoon, making an easy fire, eating a light snack, then getting strangely numb after just a little bit of the Jack Daniels and falling comfortably asleep in the zippered sleeping bag, smelling his own, and Strawberry's wild sweat. Before he knew anything, it was morning. Cold, cloudless, optimistic morning.

He'd gone about twenty-five miles the second day when he decided to make camp. It really wasn't what you'd call camping, he thought. Camping, in the contemporary sense, was something he'd never done or wanted to do. It seemed to involve a complex and abrasive ideology based on unnecessary gadgetry. Porta-lamps, porta-potties, porta-stoves, and space-age tents requiring an understanding of origami. His approach to overnighting was as simple as falling asleep at the beach. It required no more than a comfortable piece of ground, a simple fire, something to drink and something to eat.

As the day darkened quickly into purplish evening, he anticipated stopping not just for rest and refreshment (hours on horseback went by quickly, and neither anxiety or boredom, although fully expected to crash the party, ever appeared), but because he was eager to tune in the headset receiver HJ had given him. They were well into the target area now, and he might be able to pick up signals from the falcon responsible for the line of green dots seen on the map in the PRP office.

He found a swift, shallow creek and decided to camp immediately after crossing it. Strawberry moved slowly through the ankle deep water. Cooling his heels, Ben thought, and it struck him that the horse must be tired of walking even if he himself wasn't tired of riding, feeling a twinge of guilt at the inequity of their relationship. This powerful, perfect animal, spirit broken and enslaved, carrying on its back a soft prince of monkeys, sitting as on a throne. Wasn't right. But, ah, fuck it. This walk into the wilderness could be, he'd hoped, an escape—or at least a vacation—from such philosophical ramblings and the blues they can stir up.

He led Strawberry toward a patch of healthy looking, deep green grass and dismounted. He'd been told by Archie to take care of the horse *"first thing"* when making camp. He tied the reins to a sapling and pulled the hobble out of the saddlebags. Last night, when using the device to hold Strawberry's front legs together with just enough leeway to allow grazing in the immediate area, he'd thought about this curious word.

"Hobble," first heard in one of his favorite old songs, but not understood at the time. There in old cowboy hero Roy Rogers' version of *"Don't Fence Me In"* somewhere. Yeah, *". . . can't look at hobbles, and I can't stand fences . . ."* Ben had wondered, harbors? hobbies? hoboes? wobbles? Who understands all the words in a song anyway?

Now hobbles were part of his workday. He tossed the heavy leather device to the ground. The horse watched it drop, then focused on Ben in that sidelong manner horses have. A brief impassive glance.

Next to the hobble in the saddlebag had been the battery powered receiver and headset Ben was hoping to find the falcon with. Gladly forgetting the hobble and the unpleasantness it represented, Ben extracted the Walkman-like apparatus from the bag. He took off the big Stetson, enjoying a sudden rush of cool air in his hair, and spun it toward the base of a large tree where he guessed he'd set up camp for the night.

He put on the headset, clipped the tuner to his belt and flipped the power switch, hoping for beeps or clicks that might mean the bird, and Abby, were in the neighborhood. Nothing. He'd have to scan the band as HJ had explained, since they'd had no idea of the frequency on which the bird might be broadcasting.

Wearing the headphones, feeling like an ear-muffed baggage handler hustling around a parked jet plane, he unstrapped the bedroll from Strawberry's saddle and lugged it to his spot under the tree. He went back, reached into the other saddlebag for some granola bars, which he found tucked away next to the compass, matches, maps and other gear. He took two bars for now, and put them in his pocket. Then he reached back in and found the bottle of Jack Daniel's. The sun was down, and it was time for a cocktail.

He flung open the bedroll and got comfortable, resting his back against the tree, still wearing the headset. He'd make a fire and gather water later. For the moment, he just wanted to drink and listen to what was on the air out here. Tuning in a radio signal can be absorbing. When Ben was a boy, he'd owned a shortwave for a short time, and would spend hours before going to sleep tuning and fine-tuning, once picking up a program from England. The signal would fade in and out, but his interest never did. Always the possibility of picking up something. Must be like fishing, he thought, the whiskey hitting him with some force, dizzying him. Like fishing. Even if you don't get anything, you stay interested. And he tuned the little dial slowly back and forth, picking up a faint *doot-a-doot-doot*, lowering it, moving further down the band, getting it again.

Then he was asleep.

# 50.

He was awakened in the dark by an insistent, clear intermittent tone. Alarm clock? Turn it off. Where was he? There was a flash of panic reminiscent of that experienced back in that mercilessly black Denver hotel room. But here there was a sky full of stars and the shining sliver of a new moon. He had no trouble seeing where he was and quickly remembered.

He was painfully cold, and so stiff that when trying to move, it was as though his body were still soundly sleeping and had to be roused separately. What time was it? Wrist watch in saddle bag. That tone, that alarm, stop it. He flipped the radio off, pulled the earphones from his head, and the night was immediately silent. After a moment, his ears adjusted and picked up the only sound for miles, the moving water of the creek they'd splashed through hours ago. How many hours ago?

He could see quite well now in the blue-white light of the night sky. He stood and oriented himself. There's the creek. Some rocks to the right. Trees behind him. The grassy patch where he'd parked Strawberry. *Strawberry!* Shit! Guilt jumped in his chest. He'd left the saddle on. Hadn't even let the poor horse drink. He'd forgotten to follow Archie's simple instructions about seeing to the horse first. He unclipped the tuner, letting it drop with the headset onto the bedroll, and walked to the grassy area. He saw the hobble where he'd thrown it to the ground. But the horse was gone.

"Strawberry!" he called, his voice jarring in the hushed cold, steam blowing from his mouth.

"Here, boy! Strawberry!" The sound embarrassed him. No more of this calling out, this crying out. He knew instinctively, somehow seeing it in the stillness of the night grass, in the chilling indifference of the place, that the horse was long gone.

It was a situation in which a person of normal temperament would have had good reason to panic, running off breathless and bug-eyed. Yet Ben, who'd been known to panic for no good reason in the safest of environments, once even hyperventilating during a chatty coffee-klatch with his boss, finding himself unable to utter a single intelligible sentence, was at the moment, perfectly calm.

Perhaps past unprovoked anxieties had toughened him. More probably, it was that those neuroses were somehow connected to a mischievous but coldly sane part of him that liked to see him squirm when nothing truly serious was at stake. But now, this part of him, and every other, were in agreement. No time for jokes. He could get nutty later, but now had to take charge.

The lightening horizon signified that he'd had quite enough sleep. All things considered, he felt pretty good, but the chill was getting uncomfortable. He went back to the sleeping bag and eased into it, thinking ... get warm, take inventory of the situation, figure the next steps.

Gone was the ERB sending device, all his food and snacks, (except for the two granola bars), compass, maps, matches, canteen, almost everything. He had the bedroll, receiver and headset, a half bottle of whiskey and whatever he'd been wearing, including the pistol hanging loosely off his hip, fully loaded and with twelve extra bullets tucked into the little leather corrugations fitted to the gunbelt.

It was summer. Days were warm, and even though nights up there got cold enough to put frost crystals all over the ground, he had the insulated sleeping bag. He'd be okay. He assumed the horse would go back to Archie's. Riderless, it should be there in two days, even if it stopped to graze and loaf along the way. They wouldn't know Ben was here until then. He figured he might be able to follow Strawberry's trail. He had a vague idea of the direction to go and the contour of the land leading back. He rolled up the bag and realized that carrying it wouldn't be as convenient as slinging it across the horse had been.

He was thirsty. The hell with his missing water purification tablets, he thought, bending over the creek, dunking his face, sucking the water in. It was so cold it had a strange liquid density to it and hurt his teeth. In lieu of the tablets, he figured alcohol would do similarly well, so he chased the freezing creek water with a swallow of bourbon, which after a night on the ground, was just as cold, and this first hurt his teeth, then stung his throat and stomach.

But the alcohol quickly improved his outlook, and its rush magically coincided with the sun rising above the hills, illuminating everything with sharp light, making green things greener, blue sky bluer, reminding him for the moment of a long-gone detergent commercial he'd written in which colors got color-ier, and he winced at the thought. Was that him who did that? He wondered, hitching up his gunbelt, walking back to the tree where his hat lay waiting.

He picked it up and noticed the headset nearby in the grass. He remembered its shrill signal, the rude awakening just before dawn. And any thought of heading back, bedroll draped over tired shoulders, wondering... *is this the right way?* was pushed aside. It was time again to listen to the radio. The hawk and Abby could be over the next hill.

Radio switched on, headset in place, tuner re-clipped to belt, the tone still blared... DOOT-A-DOOT-A-DOOT... A clear sound. Must be close. If he walked toward it, HJ had said, the sound would grow louder. Away from it, softer. Like the childhood game, he thought, *"... No, you're cold, freezing! That's right, warmer. Warmer. Getting hot... Boiling! You're there!"* This could be fun.

He zigzagged into the countryside, taking care to keep the creek in sight, knowing it would lead him back to last night's tree and his bedroll, all the while homing in on the increasingly enthusiastic signal. DOOT-A-DOOT... really loud now, and no volume control. He looked up. DOOTS not withstanding, there was no hawk anywhere.

Probably too early to be up. Don't hawks wait for the warm, rising air of late morning? Maybe it's in a nearby tree, waiting. He saw a tight stand of white-barked trees and turned in their direction. The DOOTS in his ears became intense, almost hurting now, and he pulled the earphones off, letting them hang around his neck, faintly vibrating his collarbones.

No hawk yet. Suddenly the nearest tree moved. Something black and frantic was up there, shinnying higher, knocking a rubble of twigs and leaves to the ground. A porcupine? Some furred animal like those lonely unknowns in the unpopular small mammal house at the zoo?

Then, through the trees, at ground level, Ben's eye caught a new movement, black against shadow, coming toward him, then breaking out suddenly in the light. His understanding was instant, without words. He must have inadvertently harassed a bear cub, causing it to climb further up the tree, probably squealing notes of terror audible only to its mom, a 200-pounder, now rushing at him, all jiggling fur and streaming snout.

When she was less than fifty yards and closing, Ben, operating solely on instinct, somehow knowing not to turn and run, knowing not even to consider climbing the nearest tree (hell, she'd be right behind. And besides, it might have another cub in it. Don't they come in pairs?), simply stood and faced her, drawing his gun, waving it toward her, waving his other arm, too, making himself look bigger in her eyes. And he fired it in the air.

The noise shook the world and came back at him off the mountains, again, again, again in receding echoes. The bear skidded and jumped back, spraying forward clods of earth and pebbles. He fired again into the sky. (Hadn't this worked in the poacher's shed?) The shot. The flinch. The echoes.

It was a black bear, of course. Not as dangerous as grizzlies, unless, by chance, when protecting cubs. She stood up like a person, balancing easily on her hind legs, waving the front ones like arms. She tossed her head from side to side and a string of drool flew out, silvery and bright in the sun. Then she stared at Ben, but not straight on, looking instead out of the corners of her eyes (as Strawberry had done last night, he remembered now, but hadn't given it a thought at the time). She roared and, like his Smith & Wesson, the sound was terrifying. It, too, echoed off the landscape, multiplying, eventually dying.

He aimed the gun in her direction. Would she understand and move away? She dropped to all fours and ran, not backwards, but to the side, and quickly disappeared into the trees. As she moved Ben glimpsed a bright orange tag flapping behind her ear and clearly saw the collar she was wearing, the kind that field biologists use to carry radio transmitters.

There was only the memory of gunshots and roaring now, in the morning quiet. The bear was gone and he relaxed, enjoying the relief, but feeling strangely as though cheated somehow. Doubly cheated, in fact. The radio had led him not to the Stretch Canyon falcon, but to the bear. And this great, frightening animal that he'd stood up to was tagged and collared.

He'd have preferred a virgin.

# 51.

Ben returned to the bedroll under the tree and ate one of the granola bars. He stayed there through midday, watching the flow of the creek, the play of gray jays, finding everything about the spot relaxing.

He fantasized about living here, building a little log cabin by hand just beyond the grass where Strawberry had been. From its porch he'd be able to see the creek, and he recalled his mostly sleepless night in the PRP's line cabin, remembering it fondly now, its smell of dust and woodsmoke. He pictured "Rambo" as he'd first met her, shirtless in firelight. He imagined her bathing in the creek below. She'd look at him over her shoulder, knowing he was watching, and she'd smile.

Ben's interest in wild places, which had started in childhood with his private fascination for birds, had caused him over the years to read magazines and non-scientific books on the general topic of outdoor survival, and from these he'd picked up rudimentary tips. He knew that, now horseless and poorly supplied, he had only two options. Calmly backtrack following his own trail to Archie's, as had been his first thought that morning. Or stay put, knowing that in time rescuers would come looking for him. Local trackers, probably with dogs, would have no trouble following Strawberry's spoor to the creek, the patch of grass, and Ben himself, thinner perhaps, but in decent health, waiting under his tree.

So. To go? To stay? The sun moved slowly across the top of the sky. And Ben, by not deciding which course to take, of course, decided. So many decisions are made that way, he thought. Not to decide is to decide. No equals yes. Inaction equals action. Minus equals plus. No, yes. There's philosophic territory there waiting for someone to stake a claim.

Maybe someday he would write extensively about this in his cabin while an earthy woman tends their vegetable garden, wearing only cowboy boots and an enormous sombrero bought for her by Ben on one of his *Unreal! Advertising Versus Reality* autograph tours in the Southwest. Ben, a reality advocate? But the place was made for daydreaming.

His decision to stay was perfectly reasonable. The only thing one should *not* do under the circumstances would be to wander away from either the horse's trail, or the bedroll tree.

He rose before dusk realizing he'd enjoyed a perfect little nap, the kind you ease into when not expecting to sleep. He drank from the creek, again wincing at the shocking hardness of the cold water, again protecting against later parasitic infection with the dubious but only available water purification method at hand, a liberal dose of Jack Daniel's, now hot in the bottle from an afternoon stoppered under the sun.

He ate the other granola bar and was struck with the certainty that no matter how pleasantly he'd managed to dream away this first marooned day, he couldn't maintain such a passive strategy for the four or five days it would take before he'd be found. This scared him unexpectedly, in spite of the whiskey's friendly warmth, and he felt a slight shudder of incipient anxiety. For no clear reason, he'd assumed he had become immune to such foolishness out here and was surprised at the feeling. But this sense of surprise was, itself, surprising. Why should he have expected to be different than he'd always been?

Not wanting to explore this (it seemed inappropriate in such a robust setting, and besides he was becoming fed up with self-concern), he cast around for something with which to occupy himself. He put on the radio headset, carefully scanned the band and found mostly static, but occasionally a faint fading in and out of something that could be something. The bear still? But this was a different tone, more of a click. It was heard briefly, then nothing. Suddenly, he had a plan.

He would keep this spot with its creek and bedroll tree as his base. While waiting for rescue, he'd wander around a bit, marking his trail as he went, scouting in a different direction each day until he'd boxed the compass, listening for the Stretch Canyon hawk. Maybe—if his theory were right—he'd still be able to find it, and Abby, too. At least he'd be on the case. He would have set a mission for himself, and he'd be carrying it out.

He belched, and the whiskey came up raw and strong, burning as much as it had the first time, going down. He guessed his enthusiasm for exploration would wane when the whiskey was gone. The bottle was only a quarter full now. He'd better get started. There were still two or three more good hours of sunshine left. He adjusted the headset and headed into the lowering sun, figuring due west was as good a place as any to go.

# 52.

It was late afternoon on Abby's fourth—and her last, she'd promised herself—day in Ute's camp. Yesterday she'd gone with him to watch the bighorn rams, and she'd learned that *that* was where he went most afternoons, usually with a bottle, off to see "some friends."

She used his absence from camp to take a quick swim in Ute Creek which ran deep near the campsite, but bitterly cold. She came out of the water shivering, her nipples hard and numb, feeling against her biceps like two of the brown pebbles that lined the creek bed. She grabbed the lion skin robe and jogged to a small rise above camp, sitting on a rock shelf there, where she might see Ute from a distance as he came back from the alpine meadow.

The sun quickly dried her hair, lightening it, and she combed her fingers through it. It was thick and ropy, gritty with fools' gold silt from the swim. She wrapped the lion skin around her, enjoying its heft and heat. After awhile, she lay back resting, listening for Ute's footsteps on the scrabbly path, hearing only the slide of creek water, and soon she herself slid into sleep.

The unmistakable clicking signal excited Ben, but he was being careful. It wouldn't do to run off and get lost. He moved toward it, encouraged by the increasing volume as he headed into the lowering sun, but every fifty yards he would break a tree branch conspicuously to mark his trail or set up a little pyramid cairn of rocks. At each of these markings he'd look behind his position to make sure he could see the previous marker.

His base may be only a pathetic bedroll but it was home, with all the unreasonable sense of security any home territory has. The only possible danger he figured, was the coming of darkness. He'd never see his trail markings at night, so he'd better head back. But not just yet.

CLICK . . . CLICK . . . CLICKCLICK! The signal was getting stronger. It was a different sound from the "doot-a-doot" which had led him to this morning's bear. What if it was the Stretch Canyon hawk? Just another few hundred yards. The signal was too loud for comfort now, and he remembered this exact thing happening before he encountered the bear. Could it be a different bear? He checked his pistol, noticing the empty cartridges, ejecting them and slipping in two heavy new bullets from his gun belt.

Just a little further. He climbed a wooded rise and stopped, removing the headset now, unclipping the tuner, setting them both gently on the ground at his feet. He scanned the sky. No hawk. He scanned the trees. There! A shape silhouetted against the sun in one of the branches. The profile reminded him of the wooden carving that Altman had swung at him. He crept closer, seeing it was, in fact, a hawk of the right kind, a peregrine falcon to be precise, but suddenly not caring.

In the clearing beneath the tree a large tawny animal lay stretched out atop a redrock slab. *A mountain lion!* Ben's heart thumped in wild double-time, so loud he feared the lion might hear. It had a long sinuous tail curling into the distinctive "J" shape he'd seen before only in photos. Its head was small, surprisingly so, for such a large, full-muscled body. A white-furred paw rested under its chin and this seemed to put the animal in an unnatural posture, as though it was about to lift itself and turn.

Ben had stood like a bird dog at point, absolutely unmoving, but now sensing the lion would shift its position, he felt an instinctive need for cover and stepped behind a tree, disturbing something brittle underfoot. His radio! And the little plastic cabinet crackled clearly in the still air.

The lion rose immediately. Ben crouched behind the tree. It continued to rise, rising impossibly now, its paws spreading out, falling limply behind it, its head staring skyward, then flapping backward, no longer a head. Ben blinked stupidly, breathless, wondering, *"Have I finally lost it?"*

The lion had turned into a blonde woman, perfectly formed and utterly beautiful, wild-haired, naked, tawny as any mountain lion. And looking in his direction.

This primeval vision of Abby, perfect in the bronzing light of a setting sun, among tree shadows and silence, would dumbfound Ben for years to come, whenever he chose to replay the moment. But for now, it dumbfounded him for the first time. And he stood dumb, found.

At least he was dumb in the sense of being quiet on the outside. Found, too, now no longer a lone castaway. Although it was Abby who was more truly found, having been far more lost. (Ben, when reviewing his twelve years in labyrinthine ad offices, however, might argue that point.)

Still, on the inside Ben wasn't dumb, never had been, really. He knew it now. The young woman cocked her head, trying to see him, and he realized he was partially hidden in the trees. She had Lara's rounded lower belly, Lara's exciting full frontal view, even larger breasts, but of similar design. She called out, something that sounded like "You?"

Although this word made little sense, her voice confirmed everything. It was the voice from the answering machine. Abby Cole. This judgment was made by Ben in a microsecond while he stood— the comparisons to Lara, the voice analysis—everything between eye blinks, and that hawkish silhouette overhead had been factored in, too, obviously being the gambled-for Stretch Canyon bird, who did, in fact (*I was right!*) imprint on this wandering human, leading Ben to her with radio clicks.

Before he could instruct his voice to act, to say something simple like, "*Abby? I've been looking for you!*" Before he could even move his feet, walking out of this partial cover toward her (although these actions were immediately forthcoming, events here being measured in fragments of moments now), he first enjoyed a rush of innocent, high-spirited self-congratulations.

He was right about things! About Abby, about Altman and probably O'Brien. Right about the hawk and its radio, about not going back into the SPF conference room that day, about coming West, *Unreal! Ads Versus Reality*, Schmidt's beer, Granny Annie's uncanny taste, adults drinking more milk, right about dentists named Buzz being pricks, about Abby *being here*... He'd never felt altogether sure until now, never really comfortable with any of it. But now, being right about this big thing, and seeing this beautiful stone-age pin-up standing here, clear evidence of his rightness, he knew he was a guy who was right about things.

"Abby?" he said.

She picked up the lion skin and pulled it around her like a robe.

"Yes!" she said.

And Ben came out of the trees slowly, introducing himself, reminding her that they'd met years ago when he'd worked with her dad, this sounding bizarre there under the pines, under the circumstances. For the first time, he felt somewhat middle-aged, wanting to say that the last time he saw her she was just a kid, a cute and topless tomboy in the hotel pool.

But he squelched the impulse, sensing that in this wild twilight smelling sharply of pine, with the only other sound being the coursing of the creek now visible behind the girl, it would be best to say little. She smiled up at him, similarly word-shy, but stepped toward him and hugged him powerfully, the most honest hug Ben had ever felt. He returned her hug, enjoying the mossy scent of creek water in her tangled hair.

# 53.

Ute had not yet returned. Abby played doting hostess at the otherwise abandoned campsite, inviting Ben to sit on a log by the fire. She was dressed primly, all things considered, in her poncho although this scarcely covered her below mid thigh, and her movements or those of the wind, would occasionally cause fabric to flutter, revealing firelit skin while Abby remained unaware or unconcerned, her mind now occupied with the fable Ben had told, of her own kidnapping.

"That Darren Altman is *such* an asshole," she said, confirming Ben's opinion but dampening momentarily his growing admiration for her, finding the commonplace word ugly and blunt in her girlish voice. She gave him beers and Oreos. As the sun set, they sat close, facing the small fire, talking into it. The scene reminded him of a commercial he'd filmed years ago.

*   *   *

The product had been a new idea: Filled franks. Hot dogs injected with cheese, tomato sauce, chili, mustard-mayonnaise, or sweet-sour Oriental. He'd named them "Frankfillers, " a play on "frankfurters" although he'd had doubts about their eventual acceptance.

The commercial showed a romantic campfire, a couple roasting the Frankfillers on long forks, with close-up shots inserted to show the filling bubbling out of the fork's puncture holes. The thought made Ben hungry, and he remembered he'd only had those two granola bars all day.

But the campfire in the ad had been constructed on a Hollywood sound stage and was gas-fed. The rocks sat on by his "cookout couple" (the commercial's title) were Styrofoam, and the foliage was plastic. The Frankfillers wouldn't produce photogenic bubbles, so a food stylist had to simulate the effect by using rubber cement. The franks were darkened at the edges with paint and brushed with varnish to make them look temptingly sweaty.

These cosmetic adjustments were not strictly legal, which caused client and agency bigwigs to sweat a little themselves when, weeks later, the actress who played in Cookout Couple went on the Tonight Show and used for her mandatory spontaneous amusing anecdote, a description of her holding a spray-painted wienie, rubber cement dripping, milking the image for all its double-entendre effect. The authorities that regulate such ad fraud must not have been watching, because nothing more was said about it. The cheesy product eventually failed in test market and faded away.

*   *   *

Ben mentioned his hunger, and Abby sprang into action, enthusiastically plying him with dried trout and cold grouse, fairly fresh and juicy, which had been kept in a cooler in the creek. She joined him, and they ate with their hands, talking with full mouths, bits of food flying as they laughed, chins greasy, washing it all down with beer drunk from longneck bottles of which the camp seemed to have an endless supply, belching freely, unmannered, content.

He told her that there had been no supportable evidence that she was merely lost, especially since her voice had been heard during the ransom phone calls. That's why there were no searchers. But the Van Dyke Agency had taken a long shot, and let him check out the area where he'd noticed the hawk's straight-line movements could be suspiciously human-motivated. He gave in to the moment, feeling heroic. He aimed his sexiest smile at her, strong, but boyishly modest. "Guess it paid off, huh?"

His penalty for overconfidence had always been predictably swift.

"Hey, how'd you lose that tooth?"

This wasn't as bad a conversational turn as it first seemed, because although it might have ended any illusion he had of dazzling her with good looks by firelight, it did give him reason to relate his fight with Altman, who was, after all, the villain responsible for her father's fleecing, and her own dangerous situation.

They talked long after dark, under a cold sky and bright stars. She told him about wandering away from her things in search of a scarlet tanager she might or might not have seen, and how stupid she felt. He didn't mention his own interest in birds, thinking it would sound impossibly coincidental at this moment, like a lie, and might break the mood. Although he did flash quickly back to the flash of red he'd seen on the trail after leaving Archie's, his own displaced scarlet tanager. Better keep that to himself.

She told how she'd met the hawk and how Ute had helped her. How she'd come to his camp. How he'd told her about his life, how he'd become a real hermit who plays the cello, "just like my mother does," and goes off to drink by himself with bighorn rams every afternoon.

"I know he sounds weird," she said, laughing, clearly a little buzzed from the beers, "but he's a cool guy."

Ben wondered if such a man would describe himself that way. He doubted it, and found himself unreasonably distracted by Abby's choice of words, as he'd been when she'd called Altman "such an asshole."

After a while Abby said, "So when do we get outta here? Do you radio for help or what?"

And Ben had to explain about his abandonment by the fully equipped horse, his loss of radio, maps, compass. He faced the fire and said quietly that he, too, was kind of lost.

"Well, we've got each other," she said, scooting closer along the log. He could feel her eyes on him as he looked at the fire. She was on his good side, too. Vanity never quits.

"Until Ute comes back," she said, "And it doesn't look like he will, tonight."

A husky invitation there, no doubt about it. The beers, the gamy meat still greasy on their lips, their own gaminess, the open sweetness of this wild girl, naked but for a piece of cloth. They could take the lion skin, go down to the creek. Ben's head swooned with the planning of it, and he had to hitch a leg out to make room for the enthusiastic stretch stretching in the tight jeans. This part of him always had a prehistoric attitude, even in civilization. But now in fire smoke, animal fat, and human musk, it was in its element.

Ben turned toward Abby, allowing her eyes to lock on. He put his arm around her. She was a butterscotch girl. He actually licked his lips, remembering the snatch of dark blonde glimpsed back there in the woods.

But then Ute Sommers came back.

"Excuse me, there, little girl," he said somewhat breathlessly. They turned to see him limp into the circle of light. He used a rifle as a crutch, and his eyes were squinting and small, but the wetness in them reflected orange light from the campfire.

"Ute!" Abby shouted.

Ben stood, thinking *of course it hadn't been "You" she'd said back there when he came upon her by the creek.* Abby helped the man to the log, and he sat heavily, his heels kicking dirt and gravel forward into the fire.

"I'm okay," he said.

But there was an arrow in his calf, the pointed end extending out in back, the feathered shaft coming out of the shin, dark and wet. The man looked at Ben and said, "Mind handing me one of those beers, cowboy?"

# 54.

At first light, Ben followed Ute's sketchy map and found the meadow where bighorn males liked to spend their summer. The carcasses lay in the open, headless, bellies swollen, legs pointing out with unnatural rigidity. Frost crystals covered their brown fur just as they covered the surrounding grass and small pools of purplish blood. It was cold, and Ben noticed accumulated snow in the rock shadows. Snow in summer, he thought, what a place. And he wondered if the men would be okay after their night up here.

They were as Ute said they'd be. Cold, miserable, alive, cruelly but professionally hog-tied and staked to the ground, lying like the two dead sheep, immobile on their sides. They were close enough to the small fire Ute had made, close enough to survive one night. The fire must have burned until just recently, because a little blue smoke could be seen rising off its ashes.

Ben, following Ute's advice, and his own gut, drew the pistol and approached slowly, making sure the men were still well trussed. He stared at them, and they at him, wordlessly. Each wore a large backpack, still strapped in place. Atop each pack, they'd positioned and tied securely the head of a slain ram. Each head carried a massive curl of horn, and had open glassy eyes, strangely golden-colored.

Ben had previously seen such beasts only in pictures, but now, seeing the real thing, even though mutilated and stiff with frost, he felt the same quiet rush of privilege that came on spotting a coyote that afternoon in Hollywood and the rare tanager on the ride up. The grounded men twisted to see him better, and since their packs were securely fixed to their backs, the ram's heads moved, too. Four sets of eyes looked at Ben expectantly in the gray morning.

Ute had said, *"With that pistol you'll have no trouble from those two."* Ben kept his doubts to himself and his face cold, eyes narrowed, giving nothing away, standing over the men, breathing evenly, regaining his wind after the climb in the chill, thin air. The only sound was the distant drone of an airplane, far away. Too early for bees to be up and humming. The sun came over the horizon and moved the ground shadow out of the meadow and over the cliff, illuminating the two men brightly. Even without this clear light, Ben knew who they were.

Quietly, he said, "First you put an arrow through my friend's ass. Then you shoot another friend of mine in the leg. What am I gonna do about you two?"

He made no conscious effort to sound like Clint Eastwood and figured it wasn't his fault if he had. Standing there bearded and pissed off, in smeared boots and a beat-up Stetson, holding the six-gun in an unwashed hand. Sometimes events just create their own natural dialogue.

Ben unsheathed the knife Ute had given him and slit the raw sheep-hide straps that bound each man's ankles. He left their wrists tied, but cut the straps that held their hands to the stakes Ute had hammered into the ground with his rifle. Ute hadn't wanted them squirming over to the fire, using it to burn off their bindings during the night. Ben wondered how an old man had been able to do all this with an arrow sticking through his leg.

The poachers were stiff and cramped. The backpacks with their gory trophies off-balanced them as they tried to rise, hands pinned in back, but they eventually got to their feet at Ben's insistence. He'd mentioned something about gladly leaving them tied up for another night if they didn't cooperate and that helped. He was quite at ease with the poachers, probably, he felt, because he was utterly unconcerned with their opinion of him, they being literally beneath his contempt. Having them uncomfortable and under his control was curiously satisfying, and he could understand why cops attacked their jobs with enthusiasm even though paid little in salary.

"Walk ahead of me and do what I say, please," Ben told them calmly.

"Anything funny, I'll just shoot you in the foot and tie you up again. Okay?"

The taller man said, "You got the gun, don't you?" and walked docile to the path which led to Ute's camp. The other man gave Ben a submissive nod, criminally insincere, of course, but clearly an acknowledgment of Ben's authority here and now, and he went with his companion.

Ben followed, gun in hand, as promised, knowing there'd be no trouble. Even Ute, wounded as he was, would have been able to retrieve the defeated poachers this morning. But he wouldn't have liked the idea of taking them out of the mountains to the authorities. Ben's arrival, it seems, had been handy for Ute as well as for Abby.

They walked the easy downhill trail off the mountain, and Ben thought about the arrow wound, wondering if it would be as inconsequential as Ute thought, feeling somehow that the old man was right about such things. He recalled the cliche of childhood westerns, *"only a flesh wound,"* and couldn't help smiling, having heard it spoken just last night in total innocence.

"Hell, it's only a flesh wound," Sommers had said after Abby spotted the arrow coming out of his shin. "Let me catch my breath. I'll get to it in a minute."

She said, "Oh my god . . ." and sat on Ute's right, alternately looking at the rigid half-buried shaft, shiny with blood, and Ute's face, similarly shiny in the firelight. She grabbed a handful of hem from her poncho and used it to dab his brow, indifferent to the flash of torso under there. Ben caught sight of it and remembered how close they'd been minutes ago.

But he soon became absorbed in Sommers' story, especially because he recognized that arrow. He'd gone an entire life without seeing an arrow that wasn't a toy, and had never seen a crossbow that wasn't in a movie. Then the other night a crossbow wounds HJ and tonight, this. He had the impression that isolated as they were here, the world had suddenly shrunk, now populated by a few players who would necessarily meet and re-meet. And wasn't that truly the case?

Was it really a coincidence that crossbow poachers seen near Stretch would be out here? This is where the animals that they poach live.

Save the analysis for later, Ben thought. Besides, hadn't he noticed of late a tendency to grow away from the analytic life toward simplicity, which could clearly be measured in better emotional health? Mindless happiness. Oh, to be alone with Abby right now.

Ben said, "I saw an arrow like that the other day. Some poachers had a crossbow. Shot a friend of mine, but not seriously."

"These were poachers," Ute nodded. "Probably the same."

And Ben realized he was, incredibly, at home on this exotic topic, more than ever the heroic lawman in Abby's eyes.

"That contraption's in the gorge now, along with their rifles and knives. Threw them over the side."

Abby leaned toward Ute, hesitant, saying, "Over the side? Not the men?" Her arm encircling Ute's shoulders.

"Of course not." And he told them how he'd come upon them after they'd killed the two full-curl males, taken the heads and had packed up, ready to walk out of there. He got the drop on them, he said, coming around from behind the curve in the rock wall with his rifle in their faces.

"The man didn't even mean to shoot me. He was startled, I think, and fired the crossbow by accident. Wasn't even aimed." Before the poachers or Ute himself knew it, the arrow was there, lodged in Ute's lower leg, fortunately missing his shinbone but running right through the calf muscle.

"I got sore about that, as you might imagine," he said. He tossed their weapons over the cliff. Then made rawhide strips from the dead animals' skin and tied them up with no thought to their comfort. He knew he'd have to hobble back to camp and treat his leg before he could deal further with them.

"Was halfway home when my conscience made me go back and make those guys a fire so they wouldn't freeze overnight." By the time he'd staked them near it, the leg was really hurting, and it was completely dark. He limped back and found Ben sitting with Abby.

"Name's Sommers," he'd said then, holding out his hand. "With an oh."

Explanations and introductions were gotten out of the way and Eugene Ute Sommers spent the next hour removing the arrow. He surprised them by having an excellent medical kit on hand, including the freeze spray Ben had seen ball players use to numb an injury.

"I may live in the sticks, but I never said I was stupid," he said, rankled at their fussing over his supplies.

After numbing the leg and soaking it with peroxide, he nipped off the back end of the arrow with his knife, gripped the point in a rag and slid it out. He squeezed antiseptic ointment from a tube into both ends and then wound a clean bandage tightly around the calf, saying, "Who's got a beer for me?"

After, drinking comfortably by the fire, Ute looked at Ben, then at Abby, then back to Ben and smiled apologetically. "No offense, kids," he said. "But the neighborhood's sure getting crowded."

They agreed that Ben and Abby would leave in the morning, following Ute's directions to the highway, an easy day's walk, he'd said, and they'd take the poachers along with them. Ute figured Ben would have no trouble from the two men since he had that "big three-five-seven, and those guys were already beat-up and tied up."

Ben chose to ignore whatever slight might be read into that statement, agreeing it was true enough, saying he'd go up to the meadow at first light and collect his prisoners if Ute would make a map he could follow. With the phrase, "collect his prisoners" echoing stupidly in his mind, he heard an owl hoot fairly loudly in the blackness of trees behind him, and was struck with the impression that it was laughing at him. Well, maybe *with* him.

And he wound up being the first to go to bed, in a moldy sleeping bag Ute set up for him under the canvas awning.

# 55.

When Ben, Abby and the two poachers started walking, it had still been quite early, and birdsong filled the chilled woods. Now the sun was climbing through the eleventh hour, and the forest had taken on its midday quiet, the only sounds being the crunch of men's boots (Abby still went barefoot, preferring this to the sandals Ute offered), the groan of straps holding the poachers' top-heavy backpacks, and the insect hum of a distant plane.

No one talked, and this suited Ben, who was feeling contemplative instead of buoyant at the side of the dazzling Abby. The poachers trudged dumbly ahead, reminding Ben of draft animals, curved horns swaying above their backpacks. Their hands were still fastened behind them, but Ute had fixed them an additional binding, a length of scratchy hemp rope around their necks, yoking one to the other.

"This'll keep 'em in one place, so you can shoot them easier if they act up," he'd said, winking at Ben.

Next to Ben, Abby strode easily, silently, carrying her rolled-up cougar skin like a valise. A girl going on a trip. Her poncho was now cinched neatly at the waste by the knife belt she wore, giving this rough garment the look of a stylishly short shift. Above her the hawk could occasionally be seen circling, following.

While Ben had been bringing the poachers down from the mountain, Abby had been packing for the trail and saying goodbye to Ute. By the time Ben and the poachers arrived, everything had been made ready. Ute, incredibly not even limping, gave Ben a tiny K-Mart compass and said, "Just go north and you can't miss the road."

He also gave him a rawhide bag filled with bottles of beer, a large water bottle, some jerked meat and basic wilderness conveniences, like matches.

"Can't guess how long the walk'll take you, with those two dragging their butts and carrying the bighorn heads, but I've been able to walk there from here in a day."

Ben tried to picture what it would be like walking for a day. Define a day. When was the starting time? The ending time? Would it be light out? *What am I doing?*

Ute added, "Now you'll have to tie these two up if you don't get to the road before dark. Lash them to a tree. Make a fire, and wait out the night. When it's light, keep heading north, and you'll hit the road soon enough. Then go left until you get picked up by somebody, or just walk all the way into the town of Stretch. Won't be more than five, ten miles."

There was a weird moment when Ute jammed some food and water into the poachers' mouths, feeding them with reluctant attentiveness.

"Guess we can't have these guys running out of gas on you. See, if they can't be able to walk . . ." he said to Ben, but everyone knew he was speaking to the poachers, "you'll have to tie them to a tree and leave them for the cops to get later. But, who knows? You could forget which tree. And who could blame you?"

Then to the poachers, he whispered, loud enough for everyone to hear, "If you boys have to relieve yourselves? Go right ahead, any time. That's what you got trousers for." Then louder, to Ben, "Don't untie the bastards' hands. Ever. The sheriff'll deal with them after you turn them over, got it?"

Abby had hugged Ute. Ben shook the man's hand and thanked him. Ute said nothing more. Before they'd gone a mile, they heard the faint, smooth sound of a cello in the distance behind them. Abby and Ben exchanged a glance, smiling, listening, and kept walking. The land seemed to flatten as they moved, and the march fell into its own comfortable rhythm.

Ben watched the poachers' backs as they walked northward through the trees into increasingly frequent open areas of short, yellow grass. He realized he was about to have a strong though nearly anonymous impact on their lives by taking them in. They'd be arrested for poaching, and probably even given jail terms.

HJ had explained the seriousness of this strange crime, virtually unknown in Ben's original world. Then there was assault with a deadly weapon. HJ would surely press charges for the arrow wound, former FBI guy that he was. Yet Ben didn't know these men, not even their names, their backgrounds, anything, and he found that he liked it that way.

They belonged to a rather faceless, brutish class of human he'd known only peripherally but consistently throughout his life. High school bullies suffering from chronic smoker's cough and bad English, kids to be feared and strangely pitied.

There'd been a man in his neighborhood, a sullen, heavy-set loner who'd kept a large blue-eyed Alaskan husky confined to a small pen in his back yard, 24 hours a day, every day, winter or summer, never taking it out. The dog had been doomed to pointless incarceration year upon year. Ben's dad said the man was simply ignorant, stupid and mean, dismissing it all with a shrug. Maybe that's all you could do about such people. Shrug them off. Maybe that's why Ben had chosen to ignore these men.

Could he continue to ignore them? What if they balked at some point in this forced march? What if they counter-attacked? Was this worrying justified? Wasn't it spoiling his triumph at finding Abby, at leading her to safety? And besides, hadn't he been avoiding this exact kind of tiresome soul searching since coming into these mountains?

But to be fair, it wasn't really much like the neurotic self-concern he'd practiced for years. Practice makes perfect, his mother used to say, torturing him with piano lessons. It was only natural to dwell on such implications during his first-ever citizen's arrest, if only to be prepared to handle the unexpected dangers inherent here.

Abby looked worried herself. He'd glanced at her as they left another stand of shady pines and headed into the sunlight, coming upon a large meadow, gently sloping and covered with golden grass. Or maybe she, too, was just pensive. She felt his stare and turned, smiling suddenly. *God, she's beautiful,* he thought, but he was strangely relieved that they hadn't been permitted last night to give in to that beery body lust by the fire. Was that possible? Relieved?

"You okay?" she said.

"Fine. You?"

"Just thinking about Ute. Bet he's going to move someplace else now."

Ben said nothing, kicking at the grass as they walked, thinking briefly . . . could she have drunk beer with Ute like that? Half naked and silly under that big night sky, the firelight red on her skin?

She laughed, "He said the neighborhood's getting crowded. He's so cool."

If Ben had made love with her, wouldn't that have spoiled in some way the purity of this heroic solo rescue? And after all, wasn't she

Cole's daughter? Wasn't she too young? He'd first met her when she was a gawky kid! He guessed he was glad they hadn't done it. But as she walked next to him, squinting in the sun, her breasts moving freely inside the belted poncho, that baffling scent of her. Wild, flowery, animalistic. Maybe later, *after all . . .*

Suddenly, all this quiet musing became irrelevant.

Ben's worrying about a possible revolt of the poachers didn't matter. His concern over not knowing who they were, their names even, became pointless. His lust or restraint regarding Abby, no longer an issue. There would simply be no more marching through sun-speckled aspens. No decisions, after all, about when or where to build a fire for the night, no need to ever pour water into the tied-up poachers as though they were invalids. No more, perhaps, of this whole uncivilized mix of joy and danger.

*Of course.* He'd been hearing distant airplanes on and off since sun-up. Now the beat of a helicopter was strong in their ears, and he wondered briefly if the poachers had been in Viet Nam, thinking this sound, the sound of that war, would freak them out, causing them to break for it. But everyone just stood in the all-consuming thump of blade noise and swirling winds, stood in the yellow grass, the poachers, too, looking skyward. And Abby started waving her arms, saying something lost under the sound, her hair blowing, the same color of the grass flapping all around them.

The big army helicopter lowered into the meadow, banking sharply in a violence of new sound and flying dirt, causing the four of them to turn their heads away for the moment. And the ungainly machine hovered over them, then dropped to the ground on jiggling springs, the sound suddenly fading, the air smelling now of earth and kerosene, the door opening, HJ jumping out, and Ben thinking, *Look what I got for you, man! The girl—like I said—and, remember the guys with the crossbow . . . ?*

Then, thinking, shit, is this the end of it?

# 56.

The young peregrine falcon known to Ben as the Stretch Canyon hawk, had done well by following Abby. There had been something about her, dimly remembered, from early times when the bird was helplessly nest-bound, a scent of Abby, often on the breeze in those days, followed by the sudden arrival of food. Food, the peregrine knew with mute clarity, was the only true currency.

Things had gotten even better after Abby came to stay with the old man. His campsite on the upslope of a mountain, higher than the surrounding landscape, suited unspoken nesting sensibilities in the bird's young personality. And the man fed the bird well, raw fish liver, grouse heart and gizzard. The old man offered food in a more polite manner than Abby did, knowing instinctively that it was discomfiting to stare at the bird while it ate. He'd given food and privacy, both.

And yet, peregrines are prone to habitual behavior patterns. So having shadowed Abby in the past, the hawk mindlessly rose from the man's camp into the morning sky to follow her again. But there was an avian crankiness riding in him as he circled, not liking Abby's proximity to the three strangers, unsure of her intentions. The bird's uneasiness grew as Abby and the others moved into the woods and gradually into lower elevations, further from the warm animal guts and cool breezes to be enjoyed at the old man's place.

At midday, the peregrine falcon was irresistibly irritable. His hunger raged. Usually, Abby had given food by late morning, or, as happened in recent days, the old man did the feeding. The bird was further irritated now, because when soaring high on a late morning thermal, he glimpsed a gray, oil-smeared highway in the far distant haze, with its noisy intrusion of fuming trucks.

This was well remembered from the bird's panicked days near starvation, living on unhealthy pigeon flesh, growing weak, the days before he was reunited with the food-giver, the girl below who was now maddeningly moving toward the highway and the trucks. And, too, there was the strange truck-like noise of airplanes vibrating the air this morning. Good reasons for a hawk to be glowering and mean.

Then the helicopter raged into the space above Abby, deafening the hawk, filling the sky with turbulent winds. It came to Abby as the hawk itself once had, and she didn't move away from its commotion as the hawk felt she should, but she came to it as she'd once come to the hawk, and now all hope of being fed by her was gone.

The little falcon turned clear eyes away from the storm and stink of human machinery in the blowing meadow, and with a flick of wing, set a course for the only sensible destination in its simple world.

# 57.

Meanwhile, back at the ranch.

"Tina sends her regards," Van said. "She wanted to come along, but somebody has to watch the store. Anyhoo . . . she says *come up and see me some time,*" this last delivered in a pathetic Mae West falsetto, not becoming to a large florid man holding a sticky champagne bottle.

HJ added, "Hell, Ben, she wanted you even before you became a hero."

"Wanted. And had. Right, kid?" Van asked between swigs on the bottle, his nose fairly glowing after hours of this.

In spite of the ranch house decor with its log beams, Indian blankets and antler-clad walls, Archie's dining hall, now closed for this impromptu "Private Pardy" as the sign outside said, had the feel of a locker room scene on TV after a playoff victory. The floor, furnishings and foolish people all were tacky with sprayed champagne, voices hoarse from horseplay.

Abby sat at another table, talking with Cole and Lara. She caught Ben's stare, and smiled, giving him a cutesy little wave with a cute little hand. Can serious beauty be so jarringly cutesy, he wondered? Cole and Lara smiled at him, too, and Ben got the impression Cole would soon join him at Van's table, probably again to say something confusing or embarrassing. It was close in the room, the champagne was causing heartburn and headache, and Ben would rather have been back in the mountains somewhere under the open sky.

Cole and Lara had dropped out of the sky that day in a second roaring helicopter minutes after the first one, and this had seemed at the time to be on the order of overkill. After all, hadn't searchers merely been sent out to find Ben after Strawberry returned home riderless? That shouldn't have brought out this fleet of planes and choppers, both Van and HJ, plus the Coles and countless nameless authority figures in uniform and out.

But they were in the air, Ben eventually learned, because the night before, while Ben was sleeping alone under Ute's canvas, while Abby was consoling the bravely punctured old man about the stupid slaughter of his bighorn drinking companions, the trouble maker who started everything had made a friendly phone call to Cole from someplace cozy in South America where he'd turned a bowel-full of diamonds into a shitload of pesos.

Cole had explained that the guy was actually friendly about it. "Sorry if I caused you much trouble, he said!" Cole had told this to Ben when they'd first come to Archie's, it being the best nearby place with a likely landing area and a facility for the evening's celebration.

"Seems Altman slipped out of the country with the diamonds inside him. Had a close call in Atlanta, but the guy's tricky, as I guess you know firsthand. I heard about the fight," Cole said, mock-punching Ben's shoulder, one tough guy to another.

"Guy tells me that he's a little late calling, and says my daughter was spotted running around lost. And he gives me the details. Says she'd never been kidnapped. A harmless hoax, he called it. A shot in the dark that paid off. You got to hand it to the bastard."

Cole said he'd called Van after Altman hung up, and they organized the armada that flew down on Ben, Abby and the poachers at midday. Van had given Ben credit for guessing the truth before the facts were known. Ben had even been right about O'Brien having spotted Abby from a ridge, an accidental bit of voyeurism that took an unexpected turn, then telling Altman about her from the cabin.

Van flattered Cole for having the sense to bring this Ben Green guy in on the case, putting part of the success in his lap, which at first Ben assumed was some kind of supplier-to-client bullshit, unworthy of Van, then realizing it was simply the truth.

Lara had given Ben a warm kiss lasting perhaps a millisecond longer than appropriate, evoking an ache in him for Abby's similarly flavored flesh, but Abby had been otherwise occupied, off somewhere seeing doctors flown in by Cole and changing into fresh clothes, including a too-large University of Colorado sweatshirt, jeans and white sneakers. She was now busy talking with various police people who came and went. Reporters were waiting their turn, as were some mysteriously appearing friends of Abby's from her school and the PRP.

The poachers had been whisked off under the personal direction of HJ, who still favored his left side when sitting and had a slight limp. There'd been talk of a possible reward, but Ben waved this down, thinking privately, it should be Ute's anyway, not that he'd want it. One of the cops said Ben might be asked to testify at the poachers' trial and wanted to know where he could be reached. Ben gave his Chicago address, wondering if any guilt showed in his face as he gave each number, one by one, to the painfully slow-writing cop, knowing that he wasn't going back there for a while, if ever.

And it hit him that he had no idea where he'd be going instead. He actually liked the feeling. Never more relaxed while never more uprooted. The stranger in these parts. Goin' where the wild goose goes. *Next of kin to the wayward wind*, as an old favorite song puts it. Ben smiled expansively now at the cop, enjoying having a tooth missing there in the front, liking his new smile, too.

Van had asked him to stay on at the detective agency to work any way he wanted, part-time, full-time, special projects, whatever. Van said he guessed a weird guy with weird ideas was what was needed to solve weird cases, which is what most of them were these days.

Cole had invited Ben to come back to LA where he would put him up at the ritzy L'Ermitage for as long as Ben wanted, his treat, and he'd talk to some people about getting some quick action on Ben's *Unreal!* book, as he called it.

Ben told them he didn't know what he wanted to do just yet, and excused himself. He noticed that Abby had become, for the moment, free from the harassment of strangers, and he quickly led her out of the place, into the cool night, away from the lighted building, down the starry path to the corral where they could lean against the rails and enjoy the honest smells of horses, mud and overwhelming pine. He put an arm around her shoulder, two kids in a movie, and didn't say anything for a while.

Finally, quietly, he asked, "Still have that lion skin?"

# 58.

Ben was somewhat driven by traces of carnal frustration toward Abby. This was a carryover from their night by the campfire. They'd been high on beer, greasy from eating, sweaty and juiced from woodsmoke and their own natural heat, only to have the mood broken by Sommers and his wound, leaving Ben a victim of pre-coital interruptus.

He had, back there, envisioned the lion skin a fitting spread on which to lay in the open, and by bringing it up now he was reminding Abby of how close they'd almost come, smoothly reopening the subject. Yet, there was something perfunctory in this. The lust was there, but not pure and simple as it should be. It was dampened by things which, though related, acted together to make him both want and not want her. He'd felt obliged to seduce, but kept the effort curiously half-hearted, having doubts about both the act, and the girl.

As to the act itself, might it not be somehow wrong since Abby was, after all, the same young tomboy Ben remembered, only bigger? And worse, Cole's kid? There's this inexplicable nagging unease about having sex with friends' children. But aside from whose child she was, she was, in fact, just a child. Only twenty-one or so. (A firm, tender and tasty age, pointed out a contingent of opposition delegates in the back of Ben's mind, tossing beer cans and chicken drumsticks at him, banging their dicks on the table like gavels.) And he, a divorced man of thirty-five, almost mathematically middle-aged now. Wasn't he

The Idea People                                            241

simply too old? Wouldn't he be taking advantage? And especially after she'd been so lost and scared out there, understandably attracted to his rugged looks and clear-cut bravery.

Further, he doubted his own intentions toward her.

True, she passed every physical that man invents for woman, especially the edibility test. This was an imaginary numerical rating first devised by Ben's old office buddy Caputo, who evaluated women based on how much he wanted to "eat" them after they'd spent hours playing tennis in the hot sun.

The agency receptionist in those days, an unattainable beauty who lived with a Chicago Bear football player, got the office's only ten on Caputo's "sliding scale" as he called it, meaning he'd like to perform this particular act with her after she'd played ten hours of tennis, and all the office guys laughed. Caputo would certainly have rated Abby as high. Ben, at thirty-five, found he had misgivings about the whole sliding scale thing, on some level finding it a bit embarrassingly school boyish.

And besides, Abby really didn't make Ben's heart sing.

There was the way she talked sometimes. A jarring hint of the Valley girl, a jokey stereotype of the times. *Who cares?* Ben wondered. But it added to the weight of these doubts. So, although he stood with his arm around her, pitching the lion-skin image like some subtle ad concept to a room full of likely clients, going through the motions, doubts or not . . . out of respect for his own honest lust and with a nod to the horny Caputo wherever he might be . . . under it all there was a small, maddening part of him sitting in disapproval.

"Sure I have it," she said, keeping her voice soft in the night quiet all around them, not wanting to disturb the peace. "I'll never get rid of it. Know how Ute got it?"

And she told Ben about the old man being wrestled to the canyon floor by the largest cougar anyone ever heard of in Colorado, over ten feet from snout to tail, surely over 200 pounds. Ute hadn't wanted to kill it, thinking that the animal was a rarity (Ben nodding at hearing this), something to be honored. But still, it had been trying to kill him, Ute guessed, because it had grown too old to chase down deer, and had resorted to the demeaning practice of stalking a man.

As they wrestled, Ute's hands gripping the cat's jowls, his legs jackknifed sideways to avoid the possibility of raking claws, the lion had simply run out of life. It breathed its last into Ute's face and died. The meat, cured and smoked, had lasted nearly a year, and the hide made for warm, dry sleeping.

Interesting, Ben thought, but off the subject. And he was getting cold. She must feel the night's chill, too, so he covered more of her shoulder, encircling her, pulling her gently into him, loving the feel of her nestling in there. If an observer had happened upon them, they'd have seemed to be a particularly well-matched couple. The outdoorsy pretty blonde. The tanned and lean bearded young man. The couple you'd want on the cover of "Archie's Guest Ranch and Horsepacking Outfitters" brochure, or to sell a four-wheel drive sport truck on TV.

Somewhere in this musing, a little flag popped up. Might they be almost too good to be true? What about things not always being what they seem? *("Fronti nulla fides"* his old philosophy teacher had shouted . . . )

Abby said, "Ben, I've been thinking about our age differences. It's been bothering me."

Should he say it had momentarily worried him, too? Should he tell her not to be silly and kiss her? Again, not to decide was to decide. And again, inaction proved to be a good course.

"See, I'm twenty-one, a complete adult, sure . . . but he's probably over *sixty!*"

# 59.

At first, Cole and Lara had objected. But Abby was a pampered child, and at dawn, two days later, she left Archie's to rejoin Ute. This time she was well supplied for backcountry travel. Cole had purchased one of the ranch's best horses, Ben's old companion, Strawberry, and HJ had given her a powerful two-way radio, so she could contact Archie's in case of an emergency.

Ben had suggested that Ute might have moved, remembering that

Abby herself had believed this, but Abby surprised everyone by saying she'd find him the same way Ben found her, by homing in on the so-called Stretch Canyon hawk. The peregrine had grown familiar with Ute, and she guessed it would stick near him for food scraps.

She had a good tracking device from the PRP, which was running itself, with no replacement director, better than ever thanks to enthusiastic staffers and students, proving again the efficiency of sensible anarchy. She said she'd find both bird and man with no trouble. Her eyes flashed as she said, *man.*

In addition to just hanging with Ute for a while, she said she hoped to recruit him, bring him into the falcon release program. "He's a natural," she laughed, riding off into the hills, waving to Cole, Lara, Ben and Archie at the trailhead. Van and HJ had left for Denver the previous night. It was quiet as the horse's hoofbeats were swallowed up in the early morning stillness, and nobody said anything for a while.

Then Lara made everyone laugh by suddenly singing, *"I only have eyes for Ute . . ."*

The Coles and their new pal, Archie, who perhaps saw in their wealth an opportunity to upgrade the ranch's clientele, turned away from the now quiet trailhead, heading back to the ranch, expecting that Ben would naturally amble along, too, talking about the eggs and beans they'd have with Archie's special Bloody Marias, which he made from tequila, tomato juice and Tabasco, designed to jump start the most sluggish of aging hearts on cold mountain mornings. But Ben said to just go ahead, that he'd wander in the woods for a while, that he liked it there, alone with the magpies and jays, waiting for sunrise, thinking to himself . . . *I've got some plans to finalize.*

There was no avoiding it, he guessed. It was time to go back to work. Every two-hour, three-hour, even ten-hour (on his birthday, once) lunch comes to an end. You always have to come down and go up, through the elevator tubes, to tough out the afternoon office hours. Breaks end. Ben knew the feeling. And this one had come to a satisfying, but nonetheless conclusive, conclusion.

Abby, though now just gone off again, had been found. Van and HJ had gone back to town. The Coles had a noon plane. Van had even left the off-road Jeep at Archie's so Ben could drive them to Stapleton Airport on his own way back to Denver. And Archie was bracing for a Japanese tour group checking in this afternoon. Ben sat on a stump in the freezing woods thinking, *breaks over. That's the breaks.*

The Jeep was drafty, and I-25 was fast, so there wasn't much conversation for a while. Cole was in the bucket seat next to Ben, and Lara sat over and around their luggage in the tiny back, one boot resting against the top of Ben's seat, letting the air move up under her skirt, giving either of them a friendly view if they cared to look. Ben was actually too distracted for this, thinking about Cole's suggestions regarding *Unreal! Advertising Vs. Reality.*

Earlier, Cole said his agent, reached yesterday by phone after goodwill toward Ben reached a groundswell over tequila concoctions and Coors at an impromptu party in the ranch's dining hall, had a breakthrough idea. This was the same guy who handled the sale of Cole's own book, which still did well every year, being especially useful to the ever-increasing crops of MBAs coming along. He said, and Cole had related this, "Don't bother taking the pictures yourselves. Just sell a publisher on the concept. Take your bucks for that, and let them take their own pictures."

He told Cole, who told Ben, that a publisher would pay Ben a lump sum for the idea, then royalties for as long as the book sold. They'd surely let Ben write an introduction, even have his name on the book as its author. The publisher they'd targeted was a leader in coffee table reading.

"You make money. You don't have to do much work," Cole said. "Pretty good, huh?"

They got into Stapleton's traffic pattern, which could have been any airport's anywhere, all ramps, signs, car rental shuttles, the air charged with emotion, scented with jet fuel.

Ben said, "Do me a favor, okay? Arrange things with your agent for me. Act in my behalf? Do whatever works. I'm going to stay in Colorado for awhile."

"Van said he'd asked you to work with him. Might be fun. Sure, don't worry, I'll handle it for you."

Lara leaned in, "From ad agency to detective agency. I don't believe it!"

He dropped them at the curb, helping with their luggage, all of them standing by the idling Jeep, the Coles in their fashionable travel clothes, Ben looking like a life-long backwoods type, hugging them goodbye, again accepting their thanks, getting him to promise he'd visit them in L.A. soon.

And then they were gone, and he was again orbiting in the confusion of airport traffic, eventually spinning free, heading north on Colorado 36, away from Denver, away from Van's office, knowing now that he didn't want to ride the elevator again, didn't want to sit in Van's or anyone's conference room, and wasn't going back to Van's or anyone's version of office life.

Not just yet. Maybe not ever.

The traffic and roadside habitation both gradually thinned, and Ben could see the mountains ahead now, sharply defined against the sky. He headed toward them, knowing the back of the Jeep still had campout provisions he'd never used, not sure of where he was going, not needing to be sure. His aim, for once, was to be aimless, feeling free. Free like he'd felt after going through the wall in the SPF conference room and not going back in, liking the feeling, figuring he'd go with it. Just go with it.

# 60.

Ben himself may not have known where he was going, but the borrowed Jeep did, making all the correct turnoffs, climbing the winding two-lanes through Indian Peaks Wilderness, cutting across the great divide south of Rocky Mountain National Park, heading into the lowering sun without stopping, blowing right past an old sign saying HALFWAY 7 MI., spraying it with road grit, causing its long afternoon shadow to shake on the road shoulder long after the engine noise faded and the gas fumes drifted away.

It was after sunset, but in that corrugated landscape, sunset merely means some thrust of rock has got itself in front of the lowering sun, causing shadow to spread out, covering everything east of it, while the sky holds soft illumination overhead for hours to come. And Ben counted on this, needing the sky light, knowing the unfamiliar trail would be impassable for a novice after dark, even with the old map he'd miraculously found in the clutter of his well-traveled but little used provisions.

The downside was that if the light failed before he succeeded, he'd simply have to backtrack with the help of compass and flashlight to where he parked the Jeep and try again at dawn. Might even be better to wait and go in the crisp freeze of early morning.

But no, it wasn't dark yet, and he might still make it. He moved quickly into the mountain forest, all ears, all eyes, all nose, too, remembering something Archie had said over drinks after Ben entertained everyone with his story of following radio signals to a maternal-maniac bear. Archie had a friend who studied grizzlies, a mad intellectual vagrant of the Yellowstone area, who told him that after a few days alone in the woods, a person's senses sharpen. You don't just hear and see more, but your mostly neglected sense of smell gets so good that you can sniff a grizzly while still safely out of range.

Ben, having had some experience in the wild now, and wanting more, believed this. He drew the spiced forest air into his nose like a connoisseur, approaching it as a challenging wine. Stars became faintly visible against the soft royal blue overhead, the middle of a color gradient ranging from black on one side to pearly aqua where the sun had last been seen.

Before Ben could stop to take stock of the stars and their significance, their clear signaling of night, he thought he caught the smell of woodsmoke. And then, although it could certainly have just been imagination, a kind of olfactory mirage, he also thought there was the barest whiff of baby shampoo in the air, and he quickened his pace.

He came through a stand of trees, the path opening onto a sloping foothill of grass and fallen rock with a creek running darkly through it in the fading light. Halfway up the mountain on a wide rock shelf there was the unmistakable flicker of a campfire. It was the perfect place for a peregrine falcon hack site. He could just make out the path leading up there, and he took it without hesitation, surprising himself somewhat by his determination and by the fact that he was smiling slightly now as he walked.

And why not smile?

Rachel was surely up there, and would be quick to return the smile, her blue eyes going crinkly the way they did. But then, as he walked, he wondered . . . what if she doesn't want company? What if she doesn't like him? Or maybe, she'll shoot him. After all, he was coming up unannounced in the twilight, and she did have that big automatic. What if she's with another man? Or what if Altman's map had been just another trick, and this was someone else's camp?

*That was more like it. Worry a little.* Such thoughts as these felt familiar, comfortable as old clothes. And he walked on, smiling, knowing that this tendency toward self-doubt was a fairly harmless, probably genetic, ailment to be lived with, amused by at times, and largely ignored. Underneath, he had a simple, unarticulated gut feeling about coming here. Hadn't he been right about such feelings before? He wanted to sit with Rachel again, shoulder to shoulder. The way they'd been that night, talking quietly in the cabin. Kids at a slumber party, falling asleep against each other, her hair smelling of baby shampoo.

Ben couldn't explain this decision. Wouldn't even think of trying. But somehow, he felt he was on the right trail. Just a feeling.

# About the author

Veteran writer and creative director of New York and Chicago ad agencies, Mike Lubow has authored feature articles and the weekly column "Got a Minute" for The Chicago Tribune. His short stories have appeared in magazines around the world, including Playboy, Barcelona Review, Carve, Amarillo Bay Literary Magazine, Blue Moon Review, Etchings of Melbourne Australia, Bravado (Tauranga, N.Z.), and many others. Mike's stories have been anthologized into many books, and he is the creator and author of the online nature journal Two-Fisted Birdwatcher. Husband, father, and grandfather—he divides his time between his hometown of Chicago with frequent sojourns to Miami and Los Angeles. His heart, however, resides in the rugged pine forests, granite peaks, and secret canyons of the Rocky Mountains.

# Acknowledgements

This novel is more than the result of a lone writer's imagination. It's the result of the caring and careful attention of fiction editors at a variety of magazines, from the glossy to the literary, who encouraged me to submit stories and who published them, a real confidence builder. Sincere gratitude goes to The Chicago Tribune editor Ross Werland, who gave me a weekly column, and more confidence. Many thanks to my novelist pal Marc Davis for showing that the desire to write means nothing unless you use it and keep using it. My friend, Dr. Bob, set an example with his storytelling emails. And here's to Gatekeeper Press for their professionalism in bringing a novel out of the digital darkness of my computer files and into the world with style. Both my sons have been fans of my writing since childhood days, and that has had an immeasurable effect on my desire to keep stories coming, if only to amuse them. Thanks, guys. But none of this writing and publishing would have come about if a cute girl I met in college hadn't said she preferred to date creative guys. I started writing simply to impress her. She was encouraging back then. Today, as my wife, she still is. Without her love, literary judgment and tireless proofreading advice, this novel wouldn't have happened.

Made in the USA
Columbia, SC
07 October 2024

43680730R00143